THE MARINER OF RYL

A CORELLE OF DUR NOVEL

HAYLEY PRICE

A catalogue record for this book is available from the National Library of Australia.

National Library of Australia Cataloguing-in-Publication entry

Author: Hayley Price

Title: **The Mariner Of Ryl**

ISBN: 978-1-7637998-5-1 (Print)

ISBN: 978-1-7637998-7-5 (ePub)

ISBN: 978-1-7637998-6-8 (PDF eBook)

This book is dedicated to everyone suffering from mental health issues.
Society fails you every day, and we do too little to understand the things others are going through. May you find help, compassion, and happiness.

At times, this book will change point-of-view. Please note that each new scene does not always follow the same timeline as the last.

A note for my American readers. This book is written in UK/Australian English. Many of the words will be spelled differently from what you're used to - realised, colour, centre etc. We pronounce the "h" at the start of "herb," so we preface it with "a" rather than "an."

In addition, we do not share your fondness for the letter 'Z.' I realise you may find this difficult and offer my humble apologies. We make up for this by using a plethora of "L's" where you would make do with one. Marvellous.

All the writing and artwork in this book was created by a real person. No AI was used at any time.

ALSO BY HAYLEY PRICE

The Vermilion Saga

The Vermilion Ribbon

The Vermilion Cross

The Vermilion Triangle

Corelle Of Dur

The Blade Of Ryl

The Fan Of Ryl

THE CORELLE OF DUR SERIES RECAP (SPOILERS)

In The Blade Of Ryl, Corelle sailed south to live out her banishment from Dur with Pettra, Raolos's wife, as her lover. A cruel fate lay in wait for Pettra, but Corelle managed to kill the former Bailiff of Dur, Glailam. Corelle became more and more dependent on wine as a salve for her shattered self-esteem.

A letter from Dur summoned her home to avenge the murder of Klordia, Wilash's wife. With Synna's aid, she learned elements of the Guild still lived and were holed up on a farm in the Eastlands. Despite their best intentions and efforts, Corelle and Synna could not take the Guild's new leader, Krage, captive, and he fled south.

In the Eastlands, Corelle met a woman named Vamma. Their relationship caught the attention of the Guild, who tried to kill her. Vamma left for safety in Ort, and Corelle followed her later when she accepted the Guild had escaped.

Synna told Corelle Arella had been with child when she had urged Corelle to kill her in Zhanghar, and Corelle wavered between leaving Dur or pressing Wilash, who knew the full story, to tell her the truth.

In The Fan Of Ryl, Corelle decided to visit Wilash, but what she learned almost destroyed her. She left Dur and became a mariner.

A year later, she returned to Alcmouth aboard the ship she worked on. There, she heard some devastating news. She spoke again to Wilash, and at a meeting with the Duke and Raolos, they promised to lift her banishment if she could find the Duke's son, who had been kidnapped.

Acting on information she learned from a member of the Duke's staff, Corelle set off for the Eastlands again, where she found the Duke's son hanged by the Guild.

She reunited with Vamma, and the two left for Alcmouth together, only to learn the land had been attacked by a southern race, the Qagrue, led by Krage, who named himself the new Duke.

Due to the lack of trained fighters, Corelle felt Durfolk could not resist the barbaric southerners, and she believed all her friends in Alcmouth must have been killed. She organised a defence in Ryl, then set off to Ort to learn all she could.

She discovered Raolos, Synna, and Wilash had survived, and in Ort she found a way to kill Gillar and Sisnop, former Guild leaders from Torric. The Qagrue had turned on Krage and claimed Dur as their own territory.

With the help of some former Guild members and the Ort citizens, the Qagrue in Ort were killed, but Corelle feared recriminations against the Ortfolk at some point.

As they wavered about the correct course of action, news arrived that Ryl had fallen and Synna had been killed. Raolos, Wilash, and Vamma had fled to Malkartas.

Devastated, Corelle once more boarded a ship and resumed her life as a mariner.

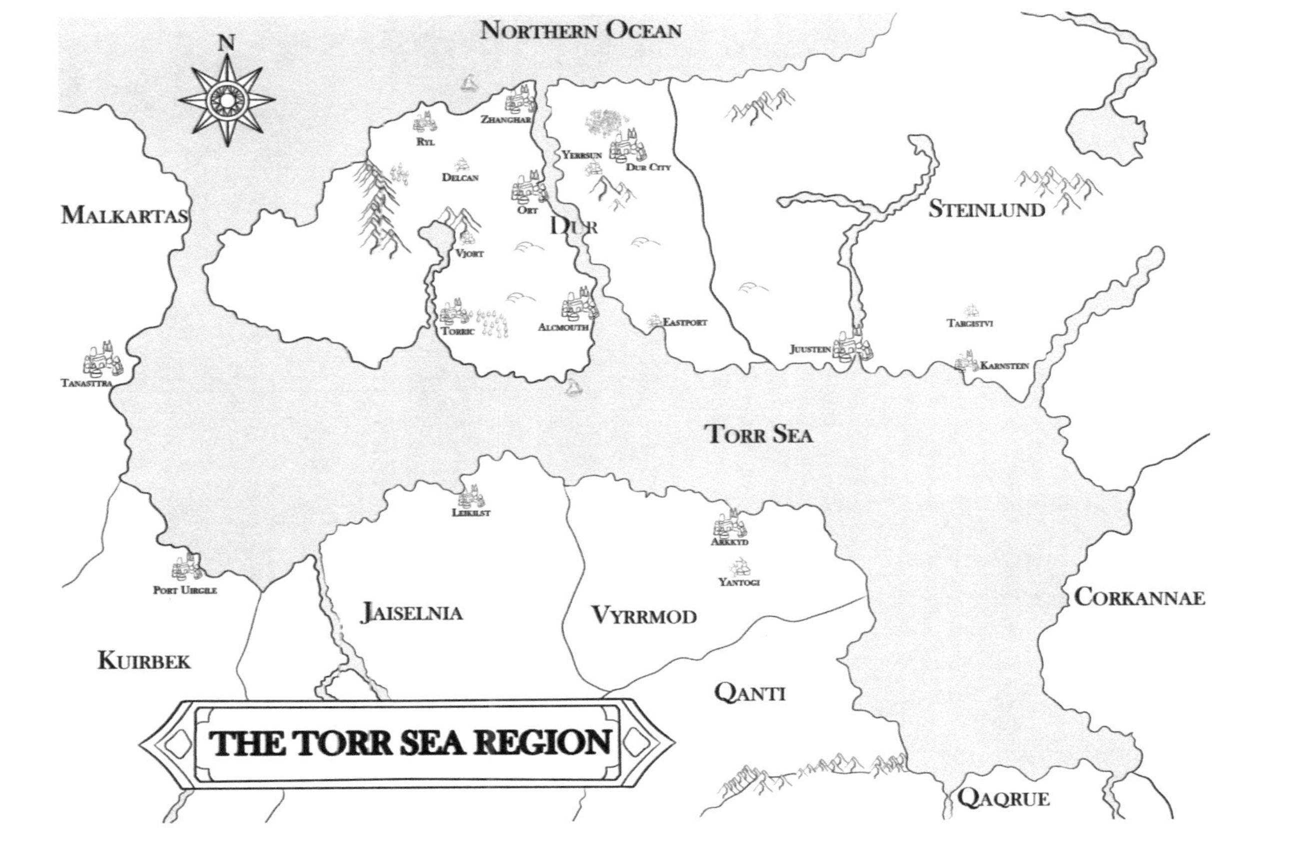

NORTHERN OCEAN
N
MALKARTAS
ZHANGHAR
RYL
DELCAN
YERRSUN
DUR CITY
ORT
DUR
VJORT
TORRIC
ALCMOUTH
EASTPORT
STEINLUND
TARGISTVI
JUUSTEIN
KARNSTEIN
TANASTTRA
TORR SEA
LEIKILST
ARKKYD
YANTOGI
PORT UIRGILE
JAISELNIA
VYRRMOD
CORKANNAE
KUIRBEK
QANTI
QAQRUE
THE TORR SEA REGION

Dur
Northern Ocean
Northlands
Zbangban
Forest of Dur
Ri
Dur City
Taro's Farms
Ort
Eastor
Yerrsun
Solgarr
Delcan
Ortlands
Mount Belram
Wantu Mountains
Eastlands
River Ale
Vjort
Freelands
Wantu River
Alcmouth
Eastport
Torre
Torr Sea

CHAPTER 1
RAOLOS

Raolos woke with a start, his eyes impotent in the darkness of the room. Cries of anger and terror, along with shouted orders, came from somewhere outside. He leapt from his bed and tore open the window shutters. The sun still slumbered, and night cloaked the city of Ryl in its black mantle. Lanterns tracked across the square outside the Portreeve's Offices, a wild, undisciplined affray, as though they were borne by dancers who each caroled to a different melody, followed a different leader.

The door to his room burst open, and lantern light poured in. Raolos raised a hand to shield his eyes from the bright stab of pain the light induced, and Synna's voice came from somewhere beyond the murderous glare. "They come. The Qagrue are here."

Two short sentences. They chilled Raolos's heart, as though Synna had immersed it in bitter cold water with six simple words. They had arrived in Ryl no more than two days ago and taken over some upper rooms in the city's Portreeve's Offices as accommodation. The city was not prepared to fight, not yet, and Raolos had hoped for more time. He had brought men with him from Delcan and many of the villages he had passed through on his journey to the small northern city, the first time he had ever visited it. Evidence of Corelle's preparations were everywhere; streets barricaded, tense-lipped men and women with fear and pride in their eyes, armed with an assortment of weapons as varied as some of them were bizarre.

Raolos shook his head. He had no time to live in the past now. The events that unfolded at this moment would define how Durfolk lived in the future. "Too soon." He muttered the words as he tugged his trousers on. "We are unready."

Synna's voice had a stern, resolute tone; it left no doubt about his state of readiness for the fight before them. "That we are, but we must fight, nonetheless. We have little time to organise our forces. Their ships approach the dock already. I must go. You must organise things here. We will make our last stand behind the barricades at the doors to these Offices if they break us elsewhere in the city."

With that, he was gone, his lantern light with him. Raolos blinked in the darkness, then shook his head. The Bailiff of Dur could not skulk in his room while people bled and died on the streets. He strode out of the room, down the stairs, and into the square. He yelled for order as he tried to remember all the instructions Synna had given him.

Carts, crates, bales of cloth, furniture; anything and everything they could lay their hands on had been piled before the doors of the Portreeve's Offices as their last barricade. With luck, Synna and the others at the docks would repel the southerners, who would lay no eyes on Ryl's square.

With help from the Portreeve's men in their deep red tunics, he organised the last defenders of the city behind the barricade. Rylfolk scurried about in the square, and soon a line of hay stood between the Offices and the few narrow entrances to the square still open. The people poured oil onto the hay, a desperate line of flame that might slow the Qagrue. If they came this far.

The sun brought long shadows from one side of the square as it rose in the east, and the Qagrue had not broken through. Grim, determined faces stared across the square even as the hands associated with those faces fiddled with weapons, anxious, afraid. The sounds of combat drew closer, the shrill cries of agony, anger, and ferocity, the clash of metal on metal. Horrified, Raolos took a step backward as a body fell from the roof of a shop across from him. How had somebody on the roof been killed? They must have lost their balance, in truth, but their fate was written; they lay in a twisted, broken heap, gone wherever they had travelled to.

When the remains of Synna's force appeared, they ran toward the Portreeve's Offices in disarray. To his relief, Raolos spotted Synna among them. He shouted orders, pointed to the barricade. Raolos stood on the tips of his toes and stretched his neck toward the sky as he stared beyond the nearest defenders. Dismay crushed him; so few remained. No more than thirty ran for the sanctuary of the last barricade. Most of them already wore the blood of combat, their own or others', Raolos could not tell which.

Behind them, the southerners emerged from the narrow streets and alleyways. Too many to count, too many for the small number of Durfolk who remained to resist; fell, violent men who waved their weapons in the air and screamed wild, guttural sounds into the square as they advanced on the Portreeve's Offices.

Somebody lit the line of hay, but too soon. The fire hurtled across the square, dark black smoke filled the air like a portent of the city's fate, but none of the Qagrue were caught in the blaze. As the flames lost their enthusiasm, disappointed by the lack of flesh they could consume with their ravenous appetite, the Qagrue leapt the fiery barrier and pressed on. Raolos yelled words of encouragement, and close by, Synna slashed and hacked at the Qagrue. He wielded a dagger in each hand. They flashed and whirled, rent flesh and clothing alike. Blood splattered and gushed everywhere his arms went, and he cried for the Durfolk to fight, resist, turn back the invaders.

Men fell before him, but still they advanced on him. When the Qagrue overwhelmed him, Raolos watched as in a dream. Synna, surrounded by a mass of the enemy, staggered as swords hacked at him, but he continued to take a terrible toll on his attackers. One of the Qagrue thrust a long pole toward Synna, a vicious metal tip at its zenith. The point drove into Synna's stomach, and he stumbled, lost his grip on one of his daggers.

With tears in his eyes, Raolos watched the demise of a man who had tried to kill the Bailiff's own wife and child before he became a loyal and devout supporter, guard, and friend. Synna lay sprawled on the ground, one dagger still beneath his lifeless hand, and blood pooled around him on the cobblestones of the square. An eerie silence fell across the square. Both sets of combatants stilled their desperate violence, and Raolos cried for those few brave defenders who still stood to throw down their weapons. The fight was lost, Synna had been killed, and the last resistance had ended. Ryl had fallen to these men and, if Corelle had the right of it, the Guild.

The Qagrue leaders acknowledged Synna's bravery, and two of them even attended his Pyre. Wilash, Vamma, and Raolos persuaded Tamgellan to sail west, beyond the known seas, beyond any chart he owned, to make for Malkartas before the Qagrue and Guild learned of the Bailiff's existence and killed him. Before he left, Raolos scribed a letter to Corelle that told of all the events in Ryl. Whether it would ever reach her, whether she even still lived, he did not believe he would ever know.

He boarded the ship and sailed away from the land he loved, the land that had claimed the lives of so many who were near and dear to him. Vamma consoled him despite her own pain; she loved Corelle, and the voyage west meant she might never meet her love again. They cried until tears would no longer come, and at last unfamiliar land appeared before them.

CHAPTER 2
YILMAY

Yilmay, who had also been known as both Corelle and Jorinda, stood on the deck of the ship, the wind in her hair and the salt smell of the river in her nostrils. She had persuaded the ship's master to hire her onto his crew, and now they sailed south from Ort down the River Alc before the ship would turn east for Corkannae and leave Dur astern. Ahead of her lay a voyage of at least two sevendays. Her work kept her busy and helped keep painful memories at bay. Dur had been lost to the Qagrue, Krage had escaped alive again, and Synna had been killed in Ryl. In quiet, dark moments in her bunk or in the nest atop the foremast, she fumed that she had seen Krage escape her vengeance a second time. He must have left Dur, but she had no idea where he had fled to. The man who had put his child into Arella had not been made to pay for the death of them both. Neither had the woman who killed them, she reminded herself. Not yet, at the least.

Once they reached Corkannae, the master paid her off and complimented her on her skills as a mariner. She had more than proved her worth during the voyage. He now planned to take some shore leave to spend time with his family, but Yilmay wanted to join another ship and leave behind all that had unravelled for her since she left Yerrsun with Vamma.

She had shaved her head once more a day after they sailed from Ort and again wore a kerchief in place of the long brown hair she used to sport. She had abandoned the name Corelle as soon as she boarded the ship. Too much pain hung from that name; friends lost, horrific deeds done. Yilmay had been the first name she thought of, and as she gazed along the docks of Corkannae, she pondered the strange choice of city name. She believed it to be the biggest city in the land, but to give the city the same name as the land seemed unusual.

A ship with the sigil of Rakulaj sat at the dockside. Authorities still sought her in Vyrrmod over the death of Pettra and her abuser. That had been almost two years earlier, and she hoped the Upholders might have forgotten her by now, occupied by more recent events. She no longer looked the same as in those days, and she had not been called Yilmay then. It might be safe to return, so she would seek work aboard Rakulaj's ship.

She strode up the ramp, head high, brimful of confidence, to seek out the master. If she had mentioned the name Corelle, she would have received a warm welcome, but she had abandoned that name. To obtain work on this vessel, she must rely on her skills and her persuasion.

Her more than adequate skills did not prove a problem, but it took all her persuasion to convince the master to hire her onto his crew. He resisted her for a time, and it seemed she might have to reveal her former name to sway his opinion, but since the ship had been rigged to depart, she guessed he would be anxious to cast off and sail south-west to Vyrrmod. She wore him down in the end, and he agreed to hire her in the lowliest capacity on the ship. Her duties would be to swab the deck, clean the heads, and help with the meal preparations, but she had been hired and would sail on to Vyrrmod.

Yilmay imagined she would soon have the chance to demonstrate her skills in other aspects of the mariners' work, and so it proved. She never missed an opportunity to help coil a rope or work with the sails, even when she should not have been on watch, and the other crew members soon included her in their work. As ever, she encountered some unwelcome attention, and as on previous occasions, she lost some fist fights to repel those advances. Not once did she surrender, and although she lost the fights, she won respect.

When the ship docked in Arkkyd, her crimes brought her no complications. By the next time the ship sailed, she had been promoted from the menial tasks and became a mariner again. Yilmay sailed around the Torr Sea for almost a year, and, as they made ready to leave Arkkyd again for yet another voyage, she noticed Rakulaj board the ship and speak to the master. She had anticipated she might see him sooner or later, in truth. He owned the ship, after all else, and she guessed he must travel for the purpose of his business, since she had first met him in Dur. Although she stayed out of sight as much as possible, there came a time, no more than a day out of Torric, when Rakulaj stood on the aft deck in conversation with the master when Yilmay came up the aft deck stairs to report to the master about a repair to a sail she had completed.

Rakulaj stared at her as though he tried to identify her, but she kept her head down and hoped he would not realise who stood before him. Her changed appearance worked in her favour, and he did not speak to her. From the corner of her eye, she watched him return to his cabin. Less than an hour later, he re-appeared and walked toward her, a determined look on his face.

He whispered as he drew alongside her. "Corelle of Dur?"

She greeted him with a despondent sigh. "I now travel by the name of Yilmay. I did not wish my life aboard to be disrupted by revelations about my past."

"I am delighted to see you. I understand your change of name, and appearance, I might add. It threw me for a time, but I knew your face. Please, join me to take a meal in my cabin after your watch."

Although hesitant, she accepted, and they talked for two hours about all that had turned since they had last met. Yilmay remained reluctant to dig up old memories she had hidden deep inside herself. There had been too much loss and too much disappointment, and her one desire had been to leave it all far behind. She revealed some aspects of her resistance to the Qagrue takeover in Dur but left large parts of the worst of the tragedy untold. He respected her wishes, and the conversation moved on to an issue he said raged throughout the lands around the Torr Sea.

"It seems learned scholars in Malkartas believe our lands—Vyrrmod, Dur, Malkartas and such, lie on a globe that extends far beyond the Torr Sea."

"I know this, or rather I have heard the theory. They name it Ictharelian."

"Do you believe them?"

His excitement surprised her. His eyes gleamed, he rubbed his palms together, and he leaned forward as he hung on every word of her reply. "I see no reason to either believe or disbelieve it. It would explain how the sun and moon replace each other every day, but in truth, I do not know."

Yilmay had never heard such wonder in a person's voice before as he continued. "I am captivated by it. Nobody has ever proved the theory. Most lack the will to gamble a large sum of coin to fund a voyage that might either prove the theory or lead to the loss of a ship with all hands. I, however, have the will and, more important, the coin. I wish to fund the voyage, and now you are a mariner, you could help me."

She gave him a confused frown. "How could I help you?"

He stared deep into her eyes as though he searched for the

answer to whatever question burned at him. "You can sail aboard my ship on this voyage. You can be its master. I know you, and I trust you."

To be on the crew of such a voyage would be an honour beyond anything Yilmay had known before. Her head swam as the idea took hold in her mind. "I have neither the desire nor the skills to be the master of any ship, but who could turn down the chance to prove Ictharelian exists as a globe we can sail around?" If Rakulaj would fund the voyage, Yilmay would sail aboard his ship. She had a new position, and the excitement of the prospect made her dizzy.

Two passes later, she left the ship she had served on and joined the crew of another. Rakulaj had taken one of his ships off the line and converted it into a ship equipped to undertake the momentous voyage required to prove the globe theory. The ship carried no cargo, the holds filled with food and barrels of fresh water. Aboard the ship were scholars, learned in the creation of maps, or the study of animals, plants, and other wonders that might be encountered in strange lands, if such existed. The mariners had been hand-picked by Rakulaj and the master. Rakulaj had settled on his most trusted and able master, Tryndeltuj, well known among those who worked aboard any ship of Vyrrmod. Those who sailed on his ships never spoke an ill word about him but praised him as the finest master among all the fleets of the lands around the Torr Sea.

They had chosen one of the newest additions to Rakulaj's fleet, built with the most current knowledge of shipbuilding. He had renamed it The Ictharelian in honour of the journey it would undertake. To Yilmay's surprise, the crew did not all come from Vyrrmod. Tryndeltuj and Rakulaj had cast a wide net, and Yilmay recognised the language or accents of at least five of the Torr Sea lands. Two of the crew came from Dur; one from Torric and one from Ort.

The food and water loaded into the holds must suffice until they sighted new lands beyond the western shores of Malkartas, the furthest west any of them had ever sailed before, and the ship sat low in the water from the weight. Nobody knew what lay beyond those shores. The scholars of Malkartas had, it seemed, determined Ictharelian might be a globe based on the curvature of the horizon as they stood on the westernmost shores of their land. Tryndeltuj and his crew and ship must prove or disprove the theory.

Some of the mariners whispered in the cabins. They said when they reached the end of the Torr Sea west of Malkartas, the ship would sail over the edge of some giant waterfall into oblivion. Yilmay did not believe them, excited to prove the tale false. Impatience gnawed at her, but an enormous ceremony took place on the dockside beforehand, with speeches and huge crowds, and time dragged on while it finished up.

At last, as the crowds waved and cheered, the master gave the order to cast off, and The Ictharelian headed north-west through the Torr Sea, onward through the The Neck, the passage of water between Malkartas and Dur, and around the north coast of Malkartas. As the coastline off their dock'ard side turned southward away from them, The Ictharelian sailed west. Yilmay and the rest of the crew stood on the deck, aware they now sailed in uncharted waters, and ahead lay fame or death. It had been a sombre moment for Yilmay, but it passed, and she returned to her work.

They sailed westward and spotted no land as the days passed. Hopes and emotions had been high at first, but as a sevenday, then a tenday passed, some small signs of nervousness appeared among some of the mariners. Yilmay did not understand the concern. They all knew it took a full tenday to sail from Alcmouth to Arkkyd, and even more to Qanti and Qagrue. They sailed west with no knowledge of what they sailed toward, out of sight beyond the horizon that circled the ship, and she thought it unreasonable to expect to encounter strange lands close to Malkartas.

Two sevendays after they entered unknown waters, Yilmay ended her overnight watch at the sunrise and descended from the small basket at the top of the foremost mast. She watched her replacement scurry up the nets to take her place and had turned toward the common room in search of some food when she heard a cry from above. She snapped her head around and up. Her replacement shouted in excitement and pointed to the dock'ard side of the ship. "Land." Elation seemed to flow from him, to infect the rest of the mariners as he cried again, "Land."

CHAPTER 3
YILMAY

Yilmay cursed the man's luck. Had he been delayed a little, she might have been the one to sight the land. She muttered frustrated words to herself, but those were the fates written. All hands rushed to the dock'ard rail and peered out as they tried to spot the land the lookout had seen. He had not been wrong. The master brought the ship around to the south and soon enough they could all see the land—tall, dark cliffs that reached upward toward the sky, taller than the masts of the ship. The water boiled at the base of the line of cliffs, which seemed impassable from this far out. The crew all burst into spontaneous cheers, relieved to see land at last. They had found a land nobody had even known existed until this moment.

Although the cliffs appeared impenetrable, there would be somewhere they could land. They all knew it, and Tryndeltuj sailed the ship along the line of the cliffs as the map makers sketched eager lines on the parch with their scribing tools. Those mariners who stood the current watch were ordered back to work, but nobody left the deck as the ship traced the line of the cliffs for several hours. Yilmay wondered whether this new land had been founded atop the cliffs, impossible to reach from the water.

The cliffs grew less lofty, and the stark walls of rock descended toward the waterline. More cheers rang out, and a small cove appeared at last. Tryndeltuj ordered the anchor dropped. He had been reluctant to sail too close to the coast without certain knowledge of the depth of the water. To have run aground could have been catastrophic.

Tenders, as the rowboats that hung from the stern and side were called, were lowered to the water, hard work at any time, but more so today as excitement and impatience flooded through every member of the crew. Yilmay knew some of the languages aboard and had picked up a few words of most of the others, but she reasoned whoever might live in this land would understand none of the curses the crew let out as they battled the tenders.

To Yilmay's excitement, Tryndeltuj chose her to help row the first tender, the one with the master and some of the scholars in it. He ordered all the mariners to arm themselves, since it could not be guessed what people or creatures lived in this land, nor how they would greet the ship's crew that rowed ashore. Yilmay kept the fan in her boot these days, not so much for protection at sea, but because in the heat of the day, she found it soothing to wave the open leaves before her face..

They rowed to the shore, as excited as children who see some carnival performer produce sweet treats from hidden places in his clothes. The tender topped each successive wave and dipped into the trough before it mounted the next. One mariner held a rope over the side with a heavy stone attached to it. A series of knots in the rope told how far below the surface the stone had sunk when it touched the bottom, and he cried out as they drew closer to the shoreline. "Ten spans. Nine spans." They were almost in the shallows where they could step out onto the solid ground of a new land; land nobody from the Torr Sea region had ever trodden before.

At last, the bow of the tender scraped on the ground beneath the water, and the crew leapt out to drag the tender up onto the yellow sand of the cove above the line of detritus at the high-water mark. They all gazed around, enthralled by what they saw.

The sun beat down from a cloudless sky above. The soft sand beneath their feet proved difficult to walk through. Yilmay did not believe she had ever seen such yellow sand before. She had never left a rowboat or ship anywhere other than a dock or a jetty, even as a mariner. Their arrival on this unfamiliar land represented a new experience for her, and she drank it in as a thirsty man will bolt down a cup of water, enthusiastic and grateful.

Thankful to be one of the first to stand on the shoreline of this new land, Yilmay held her hands up to the sky and felt the sun warm her palms, the same as it would in the summer in Dur. She now stood as far from Dur as she had ever travelled, as far as any who stood there with her had ever travelled. Some of the scholars were hard at work as they investigated every part of the cove. They had already left the sand and gazed in wonder at plants and grasses they could not have recognised.

Tryndeltuj ordered the mariners to spread themselves out and search for food they could eat, and a source of fresh water if they could find one. They would transport any food back to the ship before they returned to fill the empty water barrels. He would not risk the barrels from the ship until he could be sure of what reception they might receive, if any.

As she walked into the denser tree line, Yilmay heard one of the scholars ask Tryndeltuj what they would name this new land. He replied without hesitation. "Rakulajland." The name seemed appropriate. Rakulaj had funded the voyage, and it seemed only right they should call this land after him. If they discovered enough lands, he might name one after her, and she tried to think what it might be called. "Corejoriland." She laughed at the jest.

Yilmay did not recognise anything on this strange new shore. Bright, colourful birds flew among the trees, and she saw a small grey animal whose rear legs were much longer than its front legs. When it saw her, it bolted with a movement Yilmay could find no better word for than a hop. Its large rear legs propelled it forward, then it landed on its shorter front legs and repeated the action until it vanished from her sight.

Colourful flowers adorned a bush in every part of the cove, and they smelled wonderful, fresh, and with an aroma she could not identify. Yilmay pushed through some tall, thick grasses and almost fell into a small stream that babbled over a stony bed, the water so clear, she could see every stone it skipped over on its way from wherever it originated. She knelt and scooped up a handful of the water. She sniffed it before she sipped at it. She detected no rank odour, so she lapped some of it up with her tongue. Despite the warmth of the day, the cold temperature of the water shocked her as it danced on her tongue and down her throat with no notable taste. She decided it would be safe to take back to the ship, so she turned and followed it to learn where it emerged into the cove.

Yilmay took off her boots and enjoyed the cold of the water as it refreshed her feet, and she smiled as she continued to splash through the stream. Although it met the sea some way from the tenders, it would be safe to bring the tenders ashore near the mouth of the stream.

She turned toward her crew-mates and plodded through the yellow sand that stuck to her wet feet like a child who could not be separated from its mother. She found Tryndeltuj and told him about the stream. He nodded and appeared relieved. A ship that spends long at sea without fresh water is doomed, and before they sailed away from Rakulajland, the barrels would all be full.

Some of the mariners had found some edible fruit, but none had seen many animals they could kill and take aboard as a source of meat. Dried meat aplenty had been loaded in Vyrrmod, so the fruit had been the more important find, since it served to keep disease away from the crew as they sailed. No contact had been made with any people, however, and although the scholars begged him to stay, Tryndeltuj pointed out their objective remained the discovery of whether the globe existed and could be sailed around. Once they had confirmed that, others could come and explore any new lands as they saw fit.

They loaded the tenders with the fruit they had gathered, then rowed them back to the ship. They exchanged the fruit for empty barrels and Yilmay showed them the stream. After they rowed the barrels back to the ship, the tenders made one last trip to the cove to collect everybody who remained. They piled on sail, hauled in the anchor, and set off westward once more.

Yilmay stood at the aft of the ship and watched Rakulajland disappear behind her with some disappointment. The land had enchanted her in the short time she had been ashore, and she almost wished she had stayed behind, far from the horrors of the life she had lived up until that point.

After Rakulajland, they discovered another land some five days west where they replenished their supplies but again met no inhabitants. A tenday later, Yilmay spotted land from the nest, and she called out to advise the rest of the crew. They landed south of a small settlement and attracted the attention of the people of the land. Their language proved impossible for any of the ship's crew to understand, and all conversation took place with a combination of gestures at objects or crude pictures in the sand.

The people of this land were similar in appearance to those of Dur, but they wore bright, showy clothes, dyed with complex patterns. Clothes in Dur were often dyed, but the complicated designs dyed into the clothes of this land fascinated Yilmay. The clothes were adorned with birds and animals she did not recognise, but also with patterns such as circles and squares. She begged them to show her how they produced the patterns on the clothes, and despite the difficulty of the language difference, she learned a great deal about the methods they used to dye the clothes.

The local people made them so welcome, Tryndeltuj gave in to the scholars and agreed to rest for a few days in the land, which he named Tryngelk, a combination of his and his wife's names, it turned. Yilmay strove to learn what the people called their land but struggled to repeat the complicated name, so she settled for Tryngelk. She mangled every attempt to pronounce the name the citizens had told her so much, those around her fell about in hysterical laughter.

The locals showed them animals they could hunt and take aboard, large, vicious dog-like creatures. The locals used an unusual weapon to bring them down, a long, thin piece of wood, sharpened to a fine point. They hurled it with deadly accuracy. None of the ship's crew could become proficient in the use of the weapon, and Yilmay's attempts proved so disastrous, she abandoned them before she killed one of their new friends by accident.

On the third day, Yilmay wandered off alone to explore more of their surroundings. Separated from the other crew, she walked into what turned out to be a gap between two rocks with no other way out. As she retraced her steps, she heard a low growl ahead of her. One of the creatures crouched on the trail, its eyes fixed on her. She snapped open her fan as the creature's growls increased in ferocity. Saliva dripped from its bared fangs, and behind its head, its fur had risen in a fashion Yilmay had never seen before. If it attacked, she considered her chances slim with such a small weapon against so fierce an opponent. If she died here, the others might never find her body. She had vowed to end her life many times since she had killed Arella, and now she might meet her ruin at last, and in a manner she could never have guessed.

The creature crept forward, then leapt. Yilmay slashed at it,

Wilash's blade still as sharp as the day he had fashioned it thanks to long hours of work with a whetstone in quiet, idle periods at sea. Her blade cut its shoulder, a deep wound, but the creature knocked her backward. The air whooshed from her lungs as she landed. The beast snapped its vicious fangs at her throat as she tried to squirm out from beneath it. She continued to slash and stab at it. It lunged at her face, but she managed to turn her head and pull at its ear with her spare hand. It missed its target, but those terrible sharp teeth cut deep into her left shoulder. The animal's vile breath reeked of rotten meat and a putrid stomach. Bile burned her throat, as though the creature had lit a fire in her neck.

Yilmay screamed in anguish as the creature's jaws snapped shut on the flesh of her shoulder. No stranger to injury, wounds, and pain, Yilmay shook her head as her sight blurred and dizziness overwhelmed her. If she fainted from the waves of agony that gouged her, she would be dead in heartbeats. Blood poured from the wound, and the animal released her before it crouched once more. It moved with slow, cunning steps, side to side, its eyes fixed on her. Her strength would soon fade as her blood gushed out of her body. She guessed her ruin had come. As the creature strove to position itself for the fatal strike, it let out a high-pitched shriek and fell forward onto her battered body. A long wooden weapon pierced its head, and hands pulled at her and dragged her clear of the dead creature, her bloodied fan still gripped in her hand.

The bite had inflicted a serious wound. Scratches and cuts from the creature's clawed feet covered her body, but they were nothing compared to the bite. She had known pain, but nothing like this. Her shoulder drove hot pokers of agony into her throat that burst from her mouth in screams of distress. Locals carried her back to their settlement, but she drifted in and out of awareness as her lifeblood gushed from her. People buzzed around her at the settlement, concerned with the bite. Their voices echoed in her mind, though she understood nothing they said. She fetched up, then faded into unconsciousness again. When she came around, locals washed out her wounds with copious amounts of water and applied a salve with a pungent odour that stung almost as much as the bite. Their eyes confirmed what she feared—her ruin had come, but the pain from her shoulder did not allow her any relief to grieve for a life cut as short as the countless lives she had ended with her blade. Still the locals would not abandon her, and worked without respite to save her.

Tryndeltuj expressed his concern about her health, but his face told her he wanted to leave and would be loath to lose time while she healed. The ship carried a healer of sorts, a man who could clean a cut, close a wound, and knew a little about herbs and salves for common ailments. He checked Yilmay and told Tryndeltuj it would be best if she did not move for a few days while they saw how the terrible injury healed. She guessed his true meaning; to see whether she lived or died.

Yilmay stood at the threshold of death as razor-sharp spasms of pain throbbed through every span of her body all day with no relief. Whenever she woke, her screams rang out through the settlement, but they did not ease her agony. A fever took hold, and she dripped with sweat every hour of the day. She could not reckon how many days, only that the sunlight or daylight measured the passage of each. People came throughout the day and night to place cold wet cloths on her forehead and body as they tried to cool her. They continued to apply the rank salve, and one night, delirious with fever and in agony Yilmay no longer had the strength to endure, Deineike and Arella stood at the doorway of the small room she lay in, their hands held out toward her.

Her time had come, and tears spilled from her eyes as she addressed her two lovers. "I am sorry, Arella. I promised I would kill myself after I had killed you, yet here I am still alive. It seems I will meet my end in some strange land neither of you knew existed. I am to blame for all that has turned. I am sorry to both of you."

They seemed to smile, then they faded from her sight as she whispered, "I come to you at last."

Despite her words, she did not join them. The fever broke the next morning, and the locals seemed happier at the way the bite had healed so far.

It took another four days before she had the strength to stand and be rowed back to the ship. The wound healed itself as Deineike's had, but a scar formed behind it. It ached from time to time as they sailed west again, and she would rub at it and recall the incident. Somehow, she had lived, thanks in no small part to the residents of Tryngelk. She sat on a barrel by the rail as the ship hauled anchor and sailed off, the shore crowded with locals who all waved cheery hands in the air as the voyage of discovery continued.

CHAPTER 4
YILMAY

TWO YEARS LATER

The sails billowed and gleamed in the sunlight as the Ictharelian rode a tailwind through the water. As the wooden hull cut through the deep blue of the sea, the water turned foamy white as though enraged by the passage of the intruder that disrupted its routine. The mass of disembodied white drops threw themselves in futile anger against the sides of the ship before they fell back to rejoin the otherwise uninterrupted blue depths from which they had been so brutally sundered. At the bow, Yilmay stood and scratched at the throb in her shoulder.

Two years had passed since they had left Vyrrmod, and there were fewer crew now. Some had succumbed to illness, and one had fallen overboard and could not be located when the ship circled around the point where he had last been seen. They had discovered a land where the local people were hostile, and there had been a fight. Two of the crew had been killed, and one had sustained an injury so severe, he could not work afterward. Two more had joined them from one of the lands they had discovered, excited by the prospect of a journey to lands they had never dreamed of. They had proved to be excellent mariners despite the language difficulties.

Two years. Most of the mariners, Yilmay included, were ready to dock at Arkkyd, leave the ship to a joyous reception, carried on the shoulders of the citizens to a banquet where the drink would flow, leaving them ill in the head and stomach the next morning, with time to think and consider the next step in their lives. After Tryngelk, they never travelled more than two tendays before they found some new piece of land; vast coastlines that took a sevenday to pass, or small islands with a few trees and not a single animal. They had not yet returned to familiar land or waters, so they sailed on and urged the wind to blow stronger behind them and push them into the Torr Sea sooner. They had not fallen off the edge of the water, but each day they did not see a familiar coastline off one side or the other of the ship deepened their ache to see home again.

They had proved the globe theory, but Yilmay had grown weary of the chore. She longed for home, and her thoughts often turned to Vamma's smile, her smell, her touch.

Yilmay slapped the arm of Gaishkantah, her closest friend on the ship. He came from Steinlund and had made a jest at her expense in his own language. Yilmay had spent so much time in his company, she spoke his language as well as her own by now, the similarity between the two a mystery to her. He could speak hers also, but the jest sounded funnier in his own language. He cried out in mock pain and rubbed at his arm as everybody else in the cabin roared with laughter. He returned his attention to the game, picked up the dice, and prepared to roll them.

His jest had been brought on when Yilmay rolled ones on a

large bet. She had fallen onto her back on the cabin floor in dramatic fashion as the dice's two single eyes mocked her ill luck, and he had made his jest. Yilmay sat up as he followed his own unique style whenever he rolled the dice. He kissed each one in turn before his massive fist closed around them, and he blew through the hole between his thumb and his first finger. Then he rolled and waited to see how his luck went.

"Ones." The mariners cried aloud as one, and Gaishkantah fell onto his back as Yilmay had done.

The cabin erupted with wild cheers and laughter, and Yilmay fell onto her friend to plant a kiss on his forehead. "Bad luck, Gaish." Tears of laughter poured from her eyes as she screeched into his ear.

He groaned. "The worst. Two adjacent rolls of ones. I am fated to be cursed all my life."

The laughter at his discomfort over his bad luck increased, and Yilmay did not query the word 'adjacent.' She reasoned it meant one after the other. He smiled at her, and they sat up before Yilmay excused herself from the game. Another took her place.

She sat on her bunk and kept half an eye on the game. The ship sailed the route Tryndeltuj had planned in the belief it would carry them to the north of Dur, where they would sail down the Alc and on to Vyrrmod. Nobody aboard had ever sailed these waters before, and there were many unknowns in the course that might not bring them back where they hoped. Tryndeltuj navigated by the lights of the night sky, since he had no charts to cover this expanse of water, and somehow managed to set a course even as the sky became unfamiliar and the pattern of lights changed. They had sailed from the previous land a tenday ago and had seen no sign of land since. That was not yet a concern, and it did not weigh on the crew and officers, but the desire to be home burned in them all, the theory proved.

Yilmay had sailed to Dur several times since she had left Ort three years ago, but the Alc would be a welcome sight. The Qagrue still called it their territory the last time she had been there, but that had been two years or more ago, and they may have moved on by now for all she or anybody aboard knew.

Although she had sailed to Malkartas in the year before they had set off on The Ictharelian, she had made no effort to find Raolos, Vamma or Wilash. She yearned to see their faces now, after two years in waters their map makers sketched for the first time. They had named five new seas and oceans, along with the Torr Sea and the Northern Ocean. Seven seas, although how they made such determinations, they did not share with Yilmay.

The voyage had seemed a grandiose and noble enterprise when they had left Arkkyd, but now she had run out of patience with it. Yilmay imagined herself in Vamma's arms again, where she could feel pleasure from fingers other than her own. Throughout the voyage, she had enjoyed only one night with another woman. They had stopped for a night ashore at a new land. The woman had been forward, as had many of the local women, and as there were no other women aboard the ship, Yilmay had been overwhelmed by the attention.

Yilmay offered no resistance as the woman took her to her bed, where she abandoned herself to the vast store of lust she had found no relief for aboard the ship other than when she pleasured herself. She had given little that night and had taken all the pleasure the woman could give her without remorse, certain the woman must have enjoyed the company of another more recently than her.

The dice game continued, but Yilmay had the early watch the next day, and she had grown tired. She lay back on her bunk, and despite the rowdy noise of the game, she soon fell asleep. The mariner's life had taught her she must sleep through the noise in the cabin if she wished to have the strength to perform her duties the following day.

The watch bell woke her, and she leapt from the bunk. She always woke before the watch, but this morning, for some reason, she had slept too long. The others in the cabin all still slept, and the room smelled hideous from the mariners' body odour and the gas they passed throughout the night. Yilmay doubted she herself smelled as sweet as the flower in Rakulajland after two years at sea.

She ran past the mariners who headed to the common room or their cabin after the night watch. Yilmay loathed the night watch, and she had completed her time on it and moved to the early watch no more than three days before. If a mariner arrived late to their watch, they might get away with it if they carried a rope or a barrel, as though they had worked for some time unseen by the officers and now returned to the deck, and Yilmay swept up a coil of rope outside the cabin door in an attempt to avoid the wrath of the officer of the watch.

Her luck held; nobody called her over to deliver a stern rebuke about her tardiness. She stacked the rope with another bundle and prepared to climb the nets to the top of the mast. She would take the first two hours in the basket at the top of the mast and cast about for a sign of land, the northern shoreline of Dur or Steinlund, she hoped. With an exhausted yawn, she began her own ritual and scanned all four aspects of the horizon in turn. The sun had risen astern and warmed the day as it climbed the sky like an insect up a wall. It prepared to follow them yet again. The ship could not outpace the sun, and at the end of every day, the warmth of the yellow ball in the sky faded as the sun sank below the western horizon bound for lands The Ictharelian had yet to discover. The sails billowed from the moderate breeze that propelled them along. They had sailed west throughout the voyage, which had kept the predominant wind behind them much of the time.

An hour into the watch, she noticed the water boil off the seaward side. She stared hard at the spot in the water where she first saw it, and sure enough she saw the sign. A spout blew up into the air from the water. Most mariners believed giants expelled water from the blowhole, but Gaish had told her they breathed out air. The warm air condensed to small droplets of water as it shot up into the cooler air.

Although Yilmay trusted Gaish, she wondered how he had come by this knowledge. Regardless of what they expelled, the spout meant one thing—giants. "Blue giants, seaward side." She yelled at the top of her voice, then repeated the advice again soon after. Below her, she saw the crew turn their heads as they craned to see the animals. The wash from the enormous creatures could swamp a ship if the blue giant leapt from the water close alongside.

Some way off the seaward bow, one leaped from the water and landed with a gigantic splash. It had jumped too far away to be a problem, but as it had sailed through the air with a dancer's grace, Yilmay realised it had not been blue at all, but black and white. She had never seen such a creature before. Every giant she had ever encountered had been blue, but she corrected her earlier report. "Black and white giant off the seaward bow." Faces turned up to look at her. It seemed none of the others had ever encountered this type of giant either. All the crew stopped their work and stared out into the water as they tried to see the strange phenomenon. Some came out of the cabin area, mayhap because they had heard the last shout. She repeated the report, and even Tryndeltuj stood at the seaward rail and stared at the water.

Another leapt from the water abeam of the ship, closer this time, and Yilmay yelled a new warning. "Wash inbound. Wash inbound." As the black and white animal fell back into the water, the wash surged toward the ship, and she gripped the edge of the basket as the crew below grabbed anything they could hold on to that would help them retain their balance. In the nest, a large wash posed greater danger, since to be up at the top of the mast exaggerated any side-to-side movement of the ship. The water struck the side of the ship and churned upward in a blue and white fountain that soaked the deck and everything on it. The ship rolled dock'ard, and Yilmay clung to the basket with all the strength in her arms, desperate not to fall out into the sea.

As the ship righted itself and rolled to the seaward side, a vision she had never seen and had never expected to see appeared right before her. Yilmay stared in horror as the fates written for the ship all came at that moment and brought their ruin. Another giant burst from the water beside the ship and across The Ictharelian's track. The giant leapt straight at the ship, and its head missed the foremast nest by no more than a few spans. Yilmay stared aghast into its brown eyes before it crashed onto the deck below.

The gigantic creature wreaked total devastation as it hurtled down onto The Ictharelian. The deck of the ship split in two and flung men and equipment into the air. The crew's arms and legs flailed like the limbs of a rag doll thrown at the sky. Yilmay hurtled upward and could not retain her grip on the basket. As she flew through the air, she realised how far below her the water lay, and she resigned herself to the fact she had heartbeats left to live. She spun head over feet as the water rushed up toward her until she hit the water feet first, and her arms were wrenched upward above her head as she plunged into the depths of the sea.

The coldness of the water shocked her, despite the warmth of the morning. As she sank toward Helchik's treasure, the water tore her tunic from her body. Some instinct ordered her to swim, an automatic response that tried in vain to override the certainty of her imminent ruin. She kicked her legs with all the strength she could summon, and her descent slowed as she pushed her arms downward, then up and down again in time with the kicks of her legs, desperate to reach the surface before the small amount of air in her lungs gave out and she drowned. The panic that took over her mind exceeded any she could recall at any time in her life. Despite all her numerous vows to end her life, she could not surrender it now the moment had come. She swam upward, but she could not hold her breath a heartbeat longer. The light above her grew stronger, and she found the will and strength to kick harder.

Yilmay had no breath left and had not reached the surface. Her chest heaved as she fought against the instinct to open her mouth and breathe. As the palpitations of her reflex attempts to breathe intensified, she inhaled water through her nose. When she tried to expel it, she could find no air in her lungs with which to push it out. Her ruin had come, and she had drowned. She opened her mouth to draw in a breath that would power a frustrated scream, and her head burst above the surface of the water. With deep gasps, she sucked air into her lungs and trod water as she gulped in enormous breaths, never more grateful for each intake of air.

She looked around. Men filled the water along with equipment thrown from the ship. Some of the men bobbed up and down in the swell, while others lay face down in the water, motionless. The giant had vanished, and she reasoned it must have swum off. Whether it had landed on the ship by accident or it had been a deliberate attack she did not know, and it did not matter, after all else. The ship had been cut in half, and the aft half already sank below the waves. It tilted forward as it disappeared beneath the surface, a slow, dreadful journey to Helchik's treasure. She wondered whether Tryndeltuj had lived. His fate, and that of Gaish, she could not guess. Gaish had been in his bunk as far as she knew. Many of the men would have known nothing of what had turned as they slept in the cabin.

The forward half of the ship had a heavy list to one side, and with horror, she realised it listed toward her. As the remains of the hull filled with water, it seemed the ship sighed and rolled toward her at great speed. The basket she had been in moments before still stood at the top of the mast, and that mast now rushed toward her.

Frantic, she tried to swim out of its path, but too late. The mast cleaved the water and sent a vast plume of it into the air, then landed on top of Yilmay. She cried out in pain as the ship, the mast, and the sea were lost to sight, replaced by Deineike, who beckoned to her a heartbeat before blackness shrouded her in its merciful release.

CHAPTER 5
YILMAY

Yilmay tried to open her eyes. Warmth kissed the skin of her face, and she sensed bright light beyond her eyelids, but she lacked the strength to open them. Her head throbbed with a pain so intense, it drove fiery daggers through her brain and down into her body. She tried to recall what had turned, but nothing more than fragments of vague memories came back to her. The ship had fallen on her, she thought, and that could not be survived. She must be dead. Something did lie afterward, after all else, but she could not open her eyes to see it. For all she knew, Deineike, Arella, Klordia, Pettra, and Synna stood at her bedside, ready to greet her.

With a great effort of will, she fought the reluctance in her eyelids. Pain punctured her head with myriad blades, but she struggled against it and forced her eyes open. The light blinded her, brilliant beyond anything she could bear, and the agony increased as the intense white of whatever lay beyond her eyelids assailed her. She could see nothing at first, then two faces struggled to take shape, fuzzy and featureless, worse than the blurred vision of a night of wine. Disappointment whispered of her lack of importance; no more than two waited to greet her wherever she had travelled. It did not matter as long as Deineike had come to her again.

It hurt too much to think. Try as she might, she could not bring the faces into focus. When she had been in her cups, she had found if she closed one eye, the blurred images she gazed at came into focus somewhat, so she closed an eye.

"Yilmay?" She heard the voice but did not recognise it. It had sounded unnatural—almost as though the word itself had been blurred. It echoed around in her head, careened into every part of her brain that already hurt to create new and unbearable agony. It had not sounded like Deineike, and if it had been Deineike, how could she know Jorinda now called herself Yilmay?

It hurt too much to concentrate. Yilmay let the thought slide away, and the pain faded to a tolerable level. The faces swam into some semblance of focus, but she did not see Deineike's long dark hair on either of them. One had a beard, and they were both men. That could not be right, unless… She tried to sit up, to reach for her fan in her boot. Styrrach and some other she had killed had somehow found her here, wherever she had travelled to, and she had to defend herself if she intended to find Deineike.

The attempt to rise so fast proved too much. The faces disappeared in a flash of light more brilliant than any thus far. The bright white light burned into her skull, and she collapsed backward, exhausted by the effort. She snapped the eye closed, but the light still seared into every part of her head.

A voice came to her from far away. "Be still. You have sustained terrible injury. Do not attempt to move yet."

If she had possessed the energy, she might have laughed at the absurd comment. Terrible injury? She had died, the worst injury a person could suffer. Thirst clawed at her sand-dry mouth, and she wondered whether water could be found in this land to which she had travelled. It would not do to lie here all but blinded. Once more, she forced her eyes open.

The faces refused to come into full clarity, but they took on some semblance of familiarity when she concentrated. It hurt to focus, but she managed to squint up at the faces, and recognition dawned on her. "Gaish?" Sadness washed over her; her friend had died as well, but it felt good to have him here with her. If his eyes worked better than her own, he could help her find Deineike.

"By the fates, it is good to see you awake. We thought we had lost you." Her friend's words made no sense. She had not awoken, she had died.

The other face also seemed familiar—Faltren, one of the two mariners from Dur. The entire crew must have drowned, she guessed. "I am thirsty." She had said the words, but the croak she heard could not have come from her, feeble and scratched, like an old tabletop, worn and damaged beyond further use.

Faltren laughed. "As are we. Water we have aplenty, yet we cannot drink it. Such are the fates written for us."

It hurt too much to unravel his words. "What do you mean?"

Gaish answered her. "The sea water is too salty to drink. You know this."

"We have travelled to a sea?"

His answer made no sense. "We sailed on the sea, now we drift on it."

Faltren sounded distant, as though he spoke from some far shore. "She is confused. The blow to her head has perplexed her."

She tried to explain what they appeared not to have grasped. "I am dead. I am not perplexed. This must be the way things are wherever I have travelled to." The conversation drained what little strength she had.

"You are not dead, although I think, for a time, you walked in the shadows of that place. We found you in the water near where the ship sank. You have sustained a terrible blow to your head. The cut is deep, and we have only crude bandages torn from our tunics." Gaish's response proved too much to listen to, and it made no sense, after all else.

Faltren spoke again, and his voice sounded closer. "Also, we have a shortage of tunics, since yours became lost somehow, and we had to use one of ours to cover your modesty."

Their words were ridiculous, the babbling of infants. The effort to understand them hurt her head too much. She did not reply, and Gaish took one of her hands and drew it upward. Despite his efforts to be gentle, she cried out in pain, her entire body wracked with agony. Her head hurt so much, she had not noticed the additional pain. He lowered her hand again.

She felt the surface below her fingers. Wood, she thought. "Are we on a new ship, then?"

Faltren replied as Gaish stared at her, concern deep in his blue eyes. "That we are not. We are on a small piece of the deck of The Ictharelian that broke away intact, thank the fates. We pulled you onto it when we found you. There is scarce room for the three of us."

She could not believe him. How could this piece of wood have survived when the ship sank? Then she remembered the black and white giant had crashed down onto the deck of the ship and smashed it into pieces. How had they even crawled onto so small a piece? Concentration hurt too much; she let the thought go.

Gaish took up the incredible story. "Now we drift at the mercy of the wind and tide and hope some ship sees us as it passes, or we strike land."

"And if not?" They did not reply, and she realised why. Death. The place Yilmay had thought she had been mere moments ago now awaited, if not today or the next day, then not long. They would all die here as they floated on this piece of wood. She closed her eyes. They had rescued her, or so they thought. They had done no more than delay her death and make the piece of wood too small for them all. She whispered, defeated and breathless. "Push me in." She might as well drown now as die of thirst in a few days. At the least, the others would have more room on the little platform they must call their Pyre.

Gaish's firm answer left no doubt about his loyalty to his friend. "That we will not do, never. Do not ask it again."

Yilmay sighed. He had been a good friend, and now he would not kill her, though she asked him to. Synna had been such a friend also. She missed him.

She slept for a time, and when she woke, she thought her head hurt a little less. It proved easier to open her eyes, and her vision seemed clearer. "How long did I sleep?" To form the words took such effort, it drained her each time she spoke.

Faltren answered after a quick glance at the sun as it blazed above them. "Two hours, more or less."

"That is all? Others may be nearby, in the water. We must help them."

"I understand." Yilmay did not grasp what Faltren had understood. "You did not mean just now. You lay unconscious for the better part of a day before you awoke the first time. We felt certain you would die."

Yilmay should have died, and she knew it. Against all odds, she had been flung from the mast, and the fall had not killed her. As she sank into the depths of the water, she had not drowned. The mast had fallen onto her, but she had survived that as well. "I must be unkillable." She dragged a weak smile to her lips.

She raised a hand to her head, slow and gentle, but the effort sent fresh waves of agony through her. Why did her body ache so much? Granted, she had fallen into the water from a great height, then a mast fell onto her, but nothing more serious had turned. She smiled to herself, amused by the jest. When she ran her hand over her head, a cloth covered the top of her skull, tied at one side above an ear. She pushed her fingers under the cloth and found a gash that ran the length of the top of her head. Experience told her she had suffered a bad wound. When she pressed a finger into the cut, she felt something hard. Her scalp had been cut to the bone, she guessed. Whether all the bones of her head remained intact, she could not tell.

Yilmay sighed and withdrew the hand. "That hurts even worse than it feels." She forced another smile to her lips. Her comment about the search for the others came back to her. "Did any others survive?" She needed to know some of them had not died. The more of them scattered about this foreign sea, the better the chance one would be found, and a search made for others.

This time, Gaish answered. "Some survived the destruction of the ship. What became of them I cannot say. Some did not survive; we know this for certain."

She did not press him on how he knew this—she could guess. It must have been hard for them to see friends as they floated in the water, dead. "Could we row this platform with something?"

The defeat in Faltren's voice crushed her like the mast that had all but ended her life. "We could not rescue anything suitable. We tried to row with our hands, but it exhausted us, and we rowed little faster than we drifted. We gave up."

Everything pointed to their ruin. They had no idea where they were, had no food, and, worse, no water. Another thought came to her. "Have you tried to catch fish?"

Gaish sounded as miserable as Faltren, and who could blame him? "We have no line."

"Could we make one from our clothes? She mumbled as she turned over the possibilities in her painful mind.

Faltren sighed, a deep, defeated huff of breath, that of a man resigned to his fate. "We have no hook." That posed a more difficult problem, and one her mind could not consider without even more agony in her head.

Gaish compounded their difficulties. "Nor bait."

Yilmay knew next to nothing about how to fish, and it sounded more complicated than she had realised. She abandoned the idea. They were about to become ravenous. Yilmay ate little enough at any time, but to eat nothing, drink nothing as the sun beat down on them… They were in a desperate predicament. "Someone will sail by." Had she tried to reassure herself or her companions? "Lands in this part of the globe must trade with each other, must they not?" Gaish laughed. "What amuses you?"

"You said this part of the globe. You believe we proved the theory?"

Yilmay did not hesitate. "That I do."

He smiled at her and nodded. "We may have proved it, but none will learn of it if we die."

"Then we shall not die." She attempted to sound cheerful, but her small, croaky voice sounded no different to her ears than everything else she had said. Gaish smiled at her again.

The sun beat down on them as the platform drifted in the water, carried by the whims of wind and wave where they wished. She did not doubt it would be difficult to row with their hands, but she resolved to attempt it once her condition improved, and she recovered her strength. She pulled her fan from her boot and waved it before her face, grateful for the somewhat cooler air. After a time, she passed it to Gaish, and he wafted air over his face with it.

Faltren pulled his tunic off and passed it to Gaish, who had been bare-chested. "It is the midday. Time for the change."

Gaish nodded his appreciation and pulled the tunic on. Yilmay felt a pang of guilt. Each of them went without a tunic for half of the day so she could wear the other one. She doubted she had the strength to remove the tunic even if she had the desire. She drifted off into a restless sleep and woke thirstier, more uncomfortable and with no less pain in her head. When she turned her head, Faltren slept next to her. Gaish sat by her feet and stared out at the horizon as though he wished for sails to appear that might indicate a ship came to rescue them.

As the hours wore on, darkness closed around them and brought some relief from the heat of the sun on their faces and bodies. Yilmay stared up at the lights above her. They were not the ones she knew, but the night sky extended across the entire globe. They had observed the pattern of the lights change as they had sailed westward over the last two years. She tried to count them, but they were too numerous, and it made her head hurt more. They fascinated her. Whoever lit all the lanterns must be the busiest person there had ever been. To boil animal fat down into the flammable liquid used for the lights would be an enormous task for so many lanterns, unless they burned in a different way from those around the Torr Sea.

Sleep brought a temporary end to the pain in her head, but their dire situation had not improved when she woke the next day. Gaish and Faltren slept on, and she tried to sit up while they could not order her to rest. Already she had grown bored as she did nothing but lie on her back and stare up at the sky, and she had been awake one day, no more. Fatigue threatened to swamp her, and the pain in her head intensified so much, it made her cry, but with a great effort, she sat upright. She cradled her head in her hands and pressed her palms against her temples in a vain attempt to ease the pain that coursed through her like rivers of fire. She felt dizzy and could not leave her hands against her head for long before she needed to place them either side of her so she did not fall over into the sea. Gaish woke, and he fussed over her as soon as he saw she had sat up. She shushed his protests away as she gazed around. The small platform gave them more space than she had first thought.

"We could fashion oars from a plank torn from the outer edge of the platform." Her voice seemed to wake Faltren, who asked what she had said.

She repeated her idea, but he shook his head. Neither of the men wanted to make the platform any smaller, and Faltren expressed grave concerns that if they pulled a plank away, the entire thing might come unmade. Yilmay abandoned the idea. Where would they have rowed to in any event? They had no idea where the nearest land could be found, and no matter in which direction they rowed, they might row deeper into the depths of the sea, away from land just over the horizon.

She grew tired and had to lie down again. At the midday Gaish handed the tunic back to Faltren. They seemed to have worked out a system that kept the sun off themselves as best they could. She admired their spirit of co-operation and suggested they all make a pact not to complain about the sun, their hunger, or their thirst. They could not risk any squabble or fight. They agreed with her, and the three of them struck the bargain. She proposed her own tunic became part of the arrangement, but they would not hear of it, so she gave up her efforts to persuade them and fell into another sleep.

CHAPTER 6
YILMAY

nother day dragged by, and darkness closed around the little platform again. The night turned cold, and they huddled together for warmth. Gaish lay between the two who were fortunate enough to have a tunic, and they each wrapped him in their arms, although Yilmay could do little more than drape an arm over him, since to lie on her side brought too much pain.

They woke together. Doubtless they had disturbed each other as they moved, yawned, and stretched as people will when they awake. Yilmay felt so thirsty, she doubted she could survive another day. How long could a body go without water before it shut down and life drifted away from it? Her tongue seemed to fill her mouth, her lips cracked and dry. She could summon little saliva to moisten them with when she ran her tongue over them. Although she had not been required to pass water or any other waste under the gaze of the men since she had woken two days ago, that could not be healthy, and she reasoned it owed much to the lack of water. She stared in dejection at the sea all around her, but she knew to drink it would be a terrible mistake that could bring her ruin. On every ship she had crewed, she had heard the warning. "Do not drink seawater." The salt in the sea made it unsafe to drink, it seemed. Somebody once told her that if a person drank seawater, they became thirstier than if they had drunk nothing, since the body worked in some way to expel all the excess salt from itself, which required more water than a person took in. She could not be certain she believed the tale but had no desire to roll the dice. Not yet leastways.

As the morning wore on, she managed to sit up again. Gaish asked how she felt. If there had been any improvement in how she felt, it did not register, but she assured them she felt better. She guessed a little good news would do none of them any harm as they continued to drift along like the clouds above them that brought short periods of relief as they blocked out the sun.

Faltren crawled to the edge of the platform and dangled his legs into the water. He said it felt cooler than the air, and it brought him some relief from the sun's heat. He splashed some water onto his face despite Gaish's concern about it. Gaish believed the salt would dry on his face and might burn him more.

Yilmay thought Gaish's concern far-fetched, and Faltren did too. He laughed and splashed water at Yilmay and Gaish before he returned his attention to the horizon as he continued to kick his legs in the water. He laughed for no visible reason, but with a grin, he explained what amused him. "A fish brushed my feet. If I could lure it to—"

He did not finish his sentence. His body jerked and his hands clutched at the wooden boards. With a scream, he disappeared beneath the waves.

Yilmay and Gaish shouted his name at the same moment and crawled to the platform's edge to peer down into the water. "Did he fall?" Gaish sounded breathless with surprise.

"I do not think so. Something pulled him into the water, I think."

"Can you see him?"

She could not, though she believed some movement below the surface caught her eye. They peered into the water for some time, but Faltren did not resurface. His clothes did not rise to the top, and they could see no blood in the water.

Exhausted by the incident, Yilmay slumped back on her haunches. "What took him?"

Gaish did not reply. He continued to stare down into the dark depths for a considerable time, as if his vigilance might bring Faltren back to the platform. Yilmay lay down, and the pain in her head combined with the shock of Faltren's sudden disappearance soon made her fall asleep.

When she woke, the sun had sunk low in the sky on its journey to the western horizon. The horror of what had turned washed over her, and she felt she must cry, but no tears came to her eyes. Gaish sat next to her and stared in dismay at the wooden platform, all that lay between them and the water that seemed determined to take them down to Helchik's treasure, to snuff out their lives as they might extinguish a candle.

"We must share the tunic now." Yilmay whispered, afraid to speak too loud in case whatever had taken Faltren heard her and came back to claim her as its evening meal.

"What?"

"He wore the tunic you shared with him. We must share this one, or you will get no relief at all from the sun."

He turned to look at her. "That is his tunic."

Yilmay wondered whether he had made some point that eluded her or had spoken out of habit. "While you wear it, I will lie on my stomach. I am unconcerned if you see me without it if that concerns you."

"My thanks." He sounded distracted, and Yilmay wondered if her words had registered with him.

"Tomorrow you can wear the tunic." Yilmay lay down. She felt weak, and her thirst gnawed at her, almost unbearable. She felt hungry, hungrier than she could ever recall. The prospect she might die in the night whispered in her mind. If not tonight, tomorrow for certain, and she lay in abject misery on the piece of The Ictharelian's deck as she contemplated her life to that point. She believed she deserved little more than death here in the middle of the sea, starved, thirsty, and burned by the sun, payment for all she had done. If she had the strength in the morning, she might dangle her legs in the water and see if she could conjure up a quick death. It seemed preferable to the alternative if she lay on the platform to await her ruin.

It proved hard for Yilmay to get to sleep, although Gaish's breaths told her he had drifted into sleep long before it came to bring her any relief. The nightmares that used to plague her came less often these days, but on what might be her last ever night of sleep, they returned in force. She drifted on a platform constructed from the bodies of the people she had killed, roped together with what looked like human entrails, on a vermilion sea. Giants leapt from the water and passed over her head. They had the faces of some who had come into her life but were now gone; Deineike, Arella, Synna, Klordia, Pettra, Styrrach, Hiw.

As they passed over her, they gnashed at her with their teeth and often nipped some piece of flesh from her. Her bones appeared where the giants had eaten away at her. Arella split Yilmay's skull from forehead to the top of her neck with her vicious fangs, and Yilmay's blood flowed down over what remained of her body. At last, they had eaten all her flesh until only her bones remained, but she had not died. Still, they jumped over her and nipped at her.

Distressed, Yilmay cried aloud. "Why do you torment me?"

They all cried their answer together. "You deserve nothing less. You killed us all. We all love you."

"Free me from this life." Yilmay clenched her bony fists and waved them at the giants.

"You will never find land. You will drift here forever, far from—"

"Land." The cry brought her out of the nightmare.

She opened her eyes and struggled to sit upright. Gaish peered east and shielded his eyes from the sun as it rose. "Land."

Yilmay shielded her own eyes with a hand as she stared into the sun. She could see nothing, no matter how she squinted. "Have you imagined you see land? Your mind breaks from the lack of water."

He would not be denied. "There." He pointed eastward. Yilmay still saw nothing. She shook her head in despair and prepared to lie down, ready to await her fate.

He scampered to the edge of the platform, lay on his stomach, and paddled with his arms. With such little strength as she could summon, she pulled at him and urged him to keep his hands out of the water lest the thing that had taken Faltren return and take him. "Let it." He snarled at her and shook her feeble grip from his arm.

Yilmay peered east again, and for a heartbeat she believed she saw something—a smudge on the horizon, nothing more. When she shook her head, she could no longer see it, and guessed her mind had broken at last. Intense pain throbbed at her temples and behind her eyes, and she squeezed her temples in a bid to relieve the pressure of that intolerable agony. At that moment, she saw it again, not a smudge but a cliff. Either she stood at ruin's door and saw whatever lay where she headed, or she had seen land. She lay face down at the opposite side of the platform to Gaish and tried to paddle with one hand. The effort exhausted her, and she could manage no more than a few strokes before she had to rest as her chest heaved from the exertion. Their weakened state meant they paddled so slow, Yilmay believed their progress no faster with it than without.

Gaish hushed her even though she had not said a word. "Listen."

"Listen to what?" Yilmay could not summon the strength to turn and look at him.

He hushed her again. "Shh. Listen."

She lay still and listened as instructed but could hear nothing. With an effort, she turned her head toward Gaish. He sat upright, still as a stone as he stared ahead. Before Yilmay could ask again what he had heard, the sound came to her ears. The unmistakeable sound of water as it swept up over shallow land to break in small waves over solid, dry ground.

As one, they renewed their attempts to paddle. The prospect of land spurred Yilmay on, and from somewhere deep inside she found strength to paddle harder. The waves grew higher as the water became shallower, and their platform rode each new wave toward the white sand ahead of them. Gaish let out a whoop of delight, and they paddled with the last of their strength.

CHAPTER 7
YILMAY

The platform caught on the ground beneath the water and would go no further. Gaish pulled himself to his feet and grasped Yilmay under her arms. He dragged her step by agonised step until they were above the water line, where he collapsed to the floor, spent. Yilmay lay on her back and opened and closed her fists in the warm sand. There could have been no better moment in her life, better than the elation she had felt the first time she had seen Arella, and even better than the hot passionate nights with Deineike. They had survived. A giant had smashed their ship into tiny pieces, but they had lived to tell the tale.

"Yilmay."

"I am here."

"Why do you call me Gaish?"

She snorted. "You know why, do you not? Your name is uncomfortable on my tongue."

"Gaishkantah is difficult for you to say?"

With some effort, she threw some sand toward him. "Gaish is easier."

He fell silent for a time. "I may call you Yil then."

"Gaish my friend, you may call me whatever you like. We are alive and on dry land, after all else." She laughed despite the pain the effort brought to her head.

The sun rose higher in the sky, and Gaish staggered to his feet to wrap his arms around her again. Yilmay tried to stand but lacked the strength, so he dragged her across the sand until they reached the shade of a tall tree close to the sandy shore they had landed on. He collapsed to the floor and gasped for breath, exhausted from the effort. Yilmay luxuriated in the shade, the first time the sun had not scorched their bodies for three days—four, if she counted the day she lay unconscious on the platform.

After some time, his breaths returned to normal, and she reached out a hand to touch him, breathed her gratitude with what feeble strength remained in her broken body. "My thanks."

"We are not yet safe. We must find food and water if we are to survive. We are both at the door of our ruin. I will seek some when my breath returns."

He sat for a while, his back against the tree as he gazed around in wonder. Yilmay did not believe they had drifted long enough to have returned to the land they had left before the incident that destroyed The Ictharelian. The ship must have been little more than a day or two from where they had washed ashore. She did not recognise the plants and trees around her, so she did not think they had returned home yet, but for now they were alive and on dry land. That would suffice until her strength returned.

With a bone weary sigh, Gaish dragged himself to his feet, and Yilmay shot him an appreciative glance before he set off in search of food. Left alone, she thought back on recent days. She owed Gaish her life, and he had not deserted her as she lay in the shadow of death. Even when they came ashore, he spent the last of his strength to drag her up the sand and under the shade of the tree.

Now he had gone off in search of food and water to keep them alive. His loyalty and dedication reminded her of Synna.

Once they returned to Vyrrmod, she thought she might take some time away from the mariner's life and consider what else she could do. Although the seasons had been different and difficult to follow in strange lands, she believed she was now around twenty-seven years, and the physical work of a mariner had worn her down at times. She would seek something easier without the risk she might be landed on by giants or dragged to the bottom of the sea by some unseen monster. She could look for Vamma in Malka-rtas and see whether their paths might lie together for a time.

Gaish returned some time later, and she sat up. He carried four round, reddish-yellow coloured fruits she did not recognise. He handed her two, and she stared at them. "Are they safe to eat?"

"They are safe." He wore a grin, the first look of anything other than resignation he had turned on her for days.

Despite his answer, she made no move to eat them. "How do you know this?"

"I have already eaten one."

"You get three where I get only two?"

"Who will have to carry whom?"

"That is fair, I imagine." They both broke into laughter, unable to continue the jest any further.

She bit into the fruit and found it dry, tough, and bitter. For a moment, she thought she would spit it out, but she had eaten nothing for at least four days, so she persevered as Gaish watched her with a faint smile on his lips. Yilmay looked up at him. "This is horrible."

"It is vile, I agree." The smirk did not leave his face.

Why did he look so happy with himself as she chewed at the tough fruit? She took another, smaller bite and chewed it until she had mashed it up enough to swallow. Beneath the two bite marks, she noticed some inner part that did not resemble the outer. She dug at the inside with her finger and put a small amount of it in her mouth. The juicy inside tasted sweet, ecstasy in her mouth after so long without food or water. When she glanced up at Gaish, he had torn the outer layer off one of his fruits. The bitter outer core must form some sort of protective skin that could not be eaten. He smiled and sniggered from time to time as he pulled the cover off. "I hate you." She smiled as she spat out the insult. He had played a perfect prank, and she had fallen for it.

"I imagine you do." The mouth full of fruit muffled his words. The strange way he never replied with, "That they are," or, "That I do not," when he spoke had always intrigued Yilmay. He had dismissed it as nothing more than the way people spoke in eastern Steinlund, where he had grown up, but even when she spoke his language, Yilmay could not change the way she spoke.

Yilmay tore the covers off both her pieces of fruit. The inside consisted of smaller portions that could be pulled out and popped into the mouth. The distinctive flavour danced on her tongue, and the juices sluiced her bone-dry mouth and throat. When she had finished, she scoured the cast-off outer layers without success for some small pieces of the tender insides that might still be attached to them.

Gaish stood again. "I seem to recall that someone who has not eaten for a while ought not to eat too much at first." Yilmay waved a dismissive hand at him as she looked around for more of the fruits. "There is a stream nearby, if you can move a little more."

"That I can. I crave water. Never have I craved anything more."

He laughed. "Never?"

"Never." At that moment, she meant it.

Try as she might, she still could not stand. Dizziness overcame her, and she could not support herself as her legs buckled beneath her. She had no confidence they would not fold and deposit her on the ground, but she could not ask Gaish to expend more of what little strength remained to him to drag her, so they compromised, and she crawled forward on her hands and knees while he loitered beside her ready to assist if need be. By the time they reached the stream, they were both close to collapse, and she fell forward onto her stomach. Yilmay cupped her hands side by side and dipped them in the cold water, then took a sip. More water spilled out onto the ground than went into her mouth, but she judged it the best drink of her life. Nothing else compared, not the fine wine Bushy's brother had discovered beneath his counter many years ago in the Eastlands, nor the expensive wines Raolos had served from time to time.

Once she had taken several mouthfuls of the fresh, clear water, Yilmay splashed her face with large amounts of it to clean the salt and filth from it. The cold shocked her and even diverted attention from the pain in her head. She felt much improved with the fruit and water in her stomach and managed to sit upright with her back against a nearby tree while Gaish drank and bathed in the stream.

He sat beside her when he had finished, and she laid her head on his shoulder. "What now, Gaish?" She spoke in a feeble voice, tired from everything that had turned since the ship sank.

He stroked her hair. "We are strange friends, you and I. We are so different, and yet so alike."

"We are not so different. We do not interest each other, for one thing."

He laughed, a laugh as soft as the tinkle of a brook over a small pebble. After almost a year at sea, he had told her he found women undesirable. He said he had never told anybody before out of fear for his safety, but for some reason he had felt he could trust her. In turn, Yilmay had admitted she found only women attractive, and they had been all but inseparable from that moment.

He gave the top of her head a tender kiss. "You are in terrible condition."

"My thanks." He had the right of it, after all else, despite her jest.

"Our priority must be to find help for you. The damage to your body is bad, but it is your head I worry about the most. That is a desperate gash, and you lack the strength to stand."

"I can stand, but I am too dizzy to stand for any time. That is the true problem."

He snorted. "That fills me with more misery. That could mean your brain is affected."

She laughed, almost too tired to find the laughter within her. "Some would say it has been this way for many years."

He chuckled at her answer. "You, more than any other, little yelfret." Long ago, when he first realised how much she despised herself for all she had wrought, he had told her the story of the yelfret, a small animal from Steinlund. It seemed the animal would throw itself to its death from tall trees for reasons no scholar had ever determined. It would mate, raise its young, then jump to its death. She had been both horrified by, and sympathetic to, his description of the creature. "To return to the problem, this stream must originate further inland. We could follow it and come to a settlement where we might find some help."

She groaned. "I will attempt it, but not today. I am too tired." He kissed the top of her head again. "If you find me some more of those fruits, I will give you all the coin I have."

"All the coin? How much is that, then?"

"None."

He sniggered. "None? A handsome sum that will double my wealth. I will do it."

He stood and left her alone again for some time, and she dozed in the warm, still air. The shade of the large tree that spread a canopy of dense leaves above her shielded her from the worst of the midday sun. Gaish's return woke her, and she stretched her arms above her head with care. He carried six of the fruits, and they ate three apiece in silence, other than the dreadful noises they each made as they sucked on the food.

She took another generous drink of the water from the stream and leaned back against the tree. "Gaish, I think you should leave me here and go in search of aid."

He objected at once. "I cannot do that. If it takes me a day to find help, you will be dead before I can return."

Yilmay could not bring herself to tell him she thought she could not travel more than a few steps before she collapsed. She clung to life by the slenderest of threads, and his assessment of her chances had been on the generous side. "If it takes you a day, it will take me three. We will both be dead."

"I cannot leave you here to die alone while I save myself." Tears came to his eyes.

She smiled at him. "You have done more than enough, and more than most would have done. You saved me from the sea, dragged me here, brought me that delicious fruit, found me some water. I can ask no more of you, but this I do ask. Follow the stream alone. If you find help in time, return and save me. If not, then it is little more than I have earned in a life filled with ill deeds."

He muttered, anger in his exhausted voice. "Do not speak so. Why do you despise yourself?"

"Gaish, you know so little about me. You think me a marvellous thing, a woman who became a mariner. I became a mariner to run away from my past."

"Nobody's past can be so bad they deserve death. I cannot accept it." He seemed reluctant to think ill of his friend, more so as she lay at death's door.

"I am a killer. I have killed more people than I can count. It feels as though I have killed more people than there are lights of the night sky. Men, women, unborn children. All fell under my blade."

He stared at her. "You jest. Look at you. You are such a little thing."

She gave him a sad smile. "That I am. A small, inconspicuous bringer of death and destruction. All who touch me are introduced to my companion. It stalks me without respite. While aboard The Ictharelian, I found the most peaceful time of my life, until that giant wrote our fates as it did."

"Can you not forgive yourself for all you did before? I have known you two years. I do not care what you were before. If I am asked to give a judgement, I will say, 'Yilmay is a good and loyal friend and a hard worker. Despite her atrocious hair, she is as fine a woman as walks the land.' The globe, I mean, of course."

She flashed him a weak smile and whispered her gratitude. "My thanks. You are also a good friend. I had another friend once, and you remind me of him. Synna. He died before his time. Almost everybody who comes into contact with me does, I fear."

"I will set out early in the morning. If I can find help within a reasonable time, I will return with that help. If not, I will return alone, and we will die together."

Yilmay wiped at her eyes with the back of a hand. "There could be no finer friend to die alongside. If you bring back some of that fruit, I will let you die first."

He grinned at her. "Only so you may eat the remains of my share."

She shrugged and smiled. "You have uncovered my plan. Curses."

They settled down for the night as the darkness closed around them once more. Although she hated to sleep on the hard ground, Yilmay found the soft grass far more comfortable than the wooden platform had been. When she woke, the sun pushed its head over the nearby bushes, several of the reddish-yellow fruits lay next to her, and Gaish had gone.

Yilmay took a drink from the stream and splashed the cold water into her face. She tore the covers from three of the fruits, ate them, and revelled in their lusciousness. The juice had sprayed all around her, and she wiped it from her chin.

She leaned back against the tree and sighed. The crawl to the stream and back had exhausted her. Her time must now be measured in hours, not days. Although she had kept it from Gaish, she had realised last night that the agony in her head, the dizziness, and the pain in her body that seeped into her bones meant she could not have walked to the other side of the stream, much less for a day in search of some help, help that might be insufficient to save her, after all else. This morning, she knew it for certain. In her dreams last night, Deineike, Arella, Pettra, and Klordia came to greet her and begged her to join them. It had not been a nightmare. Rather, it had been peaceful, but it spoke of the certainty of death. She had resigned herself to it, and she hoped Gaish would survive and return home, where he might find the love of a good man. He deserved it.

An hour passed. A small, four-legged animal wandered past her and walked over her outstretched legs as though she might be nothing more troublesome than a fallen tree branch to climb over. The brown, short, squat animal had a stubby nose, and long whiskers protruded from the side of its face. Had he been here, Gaish might have found a way to kill it and provide them with some cooked meat, if they could start a fire. He had gone, and the creature wandered on, unaware of how its fate had been written.

The sun climbed the sky and passed behind the canopy of the tree. In her weakened state, Yilmay struggled to draw breath, but she felt grateful for the shade. It would not be pleasant to die in the extreme heat of direct sunlight. She rested her head against the tree and whispered aloud. "Goodbye Deineike, my love." She closed her eyes and waited for death to claim her.

CHAPTER 8
GAISHKANTAH

Gaishkantah rose before the sun. He took a long drink of the water and gathered some of the fruit from a nearby bush he had found last night. As he had returned the previous day with only two of the fruits despite a lengthy search, he had stumbled upon it. It had been laden, and he had returned to Yilmay with four of them. This morning, he scooped as many as he could carry and filled the pockets of his trousers, then took them back to the tree and dropped several of them next to Yilmay. He gazed down on her as she slept, tears in his eyes. Despite the previous night's revelations, he loved her like a sister and could not abandon her. He crouched beside her, kissed the end of one of his fingers, placed it against her cheek, then strode off alongside the stream.

In spite of his weakness, he remained determined to find help. He pushed through the vegetation and navigated his way around trees and the occasional hill, always with the stream on his right. He soon tired, but if he had found no help by the midday, Yilmay would be lost to him. She had said nothing, but he could see it in her body, in her eyes; she had all but surrendered. How she had survived this long in such pain he did not know, but she had great toughness, and she would fight until the end, he guessed.

He ate two of the fruits as he walked, and he laughed to himself as he recalled how Yilmay had tried to eat the outer skin. He had done the same thing with the first one he had eaten and had been unable to resist the jest. She had chewed at the vile, fibrous skin while he battled laughter. The look on her face when she found the inner fruit so delicious had been priceless. He longed to see that look again.

He had walked for around five hours, his strength all but spent. The sun had almost climbed to the high point of the sky, and he wondered whether he should abandon his search and return to Yilmay in the vague hope she still lived when he returned. He pushed past a tall bush and came face to face with a tall, slender man, naked apart from a cloth around his neck and over his chest. Gaishkantah could not understand why the man would leave his manhood uncovered while he covered his chest. The man looked startled but did not seem to be armed.

Gaishkantah held up his hands in a peaceful gesture and lowered his head at the same time. "My friend needs help." He had no time to waste on introductions or idle conversation. He looked up at the man, who knitted his brow. The man spoke, but Gaishkantah could not understand what he had said. To his left, Gaishkantah spotted a bare patch of ground, and he beckoned to the man to join him as he crouched down and drew in the dirt with a stick he found nearby. He drew two figures and pointed to them, then to himself and the man. The man seemed to grasp the significance, and he became animated as he pointed at each of them in turn several times.

Gaishkantah scratched with his stick again and drew a figure with two large circles just under the head. He looked up in hope as the man peered at the latest addition to the scene. His eyes opened wide, and he used his hands against his own chest as though he cupped what Gaishkantah took to be breasts. Gaishkantah nodded his head several times. How could he indicate Yilmay's injury in the picture? He decided he could not, but he could borrow a move from his new friend and mimic it. He pointed again at the representation of Yilmay in the dirt, then fell to the ground and moaned as though hurt. The man crouched, placed a hand on Gaishkantah's arm, and appeared concerned. Gaishkantah pointed at himself and shook his head as he raised himself into a crouch again, then pointed at the representation of Yilmay and repeated the fall.

The man laughed and spoke, his tone excited. Then he pointed at the drawing of Yilmay and mimicked a person in pain. Gaishkantah nodded his head again and pointed back the way he had come. The man pulled him to his feet and set off in that direction. Gaishkantah worried this one man could not render much assistance to Yilmay but had no choice but to follow him.

Not far along the stream, the man turned right and strode on. Gaishkantah tried to explain he headed in the wrong direction, but the man waved an arm in the air and increased his pace. Gaishkantah struggled to keep up with him after his recent ordeals, but he would not give up on Yilmay. They burst into a clear area in which Gaishkantah saw many huts that appeared to have been constructed from vegetation of some kind. People wandered around the settlement everywhere, men, women, children of all ages, and his guide shouted words Gaishkantah could not understand. People approached and stared at Gaishkantah in curiosity, but the man who led him pointed at some of them and clapped his hands together. Several of them scampered off, and a few moments later a cart appeared, pulled by the smallest horse Gaishkantah had ever seen. Two women sat in the cart, with a large bundle between them covered by a blanket. Three other men walked beside it and they spoke to the guide in rapid words. Gaishkantah's new friend looked at him, his eyebrows raised in a silent question.

Gaishkantah turned and headed back toward the vegetation,

but the man pulled him aside and pointed to a path Gaishkantah had not noticed. They might make faster progress, but they ran the risk they might miss Yilmay. Still, the sand fell, and Gaishkantah set out along the path as fast as he could go. One of the women called out, and the guide pointed at Gaishkantah, then at the cart. He had the right of it; it would be faster if Gaishkantah rode in the cart. In his weak and exhausted state, he could not walk at speed, and they needed speed if they were to save Yilmay's life.

He guessed they had travelled for three hours when he saw a laden bush of fruit. He hoped it was the same one. It stood no more than five paces into the vegetation from the path, and had he not been up in the cart, he may not have noticed it. He cursed his luck he had missed the path by such a small margin this morning, but he shouted for them to stop.

He struggled down from the cart and pushed into the vegetation. It had to be the bush, he thought. He could see the bare spots where he had picked the fruit that morning. Soon enough, he burst out of the tall grass and saw Yilmay. She had fallen onto her side, her eyes closed, and she lay motionless. He ran forward, his heart in his mouth. Had they come too late? Where he found the strength to run, he did not know, unless it came from his concern for Yilmay.

He crouched down beside her and whispered to her, urgent and concerned. "Yilmay." He shook her. "Yilmay, wake up. Can you hear me?" The salt sting of tears stung his eyes as the local people stood and watched. "Yilmay." He gave her another, firmer, shake.

Her eyes opened and she looked up at him. "Are we dead again, Gaish?" He strained to hear her soft, weary voice. "Is this where we travel to afterward? I am sorry, I could not wait for you."

The tears ran down his face. "We are not dead, Yilmay. We are alive, although I feared you were not. These people have come to help you. They live three hours from here. They will help me carry you to their cart."

"What cart?" Her voice was no more than the kiss of a soft breeze on his ear.

She needed help without delay, and still she might die, he feared. "It is on the path, not twenty paces from here."

"There is a path we could have travelled on?"

"There is."

Her eyes closed. "You are a terrible friend." He cried with happiness.

The two women squeezed past him and looked at Yilmay. One of them tutted and pushed at him in an indication he should move away and let them help Yilmay. He fell back onto his behind and drew his legs up, then wrapped his arms around them and watched as the women fussed over Yilmay. One of the men handed him a small piece of meat, and he chewed on it, grateful he had returned in time. He still did not know whether Yilmay could be saved, but he had done all he could. Now it lay in the hands of the fates and the two women.

CHAPTER 9
YILMAY

When Gaish woke her, Yilmay once again believed she had died. She saw the naked people behind him, and he told her they were here to help her. When the two women stared at her and shooed Gaish away, she tried to smile, but any strength she used to have had deserted her, and her facial muscles would not respond. The women unfastened the cloth from her head and gasped as they saw her wound. One of them picked up a bowl, which she filled with water from the stream. They dipped some cloth they must have brought with them into the water and used it to wipe the top of her head. An unfamiliar smell filled her nostrils as they rubbed the top of her head, and she guessed they had applied some sort of salve, like the Tryngelk people had done after her fight with the dog-like creature.

They inspected her body and manipulated her arms and legs. They appeared satisfied and spoke to the men who stood by. Yilmay could not understand what they had said and had no energy to try. Two of the men bent to lift Yilmay. They carried her through the grass and vegetation to a small cart, drawn by an animal that resembled a small version of a horse, but with bigger ears and a squarer mouth. With great care, they placed her in the back of the cart and folded her legs up so she fitted into the small space.

The women sat in the front of the cart and Gaish squeezed in the back beside her. He sat cross-legged next to her as the cart moved off with a jolt that sent bolts of agony through her entire body, and she believed her head might burst apart from the pain. She closed her eyes and felt the globe slip away from her again.

For much of the journey, Yilmay knew nothing of what turned. There were brief moments of consciousness, but in those moments, she saw nothing and nobody but Gaish, who stared at her with a worried look on his face. Then darkness would fold around her again, and she would remember nothing more for a time. Some time later, the cart stopped and jolted her awake. Men carried her from it into a hut. She noticed some other huts nearby but had no clear vision of where they were. She had not appreciated it, but darkness had almost fallen. She did not know where Gaish had gone.

Throughout the long night, she suffered from the worst pain she had ever endured. Whenever she opened her eyes, she saw the shadowy figures of at least two women who often rubbed the salve, or whatever they applied, into the gash on her head. They had removed her clothes at some point, and she lay naked beneath a heavy blanket. Her body felt as though it had been torn apart by some crazed animal and reassembled without any attempt to repair the damage caused to it.

She fetched up as the night wore on, and for the rest of the night, she got little sleep. If she did not wake to fetch up, the women would wake her with their salve. She doubted she had ever had a night so difficult to bear since the death of Deineike, and more than once she wished Gaish had not returned, and she had died.

The next morning, an older woman entered the hut with a stone bowl in her hands. She pressed it to Yilmay's lips, and though she managed a few sips of the water it held, she lacked the strength to swallow any more. A sudden, blind panic gripped her, and as she grabbed the woman's hand, she knocked the bowl onto the floor and spilled the water.

"Where am I? Where is Gaish?"

Whatever the woman said in response, Yilmay could not understand her. She spoke fast, and her language seemed to be full of short, sharp words. Yilmay could not understand any of it, and she tried to rise from the cot she lay in. The woman pushed her down, and Yilmay lacked the strength to fight her off.

The woman shouted, and Yilmay continued to struggle against her. Others entered the hut, and to her relief she saw Gaish among them. He spoke to her in a small, hushed voice. "Rest, Yilmay. You are still weak."

"Where is this place, Gaish?"

He shrugged. "I have not yet found out. I make little progress with the language difference. You are safe here though. Relax and trust these people."

"Is there any sign of Faltren or the others?"

"I have seen none of them here. That does not mean none live, however. Do not fret over it now. You need rest."

The women ushered him from the hut, but Yilmay called to him as he neared the door. "You saved my life. My thanks." Tears pooled in her eyes. He waved a hand at her as he left, as if to indicate he had done her no more than a small favour.

The days rolled on and on without end. The women tended to Yilmay daily without fail; the salve on her cut, food, water, and bathing, all provided by a procession of women. Their kindness and patience seemed endless, and they encouraged her to move around as much as she could. While she made some progress with their language, she found it complicated and difficult to grasp. She mastered a few simple phrases; how to ask for food or water, or a pot to relieve herself in, and the names of some of those who came most often, although they mispronounced her name. To Yilmay, it sounded as though they said "Yeelmah," and she reasoned her pronunciation of their own words and names must have sounded as bad to them. Both sides avoided any correction of the other after the first few attempts to rectify an error.

Gaish, on the other hand, picked up the language far better than her. In her defence, she thought, he did not struggle under the complication of insufferable headaches that made concentration for more than a moment almost impossible. He visited her often and encouraged her to move around the hut. At first, she could do nothing but crawl, but as the days passed, more strength returned to her body. With his help, she could stand, and with his arm around her waist to help keep her balance, she took a few steps. It tired her, and it confounded her how breathless she became at the slightest exertion. Gaish reminded her often how much she had been hurt, that recovery would be a slow process. She must not rush, nor undo the progress she had made. Those were only words, and they disappeared into the blackness of her mind. Yilmay had to walk so she could leave and return to Vamma. She had grown anxious to return to familiar lands, and the need tore at her like a caged animal as it fought against its constraints.

The passage of time became a blur, and Gaish did not help. Like Deineike, he did not know how many years he was and did not care to mark the passes or even the days. At her best guess, two sevendays had passed since Gaish had dragged her up the sand and off the platform. She badgered Gaish to take her out of the hut and wore him down until he relented. Her strength had improved, although she knew she had a long way to go, but she longed for some fresh air and to see something other than the four walls of the hut.

Gaish supported her at first, and the brightness of the sunshine assailed her eyes once they left the hut. She snapped them shut, and he waited while she opened them a little at a time to allow them to adjust. It surprised her how much brighter it seemed outside the hut, even though it had no windows. Lanterns spluttered in the hut, but she did not recognise the fuel they burned—some liquid the locals poured into stone bowls and set a flame to the top of. She had believed they provided good light, but the sun blinded eyes grown used to the inside of the hut for the past days.

Once she felt ready to continue, they walked on at a painful, slow pace. Many other huts stood around the one they had emerged from. She guessed the huts would be called a village in Dur, but she had no idea what these people called the settlement, nor if it had a name. People moved around the village about their chores. Two women beat what appeared to be the hide of some animal; doubtless they intended to use it for blankets or some such. They all wore so few clothes, it seemed unlikely they made clothing. Men carried large bundles of grass held together by crude ropes of leather or some similar substance. The floors of the hut were covered with the grass, and they changed it every few days. They never disturbed her when they changed the grass, but she always felt guilty.

Children ran around and played games she could not follow. A woman shouted at one group of children, and they looked guilty for a moment, then giggled and ran off. The woman shook her head, a stern look on her face, then smiled and went into a hut. On the edge of the village, Yilmay could see what appeared to be the construction of a new hut. To build it, large numbers of the villagers, men and women alike, bustled around. Some carried large pieces of wood to the area of the new building, where others cut and shaped it. It did not seem the men alone did the hard work, for many of the women also carried and positioned the wood.

Yilmay asked Gaish to let her walk unaided for a time, and he agreed, although he lingered so close to her, she felt her ire rise and snapped at him that she did not need to be babywatched. He looked hurt, and guilt prodded at her with sharp, accusatory fingers. She tried to dismiss her angry outburst, but it left her in a mood she wished to shake, so she forced herself to apologise and dragged a smile to her lips. As long as she went slow enough, she could walk without difficulty. If she tried to speed up, however, she became breathless almost at once. She put the shortness of breath down to her injuries and would not allow herself to brood on it.

As they moved around the village at Yilmay's slow, painful pace, she asked if their hosts had a reflecting glass.

"I have not seen one. Why? Do you wish to see your ugly face again?"

Yilmay laughed at his light-hearted insult. "That I do not. I am blessed with all the ugliness I could desire whenever I look upon you." She waved at one of the women who had tended her. She had emerged from a hut and seemed surprised to see Yilmay. "I wish to see this gash that gave the women such concern."

"Well, that is an ugly sight, I will confess. The gash is healed, almost, but it has left a scar that runs the length of your head and still looks angry and red to my eye. You suffered a terrible injury."

"Are my looks ruined? Will the women of Dur no longer throw themselves at my feet?"

He hesitated before he replied. "You could grow your hair again to hide it." She gave him a playful slap on the arm. He continued, more serious. "In truth, I fear your hair may not grow where the scar takes hold."

Yilmay sighed. She had never been obsessed with her own appearance, but if her hair did not grow back, she would keep it short and hide the scar with a kerchief. Such things did not matter if she could heal. "I have constant headaches. They are painful, too much to bear at times."

"That is to be expected, my guess. A mast fell on you. Most of an entire tree landed on your head." They walked on a few paces. "That poor mast."

She had waited for some jest. "I must learn to fight with my head. I will be unbeatable. Yilmay, Breaker of Masts, they will call me. My fame will spread along the globe."

"Around."

"What?"

"Your fame would spread around the globe, not along it."

She considered the riddle of movement across different shapes for a moment. "You know nothing." They laughed together for a time, a balm for Yilmay's heart. "They are all dead, are they not?"

Pain flashed across his face, but he wrestled it under control. "Hush, Yilmay. You have no way to know their fates."

"When I reached the surface, I watched the aft section disappear beneath the waves, and it carried the tenders with it. They could not have launched them fast enough. Unless they found ample pieces of wood in the sea afterward, none could have survived in those waters. Whatever took Faltren, there must have been more of them, I wager."

"I will not speculate. I will hope more than we two survived."

She placed a hand on his arm to comfort him. "Have you learned what they call this place?" Better to change the subject to something less miserable.

He brightened. "That much I have discovered. The land is called Illfarlen."

"Illfarlen." Yilmay turned the name over in her mind. She had never heard it before, but it felt less strange on her tongue than their language. "Do you know how far we are from Dur, or Steinlund?" The change of subject felt as welcome as a cool breeze on a hot day, and it lifted her spirits again.

He frowned. "They do not know of these places and cannot tell me how far away Dur is."

A thought occurred to her. "They might not call them by our names. They may know of them but call them something different."

He gave a slow, thoughtful nod of his head. "That could be so, but I have drawn a map of the Torr Sea area in the dirt, and they did not recognise it."

She shook her head and refused to lose hope. The movement sent a sharp shaft of pain across the back of her eyes. "This village is small, and these people are unlikely to be explorers. Doubtless we will find a large town where we will find better information."

"We may, I imagine." He sounded as though he held little hope she might be right.

She stopped. "I am tired. I think I will return to the hut and sleep for a time."

"A good idea. So unlike you."

She poked her tongue out at him, and they turned and made their way back to her hut. He helped her inside and saw her settled on her cot before he left. Her progress pleased her, but it disappointed her it had made her so tired. It must be a sure sign of improvement that she had walked for so long unaided. For the first time since the giant had smashed the ship to pieces beneath her, she felt optimistic, and she drifted off into a contented sleep.

CHAPTER 10
YILMAY

The door of the hut opened, and Yilmay woke as one of
the women entered. The woman carried a bowl covered
with a cloth. She smiled at Yilmay as she approached the
cot and handed her the bowl. The meal smelled delicious, and
beneath the cloth, steam rose up from a bowl of broth. The woman
handed her a wooden spoon and turned her attention to Yilmay's
head. The food had a spicy flavour, as most of their food did, and
Yilmay reasoned they used some way to cook or season it that gave
the food its spiciness. As ever, the broth contained flavours Yilmay
almost recognised but could never quite place.

Tonight, the broth had been made from fish, not meat. Yilmay
could not remember a time they had served her fish before. With a
powerful flavour and robust consistency, it resembled meat in some
ways. As Yilmay enjoyed the food, a thought occurred to her. She
caught the attention of the woman and tried to ask her where the
fish had come from. The village must be some hours from the sea
she reasoned, and she wondered how the villagers came by the fish.
Yilmay grew frustrated by her inability to make the woman understand her question, and the woman held up a hand and left the hut

The woman's own frustration must have got the better of her patience, Yilmay thought, and she tutted her annoyance. She ate more of the broth, and to her surprise, Gaish came into the hut with the woman.

"She cannot understand you."

Yilmay guessed the woman had left to bring Gaish to translate for them and felt remorseful she had misjudged her intentions. "I want to find out where the fish comes from."

He shrugged as though the question was unimportant. "The sea, my guess."

Yilmay clucked her tongue as her irritation increased. "I know that." She must keep her voice level so they would not see she had grown angry. "How do they catch it? How do they get enough of it to feed the village?"

Gaish's frown made two vertical creases above his nose. "I do not understand."

"That you do not." She sighed in exasperation. "Do they catch the fish with lines from the land? Does some ship bring it, or does somebody carry it to them after they have caught it elsewhere?"

He repeated his earlier facial expression. "Why do you wish to know this?"

Yilmay clenched her teeth as she fought down her anger. "If someone brings it to them on a ship, we could ask that ship to take us to a larger town where we might find a way home." She measured each word as she battled her impatience.

Gaish still did not seem to grasp her point, but with a shrug he turned to address the woman. He sounded hesitant, and she appeared to struggle to understand the question. His grasp of the language might not include enough words to convey Yilmay's question in full. The woman shook her head, and Yilmay's frustration grew. "Why do you not know enough of their words to ask this question?"

He shot his head around and spat angry words at her. "Why do you not? It is your question, after all else."

She glared at him, and her body shook with anger. "Forget it. It matters not." She put the bowl down, folded her arms across her breast, and stared at Gaish.

"What is wrong?" He still sounded annoyed. "Why are you angry about this?"

"Is it not obvious? I wish to return home. I do not want to stay here." The tone of her voice must sound like poison, that of a furious woman. She had lost patience with the whole affair.

His flat voice suggested he battled his temper as much as Yilmay. "As do I. I meant why are you so angry we cannot make the question understood?"

"Because I am." She balled her fists in irritation. Gaish flinched, and the woman tilted her head to one side as she looked at Yilmay in surprise. Yilmay's head pounded, and her brains seemed ready to burst from her eyes and ears. The air itself seemed to whistle around her. She raised both hands to her head and pressed on her temples with her palms. She closed her eyes and felt Gaish's hand close around one of her wrists. She shook it off and returned the palm to her temple.

The woman whispered something, but Yilmay could not tell whether Gaish had understood. He did not answer, and Yilmay fought down her fury. After a time, she quietened her voice. "Never mind. It matters not. My thanks you tried to ask the question." She lay down on the cot, exhausted by the interaction.

When they left, she wanted to scream and throw things around, to vent her anger by any and all means available, but she could not insult their hospitality no matter how annoyed she had become. Her head seethed like a ball of agony above her shoulders, and she feared the pain might drive her to madness if it did not ease. Her temper ran as hot as an iron pulled from a fire, and seemed reluctant to cool, and her body shook as she screeched, *"Why?"* in her mind. Why could she and Gaish not make themselves understood in this place? They must leave tomorrow. If they went back to the place they had come ashore and followed the coast, they must strike a large town sooner or later, with a dock from which they could sail home to a place where she could hold a conversation without...

Not for the first time in her life, she wished for some word to serve as a vessel for all the bitterness, anger and resentment in her body. Why were Durfolk so polite, curse them? She had heard arguments among mariners in other languages that involved words she did not understand. Yilmay did not doubt they had cursed one another with more fury than Durfolk did. What did she want to say? That she wished to hold a conversation these wretched people could understand? It sounded ridiculous. There must be a word she could use, but "wretched" would not suffice. She would make one up, one she alone knew, and she would use it when she could no longer contain her temper. Nobody would even know she had insulted them.

Her thoughts had strayed far beyond the important issue; how to return home. Somehow, she would persuade Gaish to leave with her in the morning. He had admitted he wanted to return home, so it would not be hard to convince him. She would tell him she felt healed, her strength had returned, and she could leave. If he would not come, she would leave alone. He could not allow that and would doubtless join her if she set off.

As her temper cooled, her exhaustion grew, and it carried her off to a restless sleep. She woke often and tossed and turned in the cot, her mind a whirl of thoughts that kept her awake longer than she wished. When her morning meal arrived, she still felt tired, shattered from the argument the previous evening and the poor sleep through the night.

Once she had eaten, she washed herself with a bowl of water near her cot and supported herself on the doorframe as she opened the door of the hut. She gazed around the village, which looked little different from yesterday. Clouds performed a skittish dance across the sky as a cool breeze chased them, the way a boy might chase a girl in search of a kiss or a favour. Or a girl might chase a girl, she reasoned, in a land that did not see these things in such a harsh light as Dur.

Yilmay had no idea in which hut Gaish slept but set off on a slow walk around the village. She waved to people she recognised or smiled at those she did not. She approached some of them. "Gaish?" They shook their heads when she asked about him. Whether they did not know or did not understand, she could not tell. Her frustration gnawed at her, and she fought it down.

Gaish's voice called to her from behind. "Yilmay. Why are you out alone?"

She pushed an unenthusiastic smile to her lips. "I desired some fresh air. And I wish to apologise for my outburst yesterday. I am not quite myself, my guess."

He returned her smile. "Do not fret. You have suffered much. I have no doubt you will soon return to your usual, somewhat less grumpy self."

The jest pleased her, and she guessed Gaish had tried to convey that no grievance lay between them over the previous day's outburst. "Gaish, I tire of life here. Let us leave. We can use the path to return to where we came ashore and follow the coastline from there. We must find a large town or city with a dock at some point."

"You are not yet strong enough for such a journey." His concern registered on his face and in his voice.

"That I am. I am far stronger now. Do you not see I can walk around without you?"

He seemed doubtful. "It is one thing to hobble around the village, but this might be a lengthy journey. I doubt you can cope yet."

"There is almost nothing I cannot do if I set myself to it." She smiled, and he hesitated, but she pressed on. "I may not move fast, I accept that. But as long as I can focus on a way to get home, and you can round up some of those fruits each day, I will be fine, I promise."

He wrinkled his nose, a sign of uncertainty, she thought. "Even if you could make the walk, we might reach this town and find that no ship sailed to Dur or any land on the Torr Sea."

"You do not know that. The first ship to depart might sail to Zhanghar."

"Or Qagrue."

She shook her head. "It matters not. We can return to Vyrrmod from Qagrue. We will bring our news to Rakulaj, and he will shower fame and coin upon us."

He laughed. "On the subject of coin, we have none. How will we secure passage?"

"We will work." His dark countenance showed his displeasure, and she corrected herself. "You will work."

He looked away and seemed to weigh the proposition. "I know not." Yilmay thought he had spoken to himself.

"I long to be home Gaish. I wish to surrender life as a mariner. I will settle down to a long, dull life and never sail again. The loss of so many friends on The Ictharelian is unbearable to me. I cannot endure it again."

He snapped his head round, his attention back on her. "You are not serious about this."

"That I am. I am as serious as a… As serious as it is possible to be."

He laughed, a snort more than a laugh, doubtless at her failure to find something to be as serious as. "What will you do? We know nothing but the life of a mariner."

Now Yilmay looked away to give herself time to frame her response before she delivered it. "I know other things. I know how to kill, although I wish to turn from that for ever. I am also a garment maker."

"I know you repaired our clothes for us." She detected a hint of mockery in his voice. "But you will need to earn real coin, not a groat here and there when you repair the seat of a pair of work pants torn in a tavern brawl."

She bristled. "I will have you know I am a garment maker of unmatched ability. Portreeves' wives have worn my making. I am exceptional." He did not appear convinced. "Gaish, I will cope. I must get home. I ache to return." A plaintive note had entered her voice. Even she could hear it.

He sighed. "You have been more sister than friend to me. I cannot bear to see you so frustrated. I believe it is this that weighs on you and makes you so irritable. Let us see if we can return you to a land that cures you of these foul tempers."

She stood up on her toes and kissed his cheek. "My thanks. When will we leave?"

"We cannot leave today. We must plan this. We need to arrange some food and water and learn as much as we can about where the nearest docks might be."

His answer disappointed her. She had been ready to set off at once, but she saw sense in being more organised before they left. "Tomorrow?"

He gave his head a frustrated shake. "Let me see what I can learn. I will come to your hut when I have spoken to some of the villagers."

She laughed, anxious to lighten the mood between them. "Do not rush. If we cannot leave today, I will walk more and prepare myself. My strength grows by the hour."

He shook his head. "This is madness." He walked away and disappeared into a hut in the centre of the village.

Yilmay walked on around the village. She decided to investigate the new hut the villagers built, and their progress surprised her.

The frame had now been built, and they trimmed finer branches before they fitted them around the framework, inside one upright, outside one, inside the next, and so on. Yilmay had no idea how to build, much less the method they used here, but she imagined all the huts had been built the same way, and the locals had sufficient experience and expertise to complete the hut.

As Yilmay continued around the edge of the village, she passed the path she believed they must have arrived along on the day they had brought her to the village. Thanks to the care and attention of the women, she had made good progress in that time, and even though she knew she might lack the strength to set off in search of a large town or city, she could not sit around here any longer. She longed to be off, to head back to Vamma's arms and a life where giants could no longer threaten to snatch all her breaths away from her in a heartbeat. She would make it to the nearest docks, or she would die in the attempt.

CHAPTER 11

YILMAY

When Gaish came to the hut that night, Yilmay pretended to feel no fatigue from her walk. She chattered about the progress of the new hut and how excited she felt to be away in the morning. He told her one of the villagers had drawn a map of the area, and a large town lay not too far away. When she asked to see the map, Gaish said it had been drawn in the dirt and existed now only in his memory. The news encouraged her, although Gaish went to great lengths to point out that the existence of a town did not equal the existence of a dock. Her enthusiasm, however, could not be quashed by details.

The villagers would give them a pack full of food and water and had implied both would be plentiful on the way. Gaish grilled Yilmay over her ability to walk the distances that might be involved so soon after a horrendous injury that had almost killed her. She remembered the extreme length of time it had taken Deineike to recover from the injuries she received when she fell from her horse outside Torric. Much of Deineike's difficulty had been that bones had needed to heal, but fortune had smiled on Yilmay, who had not broken any. She assured him she would be fine. In any event, once they had consumed all the food and water, he could carry her, since the pack would be empty. He laughed at her jest, but she saw doubt in his eyes. She said no more, afraid she might increase his suspicion if she objected to his concerns too much.

Yilmay slept well but woke early, excited to be on the path as soon as could be. She still did not know which hut Gaish stayed in, and she had no wish to use the day's energy to wander from hut to hut in search of him, so she waited, seated in the dirt outside her own hut with mounting impatience until he appeared. He stretched and yawned as he approached, and Yilmay strove to look awake and fit, in contrast to him.

The villagers gave them a morning meal, then brought a rough pack and handed it to Gaish. Yilmay embraced the women who had cared for her in so dedicated a manner, and the pair set off down the path as they yelled their thanks to the villagers. Ahead, the path turned a corner, and as they reached it, they looked back. Many of the villagers were still assembled, and they waved to them before they turned the corner. The village disappeared from sight, and they were on their way.

Despite their slow pace, Yilmay still found it hard work. She fought to conceal her struggles from Gaish and jested with him often, but after some distance, she needed to take a break. As she slumped to the grass, he gazed down on her, concern in his eyes.

She tried to reassure him. "It is the first day. I will be used to it before you know it, and you will be left in my wash."

He laughed and went to find some of the reddish-yellow fruits. As Yilmay ate two of them, she jested that she might stay here after all else, she enjoyed the fruits so much. Refreshed, she stood, and they set off again. When they came to the sandy shoreline where they had landed, the wooden platform had gone, doubtless swept back out to sea. The path curved and followed the coastline from that point, and they made their ponderous way west as the sun passed over their heads and sank toward the land before them.

They stopped twice more, and Yilmay refused to give in to her exhaustion. She gritted her teeth and drove herself onward. As darkness fell, they had found no sign of any accommodations, so they fell to the grass under a large tree, drank most of the water that remained, and ate some of the villagers' food.

Gaish asked how she felt, and she lied that she felt no serious effects from the walk. He inspected her head but found no sign of any infection. She took off her boots and rubbed her feet, which were sore on the bottom. She had not often walked this much even when she had been in perfect health, and her feet complained so much, her headache became secondary for now.

They continued the next day but found no sign of the town the villagers had suggested they would reach on the path. Despite the assurances of the villagers, water proved scarce, and they decided to ration it against the prospect they might not find enough. They found a pool early in the morning and filled the animal skin pouch the villagers had given them, but half of it had gone by nightfall, and they had found no other. The fan proved invaluable throughout the day as she waved it before her face, and Yilmay uttered many silent thanks to Wilash for its creation.

When the sun woke them the next morning, Yilmay's back ached so much, she gasped as she sat up. Gaish asked what afflicted her, and she explained about the fragility of her back when it came to nights on the ground. Instead of the sympathetic ear she had hoped for, he laughed and made fun of her. He appeared to find it funny that, after all she had been through, a night asleep on the ground seemed destined to kill her.

They found more water, drank copious amounts of it, and re-filled the water skin. From time to time, they passed a bush that bore the reddish-yellow fruit, and they picked three or four each to carry in their pockets as they tried to eke out the food the villagers had given them. Gaish told her the locals had tried to explain the name of the fruit to him, but he could not find any word in his language to represent the name, which sounded like, "Orange." Yilmay no longer tore the outer layer from the fruit. She sliced them in half with the blade in her fan and pulled the plump, juicy fruit out of the centre of each half. Gaish wondered aloud at the blade concealed in what he had believed to be a normal fan, and Yilmay lied and said a friend had made it for her as both fan and blade for such mundane purposes as cutting up fruit.

Gaish wore a leather tunic of a design Yilmay had never seen before. The villagers had made it for him, he told her. She decided a more feminine version might be a popular item in Dur and stored a study of the design in her memory. Many years before, Deineike had mentioned she wished she could wear a tunic matched with the skirt of a dress, rather than a dress, or tunic and trousers. Yilmay had said she would make such a garment, but she never had. She thought it would pair well with the tunic and vowed to try to create the items once she reached home again.

By the evening of the next day, Yilmay felt drained of all energy. They had walked for three days, and she almost regretted the suggestion they set off before she had recovered more. To turn back now could be worse, so they had little option other than to carry on, but her strength had all but deserted her as she collapsed onto the grass for another night under the lights of the night sky. They had not encountered a single person on the path, and despair ate at Yilmay. What if the villagers had been wrong and the town did not exist at all, or lay so far away, she could not manage the journey? To them, a trip might seem short that would be beyond her capability, given the extent of her injuries.

Gaish hovered over her and wrung his hands together. "What is wrong?"

Yilmay had no intention of letting him know she had come close to the end of her ability to go on. "Why were they all naked?"

"That is what consumes you? That they walk around naked? In truth, I do not know. I imagine they have never had need of clothes.

We wear them because our parents did, and their parents before them, my guess."

She grimaced. "Do not say this. People must continue to wear clothes, or I cannot make my fortune once we are home."

He looked as though he considered her statement before he replied. "I am glad we wear clothes. If we did not, I would be forced to look at your naked hideousness all day as we walk."

She muttered as she fought to repress her laughter. "Be thankful we have no reflecting glass. I have seen you with no tunic, and you are no sight to behold." A short silence followed, and they both laughed at the same moment. "Why did they make you this tunic, if they do not wear clothes?"

"They walk around naked. I do not. This is the closest my explanation and their skills could come. I think it is stylish."

Yilmay pulled a face of disdain. "We have sailed around the globe, found new lands, found and named seven seas, and all you have gained from the experience is an atrocious sense of taste."

Gaish poked his tongue out at her, but they did not speak again. Content she had deflected attention away from her weariness, Yilmay sank to the grass and closed her eyes. Gaish shook her and offered her the water skin and some food, which she accepted with thanks before she lay down again. Sleep came almost at once, and the morning found her reluctant to stir even as Gaish badgered her awake and on to her feet.

They pressed on. Yilmay had summoned and exhausted all her inner strength yesterday, and the night's sleep had done little to replenish those reserves. She stumbled often as her legs refused to obey her feeble exhortations to take each step and not betray the depth of her fatigue. Her head pounded, even worse than the day before, and she longed for more water than Gaish would allow her.

At last, he stopped and stood before her, a hand on each of her shoulders. He stared into her eyes, and she could no longer find the will to force stoicism to her face. He tutted. "Curse you Yilmay, you are spent. I said you were not ready. You would not listen."

"That I would not. I am sorry Gaish. A short rest should see me right again." She sank to the path and bowed her head. His feet turned, and she guessed he looked along the path in the direction they had been headed. She could not summon the energy to raise her head, and she feared if she did, she would find nothing but anger and recrimination in his eyes.

"Somebody approaches." Yilmay could sense the tension that seized him, and she heard wariness in the way he spoke those two words.

She struggled to raise her head and saw a lone man approach. "He is dressed."

"So he is." Gaish did not move.

Yilmay could not be concerned. If they encountered danger, she had no strength to fight it, and she doubted Gaish could wield her fan with any skill. He almost never raised his voice, much less fought. He had avoided arguments with any of the other mariners these two years past, and in truth she had defended him more than he had himself.

She hoped the man would help them. The fact he wore clothes puzzled her, but she had no capacity to find an answer to that riddle in a brain that seemed about to burst from her skull, if the agony in her head meant anything. She sat in misery on the path and waited for him to draw near enough for Gaish to speak to him.

Once the man had come within twenty paces of them, Gaish held up a hand in welcome and said, "Hello there." The man hesitated, then smiled and walked closer, but he extended an arm, mayhap some form of pleasantry here in Illfarlen. They had met nobody in three days on the path, and seen no homes of any kind, and the thought crossed her mind that the man had no business on the path she could bring to mind. He might be a robber, but he would find slim spoils on them, she thought with a grim chuckle.

The man spoke, the same short, sharp language as the villagers, and he kept his arm extended. Gaish made no move to grasp it. Confusion crossed the stranger's face, and he tilted his head to one side. Then a laugh burst from him, and he withdrew his arm and uttered one word. Yilmay recognised it as, "Hello," in his language.

Gaish attempted to explain something to him, but the man knitted his brows in confusion. When Gaish pointed to Yilmay, he appeared to notice her for the first time and crouched before her. He studied her for a moment, then shook his head, rose, and spoke to Gaish again. Gaish in turn shook his head, either because he had not understood, or to deny something the man had asked. Gaish crouched and beckoned to the man to join him. With his finger, Gaish drew a few square boxes in the dirt of the path and added triangles to the tops of them. He had drawn a crude representation of a town, and Yilmay hoped the man would recognise it. She wondered whether he ought to have drawn huts or whether the people of Illfarlen lived in houses in their towns.

Recognition seemed to come to the man, and he made a sound that sounded like, "Ah," as he nodded his head for many heartbeats. He stood and pointed back the way he had come. Relief and frustration swept over Yilmay at the same instant. A town existed, at the least, which confirmed the story the villagers had told. The man had left out the more urgent issue. Would they find the town over the next rise or a sevenday distant? Gaish spoke and moved two fingers in the air in a representation of somebody walking. Yilmay guessed he had enquired how long it would take them to walk, but the man only nodded again.

She tugged at Gaish's trouser leg, and when he glanced down at her, she shook her head. They had made little progress with the man, and her frustration grew. The man pointed at her and said something. She had had her fill of not being able to understand what the man said, and she held up a hand to indicate Gaish should help her to her feet. To her surprise, the other man pulled her to her feet and placed a hand on each of her arms, high up near the shoulder. He said something and appeared concerned. Her weak smile cost more of her strength than she had expected. "My thanks." She had no idea what she had thanked him for.

The man walked on with a cheery wave that Gaish returned. Yilmay preserved such small amounts of energy as she had for the next walk. Without a word, they set off once more. Yilmay could still see no reason for the man to have been on the path but imagined he lived somewhere nearby that could only be reached by some track they had not noticed.

Gaish slipped a supportive arm around her waist, and she flashed him a grateful smile. They walked on, although to Yilmay it seemed they walked so slow, they did little more than stand still. Gaish pressed some water on her, although they had almost emptied the skin. He would not drink any himself and Yilmay did not have the energy to argue.

Yilmay stumbled on with her head bowed and leaned on Gaish as he supported her with an arm around her waist. Without warning, he stopped, and she raised her head. A house stood ahead of them. She wanted to cheer but had no breath to force the sound from her throat. She turned to Gaish and smiled, and they pressed on. Beyond the first house, others came into view. The first house resembled the traditional design they were used to, made of wood, small, and with dull paintwork. The presence of the others suggested a settlement of some kind at last. The arduous journey had brought them somewhere they could rest, and relief lifted Yilmay's spirits. For now, they were safe again.

CHAPTER 12
YILMAY

They had no coin and would have to throw themselves on the mercy of somebody to provide food, water and shelter, but Gaish had already said he would do some work in return for any aid offered to them. They decided an inn might have need of help and would have somewhere they could sleep. They could try a townsperson's home, where they felt they might find more sympathy, but a resident might not have anywhere for the two of them to sleep and may have no need of anything Gaish could do on their behalf.

For any two steps Yilmay took, Gaish carried her for one of them, and without his help, she would have fallen to the ground and died on the spot. She cursed herself she had over-estimated what she would be capable of and under-estimated how terrible her injuries had been. Her impatience had placed them both in danger in her desperation to head for home. She vowed to be less impulsive if she came through the next day or two alive. That seemed a remote possibility, as she must now be as close to death as she had been under the tree when Gaish had gone to find help.

The town unfolded before them, a sizeable one with a hill tha rose to their right. Larger houses perched atop the hill, and their lofty position would have provided impressive views, which suggested their owners would be wealthy. That part of town would not suit them, so they stayed on the narrow street that ran through the less affluent areas. Shops and houses grew more frequent as they entered the town proper. At last, they saw an inn ahead and Gaish urged her onward. By the time they entered the tavernroom, he carried her, supported in the crook of his arm. She moved her feet as best she could; they would drag on the floor otherwise. Her legs could no longer bear her weight, and what little strength remained in her body she spent to cling to Gaish's shoulder, so she did not fall from his arms. He helped her sit on a settle near the counter, and she leaned back as she gasped for breath while her body shook with uncontrollable palpitations.

The innkeep came over as soon as they entered. He glanced at Yilmay, then turned to Gaish and spoke in his own language. Yilmay's despair deepened. She could see no way they could make their offer understood. Gaish tried to explain in a mixture of Steinlund and what little of the local language he knew. He had seemed so proficient in the language in the village, but here, with such difficult ideas to convey, he appeared out of his depth.

The innkeep shrugged, glanced at her again, and shouted some words across the tavernroom. There were ten or more people in the inn, all men. They all looked up at the innkeep's words, and one rose and crossed the tavernroom. "Which language?" He had spoken Vyrrmod, and Gaish gave him a stony stare.

It appeared Gaish had not understood, but Yilmay's time on Rakulaj's ships had given her a solid grasp of Vyrrmod. "We need a room."

All three turned to her as she spoke, and the man who spoke Vyrrmod leaned closer. "My apologies, I did not hear you."

Her words had been nowhere near loud enough to be heard, it seemed, but when he brought his ear closer, she repeated the request. He straightened and spoke to the innkeep, who replied. The man turned to her and said the cost would be three kalts. She did not know what a kalt might be, but it did not matter, after all else. They had no coin of any kind. Miserable, she answered him. "We have no kalts. We have no coin at all."

He pursed his lips before he reported the outcome to the innkeep. Yilmay fought back tears as she watched the innkeep shake his head as they spoke. When the man turned to Yilmay again, she saw no good news on his face. As she had expected, the innkeep had insisted they pay. She said Gaish would work in payment of the room.

As the man relayed her message to the innkeep, she could not keep tears of frustration from her eyes. She pressed the palms of her hands against her face and fought to get her emotions under control.

The man turned back to her. "What sort of work could he do?"

She huffed in exasperation. "I know not. Anything that needs to be done. Our ship sank, and we thought we would die. We floated here on a piece of the deck. I suffered this injury." She pointed at the top of her head, and the man winced. "I need rest. We have walked here and must attempt to find our way home, but we have no coin. We have nothing." With the back of a hand, she wiped her nose. Mucus ran from it thanks to her anger, dejection, and exasperation.

The man nodded and turned to the innkeep, and he pointed at each of them in turn as he relayed her words to him. The innkeep stared at her for some time, and she bowed her head, consumed with shame at their desperate plight. He spoke again, and when the man replied, he sounded irritated and threw his arms into the air.

The man turned to Yilmay again. "He sees you are in a drastic plight. He says you can have a room and food for the night."

Through her sobs, Yilmay strove to express her gratitude. "My thanks. What work must Gaish do in payment?"

"There is no need for him to work. It seems he will have enough to do to take care of you."

She whispered and struggled not to break down in front of them all at the generous offer. "My thanks."

"Do not thank me. Thank him." The man turned and walked back to his table. Yilmay looked up and thanked the innkeep, grateful she at least knew that simple phrase in his own language. He nodded and went to the counter, then returned with a key. He pointed to a doorway in the rear of the tavernroom, and Yilmay guessed the rooms lay in that direction. With Gaish's help, she struggled to her feet and walked toward the door.

As they passed the man who had translated for them, he grabbed her wrist and pressed something into her hand. "Take this. You will need supplies, medical things, I am sure."

Yilmay objected as she tried to return it to him. "I cannot take this."

He remained insistent. "Take it. You have more need of it than me."

"My thanks." Her tears dripped on the table. He released her wrist, wiped at the splashes, and drained his drink.

He stood. "I wish you luck. The docks are less than an hour from here. There you might find a ship that will carry you onward. You cannot reach Vyrrmod on one ship from here, I fear. You may find somebody there who can help you more, nonetheless. In the last year, more ships have sailed north from Vyrrmod with each pass. Nobody has proved the globe theory, but more people now travel to lands they never knew existed before." Yilmay had no strength to tell him the globe theory had been proved. He moved out from behind the table and walked toward the counter, where he pushed a coin across the counter, in payment for his drink, Yilmay imagined.

Gaish helped her walk through the doorway. He checked each of the four doors along the narrow passageway beyond with the key until he found one that opened. Inside the room they found a bed, a vanity stand, a chair and a window. Gaish lowered her onto the bed and rubbed her brow. "Rest. Sleep if you can." He sat in the chair and watched her.

Yilmay opened her hand and saw a deep brown coin in her palm. She could not read the words on either face. When she held it out, Gaish slipped it into his pocket, then asked what the man had said to her. She relayed the conversation, and he choked and looked out of the window. After a time, although he did not look at her, he spoke again. "I think he paid for the room. I do not think the innkeep was as generous as he suggested."

She had not imagined the outcome, but she found herself too shattered to contemplate it further. "I must sleep for an hour. What will you do?"

He smiled. "I will watch you sleep."

Yilmay wished she could make one of their familiar jests, but she lacked the energy. Soon after her eyes closed, she fell asleep. When she next opened her eyes, it had become dark outside. Gaish still sat in the chair, no more than a shadow shape in the gloom. When she spoke, he stood and lit a lantern.

"Why did you sit in the dark?"

"I did not wish to wake you."

She nodded. "My thanks. How long did I sleep?"

"Two or three hours. I will bring us some food."

He left the room, and Yilmay closed her eyes again. Her head throbbed, and her feet hurt so much she thought she might cry. At least she need walk no more tonight. She wanted to be angry at herself at how foolish she had been to believe she could complete this journey, but exhaustion and relief kept her fury at bay for now. They had been lucky to reach the town in the last moments before she could go no further, but they had a bed for the night, and Gaish had not abandoned her. She could not have blamed him had he done so. He had been correct when he told her she had not recovered enough, but she had been too stubborn. That stubbornness had almost cost her life, she guessed, and she berated herself. "You idiot."

Gaish returned with two bowls filled with a meaty broth from which steam drifted to the ceiling of the room. He helped her sit upright on the bed with her back against the wall, and she accepted the broth. The heat of the food required her to blow on each spoonful to cool it. After their arduous journey, the simple fare tasted as good as any meal she had ever eaten. Between spoonfuls, she asked Gaish how much he had learned. "What is this town called? Do you know?"

"I have not been able to find out. I struggle to understand the language I thought I had learned so well." He smiled at her as she blew on another spoonful of broth. "How do you feel?"

"I have never felt better." They laughed.

"At least you have some energy for jests again."

"That man made a generous gesture, if what you said is true."

"And he was so handsome." He seemed to realise what he had said, and his face turned red.

"Gaishkantah. Do you desire a dalliance?" It felt good to laugh after the past days, and she enjoyed the tinkle of her own laughter as it faded in the air between them. Gaish did not reply, but he concentrated on the spoonful of broth before him. She sighed, a wistful breath filled with hopes and dreams in the face of her despair. "I cannot blame you. I look forward to full health again when I can roll in Vamma's arms."

"Vamma?"

"A woman I met in Dur a while past."

"I know little enough of your loves."

"Believe me, it is better for you to know nothing of my loves. None have ended in anything but utter devastation." She fought back tears as she spoke.

"They cannot be as bad as you suggest."

Yilmay swallowed another mouthful of the broth. "They are worse. I do not wish to speak of them please." She put her head back and sniffed. One hand held the plate, the other a spoonful of broth, which left none available to wipe her nose. Distraught at the memories of the women whose lives she had destroyed, Yilmay could no longer hold back her tears. She dropped the spoon into the remains of the broth in her plate and wept. Gaish said nothing, and some time later, the spasms of her tears subsided. She returned her attention to the food. "What will we do tomorrow?"

"We will see how you are. That is the first business of the day. If you are improved enough, we may wander to the docks and investigate passage to somewhere that lies on the way home. By the sounds of it, we will need more than one voyage."

"Do you imagine that coin will be sufficient?"

He laughed. "It would be a rich man indeed who felt generous enough to fund two complete strangers so they could afford at least two journeys to come to Dur."

"He did say Vyrrmod. Dur may be possible in one voyage."

He sucked air over his lips, an affirmation she had noticed in him over the past two years. Although it sounded like an intake of breath that implied concern, she had learned he did it in agreement with something that had been said.

They had finished their meals, and he gathered up the bowls and spoons, then carried them out of the room. He returned with a tankard and a goblet. "I had the right of it. That lovely man did pay for our accommodations, and a drink each. I have ale. You have wine if you have the strength to drink it."

Gaish had brought a smile to a miserable face. They had not drunk in the lands they had visited, but she had often told him she longed for a goblet of red wine. She reached for the goblet, and he closed the door. Yilmay sipped at it, an average quality wine. She did not care—it had been so long since she had drunk wine, she relished every mouthful. Warmth and strength returned to her body from the food, and the simple pleasure of a goblet of wine relaxed her. Her head still throbbed, and her feet hurt, but she no longer felt so full of despair. The simple kindness of a stranger had in some small part helped her to heal.

She finished the wine and handed the goblet to Gaish, and he helped her settle again on the bed. He lay on the floor beside her, but she insisted he share the bed with her. It seemed unfair after all he had done to expect him to suffer the night on the hard floor. She moved close to the wall to make room for him and fell asleep almost as soon as he lay down.

Yilmay slept late, and when she woke Gaish had left the room. She sat up on the bed, weary and stiff. Her head hurt, but her feet felt better than yesterday, and she felt less fatigued. She reasoned an hour's walk should be manageable, and if that brought them to the docks, and they found a ship to sail on, she would have days of rest ahead of her. Her confidence had returned a little, and it gladdened her.

When she stood, she found that although she had thought her feet did not hurt too much, they ached as soon as she placed any weight on them. She grimaced and pulled her boots on, then made her way to the tavernroom in search of some food. Some breads and cheese stood on the counter, and she reasoned the innkeep busied himself with other matters but had left the food for his guests. She took some to a nearby table and sat.

As she ate, she wondered where Gaish had got to. He might have risen early and decided to investigate the docks while she slept. It would be a good idea, but she could not walk there on her own. As well as the risk she might miss him, she feared to take an hour's walk alone in case she fell or became fatigued. The food finished, she wondered what to do next, but Gaish entered the tavernroom at that moment. When he spotted her, he came to the table and sat opposite her.

He had been to the docks, as she had surmised. He had not

recognised any of the ships' sigils, and he had struggled again with the language. He had found a master who spoke a little Steinlund and had arranged for them to sail when the ship left at high tide, soon after the midday. He had handed over the coin the man had given them and arranged to work to cover the rest of the cost. They must sleep in the crew quarters; no exclusive cabin for them, but they had a bunk at the least. The master had sailed to Steinlund a few times and described it as a lengthy voyage. The master's Steinlund had not been good, and he could not explain how many days away Dur lay. He had held up his hands, then opened and closed his fists three times. Three times a tenday, Gaish thought. Far away, however many days it would take.

On this trip, the ship would sail to the master's own land, some way away. From there, Gaish hoped he could obtain another voyage that might take them to Dur or any of the lands of the Torr Sea. The news delighted Yilmay, and she felt they were on their way home at last. The walk from the village had almost killed her, but she now felt it had been worthwhile. Tonight, she would sleep on a ship, the waves would rock her to sleep, and home beckoned.

CHAPTER 13
YILMAY

The ship headed to Argoya. At first, they believed Argoya was the name of the land, but they were wrong. The crew were distant at first, with little fondness for strangers who could not speak their language, one of whom did little more than lie in her bunk for the first few days, eat their food, and drink their fresh water. They warmed to Gaish quicker, and his excellent deckhand skills soon earned their respect.

As her strength returned, and fortified by regular food and plenty of water, Yilmay wandered out onto the deck throughout the day and sat at the bow as she used to do in the days before she became a mariner. At one point, they sailed past some black and white giants, and her recollection of the moment one had crashed onto the deck of The Ictharelian flooded her mind. She broke into a cold sweat and stared at them in concern until they were well off the stern.

After a tenday of rest and boredom, she decided to follow Gaish around on his watches, and he encouraged her to do some light duties; tie knots, check equipment had been stowed after use— nothing strenuous, but it made her feel useful. The other mariners watched her as though she were a rodent and they some predator whenever she did anything, but they seemed less distant to her after two or three days once they saw she knew her way around the deck of a ship.

When they reached Argoya, its size stunned Yilmay, the biggest town or city she had ever seen. She did not know how this land determined town or city status, but given the endless flow of buildings that passed their seaward side as they sailed along the southern coast of the land, she felt certain it must be a city. The ship reached a harbour, turned seaward into it, and sailed for the docks. Yilmay felt sure the docks alone must equal the entire length of Ort from north to south. Even Gaish seemed in awe of Argoya, and he wondered aloud how many people must live in its houses. How had such a huge city existed for so long, unknown to any in the Torr Seas? It baffled Yilmay.

They thanked the master for the voyage, and he gave Gaish some coins. Despite his poor Steinlund, it seemed Gaish had performed beyond his expectations and the crew had spoken well of him. They thanked him and left the ship. Gaish passed the coins to Yilmay, and she slipped them into the pocket of her trousers. The coins, larger than Dur coins, felt heavy to carry in her clothing.

The docks bustled with activity. Lost for words, Yilmay watched the hordes of workers as they loaded and unloaded ships and carried away the vast quantities of goods toward what passed for tally houses here. She could not count the number of people who swarmed around the docks, and doubted even Leesant would be able to, despite that he could count to not less than two thousand. Yilmay doubted she could even count the many ships tied up at the docks.

They wandered in awe along the dockside. The noise brought on a headache Yilmay had hoped she had shaken off for good on the ship, but the hubbub of this place almost deafened her. They could not recognise the words they heard shouted all around them, but they both felt they heard more than one language, whether because the workers came from different lands, or this land had more than one language. If the other cities in the land were as big as Argoya, it would not be difficult to imagine more than one might be spoken.

They walked on and came to a stall that sold some meats that smelled irresistible. They were long, thin, and round, and they sizzled on a grate laid over a fire in a metal barrel. The smell of spices and fat made Yilmay's mouth water, and they spent some of the master's coin to buy themselves one of the meats each, which came wrapped in a piece of bread. The meats dripped with fat, and after they had eaten them, their jowls were coated in it. Yilmay licked around her mouth as far as her tongue would extend while Gaish roared with laughter at the sight, doubled up as he gasped for air. The meal reminded her of something similar she had eaten with Deineike in Ort, although the meat here had been different from the Ort meat, spicier and fattier.

They wiped the grease from their chins as best they could and continued. They both heard the language of Steinlund at the same time and stared at each other. They moved through the crowds to listen for it again. It had come from a pair of dock workers who sat on a crate to talk while they took a break from their work, it seemed.

Gaish spoke to them. "You are from Steinlund?"

One of them replied. "We are from there, indeed."

They explained they were brothers who had worked as mariners on the Torr Sea, and had arrived here four passes ago, after they sailed from Malkartas on one of the ships that now sailed further from their home. A ship that sailed to Malkartas would suit them, and Yilmay asked the men how they might find one. The men sent them to a tally house, or goods house as they were known here, owned by the person who had financed the voyage of the ship they had sailed on to reach Argoya.

They thanked the men and headed off to find the goods house. Goods houses seemed plentiful, and the words scribed on the front of each building meant nothing to either of them. Their inability to understand the language also made it difficult to ask directions among the throngs of people around the dock, but they found one man who seemed to recognise the merchant's name and pointed them to a large building.

The building must have been four times the size of Raolos's tally house in Ort at the least, with three pairs of enormous doors along the front. Colourful words had been emblazoned on the eaves of the building's face, but Yilmay and Gaish could not read them. They glanced at each other and pushed open a smaller door at one end of the building. The door opened into an office, with a large counter at one end and doors set into the wall behind it. A large window behind them looked out onto the crowded docks. Chairs and tables had been placed on their side of the counter, and four people, three women and a man, sat at desks on the other side of it. One of the women caught Yilmay's eye, smiled, and spoke.

Yilmay searched for a language one of them might understand. "Does anybody speak Dur?" Blank faces stared back at her. "Steinlund?" She had no luck with Gaish's language either. "Vyrrmod?" Again nothing, although the four people spoke to one another in their own language. She had almost run out of options. "Kuirbekian?"

At last one of the women spoke, recognition on her face. "I speak few words Kuirbekian."

Thank the fates; the year aboard The Salty Home had come to her rescue. Yilmay approached the woman. "We seek passage to Malkartas."

"No passenger ship sails of Malkartas." The woman wore an apologetic look on her face.

Yilmay glanced at Gaish and mouthed, "Passenger ships?" He shrugged. It seemed inconceivable ships would carry nothing but passengers. Every ship she had sailed on had carried cargo with only occasional passengers. She turned back to the woman to try again. "What about cargo ships? We are mariners and can work. Excellent mariners." It could not hurt to embellish their credentials.

"Yes, we do not hire crew." Two years among crew members from multiple lands had left Yilmay comfortable with the simple affirmative, "yes," or negative, "no," but she could not bring herself to use them. In this case, however, the woman had said, "yes," even though she seemed to have meant, "no."

Yilmay pressed on and ignored the mangled language. "Who does, please?"

"Masters." The woman stared at Yilmay as though she might be simple.

"You own the ships though, is that correct?"

The woman giggled behind a hand. "No. I not own ships. Ckazatch Otohen owns of ships."

"And he owns this tally… goods house?"

"She. And yes."

Yilmay glanced away and sighed in irritation. Despite the surprise revelation a woman owned this enormous and successful enterprise, Yilmay wearied of the woman's unhelpful responses. "Then why does she not recruit for the ships?"

"Master recruits of ships. Ckazatch Otohen is too busy to hire of crew."

Yilmay sighed. "Will any of her ships sail for Malkartas soon?"

"This could be."

Yilmay stared down at her feet, her teeth clenched, and her hands curled into angry fists. She focused on each of her ten toes as she counted them in her head and hoped the old Ryl trick might calm her temper. "When?" She abandoned any pretence of politeness—she would fight bluntness with bluntness.

"How to say in Kuirbekian?" The woman glanced up at the ceiling, and Yilmay looked up in case the answer to her question had been scribed there. "Next tomorrow, might be."

"The next ship leaves tomorrow?"

"No. Next tomorrow."

Yilmay gripped the legs of her trousers, worried she might otherwise reach for the woman and drag her across the counter. "Not tomorrow, the day after?"

"Yes, this is how to say. Day after."

"What is the name of this ship?"

"Rzankir, but I not know if sails of Malkartas. Master will know."

"Can you scribe that?" No doubt the word as scribed on the stern of the ship would not appear as it sounded in the local language.

"Yes, thanks you."

Yilmay exhaled a long, frustrated breath, then persisted. "Will you scribe that for me please?"

"Oh, I see. Yes. Apologise for understand bad." The woman scribed something on a piece of parch and handed it to Yilmay.

Yilmay looked at the parch. She had been correct in her guess; the word did not resemble the way she had envisaged it in her mind. "Which dock will it sail from?"

"Not known. Docks change on day. See Dock Controller." The woman pointed back along the dock, the way they had already come.

Yilmay could not comprehend the vastness of the operation of these docks, and her head throbbed after the difficult conversation. "My thanks." She turned to leave.

The woman spoke as Yilmay stamped toward the door. "That is how to say, my thanks. Goodbye."

Yilmay waved at the woman, tore open the door in fury, and stepped out onto the dock.

CHAPTER 14

YILMAY

Outside the building, Gaish laid a hand on her forearm. "What turned in there? And what did you mean by 'passenger ship?'"

"Passenger ships. It seems they have ships here that only carry passengers."

Gaish gave a low whistle. "I have never—"

"Nor me." Yilmay had become too irritated for a conversation about what they had or had not ever encountered. "A ship might sail to Malkartas the day after tomorrow. We will have to try to persuade the master to hire us as crew, unless we can come by a small fortune between now and then."

"What will we do if the master will not hire us?"

"Wait for another, my guess." Her frustration pressed on her chest like a heavy rock, and her head ached.

"That could be days or passes."

"I know this, Gaish." He took a half pace backward as she spat all her frustration at him. "Forgive me. Let us deal with one thing at a time. We will speak to the master of this ship, and if he does not hire us, we will consider our options. Before that, however, we have two nights and days to get through."

"We could try to find the tide times for that day."

Yilmay agreed with his idea, so they wandered back along the docks in search of the two Steinlund men. They could not find them, so they looked for the Dock Controller the woman had mentioned.

The building proved difficult to find, since the signs had all been scribed in the local language of Argoya. The fates intervened, and they met someone who spoke Malkartian, which sounded like Kuirbekian in certain words, and he pointed them toward a large, drab grey building some way back toward the goods house of Ckazatch Otohen. They had walked past it, so they turned and trudged back.

The language again tried to thwart them, but they managed to obtain the information they required through a series of gestures. Gaish moved his hand through the air and moved it up and down to simulate the waves, and Yilmay scribed half a circle in the air with her arm to simulate the passage of the sun across the sky. The clerk produced a bundle of parch with lines of entries scribed on them. They could not understand the words or the numbers, but the clerk pointed at an entry on the first page, then pointed between each of them in turn.

"He means this number is today, I think." Yilmay knitted her brow as she attempted to make sense of the comical dance between them.

Yilmay pointed to the entry two lines lower on the page and hoped she had indicated the day after tomorrow. The man again gestured between the two of them, then held up two fingers and pointed to the ground.

Their best guess led them to believe the man had suggested high tide in two days would be two hours earlier than the present time, which would place it around an hour before midday by Yilmay's estimation.

Gaish muttered. He sounded as frustrated as Yilmay. "We are no more certain than before. We will find the ship as soon as we awake in two days. After that, we must trust to the fates written for us."

Yilmay shuffled her feet. "Awake where though?" They had two nights to sleep and did not know how much their coins were worth.

Gaish shrugged and looked disheartened. "I know not." They thanked the clerk with no certainty he understood their gratitude and returned to the docks. "We could see whether we can afford an inn." Gaish looked from one side of the crowded dock to the other as he spoke. "Or we could sleep in the open somewhere."

Yilmay groaned. "My back."

"We could try the inns again to see if I can work in exchange for accommodation."

"That may not work a second time. I am no longer at the door of my ruin, and we would be lucky to find another person to take pity on me. I tire of the language difficulties in any event. It takes an hour to ask the simplest question."

Gaish laughed. "At the least. It vexes me."

Yilmay agreed. Her frustration, however, turned to anger at the least provocation these days, and she did not want to become embroiled in a dispute if she lost her temper with an innkeep. "Then we must sleep outside. Let us try to find somewhere comfortable, at the least."

They left the docks and wandered the streets for an hour until they came across a large green area, filled with trees. Paths ran throughout it with benches placed alongside the path at intervals. Gaish sighed as they walked through the peaceful green expanse. "This city is different from anywhere I have seen."

The path climbed a hill, and they continued to the top. From the hilltop, they looked down on the city spread out below them. They recognised the docks, and everywhere they looked, they saw houses and large buildings, shops or commercial businesses, they imagined. The city stretched as far as the eye could see as it followed the natural bay of the harbour that swept out toward the sea on either side of the docks. Behind them, the green area continued down the opposite side of the hill. More houses ran away from it, larger and no doubt owned by more affluent members of the city's population.

Yilmay sat on the bench at the top of the hill, wearied by the climb. Gaish fussed around her, but she reassured him she felt fine. The hill had taken a great deal out of her, but even though her heart pounded, and her breaths heaved from her, she felt her fitness and mobility had improved since her time in the village. Gaish suggested they should find some food and something to keep them warm overnight, so she took the coins out of her pocket and held them out to him. He wrinkled his nose as he looked at them. "How much do I need?"

She laughed despite her weariness. They might be the wealthiest pair in Argoya or the poorest, and they had no idea which. "I know not. Take them all."

He took most of them. "I will leave you a few in case I am delayed by a dalliance with a handsome young man." They both laughed, happy to find some small jest again after all they had endured.

Yilmay leaned back against the back of the bench and enjoyed the soft warmth of the sun on her face. Argoya looked splendid from the top of the hill, and its sheer size could not be guessed from lower down. She still felt amazed such a vast city could exist, and yet she had never heard of it until they boarded ship for it.

Yilmay closed her eyes, hoping Gaish had taken enough coin to find some food. He might bring back one of those greasy meats from the dock. She salivated as she thought of the flavour of it. A blanket would be a waste of scarce coin in her opinion, but they did have two nights to survive, and the weather might turn cold tomorrow for all she knew.

Voices carried up the hill, and Yilmay opened her eyes to see whether Gaish had returned with his handsome young man. He had not, but two men and a woman walked up the path toward the top of the hill and talked among themselves. One of the men carried a cask. They wore poor quality clothes that looked as though they had not been washed in a while. They all looked young, but the woman appeared to be the older of the group and wore her hair scraped back into a horsetail. She had a gaunt face and pale skin, no taller than Yilmay, but she looked too thin, unhealthy even. Her hip bones pressed against her trousers and her arms were as thin as a small branch fallen from the top of a tree.

As they approached, old instincts Yilmay had thought might be forgotten triggered concern in her. She could not decide what bothered her, but she felt mistrust in her heart. She knew better than to ignore the cold itch at the back of her neck—it had served her well in the past, almost always a portent of danger. She stood, ready to run down the hill if necessary.

The three stopped and one of the men spoke to her. Yilmay understood nothing, but she gave him a friendly smile. The other man spoke, but she did not attempt to reply, and the men separated until they stood to either side of her. It seemed her instincts had been right, and she concentrated on her breaths as she controlled her heart rate. The woman hung back and glanced around as though nervous. Yilmay kept her eyes focused on the man who had spoken first. Although she concentrated on him, she remained aware of her surroundings. She could not see Gaish or anybody else. If they intended trouble, Yilmay must deal with it alone. She glanced down at her boots and wondered whether to pull out her fan—they might be harmless, after all else.

One of the men passed the cask to the woman, spoke words Yilmay could not comprehend again, then stepped closer and reached for Yilmay's pocket, the one with the coins. He patted the bulge in her trousers, and the noisy coins gave a muffled jingle. Irritated, Yilmay slapped his hand away from her hip, and his smiled faded. The one who had spoken first took a slight step forward, and she noticed a change in his eyes.

The woman stepped close to Yilmay and leaned toward her. Yilmay did not flinch backward, and the smile never left her lips as the woman put a hand at the nape of Yilmay's neck and held her still. To Yilmay's amazement, the woman sniffed at Yilmay's face, and she grimaced as she did so. Yilmay imagined she must smell atrocious. She could not remember the last time she had soaked in a tub, but the three strangers smelled awful, in truth, and Yilmay thought it unfair the woman had frowned. *"A soak in a tub is as long overdue for her as it is for me,"* she thought. The woman's breath smelled of wine or some other drink, and Yilmay guessed the cask contained whatever they had drunk before they encountered her. The woman stepped back and said something to the men.

Yilmay dropped to a crouch and pulled the fan from her boot. When she stood, she saw confusion on the face of the man who had patted her pocket, and she sprang loose a blade that had done little more than cut the oranges in half for the last two years. To her, it seemed her movements had slowed since she had last used the fan for anything more dangerous than to feed herself, but if she was slow, the man was slower. The blade flicked up and cut his cheek, a deep wound, but not deadly. He cried aloud and fell to his knees, both hands pressed to the cut as his blood leaked through his fingers and onto the ground.

The other man reacted quicker, and he stepped close to Yilmay, then wrapped his arms around her chest. Her arms were pinned to her side, but she did not waste time on any attempt to free them. She moved her head forward as far as she could, then smashed it back into what she hoped would be his face. Blood spurted onto Yilmay's neck and shoulders as her head crashed into him. He toppled backward and released her. With luck, she had knocked him unconscious.

Only the woman remained upright. She dropped the cask, and bent to the man with the cut cheek. With an arm across his back, she spoke to him, words that carried fear and alarm. She helped him to his feet, and they turned and walked away down the hill. They had left the other, who lay motionless on the ground. Blood covered his face, his nose lay askew, and the skin around both eyes already turned purple. Yilmay dropped to her knees and felt for a pulsing. To her relief, he lived. It surprised her his friends had abandoned him to a woman with a sharp blade, but in Dur, the three would never have menaced her in the first place. This vast city must be a more violent place than Yilmay's home, where others would prey on those they thought weaker than themselves, she imagined. The three had learned a painful lesson today.

CHAPTER 15
YILMAY

Yilmay reflected on the encounter and guessed they had intended to take her coin, at the least. What other harm they wished on her she would never find out. She glanced down the hill where the woman and her blood-soaked companion had all but reached a line of houses. They soon disappeared from sight and left their friend at the hilltop, unconscious and in need of help.

Yilmay would not provide that help to her victim, and she set off down the path at a brisk pace. She had almost reached the boundary of the park when she saw Gaish walk along the street toward her with something in his hands she could not quite make out. A folded blanket, or a small chest. She quickened her pace, and he saw her. His smile froze, incomplete, as she reached him.

"What has turned? You have blood on you." He dropped the item and half-turned her around. "The back of your head and your tunic are covered in it. What has turned?"

"We cannot stay here tonight. We must move. I will explain as we walk." She checked they were alone, then took her tunic off and turned it inside out. It would hide the worst of the blood for now, she hoped.

Gaish licked the palm of his hand for moisture and rubbed at her neck and the back of her head. "That will suffice for now." She took his arm and propelled him along a street that ran parallel to the docks. As they walked, she told him all that had turned. Her story shocked him. "What were they about?" He had whispered, as though afraid other ears might overhear their conversation and betray them to the authorities.

"I know not, but they touched me, as though they wanted to learn how much coin I carried. She smelled me, Gaish. That is not normal."

"It is not." He chuckled. "Are they still alive?"

"That they are. Two of them fled, and I left the other unconscious."

"Three of them. You are so small." He sounded doubtful.

"They were not trained, they did not expect resistance, and they underestimated me. I rolled sixes."

He snorted. "It seems you did. I am sorry I could not help."

They walked on for a time in silence, and Yilmay could not shake the incident from her mind. Had she been too slow to realise the three people had posed a threat? Should she have pulled her fan as soon as she saw them? She might have been hurt had they attacked her rather than waste time as they fussed about her pocket. There could be little point in such thought, she imagined. Fates already written cannot be unwritten. She had wasted much time throughout her life on thoughts, after the fact, of what different outcomes might have prevailed. From now on, she vowed to look back less and look forward more. "I wonder what the authorities are called here."

Gaish replied in a distracted, disinterested tone. "I have seen no evidence of any uniforms here thus far. They may not have any formal authorities."

"I doubt that. Even in Dur, where there is almost no serious crime, each Portreeve has men who work for him."

"Why do they need these men if there is no crime in Dur? What do they do?"

"I know not. It is a good question. They serve to keep the small incidents at bay, my guess. At times they will come to break up a brawl in a tavern."

He walked on in silence for a moment. "A waste of coin."

As far as Yilmay knew, the Portreeve's men had always been a feature of the land, but in the four cities where Styrrach's Guild had operated, their numbers must have grown because of Styrrach's scheme. More Portreeve's men would be needed to capture a shrouded Guild member than to apprehend a street urchin who had lifted a few coins from the pocket of a merchant.

The sun had all but set, and the streets grew dark. They found a half-completed house that may have been some new property someone built, or a replacement for an older one that had been unsafe. When they put their heads inside it, it had a roof and walls but little else. They moved to the rear of the house and agreed it would serve for tonight. They would be up and away early in the morning in case those who built it arrived for work and found them asleep inside.

It grew dark inside the house. Gaish had some bread and cold meats but none of the meats from the docks. There would be another opportunity to buy some tomorrow, Yilmay reasoned, and she ate some bread and meat. They held some back for a small meal in the morning and unfolded the blanket he had brought. It smelled of horses, and he blushed as he admitted he had stolen it from outside a stable he had passed. He excused his theft as an attempt to make their coin stretch as far as he could. They could return it on the morning of the ship's departure, he pointed out. They would then only have borrowed it—a far less serious crime than theft. Yilmay laughed and agreed with him.

He shook her awake early the next day. Little light reached them in the rear of the house, and Yilmay guessed the sun may not yet have risen. They finished off the food and folded the blanket before they stepped out of the house. Neither workers nor anybody else could be seen on the street, so they hurried away from the house. Yilmay wanted to return to the green space where she had fought with the three people. Gaish thought it unwise, but she wanted to assure herself the unconscious man had not died from his injuries and lay there still, unmissed and undiscovered.

The cask still lay on the grass where the woman had dropped it, and bloodstains speckled the top of the hill, but the man had gone. Yilmay sighed with relief, and they headed down the hill in a different direction to explore Argoya further. They walked for an hour or so, and the houses became larger, which suggested they had entered the wealthy quarter. The streets grew busier, filled with women in good quality clothes and men who sported a great deal of facial hair. A particular fashion appeared to be beards that did not extend past the sides of the mouth toward the ears. Gaish had grown a full beard on The Ictharelian, and it had become as wild and unkempt as an abandoned bird's nest now. It attracted many contemptuous stares from the well-groomed men who passed by.

Their dirty clothes and faces did not fit in this quarter, and they wearied of the glances laden with distaste, so they turned back toward the sea and headed for the docks. By the time they reached them, the midday had passed at least an hour ago. The docks were no less busy than the previous day. They bought one of the circular meats each and sat on the ground in the shade of a stack of crates while they ate them. They were even more enjoyable the second time. Yilmay suggested that if she lived in Argoya, she would soon be the size of a ship as she gorged herself on the fatty meats, and Gaish confessed he felt the same way.

Ships came and went like insects on the remains of a dead animal as the tide changed later in the day. So many arrived, some had to drop anchor in the harbour and wait for another to cast off and clear a berth at the dockside. Yilmay imagined the job of Dock Controller must be a busy one, far too complicated for her to ever consider.

As the sun sank low in the west, they resisted the spicy meats and settled for some bread and cheese. They found their way back to the incomplete house with some difficulty. It lay empty again, and they settled down in the same spot as the previous night to eat the simple meal. These days, Yilmay ate bread and cheese in the once-strange way Taro ate it, and aboard the ship, Gaish had begun to copy her. She felt sorry for Taro still, but she reminded herself she must no longer look backward.

They settled down and planned to arrive at the docks early so they did not miss the ship they hoped would take them to Malkartas. Argoya had entertained her, but Yilmay did not think she could enjoy life in such a vast city.

Before they sun had risen, they dropped the blanket outside the door of the stable and ran off as though they were small children who knocked on the doors of their neighbours, then ran away before they could answer. Yilmay's headaches still returned from time to time, but not as often as in Illfarlen. She felt well enough to work her own passage with no need to depend on Gaish, as long as they could persuade the master to hire them for his crew.

They were hopeful he would hire them. Ships often sailed two or three crew short, and the other mariners would do extra work to compensate for the absent hands. Good masters would pay a small bonus to each mariner at the end of the voyage in acknowledgment of the additional work they had undertaken. Even excellent masters who had long-term, dependable crews would find one or two wished some extended shore leave from time to time. The Salty Home had almost a full crew much of the time but had sailed from Alcmouth short-handed when she had stayed behind to help search for the Duke's son.

They showed the clerk in the Dock Controller's office the piece of parch with the name of the ship, and he said something neither of them could understand. Exasperated, he scribed something on their parch and pointed toward the end of the dock where they had found the goods house of Ckazatch Otohen. They showed the parch to dock workers as they worked their way down the dock, who all pointed further along the dockside.

After a long search, they saw the ship moored at the dock. They compared the name on the stern to the piece of parch and did not doubt they had the correct ship. They hoped they could make themselves understood as they walked up the ramp and onto the aft deck. There they found a tall man with a stern appearance who wore a splendid blue coat with three stripes sown onto the shoulders that marked him as the undisputed master of the ship. One officer with two shoulder stripes spoke with him, doubtless about their route and any details of how the master wished to handle discipline and accidents aboard. Every master ran his ship in different ways, and this master had the air of a man who ran what mariners called a tight ship; a ship with well-developed practices, sailed by a master who would stand no nonsense from the crew. Yilmay thought he looked the sort of man who might be angered if the weather refused to give him favourable conditions to sail in and might be able to persuade the weather to change its mind.

Yilmay knew almost no Malkartas and nothing at all of the local tongue, so she hoped he could speak one of the languages she did know. Kuirbek bordered Malkartas, and she thought it her best chance to be understood, as it had been in the goods house. It seemed a reasonable guess; Steinlund and Dur had similar languages and customs and were joined by a common border, although neither she nor Gaish had ever crossed that border on land.

"Good day, master."

He raised his eyebrows as he glanced up at her. "You speak Kuirbekian?"

"That I do."

"You are not from there, however, or you would have said, 'Yes.' Steinlund?"

"My friend is from that fine land." She gestured at Gaish. "I am from Dur."

He nodded as though he had suspected as much. "I have never been to either of your lands. How may I help you?"

Their clothes, and their smell, might indicate they could ill afford a voyage on his ship, even if they were tied to a rope and towed behind it, but he had not insulted them by any such suggestion. "We wish to travel to Malkartas. We are mariners. In truth, we are both exceptional mariners and hope you are short-handed and might have some work we could carry out to pay for our passage. We are content to sleep in common quarters."

He gazed at her for a time, and she returned his stare. While it would be considered rude to show contempt for a master, he might doubt the character of anybody who could not meet his gaze. Yilmay believed only people who had something to hide looked away from scrutiny. At last he broke his silence. "Bring me a horn cleat."

"My apologies master, I have no tool with which to detach your horn cleats from the surfaces they are attached to." He had tried to catch her out.

He said something to the officer, who shouted to a nearby mariner. The mariner brought over a coil of rope. "Take this rope and tie a bowline to the aft cleat. Make sure we can cast off at high tide."

"My apologies again." Yilmay suppressed a smile at the game he played. "Would you prefer me to tie a cleat hitch? A cleat hitch is easier to release than a bowline if the ship pulls at the line in the swell."

"You are impertinent."

She smiled at him. "I prefer the word, 'knowledgeable.'"

"And your friend?"

She did not hesitate. "A better deckhand than any I have sailed with. He speaks only Dur and Steinlund, however."

He rubbed a finger along his teeth and Yilmay remained silent. Anybody might know a few simple things about how to sail, and thus pass his test, but experienced mariners could only prove themselves during a voyage. "You are small. Are you comfortable in the foremast nest?"

She hesitated, and his eyes widened in a silent question. "I watched from the nest not long ago. The ship met a disaster and flung me into the sea."

"Disaster?"

"A giant landed on our deck and cleaved the ship in half. All died but Gaish and me."

"I heard a similar tale from a friend, it seems. Something about a ship on a voyage to prove the globe theory, if I recall the story right."

"The Ictharelian, and we have proved it if we can return home and complete the circle."

He nodded. "Then I have good news. There are other survivors. I heard of three others who made land south of where the ship foundered."

Her heart leapt, and she turned to Gaish to relay the story. He hugged her as tears formed in his eyes. She turned back to the master. "Do you know whether the master, Tryndeltuj, might have been one of the survivors?"

He shook his head. "Alas, I do not know the names of the three. But take heart, you will meet them again one day." He paused. "If you are to prove this theory, you must complete the circular voyage that will change our view of all we know. If you are to do so, you had best stand to. We cast off in less than an hour, and your friend must haul in the fenders while you take first watch in the nest."

She turned to Gaish to give him the news. He embraced her, and they hopped around together, arms locked around one another. They were headed home, and they had proved the globe theory, after all else.

"Did I not tell you to stand to?" The master sounded stern, but the smile on his face betrayed him.

"That you did, and you will never have to repeat an order to either of us again." Yilmay almost skipped down the aft deck steps to the deck below. Their next stop would be Tanasttra, largest city in Malkartas, and from there the fates would decide what was written. This part of her life had ended, and she would serve as a mariner one more time, then settle down with Vamma somewhere. Her smile did not leave her face for the rest of the day.

CHAPTER 16
YILMAY

The voyage took more than three tendays, and they called into two docks to resupply their food and water. In the nest, Yilmay experienced many moments of concern and knew her days as a mariner were done after this journey. Her unease convinced her she could not return to the work. Whenever they were off watch together, Gaish and Yilmay talked of their excitement now they headed for home. Gaish wanted to sail straight to Vyrrmod from Malkartas and report to Rakulaj. Yilmay, on the other hand, felt content to leave that to Gaish, or the other survivors, if they reached Arkkyd before him. Her desire lay in Malkartas as far as she knew, and she thought of little beyond Tanasttra and Vamma.

One of the mariners often sang in the cabin they all shared. He had a high-pitched voice with such clarity, he could captivate any listener, no matter what he sang. He reminded Yilmay of Khittie, the singer from Ort who had sung Deineike's Sending. He had a large repertoire of songs, or so he claimed, but he often sang one he seemed to enjoy more than any other. No matter what turned in the cabin, someone would call for a song from Malialg at some point, and he always seemed happy to oblige.

Malialg's favourite song was also the favourite of many mariners, not least because it had a rousing chorus they could all join in with.

> *"The deep blue waters call my name,*
> *No matter where they flow.*
> *If I should never come here again…"*

The entire crew joined in the chorus, a discordant choir, most in a different key to their neighbour, and with a total lack of timing that resulted in the chorus starting and ending like many different conversations rather than one united song.

> *"Down to Helchik's treasure I go,*
> *Oh, down to Helchik's treasure I go."*

Malialg sang the other verses of the song, and the raucous voices of the crew in each chorus threatened to lift the deck from the ship and cast it into the wind.

At last, at the end of a long watch, Yilmay spotted the familiar coastline of Malkartas from the nest, and her shout of, "Land ahead," may have been the loudest she had ever cried from high up above the deck of any ship. The ship docked, and the master paid off the crew. He thanked Gaish and Yilmay for their work and added he would welcome them to his crew at any time in the future. He paid them the same as the other hands, and they left the ship with no belongings, but with the most coin they had had in their pockets for a long time.

When he spotted one of Rakulaj's ships moored in Tanasttra, Gaish decided he would sail on to Arkkyd without delay. It saddened Yilmay to see him go. They had been good friends aboard The Ictharelian, but they had been through so much together since the ship sank, an even stronger bond now existed between them. Yilmay borrowed parch and a scribing tool, scribed her parents' address, and urged him to send a letter whenever he could. She would always be able to collect them at some point, and if he settled anywhere in the future, she would be able to come and visit him and his handsome young man. Both in tears, they embraced before Gaish walked up the ramp to secure passage to Vyrrmod. He would not work on this voyage; his fame would guarantee him free passage now he had proved the globe theory.

As the ship departed the dock, tears poured from her eyes, and Yilmay took a moment to consider the significance of their achievement. The master of the Rzankir had said the voyage changed everything they knew, or something along those lines. It did indeed. They no longer lived in isolation in their land, or even the lands of the Torr Sea. The vast globe could be sailed around in two years, even with today's ships. In time, ships would be designed that would slash that time, she felt sure of it. Trade between new lands had been made available, and access to goods, food, animal hides, exotic gems and the like would now be possible.

The master of Rakulaj's ship had told her the body that ran civil matters in Malkartas went by the name of The Council and could be found in a building called The Rotunda. She did not recognise the term, but he advised her to start her search for Raolos there. Once she found Raolos, she hoped he would know where Vamma lived. Visions of their reunion danced through her thoughts much of the time, and her desperation to find them and Wilash had increased daily on the voyage.

Yilmay wiped away her tears. She ran a hand over her head, and the scar fouled her fingers beneath the stubby hair that grew around it. She would let her hair grow again now, she thought, as long as, or longer than, it had been when she had been with Deineike. Small scars from the days after Deineike's death, when she had dug in fury at her scalp with her fingernails, still covered her scalp, but they were insignificant compared to the reminder the mast had left behind.

Mid-morning had come already, and in spite of the broken cloud that sailed across the sky, she enjoyed the warmth of the sun as she set off. The Rotunda proved easy to locate. She could see a tall tower even from the docks, and that tower stood in the middle of The Rotunda. It stretched up toward the sky, the tallest structure she had ever seen. Yilmay had noticed it before on visits to the city but had never stayed long enough to discover anything about it. The Rotunda itself, a huge, circular building comparable to the Ducal Highhome in size and splendour, encircled the tower.

She entered the building through two enormous wooden doors that lay open, guarded by four men, two on each side. Their deep brown tunics bore the sigil of Malkartas, a leafy tree with a river that flowed through the lower half of the trunk. Inside the building, a long lobby with a desk the entire length of its rear wall welcomed visitors. The bench of the desk had been made from an ornate stone Yilmay had never seen before. Six people stood behind the desk, and a lengthy line of people waited in the lobby for the attentions of the six.

Yilmay joined the line and waited as it crept forward until she reached the front. A man beckoned her to approach, and she stepped up to the desk. In the absence of any Malkartas, she spoke Kuirbekian and asked where she might find records of some friends of hers who may have settled in Malkartas from Dur around three years earlier.

"I see." He spoke Kuirbekian better than Yilmay. "All people from other lands who wish to settle in Malkartas are welcome as long as they register their residency with the Council of the People."

His answer bewildered her, since the master had told her The

Council resided here in The Rotunda. "Is this not the building of The Council?"

"I see you are confused. The Council works for all Malkartasians, but the functions it carries out are devolved to smaller councils. The Council of the People is charged to maintain records of all who are born or die in our land, and those who wish to live here but were not born Malkartasian."

Yilmay did not know what "devolve" meant, but she thought she had grasped his explanation of the smaller councils that did the actual work of The Council. She thought it not unlike the Bailiff in Dur, whose office had two branches; Magisterial and Commercial, and she imagined these councils were similar. She asked where she would find the Council of the People, and the man gave her directions to somewhere deep in The Rotunda. The clerk assured her signs on the walls would guide her there without fail, and so it proved. The signs were scribed in Malkartasian, but key words in other languages were also included, including Kuirbekian and, to her surprise, Dur. The words for the Council of the People looked similar in Kuirbekian and Malkartasian.

She found a clerk who confirmed that for a small fee he could investigate the records and find Raolos, if he had registered. She had the coins the master of the Rzankir had given her and she held some of them out in her hand. The clerk studied a parch and tracked a line between one column of numbers and another with a finger, before he sorted through her Argoya coins, took some of them from her, and dropped them into a slot in a small chest. It appeared the councils of Malkartas accepted any coins. No doubt the amount of trade conducted in any city with a large dock meant coin of all kinds could be accepted.

She began to tell the clerk as much as she could about Raolos, but as soon as she mentioned his name, the clerk held up a hand to stop her. "Yes, yes, Raolos of Dur. He set up a trade house, I think. You call them tally houses, do you not? In Dur?"

Yilmay had not said she came from Dur. Mayhap she spoke Kuirbekian with an accent, or he thought because she searched for Raolos of Dur, she must also be from Dur. She nodded confirmation of the tally house theory. She noticed they said 'yes' here, as they had in Argoya, and other lands. As familiar as she had become with it, it still felt uncomfortable on her tongue, and she did not think she could ever adopt the practice.

In Kuirbekian, he scribed an address on a piece of parch. She cursed herself as she left the building. She could have searched the docks until she saw his tally house, or trade house, and saved herself the coin. She returned to the docks and scoured the names above all the trade houses until she saw Raolos's.

He owned a substantial trade house, and it amazed Yilmay he had built such a large business in three years. He would have fled Dur with next to nothing, she guessed. He must be the kind of man who could succeed in business against any adversity. A large sign on the eaves of the building read, "Raolos's Trades." Not the most creative of names, but Yilmay had no gift for names. She smiled, thankful she had not had ten children. She guessed she would have changed a letter here and there and called them all versions of the same thing. She might have named them One, Two, Three, and so on. She laughed to herself at her own jest.

As Yilmay approached the trade house, she wondered about the description. Here they were trade houses, in Argoya they were goods houses, while in Dur they were tally houses. It would make sense for all similar things to be called the same thing, and for all lands to speak the same language, she thought. Life would be simpler for travellers, at the least. If she ever became Duchess of Ictharelian, she would change things to this simple method. She laughed again at the foolish notion of her as the Duchess of the entire globe.

She walked in through the small door that always seemed to be set into a larger set of doors. Goods lay everywhere, sorted into neat piles, and several people bustled about as they moved crates, checked pieces of parch and so on. It seemed Raolos's business had been successful. A row of offices stood at the rear of the trade house, with windows that looked out onto the floor of the house. As she walked through the storage area, she saw two doors. One had the word, "Office," scribed on it and seemed as good a place to begin as any.

A woman seated at a desk in the office worked on a ledger, head bowed over the rows of figures, and her lips moved as she read them. Yilmay waited while the woman scribed something on a piece of parch next to the ledger and looked up, a hospitable smile on her lips. She had a strange device on her face Yilmay had never seen before. It looked like some kind of wire frame, fashioned into two small circles, each of which appeared to have a piece of glass in them. Each of the glass circles sat over one of her eyes, connected by a wire hoop, and a further piece of wire extended from the outside of each circle backward to disappear into her thick black hair. Her eyes both seemed enormous, out of all proportion to the rest of her face, and Yilmay took a step backward in surprise. Yilmay could not determine what purpose the device served unless it helped in some way with the tallies.

The woman said something, but although some of the words sounded familiar, Yilmay could not understand much of the sentence. "Do you speak Kuirbekian?"

Yilmay relaxed her clenched teeth when the woman replied, "Yes, I do."

"I would like to see Raolos please, if he is here."

The woman removed the device from her face, and her eyes returned to a more appropriate size. Through some unknown means, Malkartasians had a device to change the size of their eyes. It seemed there must be no end to the wonders to be seen on the globe. "Raolos is busy at the moment, I am afraid. Did you have an appointment?"

"Appointment?" Yilmay had not appreciated she would need one to see Raolos.

"Yes." The woman showed no sign of frustration. "Have you arranged to meet with Raolos at this hour?"

Raolos had been easier to meet with when he had been the Bailiff. "That I have not. I am an old friend." The woman continued to stare at her, and Yilmay guessed she had heard such an excuse from many others who had attempted to see Raolos. "He will see me." She adopted a firm tone; she wanted the woman to know she should not be delayed, and Raolos might even be annoyed if she denied Yilmay access to him.

"I see." The woman raised her eyebrows. "Might I ask your name?"

"My name is Yilmay." The woman stood and moved toward a door at one side of the office, but Yilmay realised Raolos would not recognise the name. "Wait. Tell him it is Corelle." She had been Yilmay for only three years, but she wore the name like a favourite tunic, comfortable in its cloak of obscurity.

The woman went through the door and closed it behind her. She seemed almost as determined as the woman in the Duke's office to prevent any interruption to her employer's important work. Through the closed door, Yilmay heard voices, but she could not hear what they said.

Yilmay jumped when she heard Raolos yell, "Corelle? Here?" A few heartbeats later, Raolos flung open the door, his smile so wide, it threatened to push his ears from his head. He gazed at her for a moment, then rushed over, swept her into his arms, and twirled her around the room as his embrace crushed the breath from her body. The woman stood in the doorway and watched the performance. She smiled, doubtless aware she had made the correct decision when she had not rejected the ragged, filthy urchin before her.

"It is good to see you." Raolos crushed her even more against himself. "We feared you had died. You stink, by the way. Tell me everything. Oh, how it gladdens me to see you alive."

"I will not be alive if you do not allow me to breathe." He laughed, then released her. She did not know where to begin her tale. "I have stood at the door of death more than once since you last saw me outside Delcan."

"Synna rode with me that day." His mood changed from ecstasy to despair in a heartbeat.

Yilmay sighed, her own heart heavy at the memory of the loss of her friend. After a brief period of silence, she forced some cheer into her voice, anxious not to spoil the joy of their reunion. "You seem to have done well for yourself."

"That I have. Wilash also. He owns a smithy in the city. He wished to return to his first love. We seldom see him these days." He paused and drew in a breath as though his excitement had tugged all the air from his lungs. "Tell me everything. Wait, do not tell me. Tell us tonight at dinner." He laid a hand on her upper arm and squeezed it in a sign of affection.

"You will send word to Wilash?"

"That I will." Lines creased his brow, as though her question had surprised him. He turned to the woman, who nodded. "The five of us will have a night of it. I may be late in the morning Bealitrice."

"Vamma is here also?" Yilmay hoped she would be among the five he had mentioned.

"That she is." He turned to Bealitrice again. "Please send word there will be five for dinner tonight."

Yilmay tried to understand the last part of the conversation. Vamma must live in the same house as Raolos. "Vamma lives in your home?"

Raolos turned back to her. "Vamma is my wife. She is a remarkable woman. I cannot thank you enough that you brought her to Ryl safe and sound."

CHAPTER 17
YILMAY

Yilmay kept the smile on her lips even as her heart felt as though it had stopped. His wife? How could that be? Vamma had waited for Yilmay to return, had she not? Had that not been what they had agreed in Ryl when Yilmay had left for Ort? It had taken her longer to return than she had expected, but she had done so at last, and Vamma had married Raolos in the meantime. She did not know what to say. She had focused all her energies on her return to Vamma, even as she lay close to death in Illfarlen. Three years, no more. Yilmay had needed to flee the sadness of Synna's death and all that had turned in Dur. The voyage around the globe had delayed her, but it had been an opportunity she could not pass up. Vamma had insisted she loved her, after all else. Yilmay had rolled ones again in affairs of the heart.

"I am happy for you both." She had paused for longer than she should have. She embraced Raolos and forced her smile not to flee into the shadows where it wished to hide. "Congratulations."

"My thanks. Vamma will be so happy to hear you are back."

Yilmay no longer felt any desire to linger in Malkartas now she knew Vamma had married Raolos. "I am not back. I will not stay, but the ship I arrived on sailed here, and I wanted to look in and see you all again." How easily the lies dripped from her tongue. Yilmay had become better at deception now than she had been throughout her time in the Guild, or when she had hidden the terrible truth from Deineike.

"That is sad news." Raolos's smile faded. "Where will you go?"

She shrugged. "Wherever the wind blows me. I may return to Ryl and see my parents."

He nodded. "The Qagrue still rule there. We trade with them now, both from Qagrue and from Dur. They drive a hard bargain and are not easy to deal with."

"Did you hear what turned in Ort when I went there, and after I left?"

"Rumours have come here. I believe some revolt left many Qagrue dead. It is rumoured the former Bailiff, Sisnop, led this revolt, infuriated when the Qagrue removed him from his position." His tone implied he did not believe the story, and Yilmay could not resist a wicked smile. "I heard townsfolk, loyal to the Qagrue, killed him afterward, and Ort is now calm. Or so the rumours tell."

"Quite the tale." She smiled. "I can scarce believe they fell for that line. Synna would have been proud of that plan. He had little confidence in most of the ideas I came up with."

His smile held only sadness. "He felt a deep pride to be your friend. You must know this."

Her throat constricted, she coughed before she spoke again, and tears burned her eyes. "Nonetheless, I believe I will visit my parents. It has been three years since I saw them."

"It is good to see you again Corelle." He half turned. "I am busy, but I look forward to an evening of outrageous tales. Not for the first time." The twinkle in his eye confirmed his sincerity.

"A ship might leave for Dur later today." She felt reluctant to go to dinner now.

Raolos would not be discouraged. "I insist. Vamma and Wilash will be desperate to see you again, no matter how awful you look. You stink. Did I tell you that?"

Yilmay laughed. "That you did. I will bathe before dinner." She feared it would become awkward if she resisted his invitation, and she valued Raolos's friendship. She would hide her disappointment and regale them with stories of Ictharelian and a life at sea. Tomorrow, she would sail for Dur.

"Excellent. Stay with us. We have spare rooms."

That would be impossible. It would be hard enough to see Vamma at dinner. To sleep in the house while she knew Raolos lay with his new wife down the corridor would be unbearable. More lies sprang to her lips, so easy, so comfortable as they slithered from her. "I have a room at a nearby inn. My thanks for the offer, nonetheless."

"Very well. Return here at the third quarter and we will travel to my home together." He embraced her again, and she took her leave of him, dejected and frustrated.

Yilmay could not guess how much an inn would cost, nor whether her coins would even cover a night, so she searched the area around the docks until she spotted an inn that seemed run down, paint faded by the sun, windows dirty and the sign that announced its name almost illegible. Yilmay thought the inn might be named The Moonlight, although the sign, scribed in Malkartasian, had faded so much, it had become one dull brown colour throughout. The inn looked as though it might be inexpensive, and that suited her requirements.

Several patrons sat at the tables in the tavernroom even this early in the day. The innkeep cast a suspicious gaze over her as she entered. She imagined he mistook her for a courtesan, she and disliked the thought more than she ought to. Yilmay had a mild headache, which she put down to the news of Vamma's marriage to Raolos. She obtained a room and arranged a tub for later in the day. She paid in advance so the innkeep would see she had coin, which might change any misconceptions he held about her status. Like the Council, he accepted her coins without question, although it crossed her mind they might both have taken advantage of her lack of knowledge of their true worth.

Since she had no belongings and filth covered her from head to foot, she imagined she might have been suspicious of herself, had she been the innkeep. It rankled her he had leapt to judgement, nonetheless. "I am no courtesan." He did not look up as he counted the coins.

"I know this."

"Then do not judge me as one."

He frowned. "I made no such judgement."

She drew in a long breath. "You looked at me as though you made the decision the moment I arrived."

He held his arms out and shrugged. "You wear filthy clothing, you have almost no hair and, to be quite honest, you smell. I am sure the tale behind your appearance would be remarkable, heard over a tankard, but I run a respectable inn, and I could not decide what that story might be as you entered. If I gave offence, I apologise."

Yilmay chewed at the inside of her mouth. Had she misjudged the look he gave her? It mattered not. Tomorrow she would sail onward to Dur to see her parents and would never see the man again. "I need the tub I have requested, I admit it. I have come from a long journey aboard ship, and I do not seek any opinion on my clothes or my hair." She turned on her heel and stomped off to find her room, her anger still unchecked despite his apology. She sat on her bed and tried to calm herself. The man had worsened her headache, and she decided fresh air might clear it away.

Although she had been to Tanasttra before, she had never

ventured further than the taverns around the docks until today. The docks soon gave way to the poorer quarter, or whatever name that part of the city carried here. She thought the area might be less wholesome than its equivalent in any city in Dur. The streets were narrow and uneven, with old clothes, boots, and other items strewn about. There were piles of waste in some of the alleyways Yilmay had no desire to investigate. The area smelled of unwashed bodies and human waste. People stood or sat around, listless, on every street, and the few children she saw wore ragged, filthy clothes. The Council must not care much about the quality of the lives of these people. She stopped to peer through the filthy window of a shop and saw little enough food on the shelves, and no customers. The houses looked untidy, with broken windows, and the faded paint-work peeled from the window and door frames. The people who stood around outside them wore poor quality clothes, torn and dirty.

Yilmay could not understand why these people seemed to have such a poor life. In Dur, the poor quarters were not magnificent, but the poor quarter of Alcmouth might be mistaken for the better quarter compared to the streets she passed through today. She shook her head and moved on.

As she passed a tavern, three men came out of the door. They stumbled and laughed aloud, and one of them staggered close to her as he turned to say something to his companions. He lost his balance and crashed into Yilmay. To the great amusement of his two friends, he knocked her to the floor, and she broke her fall with her hands, arms outstretched. She sprang back to her feet in a heart-beat, furious with the man's clumsiness, and she pushed him hard with both hands as he turned toward her. She reached for her boot, a killer's instinct, but stopped herself before she pulled out her fan. He took two steps backward before he lost his balance and landed on his behind in the street. Yilmay stood over him, maddened he had knocked her over.

One of his friends said something she could not understand, and she wheeled on him, fists clenched, a snarl on her lips. He backed away two paces as some locals helped the man whom she had knocked over back to his feet.

Somebody behind her touched her shoulder, and she spun to push at the man who stood there. "Calm yourself." The man staggered backward as he yelled at her. "They are inebriated. They meant no harm." He had spoken Malkartasian, but she believed she had understood his words.

Yilmay lowered her fists and tried to wipe the snarl from her face. Her heart raced, and her teeth were clenched so tight, her jaw ached. Her head pounded inside her skull, and she felt faint. She held both hands up to the man she had pushed and stomped away without a backward glance. Her legs drove her on faster than her normal pace, and she muttered to herself about the stupidity of the man who had knocked her over.

She strode along the street with uncharacteristic speed and soon found herself in a better quarter. The houses became larger, the people better dressed. When she saw a small green space with a bench within, she turned to enter it and sat on the bench with her head in her hands as she fought to calm her temper and slow her breaths. She stared at the ground and replayed the event in her head. While she now thought the incident had been nothing more than an unfortunate accident, her fury at the man who had collided with her would not abate. She had been so angry, she had wanted to kill him. Had she taken out her fan…

Yilmay broke the train of thought. It would be ridiculous to kill a man because he had been intoxicated and had bumped into her. How many people had she crashed into as she staggered away from a tavern in her cups? She had left the inn to seek relief from her headache, but in truth, she had made it worse. She could not understand the ease with which she had become enraged. It must have been the news about Vamma, she reasoned. The stress of all that had turned in the pass or more since The Ictharelian had sunk, her injury, the journey home. Those events, coupled with the news about Vamma, must have affected her and made her agitated. She would be fine again in a few days when recent events faded from the front of her mind.

Her heart returned to a normal rate, although it took longer than she expected. She told herself it must be because she had not used her Guild training for three years, apart from the fight in Argoya. She could soon relearn her old skills, if she ever needed to.

Yilmay pulled herself to her feet and pointed herself back toward the inn. A long soak in a hot tub might wash away many of these cares. Her clothes could go into the tub with her. She had no others and could not afford to spend coin she would need if she intended to pay for passage to Dur and avoid the need to work on the voyage.

She reached the inn without further incident, embarrassed now about how she had reacted to the inebriated man who had clattered into her. She asked for the tub to be filled, then lay in it and luxuriated in the heat of the water, the feel of the soap on her skin. Once she had washed her clothes, she lay back again to enjoy the last heat of the water. Her mind drifted to Vamma, and her hand slid between her legs to take the pleasure that had been promised to her when she arrived but had been snatched away by Raolos's news. While she would have preferred for Vamma's fingers and tongue to coax satisfaction from her, there would be others in time. Her hips bucked out of the water as her excitement peaked, and she gasped and moaned as she massaged her nub until wild excitement flooded her body. She gave one final moan of pleasure and relaxed in the water.

The water had grown almost cold before she stepped out of the tub. With no way to dry her clothes, she ran them through the two wooden rollers near the tub, a device cranked by a handle. The rollers squeezed excess water from the clothes better than she could with her bare hands alone.

She dressed in the wet clothes and returned the coins to her pocket before she headed to her room. When she looked out of the window, the sun had already sunk low in the sky. She would arrive late for the meeting with Raolos she guessed, and now the time had come, she had little appetite for the sight of his married bliss with a woman who had once professed to love her. She had said she would go, however, and it would be good to see them all again. Even Vamma.

CHAPTER 18
YILMAY

Yilmay set off for Raolos's trade house, a short journey marked by the drips of water that fell from her clothes. A carriage waited outside, and Raolos stood near it and gazed around. He waved to her once he saw her and moved to the carriage door.

He greeted her as a man in a bright red tunic pulled the carriage door open. "There you are. Vamma awaits us." He appeared to notice her clothes. "What turned? Did you fall into the sea?"

Yilmay smiled and forced a laugh to her throat. "I have but one set of clothes. With no others available, I washed these in the tub with me." With an effort, she broadened her smile. "I cannot win. First, I stink. Then, when I bathe, I am in trouble because I have not dried my clothes."

He laughed at the comment, though it had been no more than a frustrated, angry outburst clothed in a jest of flawless making. "We can resolve that situation. Come, let us away." He climbed up into the carriage and held out a hand to aid her, which she spurned. The carriage took many twists and turns as it rode through the streets. She saw none of the streets she had strolled along on her earlier walk. Soon the carriage trundled among much larger houses, better maintained and with gardens. It may not have been the wealthiest part of the city, but compared to the quarters she had seen earlier, it represented a substantial improvement.

The carriage pulled to a halt outside a large house with a neat garden. Two storeys of blue-painted windows, with a large central door, the gardens filled with flowers. Raolos lived in a beautiful house, although it seemed a pale imitation of the house he had owned in Ort. She asked what had become of that house. He still owned it, it turned, but to return and claim it did not seem important at this time. She did not mention the carpets she had destroyed with Gillar's and Sisnop's blood.

She remembered the loss of her trunk aboard The Ictharelian. "I fear I lost the key to Pettra's house."

He raised his eyebrows, then replied. "It matters not. I have another. I do not know what to do about that house. It is not mine, but we were still married when she died, in truth."

"Her parents might want it."

"Alas, they are both dead. You plan to return to Dur. Do you want the house? Pettra still professed to love you when she died, I imagine."

"That I do not." Yilmay had not hesitated. He need not know of the difficulties between her and Pettra when his first wife had taken her own life. "At whiles it has been useful to me these last few years, but I have no claim on the house, and I do not want it." How could she take it? It would remind her of Deineike and Pettra. Every room would hold memories that could bring her nothing but pain. From time to time, she had endured it in the name of convenience, but she could never live there. Two women dead because of her, and their faces on every wall, in every window. She could not live there.

They alighted from the carriage and walked up the pathway to the large door. Unlike the house in Ort, this one had no carriage drive. When the door opened, Vamma stood in the doorway in a plain dress. Yilmay thought the dress's shade of beige suited Vamma and accentuated her hair, which had been pulled into an extravagant bun on the top of her head. Vamma's warm, brown eyes drank in Yilmay, whose throat constricted at the sight of the woman she had spent most of her thoughts on for the last pass. Her legs became shaky, and she felt dizzy. Her headache had not receded, and at the sight of Vamma it pounded anew. Other parts of her ached also, and she forced her attention away from the thoughts that filled her mind.

As they reached the door, Vamma kissed Raolos on the cheek, then moved to embrace Yilmay. She stopped when she appeared to notice the damp clothes, then smiled and swept her into a lengthy embrace, her arms wrapped tight around Yilmay. Vamma smelled delicious. Some scent on her skin, different from the one Pettra had worn, filled Yilmay's nostrils. Vamma's hair smelled of apples, and Yilmay imagined the smell had something to do with a substance Vamma used to wash it. At last, Vamma released the embrace and stepped back. "Your clothes…"

Yilmay explained the story again, and Vamma offered to lend her some clothes for the night to spare their furniture. They laughed together, the three of them, but Yilmay could not guess whether the other two worked as hard to force the laughter from themselves as she had.

They entered the house, where an entryway greeted them, a set of stairs at each end of it that met in a central landing above them. Doors led off the entryway to each side and also beneath the staircase. Raolos turned left and passed through one of the doors as Vamma invited Yilmay to come to her room and choose some dry clothes. As she trudged up the stairs, Yilmay recalled the time she and Deineike had climbed the rude stairs in Taro's farmhouse to find clean clothes for the tall woman who would come to mean so much to her and whose life had been cut short by Styrrach. She choked back tears and wiped at her nose with the sleeve of her tunic. Vamma appeared not to notice.

Vamma's large bed had four tall posts, one at each corner. A mantle had been draped over the frame at the top of the posts, and it hung down at each corner like a decorative curtain. Yilmay had seen curtains before, although they were rare in Dur, but she had never seen them on a bed. Vamma crossed the room and pulled two large doors open. The cupboard held a collection of clothes so large even Pettra would not have been ashamed of it.

Vamma stepped forward and ran her hand along some of the dresses. Yilmay thought Vamma's dresses looked too fussy for her taste, but other things were on her mind, in truth. "You married him?"

Vamma stiffened, her back to Yilmay. "He is a good man." A quiver in her voice betrayed unguessed emotions she strove to control.

"That he is."

An awkward silence ensued, and Vamma took a step to one side, then bent to pull out a trunk. "There are trousers and tunics in here. I imagine my dresses will not suit you."

"That they will not." As Yilmay bent to the trunk, the clean, perfumed odour of Vamma next to her assaulted her nostrils again. Vamma smelled of dashed hopes, frustration, and the promise of future tears. Yilmay trembled with a mixture of despair and desire as she pulled out some trousers and exchanged her own for them, then repeated the process with a tunic.

Vamma picked up the wet clothes. "I will hang them near the stove. They should be dry before you leave."

Anger tore through Yilmay's veins, and she could not disguise the fury in her voice. "You could not wait for me?"

"You could not scribe to me?" Vamma stared at Yilmay, who saw anger and accusation mirrored in the brown pools of her eyes, and something else too.

Yilmay could not keep a contemptuous sneer from her face. "In truth, I could not. I did not know your new husband's address."

Vamma's mouth opened, and her eyes narrowed, but she froze and glanced down at the wet clothes in her hands. "That is not the way it turned." Her voice changed as she replied, quiet, meek. "I believed you had died. Three years, Corelle. Three years." Her eyes flashed with frustration. "Raolos scribed a letter and urged you to meet us here. I sat at the docks every day for a pass. You did not come. Where have you been?"

Yilmay took a deep breath through her nose. She did not trust her mouth to open as rage swept over her. She balled her fists and pressed her nails into the palms of her hands as she fought her temper. "You once said even if you had eight children, I could call on you. Have you forgotten those words?" Her body burned with desire again. With luck, it would sweep away her anger, at the least. As the silence lengthened, Yilmay could not deny her feelings. "You look magnificent."

Vamma blushed and stared at her for heartbeats beyond number before her breathy reply. "Not here. Not in this house. We will talk later. Raolos awaits us." She went to the door but stopped, one hand on the handle. She turned to face Yilmay, and her eyes had softened. "I have missed you. I have missed your touch." She walked back to Yilmay and kissed her, one hand pressed to the back of Yilmay's head. She pulled her tongue out of Yilmay's mouth, rested her forehead on Yilmay's cheek, and returned to the door.

As they entered the parlour, Raolos looked up from his chair. An open cask of wine stood on a small table to one side of his chair. He rose and picked up the wine. "Let us have a goblet before dinner. You have a great deal to tell us, and we are anxious to hear it all."

As he poured wine into three goblets, Vamma skipped out of the room. She returned soon afterward without Yilmay's wet clothes. They touched their goblets together, then sat down, Raolos in his chair, the women side by side on a couch.

Yilmay gave voice to a question that pushed into her mind. "Where is Wilash?"

Vamma replied. "He sent word. He has a prior engagement. It devastated him to miss you, but he urges you to call at his smithy tomorrow."

Yilmay smiled, sad beyond words. She would have welcomed the opportunity to see her old friend, and she had hoped his presence might lift the veil of awkwardness she felt as she sat so close to a woman whose body she burned for but who had married another of her friends. "I do not know where to start." Now the time had come to tell her fantastic tale, where should she begin? Things that had no place at the start of the story might serve to make sense of the decisions she had made in the last three years if she made them known from the outset. "I sailed the Torr Sea area for a year until I met Rakulaj again, by chance. He had become captivated by the thought we might exist on a globe and wished to fund an expedition that would attempt to sail around it, and I joined the ship. We set off, full of hope and anticipation."

As the story unfolded, it became clear Raolos and Vamma had no servants. Several times, Vamma asked Yilmay to pause as she ran to the scullery to fuss with the meal she prepared. Raolos suggested they all relocate to the scullery to spare the interruptions, and they did so. They leaned against cupboards in the small space as Yilmay continued the story. They consumed the wine at a prodigious rate as they listened to her tale, rapt at the stories of new lands, and laughed until they cried at some of the funnier things that had turned along the way.

Yilmay had told a story of how she had tried to make herself understood to the inhabitants of one of the lands they came across, and how she could not get them to understand Yilmay meant nothing other than her name. Raolos interrupted her and said he did not care for the name Yilmay, and Vamma agreed. They refused to address her by the name and called her Corelle all night.

The tale continued to unfold throughout the meal. Vamma had prepared a tender, juicy piece of meat, and Raolos sliced it up while Vamma served roasted vegetables and tubers to go with it. The food tasted delicious, and it served as a distraction to Yilmay, who wanted nothing more than to pull Vamma to the floor and enjoy a night of fiery passion.

When she confirmed the globe theory, it left Raolos and Vamma speechless. The concept must be difficult to grasp, and the fact that for countless years people had lived in Dur but had not known people lived in other lands far, far away almost defied their belief.

"When you were around the other side, how did you not fall off?" Vamma shook her head in disbelief. She held up a fist and pointed to the back of her hand. "If we stand upright here, then how can we not fall off here?" She pointed to the underside of her fist, where she had tucked her fingers into her palm.

The question had vexed Yilmay many times. "I do not know. I feared I would, but I did not. None of us did."

"Were you upside down, then?" Raolos leaned forward on his chair, focused on every word Yilmay said, his voice little more than an astonished whisper.

She shrugged. "I must have been, though I did not realise it. It felt as though I walked upright as I do here, or in Dur." The concept staggered them, and they could not understand how Yilmay had been upside down but had felt as though she were not.

The tales of people, animals, and customs of these other lands fascinated them, and some of the stranger traditions baffled them. They roared with laughter when they learned of a land in which the inhabitants greeted a friend with a slap to their face. They could not grasp why in one land the people dressed from head to foot in clothes and shawls, so only their eyes could be seen, yet in the next land people might walk around without any clothes at all.

When she came to the part of the tale where the ship sank, they sat entranced, their emotions visible on their faces as they rode from horror to compassion to relief along with the tale. "Thank the Council you survived." Raolos glanced to his wife as Yilmay told them about the day she arrived in Argoya

He had used an unfamiliar phrase, and Vamma explained it as a common expression in Malkartas. "Raolos has become absorbed in the culture of this land now we live here." The two women laughed while Raolos blushed.

Yilmay left out the story of the three who had attempted to rob her, or worse, in Argoya, as well as her constant desire to see Vamma as she worked her way back to Malkartas. As the night wore on, it occurred to her she had consumed a great deal of wine, and she decided she should leave and head back to the inn.

Vamma went to collect Yilmay's clothes, and while she did so Raolos suggested Yilmay might work for him for a time. He had plenty of work at the trade house or on the docks if she wished it. She thanked him and said she thought she would leave soon enough, but he insisted she come to see him at the trade house if she did wish to find work for a time.

Vamma returned with Yilmay's clothes. They had all but dried, but Vamma told her to keep the ones she wore for now as they could be returned at any time. They walked her out to the street, where the carriage stood in wait. Raolos said the driver worked for him and lived above the stable when he did not drive the carriage or perform some other chore for the business. The driver could not be found, however, and Raolos went in search of him. The stable, accessed by a small alleyway further along the street, stood at the rear of the house.

As Raolos disappeared into the alleyway, Vamma leaned close to Yilmay to whisper. "We did not talk tonight."

Yilmay corrected her. "I talked. You both listened."

Vamma smiled. She glanced around, then kissed Yilmay again.

"Meet me tomorrow. We will go to the shops. You need more clothes, so I will buy you some."

"I do not need your sympathy."

Vamma pouted. "It is not sympathy. You cannot walk around the land—my mistake, the globe, with only one set of clothes." She laughed, but Yilmay did not return the laughter, filled with despair. All she desired at that moment stood next to her, so far out of reach, it almost drove her to madness. Vamma continued in a more serious tone. "I would enjoy some more time with you, after all else."

Yilmay sighed in dejection. "I have a room at The Moonlight inn."

Horror crept into Vamma's voice. "Near the docks?" Yilmay nodded. "That is a dreadful place. You must move to a better inn."

"It suits me for now. I will not be there long."

Vamma raised her eyebrows. "As you wish. I will come for you tomorrow, once Raolos is at the trade house. Be up early. I will ride into work with him and come for you."

"Will he not suspect?"

A thoughtful expression crossed Vamma's face. "He may. He knows we lay together before I met him."

Yilmay shook her head in furious rejection of the idea. "I do not wish to create a problem in your marriage."

Vamma stared at her with earnest eyes that melted Yilmay's heart. "I want you. Now I have overcome my anger you did not come for me, I wish to tell you everything. I long for you."

Raolos and the driver appeared from the alleyway, and Vamma whispered her final plea. "Tomorrow then."

Yilmay thanked them both for the dinner and gushed about how good it had been to see them both, then kissed each of them on the cheek and climbed into the carriage. She told the driver the name of the inn, and he told her she had made a terrible choice and offered to take her somewhere better. She declined the offer. The inn cost little enough coin, and she had no other requirement at this stage.

Yilmay lay in her bed in the inn. The room spun from all the wine she had consumed. As she reflected on the kisses with Vamma, her hand slid between her legs once more.

YILMAY

When she awoke, Yilmay felt a familiar ache in her head, biliousness in her stomach, and dryness in her mouth. The wine worked its evil effect on her as it had always done the morning after a large quantity had been consumed. She forced herself out of the bed and pulled Vamma's clothes on again, and Vamma's smell on them reminded her of the kisses last night. She held the tunic under her nose for a time, but dizziness washed over her and threatened to tumble her to the floor like the inebriated man the day before, so she sat on the bed.

Yilmay left the inn and gulped large breaths of air into her lungs. She would not call the air fresh; she had breathed the pure, unspoilt air of the sea, far from any land. The air of a city no longer seemed fresh to her, but it helped settle her stomach, and she did not wish to fetch up in the street.

She wandered down to the docks with a plan to loiter some-where she could see Raolos's trade house and wait for Vamma. The morning already felt warm, and she imagined the day would turn hot later. When the carriage pulled up outside the trade house, Vamma stepped down dressed in trousers and a tunic, as she had most of the time in Yerrsun. Her hair hung loose around her fine-featured face, a faint smile on her perfect red lips, and Yilmay longed to be in her arms. Vamma crossed the dock, and her long brown hair fluttered in the breeze. Yilmay watched her walk toward her and devoured her with hungry eyes. When Vamma spotted her, a happy smile came to her face, and her eyes sparkled. She kissed Yilmay on the cheek, but her hand lingered over-long on her shoulder.

Yilmay suggested they go back to the inn, but Vamma wrinkled her nose. "It is vile. Could you not have found somewhere nicer to stay?"

"'Nicer?' It is 'nice' enough for me. It is inexpensive, and it has a bed I can sleep in. What more do I need?"

Vamma tossed her head, and her brown hair spilled around her shoulders. "Very well, if that is what you desire." Yilmay's desires ran to more than a cheap inn, but she remained silent. "Come. I will buy you something to break your fast."

Yilmay smiled what she hoped would be a suggestive smile. "I am still full after last night. I do not wish you to fill my stomach. I long for you to fill me in other ways."

"Not at that revolting place." Vamma frowned.

"Where, then?"

Vamma sighed. "Walk with me for a time. There are things I must tell you first." Despite her reluctance, Yilmay fell into step beside Vamma. "When Raolos arrived in Ryl, it surprised and delighted me. I spent the next day or two with him, Synna and Wilash, but I longed for you to return. All that had turned had devastated Raolos, and the fact his son had been killed almost destroyed him. They told me they had met you as you travelled to Ort. The fall of Ryl, and the death of Synna… I could scarce bear the heartbreak." Tears rolled down her cheek.

Yilmay reached up and wiped away her tears. "I felt the same when I received Raolos's letter."

"I understand. The two of you were good friends." Vamma laid a hand on Yilmay's arm. "After all else, we were forced to flee. The Qagrue did not know Raolos, but once they found out he had been the Bailiff, they would have killed him. He represented something the people might have followed: hope, leadership, resistance. The risk would have been too great had he stayed." She glanced at Yilmay, who gestured for her to continue "I wanted to stay in Ryl and wait for you. They insisted I must go with them. They believed you must have met your ruin in Ort. I could not..." She paused, and Yilmay remained silent. "We sailed here on the same ship you and I travelled to Ryl upon, and I waited for you. You did not come."

Yilmay felt the rage form in the pit of her stomach and fought in vain against it. "So you married Raolos. How convenient."

Vamma stopped. "That is a hurtful thing to say, Corelle. I thought about you every single day. I yearned for you to come to Malkartas. The three of us shared a house. When Wilash moved out, he left me alone with Raolos."

"Wilash lived in the house?"

"For a time." Vamma nodded in further confirmation. "He lives above his smithy now. He has met a woman here. Her name is Derkhata something. I cannot get my tongue around their names."

"You were able to get it around other things, however, or so it seems." The anger consumed Yilmay, and as hard as she tried, she could not resist the spiteful remark.

Vamma's eyes moistened. "Corelle, what is wrong with you? Why are you so hateful? You cannot know what I endured. I thought you must be dead. I found myself alone in a foreign land with no coin and nowhere of my own to live. Raolos asked me to marry him. He promised me security; something I had little enough prospect of otherwise. He is a good man, and we have grown to appreciate each other."

"Appreciation? Not love?" Yilmay asked the question, even

though the answer might destroy her. If Vamma loved Raolos and would not betray him, it would devastate her after all she had endured, all the effort she had expended to reach Malkartas, determined to settle down with this woman who dangled before her, unattainable temptation.

Emotion fled from Vamma's voice, and it raised the hairs on the backs of Yilmay's arms with its cold detachment. "He says he loves me. I tell him I love him. I do not."

"You do not love him after all it seems he has done for you?"

Vamma cupped a hand under Yilmay's chin, held her head steady, and stared deep into her eyes. "I love you. My love for you has never faded, not once. It never will. I thought you were…" Tears flowed from her eyes, and her voice dropped to a whisper, so faint it might have been no more than the sigh of silk across skin. "You did not come for me. I thought you had been killed."

The rage subsided in Yilmay almost as fast as it had risen. She stared at Vamma; eyes red as tears ran down her face. How could Yilmay be angry? How could she ever have been angry? Vamma had the right of it. Yilmay had turned her back on her, on them. Synna's death had laid her low, but she had made poor decisions from that day to this. Those decisions had almost cost her life. Would they also cost her Vamma? "I am sorry. I have been a failure to you, I see this. It should not surprise me. I have been a failure to many people."

"Corelle." Vamma gripped Yilmay's upper arms. "You did so much good in Dur. If you had been the Duke, Dur would have been the perfect place."

"Duchess."

"Duchess, then. How do you know so much about Dukes and Duchesses?" A faint smile teased at the corners of Vamma's mouth.

"Raolos's first wife." Yilmay could not claim any credit for this insignificant piece of knowledge.

"You have done so much for Dur. You saved Raolos in Ort; you brought down the Guild, then chased them from Dur. Do not say you have been a failure. Without you, the Guild would still murder people while Durfolk slept, contented and deceived by the belief almost no crime took place in the land."

"I could not kill Krage. I will regret that for the rest of my days."

Vamma squeezed Yilmay's arms. "Regret nothing. You avenged Deineike and Arella when you killed Styrrach."

"I did not avenge her unborn child."

Vamma fell silent. They walked on, and the burden of Yilmay's past returned tenfold, the guilt an unbearable weight. Her life as a mariner had eased her pain, but the brief conversation with Vamma had re-opened wounds that had never been closed, only ignored. She turned to Vamma, and the compassion in those red-rimmed brown eyes proved too much. Yilmay threw her arms around Vamma's waist and buried her head in her neck. She wept for her past, her present, and whatever future lay before her.

Yilmay sniffed as her tears dripped onto Vamma's shoulder. She no longer wished to remain in Malkartas. "Where are we headed?"

A wicked smile sprang to Vamma's face. "There is in an inn where I hear the innkeep is discreet about what turns in his rooms. I heard about it from the wife of one of Raolos's business associates. I believe she goes there for the occasional dalliance."

Vamma's face took on the look of a conspirator in some ribald tryst, and Yilmay could not help herself. Despite her misery, she smiled at Vamma's apparent excitement about the visit to the inn. "You have not been to this inn yourself for your own dalliances?"

Vamma looked stern. "There have been no others but Raolos."

"Yet you told me—"

Vamma cut her off. "I know what I told you. There have been no others. Until now, at the least."

"What about the shops?"

Vamma took Yilmay's hand and pulled her down the street. "Afterward. I want your hands on me first."

The inn in question stood in a short, quiet street, unremarkable, and with a side door almost hidden by a tall hedge. The perfect place for people who did not wish to be seen, Yilmay reasoned. To her surprise, rooms could be rented by the day rather than the night, and Vamma paid for a room.

They closed the door behind them and Vamma took two paces into the room before she turned to face Yilmay, her voice breathy with desire. "Close the shutters."

Yilmay stepped to the window and pulled the shutters closed. She turned, and in the dim light she saw Vamma slide the tunic from her shoulders to expose her breasts. Yilmay watched as Vamma caressed her breasts and pinched her nipples between a finger and thumb until they stood proud as her breaths became heavier by the moment. She slid one hand down the front of her trousers, then pulled it out and held a finger covered in her viscous juices toward Yilmay, who moved forward, took it into her mouth, and tasted the musky excitement of Vamma's sex as her own juices flowed.

As Vamma unfastened Yilmay's trousers, she breathed into her ear that it excited her to remove her own clothes from Yilmay's body. As soon as the trousers slid down Yilmay's legs, Vamma's hand dived between them, and a finger found her nub and caressed it it as Yilmay gasped. Yilmay thrust her tongue deep into Vamma's mouth and pulled her close. She felt Vamma's naked breasts against her own as Vamma coaxed Yilmay's first crescendo from her and teased the distended nub within the slit of Yilmay's sex.

That crescendo would be the first of many as they pleasured each other for almost three hours and cajoled eruption after eruption from one another with fingers and tongues. The sweat ran in rivulets from each of them as they rediscovered the joys of one another's bodies for the first time in three years. Vamma seemed as keen to receive as give. It had not always been so, but she appeared to have a primal hunger today that refused to be sated. Yilmay cried aloud in ecstasy as Vamma's tongue caressed her rear opening. She had been so aroused by the act, she returned the favour with a finger as Vamma moaned, a deep, guttural moan that stimulated Yilmay further.

Spent, they lay in each other's arms and held one another in silence. Yilmay stroked Vamma's wet hair back from her face and kissed the end of her nose. Vamma smiled and gazed deep into Yilmay's eyes. "I love you."

Yilmay wanted to reply with the same words, but she would not lie, and she could not be sure she loved Vamma. She felt content to be with her now, and even for the rest of her life. Love would come, she imagined, and would be no more pleasurable if rushed. Vamma must long to hear it, but she might hear the falsehood in it also, if Yilmay said it when it might not be true.

"I am glad you are back." Vamma nuzzled into Yilmay's neck. "These three years felt like three lifetimes. I took breaths, but they were empty without you."

"I am not back, not for long. I intend to leave for Dur. I wish to see my parents."

Vamma's lips touched Yilmay's skin, as tender as the feel of the softest breeze on a warm day. "Not straight away, I hope. We have much lost time to atone for."

Yilmay stared at the faded white of the ceiling. "I had intended to sail today."

"Please stay a day or two more, at the least. You could stay longer. Raolos has offered you work. Why not take his offer and see what turns?"

Yilmay sighed. The morning had excited her, and she would welcome more mornings like this, but the complication of Raolos remained and could not be ignored. He and Vamma were married, after all else. Yilmay wanted Vamma, wanted to live somewhere where their life would be quiet and safe. She had not enjoyed that sense of quiet satisfaction since she had left Ryl with Arella, and she longed for it now. Dalliances in a rented room in an inn would not suffice.

"You have not replied. Are you determined to leave?"

"You are married. We cannot be together."

"It is an inconvenience."

Vamma's reply shocked Yilmay. "An inconvenience? That it is, and more. He is my friend, yet I lie with his wife, and not for the first time. I am a faithless friend; I can accept that. But occasional dalliances are not what I seek. They never have been, in truth."

Vamma sighed. "We cannot resolve this situation in an hour while you wait for a ship to bear you off to Dur. If we are to find a solution, you must stay for a time. Can you not see that?"

"That I can, but if I stay, it brings nothing but pain to us all. What if he learns of us?"

Vamma propped herself up on her elbows, and her eyes swept Yilmay's face as though she sought some answers there. "We must take care he does not."

"And if he does?"

Vamma sighed. "He will be broken, my guess."

"And you? If he learns the truth, what will you do?" Another question she could not be certain she wished to hear answered. Her life had been littered with them, it seemed.

"I love you. I do not love him."

"That answer is no answer at all." In truth, the reply irritated Yilmay, and she extricated herself from the tangle of their bodies to sit up on the bed.

Vamma shuffled over and sat with her head on Yilmay's shoulder and her arms around her waist. "That it is. Let us dress and go to the shops. We will discuss it further tomorrow. If I can still speak after you are finished with me." She kissed Yilmay's shoulder.

With a sigh, Yilmay stood and retrieved her clothes. She pulled them on as she watched Vamma dress. The uncertainty of the situation distressed her, and most of the blame rested with her. She had been gone three years, and she could not have expected Vamma to wait for her for such a long time. The marriage that had snatched her dreams and plans away annoyed her, nonetheless. Although she did not wish to be resentful toward either of them, she struggled to prevent it. The unfairness of it gnawed at the pit of her stomach like some animal that burrowed its way toward her backbone.

CHAPTER 20
YILMAY

The pair walked to the better quarter, or so it seemed from Vamma's description. There were, it seemed, no defined quarters in Tanasttra, but the wealthy lived in select areas of the city, often atop a rise or behind a green space, often wooded. The shops Vamma took Yilmay to offered good quality making, but not excellent. Vamma pressed her to accept several outfits, but Yilmay restricted her to two pairs of trousers and two tunics. Vamma urged her to choose a dress, but Yilmay refused with the argument the inadequate making meant she could make herself a far superior dress. In her heart, she felt unsure she would ever wear a dress again. She had endured too much to don a dress and present herself as some respectable woman in society. Vamma insisted on an inexpensive pack to store her new clothes, although Yilmay argued she had coin and could buy it herself. It gave Vamma such obvious pleasure to buy Yilmay the few things, she had not the heart to deny her.

They wandered back toward the inn and talked of insignificant things as they avoided the serious discussion of their intent. Vamma told her about Malkartas, while Yilmay revealed some small details she had left out of the tale of her journeys of the last three years. When they reached the inn, Vamma again suggested Yilmay should move to more desirable accommodations and offered her some coin to help with the cost. Yilmay refused again. The inn would prove more than adequate accommodation for somebody who had slept in a room with ten men, none of whom had seen a tub of water for many passes.

Vamma pressed Yilmay again to think about Raolos's offer. "I will, I promise." Now it came to it, Yilmay felt reluctant to return to her room and end the day, so she walked back toward the trade house with Vamma. When they arrived, the carriage already awaited and Raolos sat inside it with some parch in his hands. He looked up, smiled as Vamma opened the door, then held out a hand to help her up into the carriage. He wanted to hear about their day, and Vamma told him all about it, although she added things that had not taken place. Yilmay stifled her amusement as the lies dripped from Vamma's tongue like honey spread too thick on a piece of bread.

Raolos's next question surprised Yilmay. "Will you take the job?"

Caught between doubt and uncertainty, she answered without thought. "That I will, for a time." She could see more of Vamma, at the least.

He smiled with satisfaction. "Please call yourself Corelle. I cannot become accustomed to this other name."

"You may call me any name you wish." She had only half teased him, annoyed by the tone of his voice.

Vamma supported her husband. "I call you stubborn. Corelle is a much nicer name."

"You used to call me Jorinda."

"I still like that name also, but Deineike called you that, and it is not my place, not ours to take that special bond from you. I prefer Corelle to this vulgar name you use now."

"A day may come when Corelle is ready to return. For now, she is forgotten."

Raolos appeared disgruntled, but he gathered himself. "Will you start tomorrow?"

Vamma spoke to her husband in a motherly tone. "Raolos, let the poor woman have a few days to recover from the hardship of such a long journey, please."

He laughed and seemed unoffended. "By the Council, I am inconsiderate. A poor friend. Very well, start when you are ready."

Yilmay felt a pang of guilt at his kindness, more so since Vamma's request had nothing to do with how well rested Yilmay might or might not be from the voyage. If Vamma had her way, Yilmay would never be rested. Until Raolos no longer... In truth, she could not permit herself such a cruel thought.

The carriage pulled away, and Yilmay watched it thread its way out of the docks toward their home. Her unexpected jealousy annoyed her, and she kicked in temper at a dog that wandered across her path. Her foot missed it, and with a yelp it ran off with its tail between its legs. She reached the inn and fell onto her bed, despondent. Visions of Vamma danced in her head; her body drenched in sweat, the heady smell of her excitement, and her gasps of pleasure. She muttered as she struck the bed either side of herself in anger. "By the fates. Curse you, Raolos. Why did you marry her?"

Darkness fell, and sleep took her. She dreamed of her and Vamma in a quaint cottage somewhere, where they tended flowers in the garden. Vamma wore a dress of Corelle's making and walked between the flowers to trim petals and flower heads that had died, while Yilmay sat in a chair near the open cottage door and watched.

All the flowers had faces in them, and as Vamma moved around the garden, the flowers turned toward her. Yilmay recognised the faces; Deineike, Arella, Klordia, Pettra, Synna, and Ibie. They grabbed at Vamma and wrapped themselves around her arms and legs as tendrils emerged from them, slid around her neck, and choked her. Vamma tried to call out to Yilmay for help, but she called her Corelle, and Yilmay denied her request for aid. "I am sorry, I cannot help. Corelle is not here." Vamma's face turned purple, and blood trickled from her ears. Her tongue protruded from her mouth, and Yilmay laughed, then poked her own tongue out at Vamma.

She woke with a start and sat up in the bed as a knock came at the door. "Who is it?"

A muffled reply came through the door. "The innkeep. A friend awaits you in the tavernroom."

"Did they give you a name?"

"Her name is Vamma." Yilmay relaxed. She had not expected Vamma to come to the inn, but it did not surprise her after all that had turned yesterday. She dressed in some of her new clothes and went down to the tavernroom. Vamma stood near the door in a dress patterned not unlike the flowers from last night's dream.

They kissed each other on the cheek, and Yilmay whispered she had not expected to see Vamma. It seemed Raolos had suggested it, consumed with guilt he had rushed Yilmay to start work and worried she would have little to do and not enough coin to enjoy the city. He had suggested Vamma spend the day with her to show her some of the key sights of Tanasttra and buy her lunch.

Vamma had acted unenthusiastic, she said, but gave in after an appropriate time. Of course, it delighted her Raolos had suggested it. She pulled Yilmay out of the inn, hurried her to The Rotunda, and pointed out some of the details of the design. Next, they visited a green space that covered a substantial area of the city beyond The Rotunda. Vamma told her they were in The Great Park and hurried her toward the centre to visit a vast lake, built by the Malkartasians, who dug the ground out and filled it with water over many passes. Small rowboats could be rented, and Yilmay smiled at the people who rowed around the lake in some of them.

They scurried through the most beautiful flower garden Yilmay had ever seen and came to a large area set aside for children's play. There were wooden structures everywhere for the children to play on. Yilmay noticed a round device children sat on while others spun it round and round. She imagined Vamma would fetch up if she rode it for even a heartbeat. A set of steps led up to a ramp children slid down, and Vamma explained a child sat at each end of a beam balanced over a central block of wood, and they each went up and down in turn. As a child, Yilmay had never played on any such devices, and the tall ramp appealed to her the most, but Vamma would not let her climb the steps, as the devices were reserved for the children.

Once Yilmay felt she could spin a tale about the sights of the city to satisfy Raolos, they headed to the inn they had visited yesterday. If the innkeep remembered them, he said nothing, in line with the discretion Vamma had referred to.

Two hours after the midday as they lay contented on the bed with arms and legs wrapped around one another, Vamma's dishevelled hair spread over the pillow, Yilmay came to a decision. "Come with me to Dur."

Vamma kissed Yilmay's cheek before she replied. "How can I do so? I am married."

"Do you love him?"

She sighed. "You know I do not, but I care for him. I cannot hurt him in this way."

Yilmay stroked Vamma's hip and chewed at her lip. "He would be hurt if he learned of our trysts." Vamma did not reply, mayhap lost in her own thoughts. "I should have come for you the moment I left Ort."

"That you should. You did not, and I cannot break his heart now. You must see this."

"Then what of us?" Yilmay's despondency grew. She yearned to leave Malkartas, where she thought she could never belong.

After a lengthy silence, Vamma replied, so quiet, Yilmay struggled to hear her words. "I do not know."

Frustration welled up inside Yilmay. She should be furious, but anger seemed ill-suited for this situation. She spat out terse words. "I will not stay here. This… arrangement is not satisfactory."

Vamma untangled her arms and lay on her side, her head supported on the hand of an arm crooked beneath it. "I waited three years for this moment. You have returned to me at last. You cannot leave now."

Yilmay shook her head in furious denial. "That I can. I must. I cannot settle for this." She waved an arm around at the room. "You cannot sneak away to lie with me for the rest of your life. I will have to work. How will we meet like this then?"

Tears dripped from Vamma's eyes, and she gazed at Yilmay. "I do not know." The same answer to the same question.

"Then come with me. There is no other solution."

Vamma wiped at her tears and words escaped between her sobs. "Raolos would be devastated."

Yilmay thought she might scream with irritation. "By the fates. If you are concerned for him, then stay. I cannot remain in this land."

"That is cruel." Vamma's face darkened with misery.

"Life is cruel. What Styrrach did to Deineike is cruel. What the Qagrue did to Dur is cruel. What I did to Arella is cruel. I want you with me, but I cannot stay here. What we do in this room is cruel. If you leave him, that is cruel. The distinction is he does not yet know of either. He will learn about us, whether you will believe it or not."

Vamma said nothing for some time as she appeared to consider all they had said. At length, she drew in a long breath. "I love you. How can I refuse? How can I stay here and watch you sail away?"

Yilmay's temper cooled. She wondered if she had been unkind or had done no more than force a decision they could not avoid for long, after all else. "I cannot work for him now. That would be a slap to the face, to take both his coin and his wife."

"On the subject of coin, how much do you have?" Yilmay slid from the bed and pulled her coins from her pocket to show to Vamma. "That is all? That will not buy us passage to Dur."

"Do you have none of your own?"

"I have a little, but it will not be enough for passage to Dur, my guess."

Yilmay frowned. "I will have to work to pay the cost of the voyage."

"Is this possible?" Vamma seemed surprised.

"I cannot work for both of us. We will pay for your passage, and I will work for mine."

"Then it is decided. How will we arrange this?"

"We will find a ship in the morning. Come to the inn after Raolos has left for the trade house. Bring no more than you need." She recalled Pettra's full trunk.

Vamma nodded. "I must tell him." Yilmay inhaled a sharp breath of shame. Vamma had the right of it, although it could involve great risk. He might try to prevent her. There could be an unpleasant scene. Vamma nodded as she went on. "I will tell him tonight." Yilmay could find no comfort in the idea, but to add deception to an already dreadful situation would be a step too far. She nodded, and Vamma stared down at the bedsheets as she continued to mutter. "Poor Raolos. He will be destroyed."

"In time he will forget you."

"That is callous." Vamma aimed a slap at Yilmay's arm.

"It is the truth. The decision is made. Are you determined to see it through?"

"What if no ship sails for Dur tomorrow?"

"We will travel there by one means or another." Yilmay forced a confident smile to her face, or so she hoped.

"I will have to sail again. I despise it."

"Eat the bread. It can help, they say, although it is vile."

"I have eaten it. I swear it made matters worse. It made me more ill than I had been before I ate it." Yilmay could not resist a small laugh, though she held up a hand in apology. Vamma managed a smile. "I do love you." She took one of Yilmay's hands and kissed it.

As they dressed, Vamma had one more request. "I will make this sacrifice for you, but I ask for one small favour in return."

"What is it?"

"Please call yourself Corelle again. I despise this other name."

Yilmay smiled. Vamma had a kind but simple heart, and although others might not think so, Yilmay thought her beautiful. Her smile reminded Yilmay of Deineike's, and it warmed Yilmay's heart. To spend the rest of her life with Vamma would be a good outcome in a life filled with few others. She would do all she could to make things work between them, as she had never done before. "That I will." She smiled, and Vamma threw her arms around Corelle's neck and kissed her.

As she buried her head in Corelle's breast, Vamma breathed, "My thanks."

CHAPTER 21
CORELLE

They reached the trade house before the carriage arrived, and they chattered as they walked into the office. Raolos invited them into his office to ask about their day. Yilmay spoke about the beauty of The Rotunda and said they had strolled The Great Park for much of the day. As she had watched the children play on the devices, she had pined for a childhood with such fun distractions. He laughed and agreed with her.

He asked her when she thought she might be ready to start work and she suggested the day after the next, which seemed to please him. "Have you been to see Wilash yet?"

More guilt took lumps from her with its sharp teeth of recrimination. "That I have not."

His mouth askew, he seemed lost in thought for a moment. "You might go to visit him tomorrow."

"He will still be here when I find the time."

"I imagine he will." He did not seem happy with the response.

Corelle grew tired of the shame he had induced in her. "I will see you in two days." She kissed Vamma on the cheek, thanked her for a wonderful day, and left the trade house.

She returned to the inn and lay on her bed for a time as she thought about the following day. She would sail from Malkartas with Vamma at her side, and they would have the settled life she had longed for as she had striven to get back to the Torr Sea. The idea excited her, and she decided to have a goblet of wine in celebration. She passed the evening at the counter in conversation with the innkeep. It had been her habit to keep to herself when in a tavernroom, but she had made the choice to start this new life, and if that meant she must put away things from the past, then she reasoned it a small enough price to pay.

The tavernroom became busier as the night wore on and kept the innkeep busy. Their conversation became sporadic, and as she stared into her half-empty goblet, Corelle decided she would finish the wine and head to her room. An early night and a good night's sleep would prepare her for tomorrow. The innkeep returned to the counter to wash tankards, but at once, he looked up in the direction of the door. Somebody had entered the tavernroom at a late hour. Corelle ignored whoever had come through the door and picked up her goblet to finish it.

"Corelle." The familiar voice shouted her name and froze the goblet part way to her mouth, and she turned her head toward the door. Raolos stood inside the tavernroom. He seemed unsteady on his feet, and his bright red face spoke of his anger. He had, it seemed, seen her as she sat at the counter, and his eyes burned into her with the unmistakeable fire of accusation. Behind him, Vamma clung to a sleeve of his tunic, anxiety clear in her face.

Corelle put the goblet onto the counter and stood, but she did not approach him, uncertain how this would turn.

"Bad enough you did it once." All eyes in the tavernroom watched Raolos as he roared his fury at her. "Twice is unforgivable."

The innkeep crossed the tavernroom in a few swift paces. "You have had enough, sir. I think it would be best if you left."

Raolos pushed him to one side, and Vamma gasped. "She has stolen my wife. Again." He pointed an accusatory finger at Corelle.

Somebody yelled, "If she has done it twice, you should work harder in the marital bed." A few laughs and sniggers broke out around the tavernroom.

Raolos continued to wrestle with the innkeep as he tried to close the distance between himself and Corelle. Vamma tried to pull him back, but he shook his arm loose from her grip. "First Pettra. Now you take Vamma from me. What manner of friend do you call yourself?"

Corelle loathed that he made such a scene in public. The patrons laughed at him, but they also directed their mockery at her and Vamma, and she snarled. "I knew her long before you."

Vamma continued to try to pull Raolos back, but he had almost reached Corelle. Spittle flew from his mouth as he spoke, and he appeared intoxicated, almost unable to stand. "Why do you do this to me? I have been a good friend to you." He hesitated, then a thought seemed to occur to him. "Why do you not kill me?"

"Raolos—"

He had not finished. "Of course, you cannot kill me. How foolish I am." He spread his arms and spun around as though he intended to address all the patrons in the tavernroom. "You cannot kill me, can you?" He returned his attention to her. "How then would you obtain your next dalliance? If I am dead, I cannot marry another for you to steal from me."

Corelle's temper boiled within her. "I did not steal either of them. You told me to take Pettra away with me, against my wishes. You married Vamma though you knew she awaited my return."

Tears ran down his cheeks, and sadness clouded his complexion. "I told you...?" He wiped at his eyes. "You have some impudence; I will grant you that. Long before I said you should take her, I caught you in bed with her." He spread his arms again. "What should I have done?"

Corelle snarled at him, her face twisted by a rage she could no longer control. "You should not have asked her to raise the son you fathered with another woman." Her voice had dropped, full of menace. Vamma drew in a sharp breath.

Raolos stared at her. "You are despicable. You are a monster."

Corelle returned his stare. "That I am. Now go home before you do something you regret."

The innkeep still struggled to pull Raolos away, but he brushed past the man and aimed a punch at her. She saw the slow strike long before it could connect, ducked beneath it, then took a half step backward.

The innkeep yelled at Raolos. "I will have no fights in my tavernroom." Raolos pulled his arm back for another punch. It came up short, but Corelle swayed backward to ensure it did not connect if he fell forward.

In spite of the attentions of the innkeep, Raolos pulled his arm back for another punch, and Corelle's rage overwhelmed her. She took one step toward him and punched him in the face. The patrons cried out, and Vamma screamed as Raolos stumbled. Blood gushed from his nose, and he tripped over one of the innkeep's feet and fell backward. The back of his head crashed into a settle, and he landed in a heap. At once, blood oozed from the back of his head.

Vamma yelled as she rushed forward and bent to Raolos. "Leave him alone."

From behind, arms pulled Corelle backward, and she did not resist. She looked down at Raolos, who lay motionless on the tavernroom floor. An eerie hush had descended upon the tavern-room as patrons gathered around Raolos. Some, Vamma among them, fussed at him. They talked to him and encouraged him to wake up and rise. Time dragged on and he did not move. Some-body went for a healer.

Corelle shook the arms away and sat on the stool she had occupied when Raolos had entered the inn. A cold dread grew in her stomach, and her heart pounded. He had not moved despite the attentions of the patrons, and the healer had not yet arrived. A large pool of blood had spread around his head, and Corelle feared the worst. She could stand the uncertainty no longer and knelt on the floor next to him. When she felt at his neck for a pulsing, she found none. Her heart sank and her head bowed. He had died. She had killed him.

She turned to face Vamma, who stared at her in search of hope. Corelle shook her head, and Vamma screamed before she fell backward. Somebody caught her and helped her sit on the floor.

With some effort, Corelle rose and gazed down at Raolos in utter despair. How had this turned? Raolos had been a good man and a good friend, but she had killed him. Yilmay would be hanged before the morning; nothing could be more certain. A tavernroom full of people had witnessed her strike the fatal blow. Three men rushed into the tavernroom. One wore black trousers and a short black tunic. He carried a leather satchel and knelt beside Raolos. The other two wore deep brown tunics and trousers to match. Yilmay guessed they must be the local equivalent of the Portreeve's men. One of them asked what had turned.

Corelle faced him, unafraid. "I killed him."

A voice Corelle did not recognise intervened. "Hold. He attacked her, something to do with his wife, he said. She did nothing more than defend herself."

Corelle denied her innocence. "That is not how it turned." To make herself heard, she had to shout above the hubbub of the tavernroom. "I killed him." Voices clamoured she had defended herself, that he had tripped and fallen, and that had killed him. "Ask this woman." Corelle pointed at Vamma. "She is his wife, after all else."

The room fell silent. Vamma looked up, still seated on the floor.

Tears of grief had turned her eyes red, and mucus ran down from her nose over her pinched lips. She wiped at her nose with her sleeve and drew in a long breath that sounded like many shorter breaths, doubtless from the turmoil that ripped through her. Her soft, hesitant voice could not be heard until the crowd fell silent. "She defended herself. He believed we indulged in a dalliance. We are good friends, but beyond that…" Her voice faded away, shock on her face.

One of the men in brown turned to Corelle. "By all accounts, you defended yourself, nothing more. The Council will need to come to a decision, but I believe you have committed no crime here."

Corelle protested. Old grief, guilt, and memories of Taro filled her mind. She had avoided any punishment for the farmer's death, though she caused it. She could not allow another death on her account to go unpunished. "That I have. I killed him. I became enraged, and I hit him."

"He hit you first." Murmurs of agreement rose up among the crowd at the protestation from another voice. It seemed as much as Corelle wished to damn herself for the death of her friend, these strangers wished to see her go free.

"He did not hit me, not once."

Yet another patron joined in. Why did they not mind their own business and let the dice fall as they should? "He tried to."

Someone else added, "Twice."

Corelle shook her head, unable to believe what she heard, unable to fathom these people who tried to manipulate the truth of what had turned. She had lost her temper, and Raolos had died on her account. She pleaded with the men in brown clothes. "I deserve to be hanged. Take me away."

Vamma screamed again and rose to her feet. She ran to Corelle and wrapped her arms tight around her, her head on Corelle's breast. Through hysterical sobs, she cried out. "You defended yourself. You did nothing wrong. He attacked you. He had consumed too much wine."

A perplexed look on his face, one of the men in brown came to a decision. "The Council will come to a conclusion tomorrow. Until then, you are free to come and go as you wish." They asked her name and where she lived, and in a voice she did not recognise, Corelle told them her name and said she could be found at the inn.

The healer arranged for some of the men in the tavernroom to carry Raolos to his chambers where he could prepare the body for the Pyre. There appeared to be no Sending in the custom of Malkartas, but Vamma wanted to give him one. Corelle whispered she would stay until the Pyre, and she would leave afterward, alone if Vamma wished it. Shock and grief numbed Corelle—yet another friend dead at her hand. She could not reconcile how the evening had turned from joy to tragedy so fast.

Vamma pressed her lips to Corelle's ears and whispered urgent words. "Come back to the house with me. The carriage is outside."

"I cannot sleep in his house after I have killed him. It is not right."

Vamma insisted, and Corelle, shaken and bewildered, could not resist her pleas. They sat in the carriage in stunned silence. Vamma buried her face in a sleeve at times as her body heaved with her tears.

They sat in the parlour, disconsolate, and Corelle wondered aloud. "How did this thing turn? It makes no sense."

"He did not take the news well. He had already begun to drink before I told him, and he drank more and more after I said we would leave tomorrow. Over and over, he complained you had stolen another wife from him. I told him I had always loved you, that I had been in love with you when I met him, and even when I married him. A poor thing to say, as it turned, and one that seemed to enrage him more. He became inebriated, and he pushed me away to call for the carriage. I rode with him and attempted to persuade him to turn around, but he would not hear of it."

Corelle laid a hand on her arm. "I am sorry. I have killed your husband and a fine man."

Vamma placed her other hand over the one Corelle rested on her arm. "You did little enough. He knew you, and he knew what to expect. You punched him, no more. The fall killed him, in truth."

Corelle shook her head, not prepared to allow herself such easy forgiveness. "I became enraged. I taunted him and drove him beyond endurance."

Vamma's tone became insistent, almost angry. "Corelle, you are not to blame. I saw the entire thing. You both became angry, and he had drunk far too much wine. Lucky for him, you did not produce your fan."

Corelle grimaced. Fortunate indeed.

The events of the evening had drained them both, and tomorrow would bring no relief. Corelle slumped back in the couch. Vamma lay her head in Corelle's lap and sniffed from time to time as she wiped at her eyes. Her breaths changed to slow and even, and Corelle reasoned she had cried herself to sleep, and soon fell asleep herself.

CHAPTER 22
CORELLE

Corelle awoke with Vamma's head in her lap. Her neck felt stiff from an awkward sleeping position, but she did not move, anxious not to wake Vamma. Despite her best efforts, Vamma's eyes opened moments after Corelle's own.

Vamma sat up and kissed Corelle. "I did not imagine we would spend the first night of our life together in this way." She tried for a half-hearted laugh.

"We must attend to Raolos's Pyre. I will speak his Sending, unless you prefer to. I must tell Wilash, although he is sure to kill me where I stand."

Misery returned to Vamma's face. "Do not say that. I could not tolerate it."

"I apologise. I do not wish to upset you further."

Vamma reached up and touched the side of Corelle's face. "Raolos is gone. We can do nothing about that. We have each other now, and that is all we need."

"That it is." Corelle found a weak smile to reassure Vamma. "Rouse yourself. We will eat something and set about our business."

Vamma snapped her fingers. "His business. What will happen to it?"

"I imagine it is yours now. You are his wife."

Vamma considered for a heartbeat. "I do not want it. I will find out what happens to it, nonetheless."

They ate, washed dried tears from their faces, and set off to accomplish their respective tasks. Aided by Vamma's directions, Corelle found Wilash's smithy, small but serviceable. A small sign hung outside with his name scribed on it. Toward the rear of the smithy, Wilash stood at the furnace as he worked the device that blew air into the fire. Corelle did not know its name, but she watched the flames leap each time he pushed down on one of the handles of the device. He turned and noticed her, although at first it seemed he did not recognise her. Then he ran out of the smithy, swept her up into his arms, twirled her around, and beamed from ear to ear. "By the fates, it is good to see you." He appeared to notice she wore no smile of her own. "What has turned? Is something awry?"

She heaved a dejected sigh. "That it is." Corelle told him the story. She left nothing out and made no attempt to avoid the blame she attached to herself.

Corelle had expected Wilash to be furious, but he dressed his face in a gown of sadness. "The fates written for you are harsh. Too harsh."

"I am death to all I encounter."

"That you are not. I still live. Vamma still lives. What will you do now?"

"I deserve to be hanged, but if I am not, we will travel to Ryl. We will plan further after we have spent some time there."

He nodded. "You wish to see your parents?"

"That I do. The last time I saw them, things were happy between us. I wish to check on them."

"Scribe their address for me before you leave. I will keep in touch as best I can." She nodded. "Do you still have the fan?"

"That I do."

"I am pleased to hear that. The Qagrue still rule Dur. You may have need of it. I will feel better if you can protect Vamma."

"I have not killed for some years." She paused, stricken with grief. "I had not, at the least, until last night."

"I hope you never have to kill again. I wish you both luck. Do not blame yourself. You did not steal Vamma from Raolos. Nobody can steal something that already belongs to them. She waited for you until she lost hope, and Raolos married her. Her heart belonged to you, and he knew it, even if he could not admit it. You did not take her from him."

"That is a convenient way to see it, after all else, I imagine." His argument did not convince her. "I see the matter in a different light, as it has brought about the death of a good friend. I have taken him from her, and from us all."

"You cannot hold yourself to account for that. In his cups, he made a poor decision. They have a phrase here. It is '*The logic leaves as the drink enters.*'"

She smiled. "They are wise, these Malkartasians."

She scribed the address of her parents' shop and told him there would be a Pyre for Raolos. He promised to be there, and she said she would send the details once Vamma confirmed them. "Take care, Corelle, and take care of Vamma. I am happy to have seen you again."

"You also." They embraced, and she walked back to the house, filled with even more sadness than last night. She had not anticipated Wilash would be so calm at her news. He had worked for Raolos for a long time, but she reasoned he had known her longer. She could not be as kind to herself about Raolos's death as everybody else seemed to.

Vamma had not returned to the house when Corelle arrived, so she let herself in with the key Vamma had given to her and sat on a couch to wait. Over an hour later, Vamma returned. She had arranged the Pyre for the next day and had also visited The Rotunda to find out what to do about Raolos's business. As Corelle had anticipated, the business passed to her as his wife under the laws of Malkartas, but Vamma had not changed her mind and did not wish to own the business. She suggested they could sell it, and Corelle pointed out it belonged to Vamma, and Corelle had no say in whether to sell it.

Vamma had a different viewpoint. "We are together, are we not?"

"That we are."

"Then what is mine is yours, and what is yours is mine." Corelle laughed and pointed out she owned nothing but one set of clothes and her fan. Everything else in her pack had been bought for her by Vamma, and the pack also. "You may not be wealthy enough to be my lover then." Vamma's eyes sparkled. "Why should I stay with you?"

Corelle kissed her as her passion mounted inside her. "I could show you."

Vamma's breaths grew heavier. "Wilash. We must let him know the information for the Pyre."

"Send your carriage driver." Corelle ran a hand over Vamma's breast and traced the erect nipple beneath the tunic.

"That I will, then we will go to bed."

Later that evening, Vamma felt hungry, and they went to the scullery. Some of the meat that had not been finished on the night Corelle had visited for dinner sat in a cupboard lined with stone walls. Corelle had never seen such a thing, and Vamma explained how the stone kept the temperature lower in the cupboard. Food could be stored within it for longer this way before it went bad and must be thrown away.

They ate some of the meat cold, with bread and cheese. Vamma wrinkled her nose as Corelle placed her cheese on a slice of the bread. "I have seen you do that before. It is a strange habit."

"I picked it up on a farm near Ort."

"A farm? You are a farmer? I did not know this."

Corelle barked a laugh of derision. "I am no farmer. What do farmers do, after all else?"

"They raise animals."

Corelle snorted. "I am unsuited to raise children or animals, I am certain."

"They dig those lines in the land with… that thing a horse pulls."

"It is called a plough, I believe."

Vamma laughed and pointed an accusatory finger at Corelle. "You *are* a farmer, you see?"

Corelle smiled. "I admit it. You have uncovered my long-lost secret. I wish to be a farmer and roll around in those lines in the land all day."

Vamma lay back on the couch and parted her legs. "Roll over here, farmer, and let us see what we can grow between us."

Exhausted by the evening of lovemaking, they slept. When they rose the next morning, an impending sense of sadness filled Corelle as she contemplated Raolos's Pyre. Vamma seemed full of trepidation also, and as they rode in the carriage neither of them could hold back their tears. As the carriage pulled to a halt and they stepped down, the mood of the previous evening seemed as far away as any of the lands Corelle had sailed to aboard The Ictharelian.

The Pyre ground appeared to be dedicated to the process, with a stone plinth similar to the ones used in Dur. Wood had been piled about and atop it, and Raolos's body lay on the wood. Men stood nearby with a lighted torch, and several other unlit torches leaned against a low wall at the perimeter of the ground.

Wilash had already arrived, accompanied by a woman Corelle did not recognise, so Corelle and Vamma trudged over to them. Wilash introduced his wife, Derkhata Perozel. It seemed Malkartasians had a family name attached to their name, a practice not found in Dur. Corelle reckoned her close to Wilash's age, soft spoken, with auburn hair piled atop her head in a neat bun, taller than Corelle and with delicate, fine hands. Her hands were not those of a smith, but she smiled often at Wilash, and they seemed relaxed together. It delighted Corelle Wilash had found happiness again after the terrible tragedy of Klordia's death.

Near Raolos's body, a man in a long black coat turned to the four of them. "I understand one of you wishes to say some words."

Vamma squeezed one of Corelle's hands, as if to remind her she had agreed she would say a Sending. "Today we send Raolos, who has gone wherever he travels to afterward. A good man, the best I have ever known. His death came too soon and leaves the globe a poorer place. I had the privilege to know him, and I count it an honour. He came to Malkartas through vile circumstances after he had worked for the people of his homeland, Dur, with no thought for his own benefit. He ought not to have died as he did. I believe he would rather have died in Dur, where his Pyre and Sending would be in the land he loved, but a different fate was written for him. Any who called him friend should be proud they could do so." She turned to face Raolos's body. "I am sorry." Tears spilled from her eyes.

The man asked who wished to light the Pyre, and Vamma stepped forward, her red-rimmed eyes and tear-streaked face a picture of grief. She took a torch and thrust it into the wood. Corelle heard her whisper, "Goodbye, Raolos," then Vamma stepped back as the hungry flames licked at the wood and climbed upward as though they were creatures desperate to feed on Raolos's flesh. They clawed at him, then leapt into his clothes and hair as they consumed him and released the scent of the oils poured on the body at a Pyre so all assembled did not fetch up at the smell of burned flesh.

CHAPTER 23
CORELLE

They returned to the carriage, and Wilash and Derkhata accepted Vamma's invitation to ride back to the house with them. They sat in the parlour, and Vamma, Corelle, and Wilash exchanged stories of Raolos as Derkhata listened in silence. She had not met him, but she said Wilash spoke of him often, and always of his good nature and fairness toward all.

Wilash and Derkhata left, and Vamma and Corelle decided to take a walk for some fresh air that might clear their grief-fogged heads. Vamma glanced up at the tower that rose above the city skyline from The Rotunda. "Do you think there would be people in The Council who would sell the business for me?"

"I know not. I have no experience of anything of this nature. I am sorry."

They walked on, and Vamma seemed thoughtful. At last, she spoke again. "Let us give it to his staff."

"Can such a transaction be made?" Corelle felt helpless and could offer no advice about the business affairs Raolos's death had unleashed on Vamma.

"Let us find out." Vamma changed direction and strode toward

The Rotunda. Three hours later, they had learned Vamma could indeed pass the business to anybody she wished, and she had signed the papers. The Council would arrange to inform the staff, and would deliver their copies of the papers.

As they left The Rotunda, Corelle turned to Vamma. "Will they know how to run the business? Which of them will take Raolos's role?"

"I care not." Vamma seemed less downcast. It seemed now the weight of how to deal with the business had been lifted from her shoulders, she felt relieved. "Tomorrow, let us sail. There is nothing here for us."

Corelle had expected Vamma to need some time to recover from her grief before they sailed for Dur, but she said neither of them had any reason to remain any longer, and Corelle visited The Moonlight one last time to gather her few belongings and settle for her accommodation.

The next morning found them at the dock, and fortune shone on them. One of Rakulaj's ships bobbed at the dockside, and they travelled to Arkkyd with no charge. Her fame had grown even greater since the news of the voyage that proved the globe theory had spread. The master even offered to give up his own cabin for them, but Corelle would not hear of it and settled for the best of the passenger cabins.

The voyage took a tenday. Vamma suffered from the effects of the swell and spent almost the entire trip either in her bunk or bent over the rail of the ship. Corelle sympathised but could not understand how the sea affected so many people the way it did. She wandered the deck and enjoyed the sensation of the ship as it pitched and rolled in the waves. Nonetheless, the voyage could not convince her she wished to return to the mariner's life, and no regrets crept into her mind.

They decided to break their journey in Arkkyd for a few days to give Vamma's stomach time to calm itself. The master recommended an inn and suggested the mention of Yilmay's name would guarantee them a high-quality room with no charge. He had spoken the truth, and they found themselves in a large hotel room with a bedroom separate from the parlour. Raolos had stayed in similar rooms in Alcmouth when she had travelled there with him, but Corelle never had. The room so impressed Vamma, she asked more than once whether they could stay there for the rest of their lives.

A letter arrived from Rakulaj, a request for them to meet him in his tavern, the one he and Corelle had met in by chance some years before. Corelle wished to leave as soon as Vamma felt able, but Vamma seemed content to live the life of luxury the name Yilmay brought wherever they went in the city, so they agreed to meet Rakulaj the next night. Corelle felt some nervousness. Somebody in the Upholder's offices might hear her name and have some recollection of events from several years ago, but it seemed none did, and they did not call on her to pay for the death of Pettra with her life.

The following night brought a warm reunion with Rakulaj. Gaish had reported everything that had turned, and the news had spread throughout the Torr Sea. Although trade already took place with a few lands to the north of the Torr Sea, merchants now planned even longer trade journeys as they sought to be the first to open up trade with the new lands The Ictharelian had discovered. Yilmay had become a much-honoured name now. Corelle told him she had reverted to her born name, but he waved a dismissive hand. Her fame would endure. He felt certain she could call herself Tree or Stone for all it mattered, and she would still be well received in any land.

He pressed her for her version of how the ship had been sunk by the giant. She told him all she could remember. "I am sorry about the ship."

"I care not for the ship itself. I had it indemnified."

"Indemnified? What does this mean?" Corelle had not heard the term before. He explained a business could pay a sum to an indemnifier; a fraction of the cost of an item such as a ship, and if catastrophe befell that item, the indemnifier would replace it with a new one. Corelle wrinkled her nose, uncertain of the concept. "That does not seem like good business. If I pay you a groat for something that is worth a regal, you will be nine groats out of pocket if it is destroyed."

"A great many people indemnify their goods each year, but only a small percentage of those goods are destroyed. The end result is the indemnifier makes their coin many times over."

The idea fascinated Corelle, but she needed other answers. She asked Rakulaj whether any others from The Ictharelian had returned. It turned that aside from her and Gaish, four others had made their way back to Arkkyd, one more than the master from Argoya had said. Tryndeltuj had not returned, and Corelle balanced her joy at the survival of four of her crew-mates against the loss of the master and so many other hands. She thought it bittersweet news and choked back tears as the faces of lost friends ran through her mind.

Rakulaj seemed captivated by Vamma, but when he heard of the death of Raolos, his own joy faded into sadness. Corelle felt compelled to tell him the entire story. He urged her not to blame herself and described it as a tragic accident, fates written in a strange way. He told them a cargo would depart for Zhanghar in two days, and they were welcome to sail aboard the ship if they wished. Vamma appeared reluctant, but Corelle accepted the offer. He pressed a small pouch of coin on her, and despite her reluctance to accept it, he insisted. "Take it as your wage, if nothing else."

The patrons delayed them when they tried to leave. They all wished to hear stories from the voyage, and more than any other, the moment the ship had been sunk captivated everybody present. Some time later, they were free, though a great many well wishes rang in their ears. They strolled back to their inn hand in hand on a warm night, heedless of what people might think. For Corelle, it still felt strange to hold hands with a woman, as she had once done with Pettra, and not fear they would be unwelcome. She had stared death in the face on the voyage, and the prospect she might incur the displeasure of some stranger now seemed so unimportant, she wondered why it had ever bothered her at all.

Out of nowhere, Vamma asked Corelle a question. "Who writes our fates?"

"I know not." The question nagged at some part of Corelle's mind, and she frowned with concentration as she tried to identify what about it troubled her. She grasped it, and Vamma raised her eyebrows in response to the snap of Corelle's fingers. "The issue of who writes them is less important than the question of why it is not 'the fates scribed for us.'"

Vamma wore a quizzical look. "You have the right of it. Nothing is written but the fates. Everything else is scribed. We may have uncovered a great mystery all the learned scholars of the globe have failed to consider."

Corelle teased her. "'We?' What part did you play in this great discovery?"

Vamma laughed. "Without my question yours would not have occurred to you. You may have all the glory, my love. After all else, you are more accustomed to fame than I."

Corelle saw the twinkle in Vamma's eye. "Do not forget that fact. I am famous."

"Will you take me to bed when we return to the inn, or will your followers occupy your time?"

"I believe I may have time to attend to your needs." Corelle dodged a slap aimed at her arm. The tingle in her sex told her she would not struggle to find the time.

Two days later, they boarded the ship for Zhanghar. The voyage across the Torr Sea turned rough, with high swells for much of the journey, and it proved hard on Vamma. Corelle had never seen anybody suffer as much as Vamma did, and her concern grew as each miserable day passed. At times, Deineike had suffered terrible sickness, but on this trip Vamma appeared to be at the door to her ruin as the ship rose and sank through the waves that battered it. Corelle pressed warm cloths to Vamma's head as she became coated in cold sweats from the turmoil in her stomach.

Three days into the voyage, Vamma fell into the relief of sleep, and Corelle went up to the deck for some air and to watch the angry water that fought the ship's attempts to drive through it. She spotted some blue giants and considered she might bring Vamma up to the deck to see them but decided it would be best to let her sleep.

The giants swam south, unlike the first time she had seen them, when they had swum north. The seasons dictated the direction of their travel, she had learned on a previous voyage. They swam north to the seas off Dur and Steinlund in the summer before they returned south to avoid the cold and wet seasons. The warmer waters to the south were more bountiful with food than the cold winter seas off Dur. Today's giants headed south, which meant summer must be close to an end in Dur.

At last, the ship sailed up the Alc, and the familiar sights of Alcmouth and Ort slipped by. The calmer water of the river eased Vamma's stomach somewhat, and she could come up to the deck for a while on most days. She expressed her disappointment she had missed the blue giants, but she looked much healthier than she had been on the voyage north across the Torr Sea, to Corelle's relief. Corelle suggested they should ride from Zhanghar to Ryl to make things easier on Vamma, and she said she would consider it when she saw how she felt when they arrived in Zhanghar.

In time, the familiar skyline of Zhanghar approached. Corelle worried her born name might put her in danger if the Qagrue sought her in connection with any of Krage's schemes. It had been three years or more ago in truth, and she hoped Krage had not given the Qagrue her name as the one who bested him at every turn and undid all he had worked for.

As the ship manoeuvred alongside the dock, a cold rain fell from a churlish grey sky. The time had come to discover what awaited them in Zhanghar. They stood together on the dock, and Vamma slid an arm around Corelle's waist and laid her head on Corelle's shoulder.

"Welcome home."

CHAPTER 24

CORELLE

hey walked down the ramp and pulled their cloaks tight about themselves as the cold rain bit at them. Their breath turned to mist before their faces in the bitter wind. All around the dockside, Qagrue and Durfolk bustled about, no doubt anxious to be out of the rain, although the two peoples did not walk together, as far as Corelle could tell. Durfolk kept to their own kind, and Qagrue did the same. It seemed an uneasy alliance at first glance, but it had been three years since the southerners had arrived and claimed Dur as their own. If resentment still lingered, the two peoples must have found a way to exist side by side.

The weather had become so cold and wet, Vamma said she did not want to set off for Ryl on horseback, so they walked the dock in search of a ship that sailed to Ryl that day. None could be found, so they took a room at an inn. Vamma would not stay at an inn close to the docks; she had no desire to lodge in accommodations as tawdry as The Moonlight had been. Corelle walked past The Ship's Yard as she could not bring herself to stay there after all that had turned in the inn. They settled for a small, quiet inn that over-looked a green park. The Park Inn, its name, thanks to the green space opposite. Corelle had never noticed either the park or the inn while she had lived in Zhanghar and imagined unexplored areas must exist in any large city, no matter how long a person lived there.

Vamma had eaten precious little throughout the journey, and to soothe her hunger, they wandered out in search of food close to the inn. They found a cenacle, although Vamma needed the concept explained to her, as Corelle had the first time Pettra had taken her to one in Ort. On that occasion, Corelle had been enriched by Styrrach's coin, and tonight they spent Rakulaj's. The food delighted Vamma, and she laughed when Corelle warned her not to get used to such expensive food.

The next day they found a Ryl-bound ship, and they took passage. Thanks to a strong wind from the east, they made excellent time, and the voyage took little more than two days. Corelle could not recall a shorter voyage between the two cities.

At last, they stood on the dockside in Ryl, and Vamma gulped down lungful after lungful of air as she tried to calm her stomach. "I will never sail again. My stomach is not suited for the sea."

Corelle could not disagree; shipboard life did not suit Vamma. As for Corelle, she also might never sail again, unable to shake the faces of her dead crew-mates from her mind. Such an unusual incident might never be repeated, but she had no desire to take the chance. They searched out an inn Corelle remembered as clean and inexpensive in the area where the poorer quarter changed to the better quarter. They agreed they would stay at the inn for a day or two while they made longer-term plans. Their coin would not last forever and an inn represented a drain on their finances they could not long sustain.

As they trudged through the rain toward the inn, Vamma said how much happier she felt now they were on dry land, and Corelle jested the land felt anything but dry as the rain poured down from the sky.

They reached the inn and took a room that seemed plain and unimpressive compared to the room in Arkkyd, but it had a bed, a chair, a vanity table and a trunk for their belongings. It would serve. Corelle could not bring herself to trade on her fame, if it had reached this far north, so she kept the name Yilmay tucked away from the innkeep's ears.

The rain did not relent for the next two days, and they could not walk far from the inn before they became drenched. They bought heavier cloaks that would keep the rain off better than the ones they already owned. Corelle bought new boots and some leather along with a new making kit with which she created a pouch inside one of the boots to hold her fan. The Qagrue did not often come up in conversation in the tavernroom at night. They reasoned any discussion on the southerners might end in a brawl between those who welcomed them and those who wished they would leave. The inn served good food in generous portions, and they did not have to venture out into the torrential rain to eat.

By the third day, they had both grown tired of the inn, so they decided to brave the rain and visit Corelle's parents. The new cloaks were better than the ones they had replaced, but the rain fell so hard, it soon saturated every part of their bodies. The constant sheet of water reduced visibility, and steam rose from the backs of the few people they encountered as the cold rain soaked through to their warm bodies.

They took any shelter they could find under shop entrances and the like, but they were soaked by the time they reached Corelle's father's shop. The window had misted up on the inside, the consequence of the difference in the temperatures within the shop and in the street. Despite the mistiness, Corelle made out her mother behind the shop counter as she worked on some making. Corelle smiled at the sight of her mother and moved toward the door.

Water flowed from them and pooled on the floor at their feet when they entered the shop. Corelle's mother looked up as they entered, and Corelle pushed the hood of her cloak down from her head. Her mother burst into tears and ran to embrace her, heedless of the saturated cloak.

Despite Corelle's joy to see her mother again, she could not fathom why her mother had become so emotional at the sight of her daughter. "Mother. It is good to see you again. Is all well?" Vamma looked on, a joyous smile on her face for the first time in many days.

Her mother looked into her eyes, and Corelle tensed. Some pain lay there, and she feared to hear it. Her mother did not wait long to lay it at Corelle's feet. "Your father has died."

Corelle took half a step backward, and her senses reeled. She stretched out a hand for the doorway, dizzy, and Vamma reached for her. Her mother and Vamma led her to a chair, where she sagged forward, head in her hands as tears gushed from her. This life had been too cruel, and she had shed too many tears. Now more must fall for her father, lost to her. The last words he had said to her had been "I love you," and those words had cost him his life, as they had everybody who had ever said them to her. She blamed herself for his death, and all for three words he had uttered to her only once in his life.

Vamma rubbed Corelle's back, and her mother sobbed, her arms around Corelle's neck and her head on the top of Corelle's own. Corelle lost track of how long she sat there, slumped and wracked by sobs. At last, some composure returned, and she turned her head to look into her mother's eyes. "How did he die?" Her voice sounded little louder than the noise an insect might make as it skittered across a counter.

"He died almost a year ago, the last cold season." Her mother tried to blink the tears from her eyes. "He developed a cough, only small at first, but soon he found it difficult to breathe and complained of a pain in his chest. After a time, he coughed up blood, and his temperature proved impossible to keep up with, as hot as a fire one moment and bitter cold the next. He ate next to nothing. Healers did all they could. He was almost sixty years, and he could not bear the pain, I think. He spent most of the time in bed. One morning, I sat on the bed to talk to him, and his breaths stopped. He died. Just like that." She snapped her fingers for emphasis.

Corelle should have been by their side to help her mother. He had only told her once he loved her, but she had been guilty of the same crime. The only time she had told her parents she loved them had been that same day, as she left the shop. Now she had no more chances to tell him, no opportunity to sit beside a warm fire and enjoy his quiet humour, could never present her latest gown to him and see the unspoken pride in his eyes at her making. Those things had all been snatched away from her. Devastated, she wanted it back. She wanted to tell him she loved him and beg him not to leave them. She had left it too late, and he had gone. "I did not tell him I loved him often enough." She sobbed, and Vamma took her hand.

"He knew." Her mother placed a hand on Corelle's head. Corelle looked up at her and saw a smile she did not have the wherewithal to return. Her father's death had broken her into pieces and scattered her around the shop, where she mingled with memories of him in every floorboard, every gown on the rack, every cast-off piece of thread abandoned on the floor. "Who is this?" Her mother smiled as she turned to Vamma, who had stood in silence the entire time as she rubbed Corelle's back.

"This is Vamma. I told you about her the last time I visited."

Corelle's mother spoke quiet words to Vamma. "We wanted Corelle to bring you to dinner with us. I think she felt embarrassed. I meet you at last."

Vamma moved and embraced Corelle's mother. "It is such an honour to meet you. I am so sorry about your husband."

"Thank you, dear." Corelle's mother stroked a hand down Vamma's long hair. "I am Lembell. I doubt she has ever told you."

Vamma laughed, a joyous sound in such a sombre occasion. "That she has not."

Corelle's mother released Vamma from her embrace and smiled at them. "Will you stay for dinner tonight? Both of you?"

"That we will, and I will cook." Vamma placed a hand on Corelle's back.

Corelle sniffed back her misery. "You kept the shop open?"

"How else could I eat?"

"Another failure," Corelle thought. *"I should have been here to help her. I thought of nobody but myself, of nothing but the glory of the voyage around the globe, so I left my father to die and my mother to struggle along in the shop alone."*

Her mother crossed the shop and locked the door. "We will close early tonight, I think." She smiled as she returned to the two younger women. "Come, we will prepare dinner together."

As they prepared the meal and sat at the table in the parlour to eat it, Corelle asked her mother what she planned to do with the shop.

"I get by." She had not answered the question Corelle had asked. "Things are different under these Qagrue people. It is not good. There is still some demand, but there is no longer a Portreeve. Some southerner rules the city, and he favours the Qagrue businesses. They all do." She sounded resentful, bitter almost, but she smiled away her emotions. "Some people still make plenty of coin, after all else. Some people always will.

"For the most part, Durfolk only do business with other Durfolk, so I have some customers still, but not as it used to be when..." She fell silent for a moment, as though lost in her thoughts. "I get by. I could use some help, in truth. I am too old now."

Laughter tinkled through Vamma's voice. "Did I hear you offer Corelle a job?"

Lembell laughed in turn. "That you did not." Her face was a mask that betrayed nothing of her thoughts. "I offered her the shop." Corelle whipped her head up from her food, but her mother had not finished. "I will help with the making, but you can make of the shop what you will."

Corelle spluttered words of protest. "Mother, I know nothing about how to run a shop. Father took care of all that."

She nodded. "I know that, dear, and I have made a terrible job of it since he has been gone. There is no Portreeve now, and the levies are no longer required." She turned to Vamma. "Do you know anything of how to run a shop?"

"I…" Vamma hesitated, and Corelle wondered whether she intended to lie. "I ran a stall in Yerrsun. It is not the same, but I could help, I am certain."

Surprised and thoughtful, Corelle pondered the opportunity. "I do not know what to make of this offer. It is unexpected."

Vamma's tone was earnest. "You have no other plan. If you take over the shop, we can spend time with your mother."

Corelle's mother smiled at this, but the argument did not convince Corelle. "And what of your own mother? When would you see her?"

"My parents are dead. My grandfather is all that remains of my family if he still lives. I do not wish to return to Yerrsun." She stopped and lowered her head.

Corelle suspected more lay in the tale but did not wish to press her on a story she had shared no part of before this moment. She turned to her mother. "I will think on it." She worked to force some cheer into her voice.

Her mother's mind seemed made up. "You can move in here. I will take your old room now your father is gone. You can both have our room."

Her mother pushed her hard to accept the offer, even though she could not have entertained it until today. Until the moment Corelle walked into the shop, soaked and unaware of the tragic news she would hear, her mother could have only hoped her daughter might return and take over the shop. Vamma had the right of it when she said they had no certain plan, but Corelle had done no serious making other than to repair a mariner's trousers for many years now. She might no longer have the skills she once possessed. After all else, to run the shop would involve much more than the making. Even though Corelle knew it would provide some security in her mother's life for however long she still had to live, the prospect seemed formidable, and it frightened her. "I do not know." She could find nothing more to say.

Vamma came to her rescue. "We will talk the matter over."

The hour had grown late, and they said fond farewells with a promise they would deliver an answer soon. Corelle clung to her mother in case she did not have another opportunity. "Goodnight, Mother. I love you."

Her mother beamed at her. "I love you too, dear. I am so happy to have met you at long last, Vamma." She planted a kiss on Vamma's cheek. Corelle ground her teeth together, delighted to hear her mother's affirmation of her love, frightened it would condemn her to a hideous fate. Such a burden should not be anybody's to carry, but Corelle could do nothing about these fates. They were written, and she must endure them until her own gave her peace at last.

CHAPTER 25
CORELLE

The rain had not eased while they had been at the shop, and they toiled through it back to the inn. The plethora of puddles led them on a back and forth dance as they strove to avoid the worst of them. The street had become a sea of mud, churned up by countless feet, horses' hooves and carts' wheels. Their boots were caked in mud by the time they reached their room, and the hems of their cloaks were filthy. Water ran from them and formed puddles on the floor to rival some of those they had avoided in the street.

"A beautiful evening." Corelle spat out the sarcastic words as they dried one another with the cloths provided by the inn.

"Indeed. For ships." They laughed at Vamma's jest.

Laughter did not linger overlong on Corelle's lips. The memory of her father drove it away and replaced it with guilt she had allowed happiness to help itself to a place in her heart, no matter how small.

Vamma held her tight, mayhap because she saw the pain that ate at Corelle. "To take over the shop might be a good thing for you." Her voice sounded soft and calm, like a supportive touch from a parent after a child's nightmare. "It may take your mind off the things that eat at you."

Corelle remained unconvinced. "I would spend every day at work in my father's shop. Everything I see would speak to me of him."

Vamma acknowledged the point. She stroked Corelle's cheek with the back of a hand. "I can see how that could be painful, but you would also see more of your mother. I sense that might help you. Your back is bent beneath the unbearable weight of so much guilt for things both done and left undone, but they are not all yours to carry. I think time spent with your mother would help you both for now."

Corelle squeezed her temples. "I have a headache. This has been a difficult night. I will consider the shop, I promise. For now, I must sleep." She crawled into the bed, and sleep brought relief from the ache in her heart and in her head.

When Corelle woke, she lay confused in the bed for a moment as she tried to decide what unsettled her. She realised the relentless pitter-patter of the rain on the roof above them had gone, and it did not knock at the window glass like a visitor who cannot be deterred.

"The rain has stopped." Vamma's sleepy voice from beside her startled Corelle. She had not realised her lover had woken. "We should go for a walk."

"Your thoughts turn to a walk rather than other activities?" Corelle tried for a jest, although her mood had improved little from the previous night.

"That can wait until the rain returns." Vamma moved closer and kissed Corelle's shoulder. "A walk will be more pleasant while the rain has gone." She pushed at Corelle. "Up, sluggard. Let us dress, and you can show me your home city."

"Sluggard?" Corelle laughed. "Is that some Eastlands word?"

Vamma pushed harder. "I know not. You are heavy for one so short."

"That I am." Corelle smiled, but she allowed herself to be bullied from the warmth of the bed. Although the rain had stopped, the day remained cold and grey. Their clothes from last night had not dried, so they pulled on clean trousers and tunics and dug their old cloaks out of their packs before they headed out into the street.

Water pooled everywhere still, and the air smelled of rain and moisture. The streets were busier than the previous day as people rushed to complete chores before the rain returned. The damp air and ominous grey clouds above them gave the city a sullen feel. They found a shop where they could buy some pastries and ate them as they walked. Corelle led them to the square. The former Portreeve's Offices had not changed, although the Qagrue guarded them now. Corelle guessed they now housed whichever Qagrue controlled the city.

Corelle steered them along familiar streets and pointed out buildings she remembered from her childhood. To her surprise, Orgel's shop still stood where it always had been. Corelle persuaded Vamma to take a cup of Orgel's brew, and they entered through the same door Corelle had opened so long ago, the day she had first seen Arella, the woman of her dreams, but her dreams had turned to nightmares. Nobody sat at the table Arella had occupied that day.

Nothing in the shop had changed except Orgel herself. She looked frailer, and her hair had grown into an untidy shock of grey that hung past her shoulders. Corelle ordered two cups of her brew and paid for them. Orgel gave no indication she remembered Corelle as she placed the two cups on her counter. The hour was early, and there were no other patrons. They sat near the door, and Corelle blew on her drink to cool it. Steam rose from it, too hot to drink yet. "This is where I first met Arella.

That marked the start of all the terrible things that have plagued me since."

"This is where you first met Arella and set off down a path that brought you to me." Vamma smiled at her, a twinkle in her eye.

"Does nothing ever disappoint you?" Corelle frowned at the unbridled optimism of Vamma's reply.

Her lover pouted as she pondered the question. "Things do disappoint me. My disappointment does not change them, and I do not waste time on it. Things worry me. You worry me. You are not yourself." She reached across the table to lay a hand atop Corelle's.

"My father has just died. Or rather, I have just learned my father died."

Vamma nodded. "I understand, but I did not refer only to today. You are quicker to anger, and your mood changes more than it used to."

Corelle shrugged. "I suffered a terrible injury. That may have brought some effect that lingers. Before Deineike died..." She paused to blink back the tears that threatened to pour from her eyes. "Before Deineike died, she suffered a terrible beating, and the healers told me damage to the head can disturb a person's brain. The mast may have damaged me in some way."

Vamma's infectious laughter dragged a smile to Corelle's face. "You were already damaged." Her voice became serious. "We should seek some advice."

Corelle picked up her cup and sipped at the brew. It had not changed in the years since she last came to the shop to drink it. The spiciness and the flavour still soothed her body, and she savoured it as she drank. Vamma watched her for a time, picked up her own cup, sniffed at the brew, and wrinkled her nose.

Corelle tried to reassure her. "It tastes better than it smells."

Vamma took a mouthful of the brew, and her face contorted into such an expression of revulsion, Corelle could not help but laugh out loud. Vamma threw her a guilty look. "Shh. She may take offence." Corelle could not speak for some time as her laughter accompanied Vamma's pained journey to the bottom of her cup. "That is hideous." Vamma wiped at her lips as she whispered her verdict on the drink.

"It will help with your moon cycle, when it comes. We will come here then, and you will beg me to bring you here every day that wretched curse lays upon you."

Vamma poked her tongue out at Corelle and rejected the offer of a second cup. "Have you thought any more about the shop?"

"I have had little time to do so." It irritated her Vamma pressed her on the issue again so soon.

"I understand." Vamma seemed embarrassed.

Corelle struggled to find words to explain the whirl of her thoughts. She did not want to upset Vamma, but the question had annoyed her. She had slept all night and walked the streets for an hour or two. Such an important decision ought not to be rushed, she felt. When Vamma had suggested it would be an opportunity for Corelle to spend time with her mother, it had made more sense than any other consideration about the shop, but the commitment felt like more than she should take on. "I am sorry, I did not mean to snap. It is an important decision. I am not even sure we intend to remain in Dur, ruled by these southerners."

Resolution sprang to Vamma's face. "I cannot leave Dur. I will never sail again. Never."

"Never?" Corelle fought to keep a smile from her face at Vamma's determined opposition to any further voyages aboard a ship.

"Never. And do not laugh. I can see your lips twitch."

Corelle could not suppress her laughter anymore. She tried to apologise through the laughter, but Vamma's face wore disgruntled determination. Corelle spluttered between her laughter. "If you will not sail again, I may as well take over the shop."

"Do you mean this?" Vamma's eyes searched for something in Corelle's face.

"It is the lesser of two evils. If I do not wish to remain in Ryl, I must leave alone, it seems. If I stay, I must earn coin, and the shop will provide that. If we can make a success of it."

Vamma clapped her hands together. "I am so pleased. I feel this will be good for you, and your mother will be delighted."

"We will see." Corelle smiled, content. Vamma's face had lit up at the news, and her joy had driven away Corelle's irritation. "Let us walk some more. I fear the rain intends to put in another appearance."

As they walked, they discussed Vamma's role at the shop. She felt her making would not be of a good enough standard, and she thought work on the garments would be a bad idea. To run a garment shop involved more than the making, nonetheless, and Vamma already had some business experience with her stall. Vamma worried it might seem as though she had taken over from Lembell, and Corelle's mother might feel left out of the shop that had been such a huge part of her adult life.

Corelle disagreed. "I believe she will be happy to step back. She said as much; she does not know how to run a business. I am sure she will be content to help with the making when she can. My father always ran the shop, and Mother took no interest in it other than making and fitting the clothes."

"Then I will help, if it makes you happy. Let us hope there is enough for me to do, and there is enough coin to feed us all."

"The shop always fed the three of us. It may not do so well now Dur is so changed. We will see." Spots of rain splashed onto their hands and cloaks, and the skies threatened heavier downpours. "Let us return to the inn. I wish to ask you something."

The deaths of Raolos and her father, and now the decision to take over the shop, had an air of permanence Corelle struggled to come to grips with. As the voyage on The Ictharelian stretched on, she had longed to see Vamma and had believed herself ready to settle down, but that had grown far beyond an idle thought. It had become reality now, but one aspect of the relationship between them still needed to be addressed. It had nagged at her since the first day in the inn in Tanasttra.

Once they reached the inn and had dried themselves, Vamma sat on the bed with an expectant air, her head tilted to one side. Corelle took a deep breath before she began. "Long ago, in Ort, you told me you could not devote your life to one person, to the exclusion of other fruits. I think that is how you described it. I told you then I would not be able to accept it, and I have not changed my opinion. I do not demand any change from you. It is not my place to do so, but I cannot face the long days ahead if I feel I cannot depend on your faithfulness."

Vamma's head nodded back and forth. Corelle believed she nodded not in agreement, but rather as something she did as she thought. She answered after many moments. "Then I must."

"You must what?" The answer had been no reply at all.

"I must change. I love you, and I wish to be with you. I longed to be with you for every heartbeat of the three years you were gone. I had all but given up hope, but you came back. You are complicated, and there is much I do not understand about you, but I cannot trust to hope again as I did for those three years. I must keep you near me, and to do so, I must change. I will not stray from our bed. You have my word."

Corelle pushed her back on the bed. "Then stray into our bed now." Her tongue dived into Vamma's mouth. Vamma moaned deep in her throat as her own tongue fought its way into Corelle's mouth. As Vamma fumbled with Corelle's trousers, Corelle lifted her lover's legs onto the bed and slid between them. Corelle thrust her pelvis down on Vamma's, and gasped as she pulled Vamma's tunic up over her breasts to lick at a nipple.

Vamma coaxed her to the heights of desire, and even when

Corelle felt her warm juices gush out onto Vamma's hand as she cried aloud in satisfaction, Vamma drove her fingers deeper into her sex and did not allow her any pause from the waves of agonised ecstasy that tore through her body. Corelle threw her head back and gasped in pleasure with each stroke of Vamma's fingers. The rain beat on the roof and drowned out her moans until she fell forward onto Vamma, and her body shook with one last eruption that drove a long, guttural moan from her throat.

Spent, Corelle lay for close to an hour wrapped in Vamma's arms. They whispered to each other, but Corelle had no memory of the words. She had never enjoyed sex as much as she did with Vamma, and today she had reached a new peak never felt before. The rain continued to fall, and the room darkened. Vamma asked if Corelle felt hungry, but Corelle had no need of sustenance at that moment. She fell asleep in Vamma's arms, content.

CHAPTER 26
VAMMA (CONTAINS INCEST)

Vamma listened to Corelle's soft, rhythmic breaths, but sleep took its time to come for her. Corelle had not touched Vamma's sex during the furious lovemaking earlier, but it did not matter. Vamma found almost as much satisfaction when she gave Corelle pleasure as she did when she took pleasure in turn.

Her delight that Corelle had agreed to take over the shop could not be measured. She had expected it to be more difficult to persuade her, but in the end the frailty of Vamma's stomach had carried the day. The lie she had told the previous day, however, had brought her no delight. She had told Corelle only her grandfather remained from her family, but that had not been the truth. Her parents had died, but her brother still lived—or had, six years earlier.

Her parents had died at her brother's hand. Vamma closed her eyes and tried to force the memories to leave, to cease to torment her. She had never told anybody about the events that had led to their death, but two nights ago in Lembell's scullery, when Corelle had asked her about her mother, she had wanted to pour the story out for the first time in her life, to free herself of the encumbrance of the years she had carried it around, unspoken.

Her brother had been born after her, younger than her by a year or two. As they grew up, they were close, but as her body developed, she became more uncomfortable about how close they were. He would sneak into her bed at night, and oftentimes he would kiss her.

Vamma wanted to push Corelle away and leap from the bed, to find something to distract her from the memories the innocent and well-intentioned question two nights before had awakened in her, but those memories would not be kept at bay. She would not wake Corelle, who seemed to balance on the knife edge of her sanity. The temper outbursts, the headaches, the irrational wish to be hanged for Raolos's death; they all spoke of a woman who had come to the edge of some abyss. Vamma hoped the responsibility of the shop might calm Corelle down and give her a new focus. She loved making, and if she threw herself into the shop to return it to something that approached its former reputation, it could only be good for her. In the meantime, Vamma wanted Corelle to sleep whenever she could.

Vamma had wanted to sleep the night her brother had killed their parents. Instead, he had again crept into her bed, as he had done for three years or more. She was sixteen or seventeen years by then, and he had long been fascinated by her breasts as they developed. He would squeeze and fondle them, and bite at her nipples while she pressed her pillow against her face to muffle any cries of pain. Such cries might bring her parents into the room and land her in trouble, and her father might beat her with his belt, not for the first time.

This night, her brother's manhood sprang to life as it always did, and she reached for it, certain he would demand she pleasure him in their normal routine. He knocked her arm away instead, climbed on top of her, and forced her legs apart with his knees. As he entered her, she screamed. She had not intended to, but it had hurt, and she had no time to press the pillow over her face.

He hissed at her. "You stupid little..." He slapped her hard across the face.

Their parents burst into the room before he could climb off her, and his manhood still stood proud near her bush. Vamma's tears gushed from her as she prepared for her father to beat her. Her mother screamed, and her father stared at the scene before him in apparent disbelief. Her father crossed the room, dragged her brother from her bed, and punched him in the head over and over again. Vamma watched in horror as her mother, a lantern in her hand, moved toward the pair, but her father cried aloud and fell onto his back. Blood poured from his stomach.

When her brother stood, he held a knife in his hand. Vamma had never learned where he had obtained it from. Their mother reached for her son, and he thrust the dagger into her throat. Vamma screamed as her mother fell to her knees and dropped the lantern. Her brother threw the knife aside and ran from the room, and the flames from the lantern licked at her mother's nightgown.

Vamma shook her head and scattered teardrops from her cheeks, but the memory refused to be dislodged. Vamma had climbed from her bedroom window as the flames engulfed the room. She lost her grip, and the heavy fall damaged her ankle. The Portreeve's men arrived, but the house had been devoured by a solid sheet of flame by then. They had taken her away and tended to her ankle, but she had said nothing of what turned. They found her brother, and the pair of them were left alone, as she had been deemed old enough to care for them both. Her brother said he would kill her if she ever told the truth about that night, and she had been too frightened of him to tell anyone. She left him and tried to avoid him, but at times, he would learn where she lived and visit her to force himself on her. Tired of his attentions, she had fled to Yerrsun and her grandfather's house, where her life had improved over the years.

Her brother never came to Yerrsun, to her relief, but she never forgot him and lived in fear of him, afraid she would see his face leer down at her whenever she woke during the night. She always lied about her past, told people she came from Yerrsun, and never mentioned the night her parents had been killed or the many times afterward her brother had mounted her like a ram will mount a mutton, callous, bent only on his own satisfaction.

Vamma had not lied when she said she did not wish to return to Yerrsun. Corelle brought her happiness, and one day she might tell her the entire story, admit to the lie. She felt certain Corelle would understand and would not be angry with her. More, if her brother ever found her, Vamma believed Corelle would kill him before she would see him harm her, and who could argue he did not deserve the fate?

Ryl would suffice. She had no reason to return to Yerrsun, and one excellent reason never to return to her original home, where her brother might find her. She would never again set foot in Dur City.

CHAPTER 27
CORELLE

The next morning, they walked to the shop and told Corelle's mother she would take over the shop. They moved their belongings out of the inn and into her parent's room, while her mother moved into the room Corelle had slept in until she had sailed to Zhanghar with Arella.

Vamma looked for some way they could track how well the shop performed. Corelle's father had kept good records until his death, but her mother had kept almost none at all since. Corelle checked the stock of clothes that remained in the shop, most of which could be sold with no issues.

Corelle and Vamma strolled around the wealthy quarter and watched the rich women as they walked around the area whenever the weather stayed dry enough to tempt them outdoors. From these trips, Corelle formed an opinion of the current fashions and where those fashions might move to next. Nothing stays the same in garment making, she told Vamma. What is popular this year might be cast off to a servant next year. "Fashion is a game, nothing more. To play it well, we need to be at the forefront of the new ideas, not follow along behind."

They used all they learned on their strolls to determine what direction Corelle's making should take. Corelle began a gown she felt would be the next step. Tight bodices had always been fashionable as long as they did not reveal too much, but Corelle decided with the arrival of the Qagrue, whose culture might be more relaxed than Dur's, women might become bolder. She made the new gown with only one shoulder strap and left the other shoulder bare. The design would reveal a hint of cleavage, but nothing too bold. It did not pay to leap too far ahead of current standards, she explained.

When they discussed what made any new trend in fashions desirable, Corelle said the moment a new trend appeared would be the time to carry the most stock of it. At that time, there would be few available dresses that reflected the new direction, and the wealthy women would fall over each other in the battle to own the first of the new designs.

Vamma suggested they could display the new design in the window, but with a "Sold" sign pinned to it. That would give the bold new idea some semblance of desirability. Somebody had bought it, but who? The gossips would gather at Orgel's shop and other popular locations as they tried to decide which adventurous trend-setter had bought the gown. Those who wished to be among the first to wear the new fashion would beat a path to the shop, she reasoned, to beg for the next gown Corelle would make.

Vamma had the right of it, but she had not foreseen how successful the ruse would be. They had to buy a journal in which to scribe the orders they accepted, and Corelle became swamped by the making. They could not keep any stock of the gowns that flew out of the door almost the moment Corelle applied the final stitch, and indeed they needed to close the journal to any new commissions, but that only increased their custom. As soon as word spread Corelle would not accept any new business other than that already in the journal, more and more of Ryl's rich women arrived at the shop and begged to be allowed into the journal. Some offered outrageous sums for the privilege, anything to wear Corelle's latest design at some imminent ball or festivity.

To retain the sense of exclusivity, Corelle and Vamma refused to accept new business until the journal cleared somewhat, and they created a second list of commissions that would flow on from the accepted orders.

Two passes had gone by, and the journal continued to be full. Corelle's mother's making lacked the quality for the work the wealthiest women in Ryl demanded, but her making still proved popular, so they installed a two-tier system. Corelle would make the most expensive designs while her mother created similar, but lower quality, versions they sold once the first gown had been seen around the city a few times. It would not do to flood the city with cheaper, less well-made copies of the gown before the purchaser of the original had been given sufficient opportunity to flaunt it.

Each day exhausted Corelle, as the making occupied every hour she could devote to it. She had finished an intricate design one night and worked well after the shop had closed in order to have the gown ready for an imminent ball. Vamma came into the shop and gazed out of the window as Corelle folded the gown with care and placed it between two sheets of soft, expensive paper.

Corelle exhaled as she placed it out of sight behind the counter, and Vamma looked round. "You look tired."

Corelle gave an ironic laugh. "That I am. I am exhausted."

Vamma turned back to the window. "There is a beautiful moon tonight. The clouds have blown away. Let us go for a walk and take the night air before we eat."

"That is an excellent idea." They retrieved their cloaks, then stepped out of the rear door and locked it behind themselves. The shop wrapped around the corner at the intersection of four streets. It commanded an excellent position, and Corelle guessed that explained why her father had bought it all those years ago. One of the streets ran onward to the square, and the street that crossed it ran toward the wealthy quarter. Plenty of wealthy people passed the shop every day.

They crossed the street and walked away from the square toward the northern part of the city. If they followed the street far enough, it would lead through the better quarter and, in time, to the Northern Ocean. If they jumped into the sea and swam, Corelle imagined they might come to Argoya in time, if whatever had taken Faltren from the platform did not drag them beneath the waves first. Vamma looked up at the night sky and stopped. "The moon is full. It is beautiful."

Corelle looked up at the moon, a fat circle among the lights of the night sky. "That it is. I saw a full moon through the rain clouds a few days after we arrived, and another since. We have been here for two passes."

"That we have." Vamma slipped an arm through Corelle's.

They walked again, but the brief conversation had unravelled something in Corelle's mind. She strove to keep her words casual. "My moon cycle ended a tenday since."

"That it did." Vamma sounded guarded.

"Yet we have been here for two passes, and I do not remember yours."

Vamma laughed, a little too loud, a little too hasty. "I have been late before. It is nothing."

"When did you last have your moon cycle, then?"

"On the ship to Arkkyd."

"I must have forgotten. I do not remember it."

"Why would you? I could not leave my bed for a tenday. My moon cycle seemed but a trivial concern compared to how I felt."

Corelle thought back to the voyage. Vamma had been ill on the river, but she had been worse on the journey north from Arkkyd. She could not recall the exact details.

Vamma gave a short laugh. "Let us not worry about this. We should return to the shop. I am hungry."

The subject did not arise again that night, and the next day Corelle began work on the next commission. Close to the midday, the shop door opened, and Corelle glanced up. A Qagrue woman entered the shop, dressed in fine clothes of good making, albeit not as good as Corelle's. She recognised the style of the maker and knew the clothes had come from Ryl.

The woman walked to a rack of her mother's making and inspected some of the dresses and shawls there, and Corelle returned to her work. She left the woman to Vamma's care.

"Good day to you." The Qagrue woman spoke perfect Dur. Her accent gave the words a strange sound, but she had a good grasp of the language.

Vamma replied, polite and businesslike. "And to you. How may I help you?"

The woman paused before she continued. "I have heard of this shop. Some say it has the finest making in Ryl. These are excellent quality indeed." Corelle glanced up. The woman pointed at her mother's work. Corelle smiled and returned her attention to her making.

Vamma's amusement could not be disguised when she replied. "Not as good as you expected though?"

The woman sighed. "Not as good at all, if I am honest. It had been suggested to me the making in this shop surpassed all other shops in the city. These do not, I fear."

Vamma laughed. "You have a good eye. The clothes you see there are not our most exclusive line. There are two standards of making here. Many desire our exclusive items, which do indeed surpass all other making in the city." Corelle smiled again at Vamma's flattery, and her cheeks warmed up as ever. "Few can pay the price for these items, I regret to say."

The woman gave a stilted laugh. "My, you are forward."

"The items we discuss are made to order. We do not have them on display since most customers collect them as soon as they are ready. Such items can be ordered, but our order list is always full."

Corelle stopped her work and looked up at the scene. The two women stared at each other across the counter. Vamma had been polite so far, but Corelle believed she had stalled the woman, doubtless uncertain she could afford the making she desired.

If that had been Vamma's belief, the woman dispelled it. "I can afford it. You need not worry on that account. Can you show me an example, at the least?"

Vamma glanced backward at Corelle, who decided to become involved in the conversation. She stood, and the woman's eyes turned toward her. Corelle gave her a polite smile. "I am Corelle, the owner of this shop. May I ask what sort of garment you require?"

"I need a dress."

The inadequate reply irritated Corelle. She needed more detail. "For a special occasion?"

"Every day is a special occasion." The woman's voice held a tone of superiority. Corelle had heard that tone many times in the shop—wealthy woman who fancied themselves far above the people with whom they dealt.

She smiled. "I see you wear Dur making."

The woman tilted her head to one side. "And how do you know the difference?"

"I recognise the maker's work. It is by Pomto, is it not?"

The woman nodded her head, almost imperceptible. "Yes, it is. How observant of you."

The Qagrue, it seemed, used 'Yes' and 'No' rather than the typical Dur response. She did not speak flawless Dur, after all else. "I mean no disrespect, but it is unusual to find someone from Qagrue who wears Dur making."

The woman's face betrayed no emotion. "I take no offence,

although many would, I am sure, my husband among them." She glanced around as if to imply the conversation bored her. "Is it not better for us to live together and break down any barriers between us?"

Beside her, Vamma stiffened. The conversation veered toward the dangerous, and Vamma sensed it also, but Corelle kept her tone friendly. "That is a noble thought. I suspect many Durfolk would say it would be better if you went back to Qagrue and returned our land to us." Vamma took Corelle's hand beneath the counter and squeezed it hard.

The woman's face set in a firm line, and her tone became curt. "I cannot express an opinion on that matter. Come. We are here together, you and I, by fates not of our own design."

Corelle remained polite. "That we are." Vamma released the pressure on Corelle's hand.

"I have heard nothing but good things about the garments from this shop from some of the women I have spoken to in Orgel's shop. Do you know of it?"

"That I do. We often visit there when our moon cycles are upon us." The words reminded Corelle of the conversation the previous night, and she paused as she replayed it in her mind. The woman shifted her weight as though she waited for Corelle to continue. Tired of the standoff, Corelle relented. "Very well. I have a ball-gown I completed last night that has not been collected yet. I will show it to you, but I must ask you not to touch the fabric. It is delicate and will mark with ease."

The woman nodded, and Corelle reached beneath the counter to take out the gown. With great care, she took the soft paper from around the gown and carried it around the counter. As she held it up, she said, "I will not take it nearer to the window if you do not mind. It is delicate."

The woman examined the gown in some detail but did not touch it, as requested. She studied the flared skirt and the fitted bodice, with small, intricate flower-shaped designs stitched onto it. The single shoulder strap came from within the front of the bodice and returned within it at the back to create the impression it might be attached somewhere near the skirt and held the dress up from within.

The Qagrue woman looked into Corelle's eyes. "It is magnificent." She had whispered, as though she feared to speak any louder in case she shattered the gown into myriad pieces. "I have never seen its like anywhere. How do you achieve such fine making?"

If she had never seen any of Corelle's work before today, she did not move in the correct circles, Corelle guessed. The woman's "friends" in Orgel's shop must not value her friendship enough to have invited her to any of their recent balls. Did she want one of Corelle's gowns so they might be more prepared to accept her? Who could know? "My father taught me the making skills from an early age. He had extraordinary skill. Those skills, of course, could be learned by anybody who had the patience to suffer the incessant repetition I possessed as a child. My designs are my own, and it is those that set my work apart."

"It is a spectacular design, I see this." The woman stood upright and bristled with pride. "What would you suggest for me?"

Corelle hesitated before she replied. "I would suggest you set aside fifty regals."

CHAPTER 28
CORELLE

The Qagrue woman smiled at the mention of the coin. "That price seems low for such fine work."

"That it does, but I have not yet finished. That price is for the consultation. I will determine what suits you; what style, shape, material. Where it will accent, where it will enhance, where it must… diminish. Then I will provide a sketch and some sample cloths. If you wish the dress to be made, the price will be far more than fifty regals, but the fifty will be deducted from the final price. If you do not proceed, you are fifty regals worse off, and I am a great many hours poorer."

"But fifty regals richer." The woman laughed, and her dark eyes twinkled.

Corelle nodded in confirmation. "I will be unable to take the regals with me where I travel to afterward."

The woman's laugh became more sincere and lasted longer. "I am Ingastdrek Sterhel Akh Drek."

"Corelle." She extended her hand.

The woman did not hesitate to shake Corelle's hand, and she laughed as she did so. "Such simple names."

Corelle bit her tongue before she replied with a smile of condescension. "Such complex ones."

The woman nodded, as though she appreciated the retort. "I do not carry such large sums of coin with me. I will send somebody with the coins later today. May we make an appointment for my consultation?"

"Before we discuss that, you should know I work on one commission at a time, and they can take a week and more for the making alone. I could not start your dress for close to two passes."

Ingastdrek Sterhel Akh Drek raised her eyebrows. "I expected two years."

"I reject more commissions than I accept. A gown that takes a year to deliver will either disappoint, not fit, or not be required any longer."

"Then why do you accept my commission?"

"I have not yet said I do."

"No, no you have not. Will you?"

Corelle looked the woman up and down and considered the offer. It would be a challenge. Qagrue were a similar shape to Durfolk, but they tended to have broad shoulders and short legs that meant they were not what would be considered statuesque in wealthy Dur society. Ingastdrek Sterhel Akh Drek had been struck from that same mould. The challenge would be to reduce the appearance of the broad shoulders but not thicken some other part of the body, and to create statuesque tallness below the waist from legs that might have been a span longer on a Dur born woman. Corelle could not resist the challenge. "That I will."

They made an appointment at Ingastdrek Sterhel Akh Drek's house for four days' time at which Corelle would explain her idea and take measurements of Ingastdrek's body, and the Qagrue woman walked to the door. As she reached for it, she stopped and turned. "Corelle?" Corelle did not speak but inclined her head in acknowledgement. "You do not like us, do you?"

Vamma squeezed Corelle's hand again, a caution to be careful how she replied, Corelle guessed. "That I do not."

The woman nodded as though she had expected the reply. "Is there a reason for your distaste?"

Corelle hesitated. She now trod even more dangerous ground and must not slip. Unless she took care, she would fall, not down but up, as a rope cast over the branch of a tree stretched her neck. "Your people killed my Duke." She measured each word against the damage it might cause.

The woman's response had no hint of malice in its tone. "In truth, we did not kill the Duke. One whom we trusted killed him. We did not wish that violence."

Corelle did not doubt the story had been told to Ingastdrek Sterhel Akh Drek that way, but she had her own opinions on the matter. "I knew the Duke."

"Then I offer my sorrow, and my apologies on behalf of the people of Qagrue and Dur."

"Is that how you refer to yourselves these days?"

"Is that not the way it is?"

Vamma squeezed her hand so hard, Corelle feared she might tear it off at the wrist. "That it is. I will see you in four days."

Ingastdrek assured them the coin would be delivered later that day, then left.

Vamma heaved an enormous sigh once the woman passed from sight. "You will make a dress for one of them?" She almost spat out the word, "them."

"It is a challenge." Corelle kissed Vamma on the nose. "If I can make her appear less square, I can retire. I could not exceed that achievement if I lived for ever."

"Square?" Vamma snorted, and they both laughed.

Corelle returned to the gown she had started earlier in the day. She had begun with the shoulder strap, which required some intricate patterned stitching, and the work took intense concentration. A headache formed behind her eyes, and she considered an early finish; to close up the shop and take Vamma to their room to drive her headache away with an hour or two of passion. It would frustrate her if she made a mistake in such detailed work because of tiredness.

The door opened again, but Corelle did not allow it to break her concentration. Vamma tidied up the racks of displayed clothes, but she could deal with whoever had entered. She hoped it would be the fifty regals from Ingastdrek Sterhel Akh Drek.

"Corelle."

Corelle had heard the voice before. She finished the stitch she worked on before she looked up. A short, thin man in a dull grey cloak stood at the counter. Vamma hovered close behind him and looked at Corelle, puzzled. The man's face looked familiar, but at first, Corelle could not place him, nor put a name to the face. He did not introduce himself, but recognition came to her at that moment—Denstal, the Guild member she had met in Ort when they were allied together for a few days to kill Qagrue. It had been three years, and now he stood in her shop in Ryl. Corelle disliked coincidences, and she disliked one this big even less. She placed a casual arm over her making scissors, which lay on the desk before her, then smiled at him. "Denstal. What brings you to my little shop? Do you seek some finery for a grand occasion?"

His face remained a blank parch, no emotions scribed on it. "That I do not. I come to talk to you about a customer who has been observed in your shop."

He did not take his eyes from her, and she made no move to manoeuvre the scissors into a more convenient position. "Which customer might that be? We have a great many."

"A Qagrue woman came to your shop no more than two hours ago."

Corelle ignored his words. "You are here in Ryl but only now wish to come and pay your respects to me? Some would consider that impolite."

"That they would. I have known you were here for almost a pass. The work I do these days is… of a sensitive nature, shall we say? I had no wish to embroil you and your friend in it."

"Vamma is my lover, not my friend."

He turned to Vamma. "Please, accept my apologies." Vamma did not answer, and Corelle waited. He had some purpose and would reveal it in his own time. "We have watched several of the Qagrue for some time as we seek opportunities to discuss some matters with them."

Corelle sucked air across her lips, as Gaish had done in lieu of an acknowledgement at times. "What does this have to do with me?"

"One of those whom we watch is the commander of the forces the Qagrue maintain here to ensure their rule is not challenged." Corelle said nothing. "If their rule is challenged, they enforce their control without mercy, as some have found to their ultimate cost. The woman who came to your shop is this commander's wife."

Corelle wanted Denstal to reveal why he had come to the shop and did not want to guess at his intent. "If by this you mean she has requested a dress for her husband, then the challenge will be greater than I imagined."

He laughed. "You are a close one, Corelle. You have changed little."

"I have changed a great deal, in truth. But I have not yet heard what brings you to my shop. I am certain you did not come here to praise my caution with words."

At that moment, the shop door opened. Vamma turned to look at whoever had entered, but Denstal did not take his eyes from Corelle. Corelle's eyes flicked to the door, where a man in a Qagrue uniform stood and gazed at the three of them. Her heart beat faster.

The situation had turned dangerous, and they must all now be careful. The Qagrue approached the counter.

Vamma greeted him, calm and relaxed. "Good day to you." Corelle admired Vamma's control.

"I bring pouch for you from Ingastdrek Sterhel Akh Drek."

"Ah. My thanks." Vamma took the pouch he offered her. The man glanced at Denstal, turned, and left. Vamma released her tension in a lengthy exhalation of breath.

"I take it you intend to make this woman a dress." Denstal appeared unperturbed by the appearance of the Qagrue man.

"Such matters must remain between my customers and me."

Denstal stared at her, still with no emotion on his face. He did not tap his fingers or a foot, as people were wont to do when frustrated or impatient. "You may remember I asked you to lead us in Ort."

Corelle had not forgotten. "This is Ryl."

His smile lacked any warmth, as cold as a bitter day in the depths of the cold season. "Ryl is smaller. It is an easier place to start."

She snorted in amusement. "Start? It has been three years since you asked me to lead you, if I remember aright. You are in no rush, it would appear."

"Much has turned, but to hurry things would have been rash, I am sure you agree."

"What does that request have to do with your visit to my shop, after all else?"

"I still ask it." No trace of emotion betrayed his inner thoughts.

She frowned. "And I say again I will not lead the Guild."

"Then help us, at the least."

"And how would I do that?"

He looked around the shop, and Corelle moved the scissors so they lay under her wrist and outspread hand. He asked her if she would have to visit Ingastdrek Sterhel Akh Drek's home for a consultation, and Corelle asked him how he knew so much about dressmaking. "I have my sources." He left a dramatic pause before he continued. "While you are there, her husband may also be there. Kill him if he is."

Corelle barked a short sharp laugh. "I would not leave the house alive."

He shrugged. "Neither would he."

"And how many Rylfolk would they hang in the square in reprisal?"

"None, my guess. You would be the killer, not the people of the city."

Vamma broke her silence at last. "You jest, do you not? You ask Corelle to lay down her life for you, all to kill one man? What would it achieve, even if she took leave of her senses enough to agree?"

"It would show them they are vulnerable. It would strike a blow for the people of Dur."

"It would strike a blow for nobody." Vamma's face had grown red, her voice louder. "The next day another would rule the city, one who might be more vicious and vengeful than his predecessor. You have lost your mind. Is this the plan you have worked for three years to create? It is ridiculous."

Rather than address his answer to Vamma, Denstal continued to stare at Corelle. "Corelle, be sensible. This shop is your livelihood. What if you lost all your customers?"

Corelle glared at him, irritated. "Explain yourself."

"We have connections among those wealthy patrons of yours."

Corelle stood, and her temper heated. She left the scissors on the desk. "Do you threaten me?"

He held up his hands in appeasement. "I ask you to help us, and yourself in the bargain."

Her rage grew with every word he spoke. "I should kill you where you stand."

"Believe me Corelle, I would rather keep you out of this." He spoke as though she had not threatened him. "This is an uncommon opportunity. Join us or help us. Please."

"If I help you as you ask, I would throw away my life. When I am dead, what of my mother and Vamma?"

"The shop will find its patronage sustained by wealthy customers who will be delighted to wear your mother's making."

Vamma spat poison at him in her words. "Do not treat us with such condescension."

Corelle struggled to keep her voice level and her anger in check. "You should leave before I am forced to do something you will regret."

He allowed a smug smile to his face at last. "Do you think you are capable after three years?"

Corelle focused on her heart rate, her voice steady, her eyes on his. "I am more than capable."

"And yet you make dresses on demand for rich women whom you despise."

His words stung her. "I chose this life. I have turned my back on death, but it has not yet turned its back on me. You should choose your next words with caution. I have never been reluctant to take the lives of those I loathe."

He exhaled. "Corelle, this need not be unpleasant. I respect you. I have asked you to lead us, but you have chosen another path. I ask you to help because you have a unique opportunity that may not be available again. If anybody can kill him and escape with their life, it is you. I do not doubt it, though Styrrach, Gillar, and Sisnop did, to their cost."

"You omit many names from that list. This idea is madness. Go. Leave us in peace."

He hesitated, and Corelle sensed he held a high card hidden in his sleeve. "We know where Krage is."

Corelle stared at him in silence, her lips pressed together. She weighed all his words since he had entered the shop. Vamma begged him to leave, but Corelle had drawn an inevitable conclusion. "How convenient. This woman enters my store, a woman whose husband you wish to kill. Two hours later you appear and beg me to kill him in your stead. In exchange, you offer me the knowledge of Krage's whereabouts."

"Wealth also. You forget the benefits for your shop."

"That does not interest me, as you know. I have experienced coincidences in my life that have worked to my favour and against it. This coincidence is one of the most spectacular ones I have ever come across."

He gave a slight nod. "There is no coincidence, as you have guessed. Our contacts among the wealthy women of the city have worked their way into Ingastdrek Sterhel Akh Drek's favour. It proved easy to ensure they all billed and cooed about your shop, and to plant an idea in the ears of the wife of a man we wish to see dead. It has a certain charm, you must agree."

Furious, Corelle walked around the counter, and he took a pace backward, a startled look on his face. She pushed a hand into his chest that sent him two further paces backward toward the door of the shop and snarled at him. "You threaten everything I have for your own end? I should kill you here, in my own shop, and hang your body in the window among my mother's making." Her face twisted with rage. "Get out."

CHAPTER 29
VAMMA

From the moment the man had entered the shop, Vamma had disliked and distrusted him. He spoke to Corelle, and Vamma could tell they knew one another. What he asked of her, Vamma found difficult to believe. He asked her to kill an important man in the Qagrue system it seemed, the husband of the unpleasant woman from whom Corelle had accepted a commission earlier in the day.

Vamma listened as the man tried to persuade the woman she loved to kill this man on his behalf even though she might die in the process, from all she could fathom of his words. His request seemed unreasonable, and when Corelle seemed reluctant to oblige him, he threatened their business.

Vamma joined in the conversation at times and grew concerned as she watched Corelle, who sat at her making table while her temples throbbed, a sure sign her temper boiled. Vamma worried blood might be spilled in the shop as the argument between the three of them became more heated.

The arrival of the Qagrue man with the coin from the commission could not have been timed any worse. Vamma did not trust the short man in his dull clothes, and she did not trust Corelle to retain an even temper, so she spoke to the Qagrue man as he entered the shop, and she took the pouch. She had remained calm as she spoke to him, but her nervousness consumed her as he left. Her body shook with fear as he passed from sight beyond the window.

Corelle rose, and Vamma's concern increased. What would she do? Might she attack the visitor? Vamma had seen both Corelle's anger and her cold detachment at other times when under duress, and she came close to panic as Corelle glowered at the man. When the man mentioned the name Krage, Corelle became more enraged. Vamma could see the anger in Corelle's face. Her jaw clenched and her eyes blazed. Vamma believed her ears must have betrayed her, because the man then admitted he had driven the woman to the shop as part of his plan to have her husband killed. In horror, she watched Corelle advance on him in fury and push him backward.

Corelle's face radiated outrage as she glared at him. "Get out." She spat the two words between clenched teeth and tense lips. What turned next almost stilled Vamma's heart in her breast.

Denstal half-turned toward Vamma and winked at her, but his hand dropped to his belt, hidden from Corelle by his body. She cried in alarm. "Corelle." The man moved fast, and no sooner had the word left her mouth than the man had a dagger pressed to Corelle's side while another hand balled the front of her tunic.

"Calm yourself, Corelle." He seemed angry himself, a change from the composed, collected man he had been to this point. "I do not wish to hurt you. Besides, you have left your scissors on your desk." Vamma's eyes flicked to the making table. The scissors still lay on it, and she gasped. Corelle had no weapon, and things had taken a sorry turn. Should Vamma leap on him and attempt to distract him while Corelle ran for the scissors?

Corelle smiled, but to Vamma the smile seemed like the lips of a dog drawn back from its teeth in a threat. The anger seemed to have otherwise floated away from Corelle, and she appeared calm, cold, and detached. Vamma had seen this ominous serenity before but could not guess what might happen next. The man pushed his dagger into her side as if to emphasise his words, and a spot of blood appeared on Corelle's tunic.

The icy smile did not fade as Corelle spoke, quiet and slow. "You are a smart one, Denstal. Not smart enough though. Not smart enough by some margin." Vamma had thought the man quick to act, but Corelle moved so fast, she seemed nothing more than a blur as Vamma fought down her fear. Corelle's right hand flicked up to the man's head, and he released his grip on her tunic to move his hand toward his bloodied cheek with surprise on his face. His hand froze in mid-air, and Corelle held her fan pressed tight against his throat, blood on its blade. Corelle growled at him. "You focused too much on the scissors. So much, in truth, you did not see me pull my fan out of my boot."

Vamma had never been so horrified in her life. Only the death of her parents could compare. The man compounded her surprise. He laughed. "That I did. You have lost none of your art, Corelle, and I am pleased to see it. He lowered his dagger to his side as blood spread on Corelle's tunic. He breathed words that chilled Vamma's blood in her veins. "Do it. If I must meet my ruin today, it will be no dishonour to meet it at the hands of the famous Corelle."

Corelle snarled again, her eyes fixed on his. "Get out."

"Think on my words, Corelle. You will see the sense in them."

"Leave with your life before I change my mind and take it from you." The man turned, gave Vamma a small nod, then pulled the door open and walked out. The cut on his cheek trickled blood down his neck.

Vamma exhaled a sharp breath, the suspense of the moment expelled with it. "What a disgraceful thing this man has done."

Corelle remained still and stared at the door. She shrugged. "I would have tried the same thing if I could. He played a decent hand."

Her words stunned Vamma. "You cannot agree to his sugges-tion. It is madness."

"That is not what I said. I admire the plan, but I dislike being used."

Vamma stepped forward and placed a hand on Corelle's hip. "Would you have killed him?" She could not comprehend what it must be like at that moment, to be prepared to end another's life.

"That I would. He stood at the counter and laid out his scheme when one of the Qagrue entered the shop. He put us all at risk."

Vamma loosed another heavy breath. "You seemed so angry."

"That I was." Corelle seemed to relax, and she stooped to replace the fan in her boot.

"It seems so much more frequent these days. We must find somebody who understands these things. They may be able to help you."

"I believe the healers know little about the inner depths of the brain. I will be fine. Do not worry." Corelle kissed Vamma's cheek.

Her assurance did not satisfy Vamma. "The other day you had to start that gown again. I have never seen you so angry as at that moment, I do not think."

Corelle shrugged. "I had wasted a great deal of work, and no extra coin came from it. I lost my way and needed to start again. I am to blame for the mistake."

"Corelle, you threw your stool across the shop." Corelle said nothing in reply. "Are you all right? Is something awry?"

"You know the details already. I sometimes get terrible headaches. At times my sight blurs. Not often, but it does happen."

Vamma chewed at her lower lip. "These things may all be linked. We must find somebody for you to speak to about them."

"Deineike suffered similar things. I have told you this." Corelle paused. "Deineike died."

Something crossed Corelle's face that might have been fear, and Vamma tried to reassure her. "She died after Styrrach's attack. The two need not be the same. Please say you will see a healer. You have been battered and bruised almost your entire life, and now a mast has fallen on you. You had no healer attend that injury for days."

"I will see a healer, I promise." Corelle pulled Vamma closer and kissed her nose. "You need not fear me."

Vamma hesitated. She had lied twice to Corelle in the last few days. She could not yet reveal the story of her brother and parents, but the other lie must be corrected. "I must tell you something, but I am afraid you will become angry again."

"What is it?"

"Promise me you will not become angry with me."

Corelle kissed her, a tender kiss on the forehead, as though an insect had landed there. "Did I not just say I would not harm you?"

Vamma drew in a deep breath. "I think you were right last night. I think I am with child."

Corelle took a backward step and stared at Vamma in obvious shock. "What?"

"I have not had my moon cycle since before we left Malkartas."

"Last night you said—"

Vamma interrupted her. "I lied. It has been almost three passes. I am sorry."

Vamma had suspected for over a pass, and the last two mornings she had fetched up after Corelle had gone down to the shop to start work. It could no longer be denied, and although she had wanted to keep it from Corelle, the time had come to tell her. The cat was out of the sack.

CHAPTER 30
CORELLE

Corelle's life had swirled through a tumultuous frenzy of emotions. Highs that had lifted her beyond the lights of the night sky, lows that had threatened to crush her into the dirt and bury her so deep, none could ever dig her out. The shy, awkward girl who took such pleasure from the design and making of exquisite gowns for the wealthy women of Ryl had disappeared, replaced by a cold, cruel killer who walked a road littered with the bodies of friend and foe alike. Death stalked her and took all who crossed her path. She had returned to Ryl in the hope she would at last settle to a simple life with Vamma, free of complications and, with luck, free of death.

How wrong she had been when she had imagined that outcome. Already the Guild reborn called on her to kill, and die in all likelihood, in their service. Now Vamma claimed a child grew within her, even though such a thing ought not to have been possible between two women. Had she strayed? A pass ago, she had promised never to do so again, but before that, who could know? Vamma once declared it a part of her nature; she must have found some man to lie with and had become with child. It could not be endured. Corelle could not do what Pettra had done; to raise a child born from a dalliance with a stranger that did not involve her.

Dizziness washed over her and threatened to dash her to the floor, and she reached for the chair at her making table, collapsed into it, and lowered her head into her hands. Vamma said no more. "How can you be with child? It is impossible between us. It makes no sense unless you have lain with another since we left Malkartas." She looked up and shot a glance of accusation at Vamma, who fidgeted before her.

"I have not strayed."

Vamma had kept her voice soft. Had she not wished to anger Corelle? She appeared to have suspected this news would rile Corelle, but the thought only strengthened her suspicions. "Then how is this possible?"

"You forget I had a husband when you returned."

Corelle sat upright and stared at Vamma in disbelief, breathless with anguish. "Raolos's child is within you?" Raolos had created this child? The man she had killed in a pointless brawl over Vamma, who must have carried his child at the precise moment the deadly incident in Tanasttra took place?

"It can be nobody else's. I promised I would not stray, and I have not." Vamma's tears dripped from her chin past Raolos's unborn child on their journey to the floor.

"Then what will we do?" Corelle had never desired children, and her attraction to women had long convinced her she would have none. Now a second child had entered her life unbidden, and this one's fate would not be written by Corelle's blade.

"I know nothing about children nor how to raise them." Vamma's voice rasped in her throat.

"I reason you know more than I." Could this day hold any more nightmares? "What will we do?"

Vamma hesitated, and Corelle's heart became heavier with

premonition. "Can anything be done to stop it?" Vamma spoke so quiet, it almost seemed she feared to give the thought voice.

"I know not. Of all the people in Dur, I am the worst person to ask such a question."

Vamma appeared to reach for shadows. "I could ask your mother."

"By the fates, do not mention this to her, I beg you." Corelle shot an anxious glance behind her to be sure her mother did not stand in the doorway and listen to the entire exchange. "She must not know yet, not before we have decided what we will do."

"There must be people who know of ways to stop these things."

Things? It seemed callous to label the child so. Vamma must have intended to imply something different than her words suggested. Corelle's head spun. If something threatened her life, she could remain calm, detached, deliberate. Never had she experienced anything like this moment in her life before, and she had no concept of the right thing to do, nor how to do it. "Is that what you want?" Corelle was afraid to speak too loud herself now they discussed it.

"I know not." Vamma crouched, and her hands pulled Corelle's own down to her thighs and held them tight. "What do you want?"

Arella had not asked her opinion, and Corelle had stilled the child's breaths long before it took any of its own. She would not write this child's fate. She pursed her lips and blew out a long, slow breath. "It seems my wishes are unimportant. It is your choice. I am not the one who would have to carry and birth it."

Vamma raised one of Corelle's hands and kissed it, distracted, as if out of some habit. "I thought you might want it stopped because..." She paused, gazed into Corelle's lap, then whispered, "It is Raolos's child."

"What in the Five Cities would lead you to that thought? Until that night in the inn, I bore him nothing but friendship, though it proved faithless. I still do. I bear him no ill will. Although I said cruel things to him that night, I wish now I had not."

"I understand." Vamma squeezed Corelle's hands as though to reassure her. "He angered you in his intoxication. Boiling water scalds—"

"But boiling blood scalds the more." Corelle finished off the old expression. She sighed, her mind made up. "You must make the decision. It is your choice to make. The child is in your body. I will aid you in any way I can, whichever way you decide."

Vamma shook her head. "My love, we decide. I could not inflict a child on you against your wishes." She smiled, and her eyes were lit with mischief. "It might be fun, in truth."

Corelle returned the smile and sensed Vamma had made up her mind. "It will be a beautiful child. It had a handsome father, and its mother is not unattractive."

Vamma placed a hand on her breasts and turned her eyes to the ceiling. "Such compliments. I may swoon."

Corelle smiled, amused by Vamma's act. "This has been quite a day."

"That it has." Vamma loosed a short, ironic laugh.

"Before Denstal arrived, I thought I might finish work early. I had thought we could…" A terrible thought crossed her mind. "Are we still able to?"

"That we are." A suggestive smile sprang to Vamma's face. "I will lock the shop door."

Corelle worried sex might be harmful to the baby that grew in Vamma's womb. "It will not hurt the child?"

"I care not if it does." Vamma pulled Corelle to her feet. "I am on fire for you. I wish to have my way with you, and the child will not prevent that."

They ran up the stairs to the bedroom, closed the door, and tumbled onto the bed. They tore at each other's clothes, their tongues entwined in a familiar dance. Vamma's hand dived between Corelle's legs and searched for her nub. Such a small thing, but the pleasure it could bring overwhelmed Corelle as Vamma's fingers fondled it, and she gasped as she took a handful of Vamma's hair in each hand and pressed her head back on the bed. Her guttural moans of desire built to a crescendo as her body rose from the blankets in response to fingers that coaxed her with an urgency that tantalised. Visceral cries burst from Corelle's throat, and she reached the peak of her excitement. Her body shuddered as the sensations that swept through her drove her beyond the brink of pleasure and into a darkness where nothing existed but Vamma and the gratification her fingers created.

One hour, two hours. Neither could guess as time passed, unmarked and irrelevant. They explored the limits to which they could drive one another and found the other always hungry for more. They lay in each other's arms exhausted afterward. Corelle kissed Vamma's forehead and tasted the salt of her sweat. "Do you plan to keep the child?" Her mind had returned to the earlier conversation.

Vamma gave one sharp nod of her head. "I think I will, if you are happy with that decision."

Corelle's opinion had not moved from her position earlier. "It is you who must carry it to birth. I will do all I can to aid you in this."

Vamma's nose wrinkled. "Thank you. I love you. How could I not love a woman who brings me such pleasure, would kill to protect me, and will raise my child with me?" She kissed Corelle on the lips, soft as the touch of the first raindrop at the start of a downpour. "I am hungry. Let us help your mother prepare the meal."

Corelle did not want to leave the bed and the warm closeness of Vamma's body, but they dressed themselves and went to offer their assistance with the evening meal. They sat and talked with Corelle's mother for a time after they had eaten, washed the dishes they had used, then returned to their bed. Sleep took them, but not before Vamma had again taken Corelle on a journey of lust they seemed never to tire of.

Corelle spent the three days afterward busy at her table as she continued to work on her next commission. Denstal did not visit again, nor the Qagrue, and she made good progress on the gown. They told her mother Vamma carried the child. Corelle's mother listened in silent surprise to the story of how it turned that Vamma had been married while Corelle had travelled the globe on The Ictharelian, but she seemed happy for Vamma. She said she admired them both for their commitment to the child's birth and promised to share her experience with them to help with the child's early days once it arrived.

CHAPTER 31
CORELLE

The day arrived for Corelle to visit Ingastdrek Sterhel Akh Drek for the initial measurements and to see if the Qagrue woman would be happy with Corelle's suggestions. Corelle's design combined a wide scooped neck with sleeves that expanded into a bell shape lower down the arm. She felt the neckline would draw the eye to the wearer's collarbone and the sleeves would serve as a further focal point that would distract the eyes of observers away from the woman's broad shoulders. Corelle had wanted to cinch the waist as close as possible to accentuate the woman's hip as another focal point but had decided if she incorporated a false belt a finger or two above her natural waistline, it would create the impression her torso and legs were more in proportion.

The skirt of the dress would fit snug over the hips and fall straight down to her ankles. The straight skirt would help to disguise Ingastdrek Sterhel Akh Drek's shorter legs, and if the woman could find some shoes with raised heels and in the same colour as the dress, they would create the impression of longer legs to the casual observer. A small train at the rear of the skirt would drape over the shoes to disguise the heels.

Corelle and Vamma both felt the design would help minimise the woman's unusual shape, and while Vamma found the devices incorporated into the design outstanding, clever work, Corelle hoped only that the woman would like the dress. Some people might not like the ankle length skirt, designed to create the impression her shoes were an extension of her legs. The higher shoes would also make her appear taller.

Other concerns ate at Corelle. The visit from Denstal had unnerved her, and she wondered if the Guild would make some further attempt to persuade her to kill Ingastdrek Sterhel Akh Drek's husband. She did not doubt they watched the shop, and they would see her leave, but she must roll the dice. She slipped her fan into her boot in case things turned awry.

She kissed Vamma as she left the shop, her designs and some sample cloths in her pack. The woman and her husband lived in the house the Portreeve used to occupy. In some cities, the Portreeve lived in his own house and would have retained it even after the Qagrue removed him from office, she guessed. In Ryl, the city had owned the Portreeve's home, and the Qagrue must have commandeered it for their highest ranked officer. As she walked toward the house, she thought about the Portreeve who had visited her father's shop when she had still been a young girl. She wondered what had become of the dress his wife had taken. Those days seemed such a long time ago. She laughed to herself as she remembered her indignation when the woman had taken the dress she had made, and not a groat paid for all Corelle's efforts.

A servant opened the door and confirmed they expected her. The large, airy house could not match the one Raolos had owned in Ort. What would happen to that house, and to Pettra's, Corelle did not know and no longer cared. The servant led her up to the main bedroom on the first floor, where Ingastdrek Sterhel Akh Drek waited for her, excited, restless with impatience.

Corelle spread her sketches on the bed. She could not draw a person well, and the figures in her sketches were no better than some of Deineike's abysmal work. Despite her limited abilities, she could draw clothes, and the detail of the work required in some more complicated areas, along with sketches of any designs or baubles that would be stitched to the dress, were drawn to a larger scale on the design template. Ingastdrek Sterhel Akh Drek loved the concepts of the design, although she expressed some nervousness about the scooped neckline. She said Qagrue men were jealous of their wives' bodies and did not care for others to see them. Corelle resisted a chuckle at this. By Dur tastes, Qagrue women had odd shaped bodies, nothing to be jealous of. It seemed, regardless of her opinions about Qagrue women's bodies, she had been wrong when she had believed the invaders might bring a more relaxed attitude to the way women dressed.

Ingastdrek Sterhel Akh Drek understood the concept despite her concern about her husband's reaction, and Corelle agreed a compromise that would raise the scoop of the neckline a little. The change left her disgruntled, since if the collarbones could not be seen, the dress's ability to distract might be lost. Ingastdrek Sterhel Akh Drek would pay for the dress, however, and the customer must be happy with the finished product. The woman chose a deep crimson silk for the material, and Corelle approved of the dramatic colour. It reminded her somewhat of the material of the dress Pettra had had made with the coin Corelle had left her when she sailed to Alcmouth.

When it came time to take the accurate measurements that would be needed to make the dress fit to perfection, Qagrue traditions demanded modesty could not be compromised unless a female servant remained in the room. Corelle thought it a ridiculous convention, but the Durfolk servant chatted away as they waited for Ingastdrek Sterhel Akh Drek to disrobe, and Corelle took the measurements she would need. She had made a new measuring string. The span might not be the same as the one she had used for so many years until the ship sank and took it to Helchik's treasure, but that did not matter as long as she used it in both the measurement and creation of the dress.

Corelle crouched behind the woman to measure the drop from where she intended to position the false belt to the point at which she wished the hem to stop and the train to begin, and the bedroom door opened. When she peered around Ingastdrek Sterhel Akh Drek's legs, a man in a Qagrue tunic adorned with braid entered the bedroom with some letters and a knife in his hand.

"Husband." Corelle did not miss the sharp thorn of surprise in Ingastdrek Sterhel Akh Drek's voice. Something else lingered there. Fear? Disappointment? "I did not expect you to return so early."

"I see this." Corelle did not care for his gruff tone. It sounded terse to her and gave the immediate impression the man found the presence of an unknown woman of Dur in his home unacceptable. "Who is this woman?"

"My dressmaker, my sweet. I told you she would come to measure me today."

He grunted. Corelle continued with her work, anxious not to be involved in their domestic dispute, but she bridled at the way he had referred to her. "Must she measure you in your bareness?"

The word, "bareness," seemed strange to Corelle, but they spoke Dur, mayhap only because Ingastdrek Sterhel Akh Drek had spoken first, and it might have been a poor translation from their own language. Corelle answered his question. "That I must, if the dress is to fit." The servant had fallen silent as soon as the man had entered, she noticed. "It would be a waste of coin to pay so much for a dress that did not fit."

She had tried to come to the woman's aid by means of an excuse for her nakedness, but it soon became obvious she had touched a different nerve in the man. "I see. And how much will this latest plaything cost me?"

His wife intervened. "We have not yet agreed on a price. Do not worry, it will be excellent value for such wonderful work, and we can afford it with ease." Corelle wondered if the last sentence had been for her benefit or his.

"I know we can afford it, but you spend altogether too much coin on clothes. It is wasteful." Corelle had finished with the measurements, so she crossed to the table and the parch on which she scribed all the measurements. He waved an arm toward a door in the bedroom. "You have a room full of them, yet still you wish for more." The gruffness in his voice had increased, and Corelle guessed she would be caught up in a domestic argument, after all else. "You, dressmaker. How much will this cost me?"

Corelle stiffened, her back to him as she scribed on her parch. Anger welled up in her, and she struggled to contain it. Things might turn awry for her if she allowed her temper to control her tongue. At that moment, she decided she had no further interest in the commission. The Qagrue were an unpleasant people, as Raolos had told her, and this man seemed more obnoxious than most. If Ingastdrek Sterhel Akh Drek tolerated this man's rudeness, she did not deserve a dress made by Corelle of Ryl.

She turned to him and stood straight and proud. Her eyes glared into his. "Five hundred regals."

"Five hundred regals?" He gave a raucous laugh. "Do any of you Durfolk even possess such an amount?"

Corelle replied without hesitation. "That we do. I once paid a man two thousand regals to carry letters for me."

His face suggested he found her reply difficult to believe, but he appeared to settle for an insult. "Then you were marked a fool before the negotiation."

She did not recognise the phrase but believed she understood what he had meant. "If the price is too high…"

He used his knife to slit the seal of one of the letters with a casual indifference. He glanced at it, then crumpled it in his hand and dropped it to the floor. The servant took a step forward, and seemed about to pick up the discarded parch, but he held up a hand to stop her. "The price is not too high, but I would see this wondrous dress before I pay it. You have sketches of this item?"

"That I do." Corelle spoke through clenched teeth—her temper had risen to fever pitch. She handed him the designs she had sketched.

He flicked through the parches. "Did your daughter draw these?" He did not deign to glance at her.

"I drew them." Her simple response disguised the rage that urged her to pull her fan from her boot and end his rudeness. She clenched her fists and pressed her nails into her palm as she fought to control her resentment of him.

"I trust your dressmaking is better than your sketches." He laughed again, an unpleasant laugh, full of mockery and contempt, it seemed to Corelle.

Ingastdrek Sterhel Akh Drek had stood by throughout the exchange between her husband and Corelle, but now she intervened. "Why must you speak to her so? It is rude." A hint of anger had crept into her voice, her face had turned red, and the veins at her temple throbbed.

"Do not raise your voice to me." A dark menace crept into his tone.

"I did not raise my voice. I asked only—"

He took a step forward and slapped her face. Her cheek reddened at once, and her head snapped to one side. "Remember your place." He turned to the servant, who fidgeted in discomfort nearby, her face bright red with embarrassment at what turned in the room. Corelle pressed her lips together as she battled her fury. He growled at the servant. "Leave us. I will chaperone."

Chaperone. Another word Corelle did not know. She guessed it referred to the modesty element of their culture. The servant bowed and left the room, her head down and her eyes fixed on the floor. She did not meet his stern gaze.

Tears ran down Ingastdrek Sterhel Akh Drek's cheeks, and Corelle could no longer tolerate such disgraceful behaviour. "You should not have struck your wife." She imagined how angry her voice must have sounded. Memories of the day Pettra had slapped her own face had gushed into Corelle's mind as the slap of his hand had reverberated around the bedroom, and those memories only served to incense her further.

"This is no concern of yours, dressmaker." His vitriolic reply had been intended to intimidate her, she guessed. He thrust his face into that of his wife. "You should know better than to embarrass me in front of the staff."

His wife glowered at him, hatred in her eyes. Ingastdrek Sterhel Akh Drek raised her voice, no longer the submissive wife she had been before he had struck her. "You are intolerable at times. You hurt me." Her cheek had turned bright red, and blood trickled from a small cut on her cheekbone.

"I intended to. How else will you learn the lessons I must teach you?" Corelle could constrain her ire no longer, and she drew in a breath to speak. He must have heard it, and although he did not glance in her direction, he raised an arm and pointed at her, the knife clutched in his closed fist. "Shut up. Leave us."

Corelle reacted as she always had done whenever danger threatened and she might need to kill. She slowed her breaths, relaxed her shoulders and arms, focused on his eyes. "So you may strike her again?"

He turned to face her, eyes wide in apparent shock. "Who are you to speak to me this way? You are but a common dressmaker, yet you are as insolent to me as though you are my superior."

She resisted the urge to bend to her boot and pull out her fan. "I am an exceptional dressmaker." Her gaze trekked from his boots to his eyes. "You, however, are less than a man."

He waved the knife at her and flexed his fingers on its handle. "Would you like a taste of my wrath?" Spittle flew from his taut lips with every word, his face red with rage.

Corelle's tolerance snapped. She took a step forward before he could react and snatched the knife from his hand. She reversed it and slashed in one smooth movement. A vermilion ribbon opened across his throat, and his eyes opened wide with surprise. He reached up to his throat and pressed the palms of both hands to the gash, as though he hoped to stem the flow of blood that gushed from it. The letters and her designs fluttered to the floor. The blunted knife had been inferior to Wilash's work, but it had been wielded with easy familiarity and had wrought his ruin.

Ingastdrek Sterhel Akh Drek screamed as her husband's blood oozed from his throat. As he crumpled to the floor and streams of his life pumped from his severed artery, Corelle turned to her without hesitation and drove the knife into the side of her neck with all the strength in her body. Her aim did not fail her; crimson blood pumped from the woman's neck to the floor and spattered the body of her husband. The knife had found her vein, wielded by a peerless killer. The Qagrue woman hung on the knife for a moment, but Corelle had not the strength to support her weight and pulled the knife from her neck. The woman collapsed to the floor and lay still, empty eyes fixed on the ceiling.

CHAPTER 32
CORELLE

The woman's scream had been unfortunate. It would bring guards, and Corelle must act fast, or she would join the couple, dead on the floor. She reversed the knife again and thrust it into her chest with both hands. It penetrated deep into her flesh, high up toward her right shoulder. She grimaced at the pain and grunted as she threw the knife down near the dead hand of Ingastdrek Sterhel Akh Drek. She took a pace backward and dropped to the floor, her upper back supported by the end of the bed and both hands pressed tight against the wound, from which blood poured at an unexpected rate. Her tunic turned red in moments, and she hoped she had not inflicted a worse injury than intended.

The door burst open, and three guards rushed into the room. They came to an abrupt halt as they saw the scene, and gazed around, aghast. Blood covered the carpeted floor, pooled around the couple's bodies, and merged as their life sources embraced in one final kiss. Corelle's own blood poured from her wound, and she felt both concerned and in considerable pain.

One of the guards pointed a finger at Corelle and roared orders. "Seize her. She will hang for this."

He had made up his mind, and Corelle rolled the dice in desperation. "I did not kill him." Her voice sounded thin and weak, and she felt light-headed. Loss of blood sapped her strength, and she fought against the desire to close her eyes and fall asleep. One mistake now, and she believed she would wake up dead. "He stabbed me. He struck Ingastdrek Sterhel Akh Drek and stabbed me when I tried to intervene. He stabbed me." Had she already said that? She could not recall as her mind turned to fog in cadence with the blood that ran through her hands and over her body. "She screamed and grappled with him, but he stabbed her too. She pulled the knife out and slashed at him. Such a horrible sight. Help me, please." Corelle cried, and her tears were not faked. Agony coursed through her, the wound throbbed, and she struggled to focus on her words.

"A likely story." As the guard spoke, darkness threatened to overcome Corelle.

A woman's voice came from somewhere. "They fought. He struck his wife." To Corelle, the voice sounded distant, and she struggled to remain conscious. "He brought the knife with him. He opened the letters with it. He insulted the dressmaker."

The guards looked around the room. The letters and designs lay scattered across the floor. The servant had done all she could to help, Corelle imagined. The Durfolk woman may not be sad to see the two Qagrue lie dead in the room, but her opinions were the last thing on Corelle's mind, and in a croak, she begged for aid. "Help me, please. I am close to death."

Somebody shouted for a healer. They used a name, but it entered her consciousness, failed to find anywhere to land, and flew out as swift as it had arrived. Corelle felt her heart beat faster than normal, and she gasped for breath. She had concocted a plan to avoid being hanged, but it seemed she had killed herself in the execution of her own plan. How Synna would laugh when she told him. She gazed around and blinked in confusion. "Where am I?"

A shadow crossed before her eyes, bent to her, and spoke in a calm voice. "I am a healer. Let me see that wound." He pulled her hands away from the puncture she had made in her own body. "Nasty. Not fatal, but I must stop this blood loss, or I may be mistaken in that determination."

He turned, spoke in his own language, and one of the guards crouched beside her and pressed his hands hard on her chest. She had struggled to breathe before, and the pressure from the guard made it worse. "Can—not—breathe." Nobody took any notice. The healer barked instructions in his own language. He must be Qagrue, Corelle realised. He might let her die where a Dur man would fight to save her, curse it. She ought to have rejected the woman's offer to make her a dress. Why had she come to this house? She had lost her mind. Corelle closed her eyes and abandoned herself to whatever fates were written for her.

When Corelle opened her eyes again, she lay on a cot in a small room with little furniture and blank walls. Her shoulder screamed at her and burned in agony. When she raised her head, a blood red tunic covered her. She lifted it and gazed beneath. A large bandage had been wrapped around her, and blood seeped through it. She struggled to recall the events and sat upright at the memory but winced as flames of agony burned through her. She needed to leave the Qagrue house at once. Her life hung in the balance while she remained here. Her head swam, and she felt so weak, the temptation to lie back in the bed and sleep threatened to seduce her, but she forced her feet to the floor and sat on the bed, her face contorted against the pain.

At that, the door opened, and a woman's face peered round it. "You are awake. That is good. How do you feel?"

Corelle replied through clenched teeth. "I have never felt better."

The woman laughed. "Drink." She pointed to a pitcher and goblet on a small table beside the bed.

"Where am I?" Corelle poured a goblet of the water and drank it in one swallow. She had not realised how thirsty she had become.

"In the house of Wimstredor Sumbrid Akh Stredor."

"What turned?"

"You do not recall? You were injured in a disagreement. Wimstredor Sumbrid Akh Stredor and his wife are dead. You are to be questioned before you are allowed to leave. If you are allowed to, that is."

Corelle nodded, guarded. "I have already told them the story."

"Do you remember all the details of the incident?"

Corelle cast her mind back as she tried to recall how she had described the so-called fight. "I believe so."

"You must sound more confident if you are to convince them." The woman gave her a cunning smile. She glanced around before she continued. "It is important to recount the same story you told the first time." Her voice became quieter as she spoke again. "You have killed the most senior Qagrue in Ryl, and they will hang you if they learn the truth. Remember; he stabbed you, then her, then she killed him. You must tell it that way."

"Why do you help me?" It puzzled Corelle the woman would take such a risk for a stranger.

The woman smiled, a cold smile that did not reach her eyes. "You killed a vile creature, and there are two fewer of them now, thanks to you. I would not see you hanged for the service you did for Dur today." Her lips tautened. "Would that you could rid us of them all." Then her smile brightened, and she headed for the door. "We will summon the sergeant, and you might be allowed to return to your home."

With the woman gone, Corelle played the scene over in her mind in the order she must describe it. She saw no flaw with the tale—a lie, but a plausible lie, and it would suffice. Indeed, it must suffice if she had already told it once.

Corelle drank two more goblets of the water, still light-headed. Her body trembled, and she guessed she had lost much blood, but she lived and would recover in time. Her body screamed at her to lay down again, since it would be better to rest if she must wait for a time before she could leave, and she gave in to its demands. The desire to be back at the shop with Vamma ate at her. Vamma must be worried by now at how long the consultation for the dress had taken, though Corelle had no idea how long she had been at the house.

The door opened again, and three men entered. One of them headed straight for the bedside while the others lingered near the door. The man who approached stopped at her bedside. "How do you feel?"

"In great pain, but grateful to your healer." She hoped she sounded as thankful as she intended.

He smiled. "Tell me what happened today, if you please."

Corelle tried to sound as weak as possible. "I have already told your men." He must be the superior man in the room, or she had missed her guess.

He nodded, no emotion in his eyes. "That is what they tell me. Please tell me again. I am anxious to detain you no longer than we must."

Cautious and slow, Corelle recounted the tale she had rehearsed in her head. She grimaced often, and paused from time to time with a well-timed clutch at the wound to reinforce the seriousness of her injury.

When she had finished, he stood motionless for a moment. To her relief, he nodded. "That is as I have heard it already. The servants tell me such violent outbursts were not uncommon, and the healer stated both your wound and that of the unfortunate

Ingastdrek Sterhel Akh Drek were deep enough to suggest a man of his strength might have made them. You are small and slight." He stared at her for a time, and she judged it prudent to remain silent. "We will detain you no longer. Please tell my men here your address before you leave. Your things will be returned to you, such as they are. We will deliberate and will inform you of the outcome of those deliberations in due course. I am happy you lived and offer my apologies for all you have been through here today."

She must not reveal the relief that flowed through her. "My thanks." He offered an arm, and she used it to raise herself and sit on the edge of the bed again. Her boots lay nearby, and she slipped her feet into them as he turned for the door.

He stopped. "One more thing." Corelle's heart fluttered in anxiety. Had there been a flaw in her tale? He turned toward her. "We found a fan in your boot." He did not elaborate.

Her mind searched for something to say—how to explain it? She settled for the truth, or a version of it at the least. "I carry it against the warmth of the summer."

"It is fine craftwork. Its maker is talented." He paused, and she sensed he had not yet abandoned the issue of the fan. "It is bitter cold. The winter." He gestured toward the window.

She had made a mistake, and she needed a quick recovery. "A dear friend gave it to me as a gift, and I cannot bear to leave it behind even in the winter." The dice had been rolled, and she hoped she would not roll ones. It had been the only excuse she could come up with.

"I see." He thrust a hand into a pocket and pulled out the fan. He turned it over in his hands and stared at it. He opened the leaves with a clumsy shake, then snapped them closed and handed it to her. "Have a safe journey home." Corelle offered up silent thanks to Wilash. His skill had made the fan undetectable to the scant inspection the Qagrue had given the fan.

The Qagrue left with his men. Soon after, a guard carried in her pack and left it on the bed as she struggled to her feet. She found it difficult to walk, and each step stabbed the wound in her shoulder as if the knife once more cleaved her flesh.

By the time she reached the shop, exhaustion had all but brought her to a standstill. She had stopped for rests many times along the route, and she laboured to breathe as she pushed open the shop door. Blood seeped from her wound again, doubtless from the movement of her shoulder as she staggered along the streets.

Vamma looked up from the counter and ran to her, a horrified expression on her face. Corelle's tunic glistened with her blood, and precious little of its original colour remained. "What has turned?" Vamma took one of Corelle's arms and helped her to a chair.

Corelle gave a short version of events, then begged Vamma to help her up the stairs and into their bed. The exertions of the walk home had drained her. She leaned on her lover as they climbed the stairs. Her mother heard them and came out from the parlour where she had been about some chore, Corelle guessed. Her reaction tore at Corelle's heart, and tears streamed down her mother's face as the two women helped Corelle into the bed.

They brought a bowl of water, and her mother removed the bandages from the wound. She gasped when she saw it but used a damp cloth to clean it. Vamma ran for clean bandages, which Corelle's mother told her were stored in the scullery. Her mother dressed the wound again and urged Corelle to drink some water before she slept. She said she would call a healer the next morning, then left Corelle and Vamma alone.

Vamma sat on the bed beside Corelle and encouraged her to drink some water while she rubbed Corelle's short hair. "You should be more careful. They might have hanged you." She sounded, and looked, furious.

"That they might. I lost my temper, I admit it. But the way he spoke to me, the way he treated her. I could not tolerate it."

Vamma did not reply for some time. "It sounds awful, but it is not your concern. You took a great risk. What if I had lost you?"

"You did not." Corelle guessed only her weakened state had saved her from a slap. She mumbled, anxious to calm Vamma's temper. "I am sorry."

"Sleep now. We will talk more when you are awake." Vamma kissed Corelle's forehead and closed the door behind her as she returned to the shop. Corelle fell asleep before Vamma's footsteps reached the bottom of the stairs.

Corelle did not wake until the next morning. She lay alone in the bed, unsure whether Vamma had slept in the room the previous night. Though she felt improved from the day before, the pain in her shoulder remained intense.

Her mother popped her head around the door. "You are awake. How do you feel?"

"I am sore but otherwise fine."

Her mother appeared agitated and concerned. "That is good. Drink some water It will help your recovery. I will send for a healer. Will you take some food?"

"I am hungry, in truth." Corelle had not eaten since the previous morning, and her body had been through considerable distress in that time. Her mother brought her some bread and cheese and helped her sit up in the bed with the aid of two pillows propped behind her back. Corelle ate the food and drank more water, and some time later Vamma came in to sit on the bed beside her.

Vamma leaned forward to kiss her, then smiled, calmer than yesterday. "Good morning." It felt good to see her. Corelle longed to pull her close and hold her tight, run her hands through her light brown hair, and feel Vamma's hands on her body. In truth, it might be some time before they could be intimate. The wound must be allowed to heal, and Corelle could not risk any aggravation of it that might impair her movement over time. Her intention had been to stab herself in an area where there would be little risk of serious damage, but she had gambled, nonetheless. A calculated risk that had so far kept her from a hangman's noose. So far.

Later in the morning, with her mother's help, Corelle rose from the bed and dressed so she could sit in the parlour with her and tell her the version of events she had told the Qagrue. Her mother must be protected from the horror of the monster her daughter had become and kept from harm if the Qagrue or anybody else happened to question her about the incident. If she believed the same version other people believed, she could not be pressured to lie, or misremember some part of the tale.

A healer arrived and inspected the injury. He closed the wound and advised them to keep it clean and change the bandages often. Because of the area of the body the knife had entered, he doubted any important internal organs would have been impacted and, other than a scar, he saw no reason to suspect she would not make a full recovery. Rest, water, and gradual exercise of the arm were his recommendations.

Once he had left, Corelle picked her way down the stairs and through her father's old office into the shop. Vamma cleaned the floor near the rack of clothes her mother had made. The supply of her mother's work had already diminished to a trickle, and Corelle suspected her mother's interest in the making had waned within a tenday of Corelle's ownership of the shop. Without her, Corelle did not know whether they could sustain the two-tier quality system.

Vamma looked up as Corelle entered. "How do you feel?"

"I feel tired of being asked that question already." Corelle laughed, embarrassed she had complained. "I am fine, I swear. Sore, but I slept well and feel stronger today."

"That is good." Vamma crossed the shop to take Corelle's hands in her own. "We worried about you."

Corelle gave a scornful snort. "It will take more than that bully to finish me. Have no fear."

Vamma kissed her before she replied. "Let us hope you need kill no more."

Corelle doubted Vamma's wish would be granted by the fates, but she remained silent. Two days later, her doubts increased when Denstal came to the shop again.

CORELLE

Vamma spat her fury at Denstal as soon as she saw him. "You are not welcome here."

He marched to the counter as though undeterred by the less than enthusiastic greeting. "Corelle. Are you recovered?"

Corelle sat at her making table. She had returned to as much simple work as she could cope with each day, bored of the bed and the parlour. The wound still hurt, but the simple tasks she undertook each day took no toll on her and distracted her mind from thoughts of the incident and any possible repercussions. The arrival of Denstal, while not unexpected, concerned her both because of the unpleasantness on the last occasion they had met, and because it stirred her anxiety about the implications of her actions. "That I am."

"That is good to hear. What turned? Rumours fly, but I find it best to go direct to the source in such matters."

Vamma made no effort to disguise her animosity. "That is not your business."

He bowed, but Corelle could not tell whether in respect or mockery. "That it is not, but the story fascinates me. When I asked

Corelle to kill this man, she sent me on my way, and I felt grateful to escape with my life. I now hear she had a change of heart and slit his throat. The story intrigues me."

"That is not the way of it." Corelle had no desire to tell Denstal the story, but she had less desire to allow dangerous rumours abroad in the city about her part in the deaths. If those rumours came to Qagrue ears, she might still be hanged. She told Denstal the same story she had told the Qagrue and her mother.

He pursed his lips when she had finished. "I hear his wife slit his throat so clean, it must have been remarkable fortune a woman could make such a stroke heartbeats before she fell dead." He winked at Corelle. "Your secret is safe with me."

"There is no secret." Corelle fought her anger at his belief she had lied to him, even though she had. It could prove dangerous for anybody to think she had not spoken the truth. Words spilled from such mouths could bring the Qagrue to her door.

"That there is not." He gave her a smug smile. "Have you rethought my offer? I still wish you to lead us."

"I have given the matter no thought at all. I do not need to. My answer is unchanged."

"You are not welcome here." Vamma spat the words out again. Corelle could not recall a time when such malice had dripped from Vamma's words.

"Then I will take my leave. I bid you both a good day." He turned and left without another word.

He did not reappear, and no Qagrue came to the shop. Day by day, Corelle's health improved, and she returned to her work. Although she tired early some days, she resumed the commissions she had already accepted. New commissions still came in. It seemed whatever rumours swirled around Ryl about the deaths of the two Qagrue, the shop suffered no ill effects as a result. A pass had gone by since the incident, and Corelle and Vamma hoped they had heard the last of it. They had resumed their physical lovemaking and Corelle had persevered with the exercises recommended by the healer, which had helped her strength to return over the pass. Their life had settled again, and she hoped it would remain that way for some time. If the Qagrue left them alone and Denstal paid them no more attention, nothing now could turn awry for them, she told herself.

A letter arrived from Gaish. Corelle read it aloud to Vamma. He had met somebody, and they seemed happy. His new man went by the name of Takishtah, and they lived somewhere to the east of Steinlund. Corelle smiled, pleased he had found happiness, and stored the letter away, intent on a reply at some point to bring him up to date on all that had turned since he had sailed off for Arkkyd and left her in Tanasttra.

The idea of the tunic and separate skirt cropped up from time to time, and the memory of the leather tunic the villagers had made for Gaish came to her at times, but the demand for her gowns left her no time to do anything other than dream of the concept and vow to revisit it at some future date.

Vamma's stomach now showed visible signs of the child she carried, and a noticeable bump projected before her. She complained she found trousers uncomfortable and turned instead to dresses. Both Corelle and her mother offered to adjust Vamma's trousers, but she seemed more content with dresses.

They had spoken at length about all that would be involved as she carried the child to birth and had involved Corelle's mother in their conversations. On her advice, they had decided to seek out a birthwife who could assist them as the day of delivery came nearer and be on hand to deliver the child on the day itself.

The issue of Corelle's anger, headaches and blurred vision cropped up in the conversations at whiles, but they had not been lucky in their search for a healer who understood matters of the brain in any depth or who could help Corelle. The headaches continued, and her temper tantrums reappeared from time to time.

They learned of a good birthwife who might serve well for the passes until the child appeared, and they arranged to meet her. They left Corelle's mother in charge of the shop and walked to the birthwife's home. They stopped to look in many of the shop windows they passed along the way. Corelle felt they were watched but did not mention her concerns to Vamma. She guessed Denstal would still be interested enough in her to have the shop watched, but it surprised her they would follow her, although she gave no indication she noticed, and did nothing to attempt to throw them off.

The birthwife checked Vamma with care and asked many questions. When she asked about the father, Vamma told her he had died, genuine sadness in her voice. The birthwife said she might be close to the halfway stage. It seemed Vamma could expect some relief from the biliousness that had afflicted her in the early passes, although it might return.

The birthwife assured them the progress of the child seemed normal so far, and Vamma's health appeared to be excellent. She agreed to meet them in three passes but urged them to visit her if anything turned awry at any time. They thanked her for her time, paid her for the visit, and set off for the return trip to the shop.

They had almost reached the shop when they passed an alleyway, and Corelle noticed movement from the corner of her eye. It came from deep in the dark of the alleyway, and she showed no reaction. They walked on several paces, and she heard a boot or shoe scrape on the street behind her. They continued onward with no visible sign Corelle had heard anything untoward, but she spotted a woman across the street who leaned on the wall of a house. As Corelle glanced at her, the woman pushed herself away from the wall and walked away on her side of the street.

Corelle tried to convince herself she had nothing to be concerned about. The person in the alleyway might have gone into the shadow to relieve themselves, and the woman doubtless had business unrelated to them and continued her journey after a rest. As the woman passed opposite an alleyway ahead of Vamma and Corelle, a figure emerged from it. The woman did not glance at the figure, and the figure did not seem to pay the woman any attention. Two coincidences alarmed Corelle. Three coincidences were no longer coincidences, not to someone with Corelle's Guild training.

The person ahead of them wore a cloak with the hood pulled over their head. The wet season had all but ended, and the day, although dry, felt cool, so a cloak did not seem unusual. The person moved in a way Corelle recognised, however, and she felt certain it must be someone from the Guild. No particular stride or movement gave them away; more that they were lithe and carried themselves in an apparent state of readiness, arms relaxed but never far from a belt. Their body seemed attuned to their surroundings as though they listened for any sound out of the ordinary, as Corelle had when she had heard the scrape of footwear behind them.

Corelle stopped outside a shop. She pulled Vamma close as she pointed to a small ornament in the shop's display. Vamma gazed at it, a look of surprise on her face, and Corelle knelt. She fussed with the hem of Vamma's dress below her cloak and slid her fan out of her boot. The Guild member had drawn close now, and Corelle must act.

She straightened and suggested they should go into the shop to look at a chair from the display. Despite Vamma's surprise, Corelle ushered her into the shop and whispered to her to remain inside with the shopkeeper and not come out until she returned.

With no time to check Vamma had understood the instructions, Corelle stepped back into the street and looked left at the person who had emerged from the alleyway. He did not move like a Guild member, and he seemed tall for a Guild man also. Corelle decided he would be easier to deal with, so she turned and strode toward him. He stopped and stared at her.

When she reached him, she hissed, "Why do you follow us?"

His mouth opened to reply, but his eyes flicked behind her. Corelle heard the lighter footfalls of the other and realised they must have quickened their pace as she had approached the other. She turned so the two were on either side of her and pressed her back to the wall to make herself as small a target as possible if she must take them on together.

To her surprise, the cloaked figure brushed past her, produced a dagger they thrust upward under the other's chin, and drove it up into his head. Blood spurted from his mouth and from beneath his chin as his eyes glazed over. The cloaked figure pulled the dagger out as the man collapsed to the street.

Corelle prepared to strike, but the figure pulled the hood back from its head. Denstal. Corelle did not relax as he turned to face her. She kept her voice quiet as she checked the street for anybody who might have observed. "What turns here?" Nobody else could be seen on the street, but as soon as somebody came along, the man who lay in a pool of his own blood would be difficult for them to miss.

"This vermin worked with us, but he sold you to the Qagrue. He told the Qagrue who you are and all you wrought in Ort. I wish I had learned this before he approached them."

"How did he find out who I am? He did not seem like a member of the Guild you and I once served. He did not move with the stealth we were taught, and he did not seem prepared for your attack."

"There are no secrets in the Guild. You know this. We keep nothing from any who ask us, and you have been in our conversations of late."

"Why kill him here, on the street where anybody might see?" She could not work out what gnawed at her mind, but instinct told her something had turned awry.

"He planned to mislead you into going to the Qagrue with him with a tale they had completed their deliberations in the matter of the death of Wimstredor Sumbrid Akh Stredor and his wife. There you would have been slain and your body dropped into the Northern Ocean in the dead of night." Corelle still felt uneasy. His words sounded plausible, but they did not ring true, and she could not decide why.

"More urgent news I bring. I am sorry to tell you the Qagrue went to your shop this morning. They were seen inside and have laid waste to the goods and fixtures."

The news stopped Corelle's blood in her veins and chilled her to the heart. "My mother?"

"I know not."

Corelle pushed him to one side and ran toward the shop as she called for Vamma. She tugged the door open and called for Vamma again. The shopkeeper appeared from a rear door, and behind him Corelle saw Vamma peer out, anxiety on her face. "Vamma, come with me. We must hurry. The Qagrue have been to the shop this morning."

Vamma had come out from the rear of the shop and walked toward Corelle, but she stopped at the words and raised a hand to her mouth. "What?"

"Come, we must hurry." Corelle extended a hand toward Vamma to encourage her to move faster.

Vamma took her hand, and Corelle pulled her out of the shop. Vamma glanced up the street and gasped. "There is a man on the ground surrounded by blood. What has turned?"

"There is no time for that now. I will tell you later. We must hurry."

Between the two of them, they could not walk as fast as Corelle desired, Vamma hampered by the discomfort of the child in her stomach, and Corelle by the pain from her wound, which still ached when she tried to walk at speed. It took longer than Corelle would have liked before they reached the shop. A crowd of people in the street loitered outside, and the door stood open. Corelle pushed past the onlookers and entered the shop.

A group of people near the counter were bent over Corelle's mother, who lay on the floor in a pool of blood. Panic swept over Corelle, and she pushed and pulled people out of the way to reach her mother. A vicious gash had opened her mother's stomach, a blow from a sword, Corelle thought. Blood covered her, her flesh had turned a dirty white colour, and her eyes were closed.

Corelle reached for her mother's neck to feel for a pulsing but found none. Her mind searched for something she could do, but nothing of any value came to her. "Mother." Corelle sobbed, her heart shattered in her breast. "Mother." Vamma laid a hand on top of her own, and Corelle turned to her. "She has gone." Tears gushed from Vamma's eyes. Corelle tilted her head back and screamed. All her pain and grief poured from her lips in that anguished cry.

"Corelle." Vamma's plaintive voice cut through her anger. "Who did this? Who could do this to an old woman?"

"The Qagrue." Corelle's heart filled with hatred. She stood and turned to face the stunned crowd. "Did anybody see anything?" Nobody had, it seemed. Somebody had come past and found the door open and her mother on the floor. The crowd had gathered as word spread. Nobody had seen the people who had killed Corelle's mother. Nobody could describe them so she could track them down and carve them into pieces by way of vengeance. "Please leave." They were no use to her. Nobody moved, and she screeched with all the breath in her lungs. "Get out."

The crowd dispersed. They left the shop in small groups and muttered inaudible comments to one another about the horror that had unfolded here. As the shop emptied, Corelle noticed the dresses her mother had spent so much time and skill on lay strewn about the floor. The making table had been tipped over and Corelle's tools lay scattered around. As the last of the people passed through the door, she saw Denstal in the doorway, and he gazed in apparent horror on the body of Corelle's mother.

He breathed words, but they were chaff in the wind. "I am so sorry." The colour had drained from his face, and he stood motionless as he surveyed the terrible scene.

"They killed her. They killed my mother. She never hurt another person, nor an animal, in her entire life, and they killed her." Vamma's arms slid around Corelle's waist, and she laid her head on the back of Corelle's shoulder. Her tearful convulsions shook Corelle and mingled with the spasms of her own rage. "I will avenge her. I will kill every one of them,"

Vamma sighed into her ear. "Corelle, that is not possible. You will meet your ruin."

"I do not care." Corelle balled her fists against her thighs. "I will have my revenge." She glanced up at Denstal again. "Can you identify the ones who did this?"

He shook his head. "I doubt it, but I will make enquiries. Word came to my ears from one of our couriers who passed the shop, as it turned."

Corelle muttered grim words, her rage in each one. "They will pay. Whoever killed her will wish they had never come to Ryl when I find them."

Denstal nodded. "You may count on us for any help we can provide. Our objectives are aligned in this regard. I am sorry about your mother." Corelle said nothing in response. "I will arrange for a courier to be made available to you. You may send a message to me any time you have need of our help."

Vamma seemed the only one focused on the practical details. "We must arrange a Pyre."

Corelle turned and embraced her. Vamma looked tired and stressed, and Corelle whispered, "You should lie down and rest."

"A Pyre must be arranged." Determination flashed in Vamma's eyes.

"Then I will arrange it. You are with child and must rest." She ushered Vamma out of the rear door of the shop and up the stairs.

When she turned, Denstal had not left. "She is with child?"

"That she is." Corelle could not hide her disappointment he had heard the exchange, although she could not say why. "Excuse me, I must arrange a Pyre for my mother."

"I understand. I will leave you to your grief." He turned and strode away.

Corelle wandered, morose and tearful, to the nearest business that arranged Pyres. Together, they organised the Pyre, and four men accompanied her back to the shop. They took her mother's body away and promised she would be ready for her Pyre the following day. Exhausted and drained, Corelle dragged herself up the stairs, step by weary step. Vamma lay asleep in their bed and Corelle crawled in beside her.

In her nightmare, her mother lay on the deck of a ship, her stomach gashed open, and her intestines spilled from her. When she stood, the top half of her body toppled forward and landed on the deck with an ugly splat. Corelle urged her mother to come to her. The upper half of her mother crawled toward her while her legs remained rooted to the spot. Vamma appeared from behind her mother's legs, her stomach huge and distended.

Her mother's torso had reached Corelle's feet, and her frail hands gripped Corelle's ankles as Vamma's stomach burst open. Arella fell to the deck from Vamma's body, her own body swollen in the same way, and she stood as Corelle's mother began to climb up Corelle's legs. Arella's stomach burst open also, and Deineike fell out. Deineike pounced on Corelle's mother's body and devoured the intestines that dragged behind her across the deck.

Corelle screamed, and the four other women stared at her before they cried aloud in unison. "I love you." A blue giant fell onto the ship. It had Styrrach's face, and it laughed as it lay in the water nearby and watched Vamma, Deineike, Arella, and Corelle's mother as they drowned. Corelle looked down and saw a large sword protrude from her own stomach. It had passed right through her from behind, shaped like a man's member.

She screamed again, and Vamma shook her awake. "You have had a bad dream my love." Vamma wrapped her arms about Corelle. A grey day had dawned outside the window. Night had passed, but clouds and rain had replaced it. The two women lay close for some time but said nothing. The morning could not be ignored; they must rise and head to Corelle's mother's Pyre.

Tears spilled from their eyes as they dressed and ate some bread. They made their way to the small grassy area where Pyres took place in that part of the city. Corelle's mother lay among the wood stacked in neat rows, her stomach covered by a grey shawl. The sight of her body, her face white and drawn, proved too much for Corelle, who collapsed to the ground despite Vamma's attempt to catch her. Two men rushed forward to help her as she sobbed in desperation on the wet grass. Corelle swatted their hands away as they reached down toward her, and she heard Vamma say something she could not catch.

Corelle's legs had failed her, and she could not rise. Vamma stood nearby, no doubt consumed by grief in her own way. Nobody moved for a time, and Corelle's tears mingled with the raindrops. They ran down her face onto her tunic and disappeared as they were absorbed into the rain-soaked cloth, forever trapped in the fibre of the tunic. After some time, another man approached her. "Will someone say a Sending?"

What could Corelle say about her own mother? For too many years, she had not come home to see her or her father and had become a monster her mother would not recognise as her own daughter. None of those things were suitable for the Sending of a kind woman whose dedication to her husband ran to endless hours every day in the shop, even as she found the time to care for a daughter who went her own way in life. Her mother always put a meal on the table at the end of each day and would often sit for hours in the parlour afterward as she completed some piece of making on another garment for those wealthy folk who knew nothing of the way she worked and provided for her family.

Corelle reached up a hand and one of the men helped her to her feet. Nobody other than Corelle and Vamma had come to the Pyre. None of the people whose gowns and fancy coats, whose trousers and shawls were made by her mother's hand were there to farewell her. None of the children to whom she had given sweet treats as they ran into the shop from the street came. The girl with whom Corelle had wanted an inappropriate friendship did not come.

Her mother had had no fancy carriages or processions, as Deineike had. The only people at the Pyre were a daughter who did not deserve such a fine mother and a woman who had known her for so few passes but had told her she loved her more in that time than her own daughter had in her entire life.

"There is little to say." Corelle choked through her tears. "As fine a woman as any that have lived, and a better one than I can ever aspire to be. I failed her, and she lost her life because of me and knew nothing of why. It is unfair." She paused, unable to continue for a time as her emotions overwhelmed her. "I send my mother. Few called her friend, and most did not have the character to be able to do so." She recalled some of the words she had said at Raolos's Sending. "Forgive me, Mother. I love you. I am sorry." She took two torches and passed one to Vamma. Together they thrust the torches into the wood, which crackled and spluttered, reluctant to burst into flame in the persistent rain.

They stood back and watched the slow spread of the flames until they had climbed over the wood to reach that which they most desired—human flesh. The fire consumed Corelle's mother, and it consumed a part of Corelle for ever as it did so.

CHAPTER 34
VAMMA

Vamma, her long hair sprawled around her face, soaked and plastered to her neck, her cheeks, her forehead, listened to Corelle say the Sending. Devastation tore her apart, not only for the loss of Lembell, but for the loss of something she saw in Corelle as her lover collapsed to the grass, then said such a mournful Sending for her mother.

Corelle's angry outbursts had become commonplace, and they concerned Vamma. The murder of Lembell seemed certain to fill her with ferocious rage and a desire for vengeance, a fire Vamma feared could not be extinguished. Corelle needed her now, more than ever. Vamma must stay and do all she could to help Corelle. She loved her and could not imagine her life would ever be complete from this day until she went wherever she travelled to afterward if she did not have Corelle by her side. Nonetheless, Vamma had a child to think of now, and she could not sit by and watch Corelle self-destruct or be killed by the Qagrue as she quested for a vengeance, a thirst that could never be slaked.

As the flames consumed Lembell, Vamma believed one day she and Corelle would be sundered. Either the injuries sustained in a lifetime of violence would claim her as they had Deineike, or Corelle would leave her. Corelle searched for vengeance, relentless and determined in its pursuit, and a time would come when she would draw a line Vamma would not cross. At that time, Corelle would go on alone and abandon Vamma, who knew in her heart she would not follow.

They trudged back to the shop, miserable beyond words, for no words could lift the pall of dejection from either of them. They locked the shop door, stepped through the chaos of the floor, and climbed the stairs. Vamma could not glance at the blood stain where Lembell's life had been stolen from her. It would need to be cleaned, she guessed, but not today. They sat before the fire Vamma lit, and steam rose from their saturated clothes as the warmth of the fire spread around the two women. Vamma stared into the fire and imagined she could see Lembell's body as the flames licked at it like a child will lick its lips after a sweet treat. She shook the vision from her head, and water from her still-wet hair flicked around the parlour.

The silence must be broken before it crushed them beneath the weight of the tragedy that had spawned it. "What will you do with the shop?" Corelle shrugged and said nothing. "You cannot leave it as it is, my love. You have two commissions to complete even if you take no others."

"I imagine I will sell it, as you planned to sell Raolos's trade house."

"Where will we go afterward? We will have the child to—"

"I know not, Vamma. Let us address this another time. Please."

"I am sorry." Vamma sniffed, misery piled on misery. Her attempt at mundane conversation had only served to irritate Corelle.

"Do not be. You have the right of it, decisions must be made. Not tonight though. Not tonight."

They again sat in silence for a time. Corelle reached forward and threw a fresh piece of wood onto the fire. Vamma rubbed a hand along Corelle's forearm. "Why not bring your work up here and work on it in front of the fire for a time? I will prepare some food for us."

Corelle sat in her chair for a moment, then pulled herself to her feet and went down the stairs. Vamma busied herself with the preparation of a broth. She chopped up vegetables and tubers, seasoned them with herbs, and diced some meat to add into the pot. Behind her, Corelle came back up the stairs and settled in the chair again. When Vamma glanced over her shoulder, Corelle had set a lantern on a table she had pulled next to her chair. She had a gown on her lap as her hands flitted to and fro with a needle. It fascinated Vamma to watch Corelle create her designs, how simple pieces of cloth came together to form the gown she had already created in her mind.

Vamma hung the pot over the fire to heat up and sat down to watch Corelle. The concentration on the face of this skilful dress-maker must be seen to be believed. As the needle skipped through the cloth, Vamma could not grasp how Corelle knew which piece of cloth must be sewn to which. It might be easy enough to make a crude pair of trousers or a tunic, even a simple dress, but the gowns Corelle created were so complex in their design and creation, her ability left Vamma awestruck.

Corelle put aside her work once Vamma ladled out two bowls of the broth and handed her one bowl and a spoon. She thanked her as she blew on the broth and sent the steam that rose from it across the table like a wind disperses a morning mist. They ate a few mouthfuls before Corelle spoke. "I am sorry about earlier. I should not have snapped."

Vamma laid a hand on Corelle's arm in reassurance. "You did not snap. I pestered you."

"You will do so." Corelle managed a half-hearted smile. "In the bedroom most of all."

"It would be a shame to waste this broth." Vamma tried to sound playful. She felt guilty she had introduced joviality into the room so soon after the Pyre.

"That it would." Corelle returned to the broth, and when they were done, Vamma scooped up both bowls and spoons, then washed them in the small basin in the corner of the room with some water she heated on the fire. They had eaten less than half the broth, and they could reheat it tomorrow for their evening meal, she reasoned.

Corelle returned to her work, and Vamma drifted off to sleep in the warmth of the chair. When she woke, darkness had fallen outside, but Corelle still worked by the light of the lantern. Vamma stretched her arms into the air. "I will go to bed."

"I will join you soon." Corelle looked up as Vamma kissed her.

Vamma crawled into the bed alone. She hoped Corelle would come to bed soon. She must be exhausted by the trials of the day, but once she became focused on her work, it could be hard to stop her.

Corelle slid into the bed beside her and woke her. Vamma turned and slid her arms around the woman she loved and the sobs that tore Corelle apart squeezed at her own heart. She kissed the nape of Corelle's neck. "Goodnight, my love."

Corelle's tears continued, and Vamma could not keep her eyes open. Heartbeats before she fell asleep again, she heard Corelle whisper, "Goodnight." Vamma smiled even as she fell asleep

CHAPTER 35
CORELLE

When they woke, they lay for some time in the bed together and made insignificant conversation. Corelle's mind screamed thoughts of vengeance, but she must also take care of Vamma. The child would arrive in time, and both Vamma and the newborn would have need of her. Her mother must be avenged, however, and she would do all she could to bring that vengeance about.

When they rose, Vamma prepared a simple meal to start their day. Corelle watched as Vamma pulled the meal together, bread, cheese and some dried meat she had found in a local shop. Corelle must keep Vamma safe; that must be her priority. She yearned to kill also, to find those responsible for the death of her mother and leave their blood in the streets, to watch as it flowed into the culverts that led to the ocean. Until her mother had been avenged, she would not be satisfied.

Vamma frowned at her. "What is on your mind?"

Corelle's face must have betrayed her, she guessed. "You. I cannot fathom a way to keep you safe now."

"I am in no danger, am I?"

"That you are. They came to the shop in search of me, but did not capture or kill me. They will be back, and that will place you in danger also."

Vamma sat silent and ponderous. "How much coin do we have?"

Corelle did not have an exact answer, so she guessed. "Around three hundred regals."

"We could move into a different house for a time while you finish the commissions. After that, we could leave Ryl. We could leave Dur if we wanted to."

"Leave for where?"

"Anywhere, my love, provided we are together, and we are safe. You have discovered a host of new lands. One of them might suit us."

"You would need to sail if we were to reach those lands."

Vamma's face creased in concentration. "Hmm. A good point I had failed to consider. What lies to the west of Ryl?"

"Sea, then Malkartas." Vamma's thoughts amused Corelle, and a smile fought through the mask of her misery.

"Wipe that grin from your face." Vamma had a twinkle in her eyes in spite of her stern words. "What lies to the east?"

"The Eastlands, and beyond them Steinlund."

"Is there a land crossing to Steinlund?"

"That there is. Dur is connected to Steinlund, to the south, at the least. Mayhap the entire length of Dur, though I confess I do not know for certain." The discussion about Steinlund reminded Corelle of Gaish, and she told herself she must answer his letter soon. "Do you know they have an animal there called the yelfret that births its young, then climbs a tree and throws itself to its death?"

"We have this animal in the Eastlands, although we call it the necrel."

Corelle could not believe the animal could be found in Dur, and she had never heard of it. "You tease me. This animal does not exist in Dur. I have never heard of it."

Vamma wore a curious look. "You have not? It may be native to the Eastlands."

"Why would it exist in the Eastlands, yet nobody in the west has heard of it?"

Vamma snorted. "Because you have not heard of it does not imply that none have. You are everything to me, but you are only one person to the rest of the Duchy."

The conversation had strayed far from its origin, but the animal puzzled Corelle. "The river might keep it to the east if it cannot swim."

Vamma raised her eyebrows and puckered her lips. "You could be right. That would explain why it is not seen west of the Alc. It also suggests Steinlund is accessible from Dur by land."

"That it does. Now we have returned to the matter at hand, I would be prepared to consider a move to Steinlund, but I cannot leave Dur without some vengeance for my mother."

"That vengeance might cost your life."

"If that is the fate written for me, so be it." Corelle's bloodlust must be sated. Whoever had killed her mother could not be allowed to live.

Vamma studied her face for a time and appeared not to like what she found there. "I waited three years, certain you would not return, yet here you are. We have a child on the way, and we are together once more. You cannot leave me again. I could not stand it, not now."

Vamma had neglected to mention that in the three years she had waited, she had married Raolos, and the child under discussion had been fathered by him. She played the best hand she had in the circumstances, Corelle reasoned. "We need make no decision at this moment. I would prefer to finish the two commissions, at the least. Once they are completed, we can return to the idea." The bluff might buy time for her to acquire some information that might point to the person who had slain her mother in such a brutal manner.

Vamma smiled. "What is scribed, must be. If you intend to work on the dress this morning, I will clean up the shop."

Corelle had made good progress on the first of the dresses last night and agreed she should work on it again this morning. She picked up her work and carried it down to her table in the shop. She focused on her work, and Vamma appeared with a pail of water and some cloths to set to work on the dried blood on the floor of the shop. Vamma rubbed at the blood with such fury, sweat formed on her brow, but Corelle did not watch for more than a heartbeat. It saddened her to see her mother's blood on the floor, and it ignited the fire of her rage also. She returned to her work as Vamma rubbed at the bloodstain, the sounds of water being squeezed from the cloth interspersed with grunts of effort as she worked.

"There." Vamma's voice interrupted Corelle. She looked up at Vamma, who knelt on the floor and wiped at her forehead with the back of a hand. Vamma sat backward onto her heels and smiled at Corelle as though she sought an opinion on the result of her labours. She had piled her hair into a bun earlier, but strands of it had escaped and hung about her head and face, and as she blew one of them away from an eye, her mouth crooked, she looked wonderful; homely yet beautiful.

The light through the window shimmered in the water stain that had replaced the blood. Corelle could not be certain all the blood had been removed until the floor dried, but she wished to compliment Vamma on her efforts. "The floor looks almost as good as you." She blew Vamma a kiss.

Vamma rose from her haunches and shuffled across the shop on her knees, then slid her arms around Corelle's waist and kissed her. Corelle brushed some of the stray hairs back from Vamma's face and gazed into her eyes. Could she ever love Vamma? As well as the excitement Vamma brought to their bed, she had a kind heart. Such a fine woman, easy company and wise; not unlike Deineike in many respects, Corelle believed.

Vamma interrupted her thoughts. "What?"

"Are we finished here? Shall we go upstairs?" Corelle deflected, unprepared to share the thoughts that had occupied her.

Vamma slapped Corelle's thigh. "You are insatiable."

"For you I am." Corelle nuzzled Vamma's neck.

At that moment, a knock on the shop door drew their attention. A Qagrue stood outside the locked door. Corelle tensed at the sight of him, and Vamma turned to look at her, concern in her eyes.

Corelle had left her fan upstairs. She had expected no visitors with the shop in disarray, closed and locked, and had no shoes on her feet. Vamma's whisper carried all her uncertainty. "What could he want?"

The man stared through the glass of the door at them. They could not pretend to be away from home. Corelle eased Vamma away and crossed to the door. "What is it?"

The man shouted through the glass. "Are you Corelle?"

"Why do you wish to know?" His braided tunic marked him as some higher ranked man in the Qagrue organisation. Two others in plainer tunics stood behind him, silent and respectful. A sorry turn, she thought, to be confronted by three of them while unarmed.

"I have some information I must discuss with you."

Corelle tutted. She needed her blade, so she lied. "The key is upstairs. I will return in a moment."

He nodded and turned to the other two men. Corelle ran upstairs, retrieved her fan from her boot, and called to Vamma from the top of the stairs. Vamma's head peered around the doorway. Corelle whispered for her to come upstairs and take shelter in the parlour.

"That I will not. I will hear what they have to say."

Corelle exhaled in frustration. Vamma could be stubborn, but she had little time to argue while the men waited outside the shop, so she hurried down the stairs again, the fan in her belt behind her back. She pretended to walk into the counter in her haste and slipped the key into her hand as she bent to rub at her knee with a grimace of fake pain, then limped to the door and unlocked it. "Come in." She returned to the counter so it stood between her and the men.

To her surprise, only the one with the braided tunic entered the shop. He walked in, then stopped as his gaze took in the devastation. When he turned to Corelle again, he wore shocked surprise on his face. "What happened here?"

"You should know, of all people." Corelle's instincts urged her to leap the counter and slit his throat before his men could intervene. With him dead, the other two should be simple enough to kill, some vengeance for her mother. They would need to leave Dur without delay, of course, or they would be hanged.

His words cut through her thoughts, and he frowned as he replied. "What do you mean by these words?" He spoke Dur well but with a clear southern accent.

"Your men did this." Corelle swept her arm about the shop. "They destroyed a lifetime of my family's work and murdered my mother into the bargain."

His frown intensified. "Why would we do this?"

Corelle could no longer maintain the veneer of politeness. "For the same reasons you do everything here. This is not your land; it is ours by birthright. Return to Qagrue and leave us to our own ways. You have no right to be here."

He bristled and stood up straight and proud. "We were invited here by one of your own."

She blew a contemptuous breath through her lips. "The man you speak of is filth. If he entered this shop behind you, I would cut him to pieces where he stood. Krage..." She stopped, concerned she had gone too far. The mere thought of Krage had riled her beyond control.

He waited a moment before he replied. "It has not been our way to interfere with Dur businesses. We act with violence against those who oppose us, nothing more."

"Then you admit you did this in revenge for the death of that woman and her husband?"

"You refer to Wimstredor Sumbrid Akh Stredor and his wife?" Corelle nodded in confirmation. "Then you are wrong in your assumption. I have come here to tell you our deliberations have concluded, and you are no longer implicated in their deaths." As Corelle's jaw dropped, his face softened. "His staff all confirm he had a history of violence. We have heard stories of improper behaviour from one of such high rank. He attacked you and his wife as you said, and she killed him. Or you did. It matters not; he earned his fate."

CORELLE

orelle struggled to understand him. Had she misheard? Had they decided she had not killed the man, after all else? Why then… "Then why did you destroy my shop? Why did you kill my mother?" The words flowed out from her thoughts. What he had said confused her, and she had no more patience for the careful selection of her words.

"I do not believe we did, but I assure you I will make full enquiries. If one of our soldiers has killed your mother, he will be hanged. We will fight if provoked, but we do not support the cold-blooded murder of an old woman. You may kick the stool from beneath the killer's feet, you have my word." Corelle glanced at Vamma, who held her hands to her mouth, eyes wide. "We would not have ordered any reprisal before we reached a decision, regardless." His surprise at the accusation seemed genuine. "Under no"—he hesitated, as though he searched for the correct word—"circumstances would we order reprisals against one whom our deliberation had found to be innocent of any offence."

For some perverse reason, although Corelle had heard all he had said, her mind nibbled at the unfamiliar word, "soldiers."

What did the word mean? She shook it from her. "What turned here then? Who killed my mother?"

He shrugged an apology. "I cannot tell you. Do you have any jealousy from a competitor in your field?"

"None I am aware of." Corelle's mind chased multiple thoughts, all in circles, like a dog that chases its tail. It astounded her to think the Qagrue might not have killed her mother.

"Ingastdrek Sterhel Akh Drek commissioned you to make a dress for her, is this correct?"

"That she did."

He rubbed his chin. "We know not all Durfolk admire us. We hear reports some businesses that worked for us have encountered some resentment from other Durfolk. Might such a motive be behind the attack?"

It was impossible to believe Durfolk would commit such an act of terrible violence. Another garment maker might be jealous of the business her designs won in place of their own, but they would never stoop to murder. Nobody even knew she had agreed to create a dress for the Qagrue woman, after all else.

Nobody except Denstal. She pushed the thought from her head. He had nothing to be resentful over. Quite the opposite; he had been delighted Corelle had killed the two Qagrue, and he had attempted to recruit Corelle to do the job for him after all else. Despite her refusal, the fates had been written in such a way, she had, by accident, done the exact thing he wanted from her. Denstal had said the man he had killed mere moments before Corelle discovered her mother's murder had worked with the Qagrue to betray her, so she described the dead man to the Qagrue who stood in her shop.

The Qagrue rubbed his chin, deep in thought. "Do you know this man's name?"

"That I do not. I met him but the once."

He sighed. "I will make my enquiries. If I uncover any information, I will let you know. I am sorry about your mother. That is something that must have been horrible to see, and if we can prove who did such a despicable thing, we will hang them, I assure you. My name is Karaftaraluq Sumbrid Akh Aluq. Please let me know if there is any way I can be of assistance."

He extended a hand, and Corelle shook it, unable to unravel all she had heard. When he had entered the shop, she had been prepared to kill him. Now she shook hands with him and hoped he could find some information that would help her to identify her mother's killer. He turned and left, and his two companions followed him.

Vamma knitted her brow in confusion. "I am baffled. This whole episode makes no sense. Who killed Lembell, if not the Qagrue?"

In her mind, Corelle replayed the incident when Denstal had killed the other man. She wondered what the man had been about to say when he saw Denstal. The woman from across the road—another thorn in Corelle's thumb. Did she play some role in the meeting or had she been there by coincidence? She might have moved as some signal to the man or to Denstal, but to signal what? If the man had been in the Guild, he had not been well trained. Little wonder Denstal had wanted Corelle to lead them, if this man represented the killers he now recruited and trained. Unless, of course, the man had tried to get a message to her, anxious to be seen and heard in advance so she would not kill him. And what if that message differed from the one Denstal had alleged?

All Corelle's thoughts pointed to Denstal, although the argument proved difficult to accept. He had tried to get her to lead the reformed Guild on at least three occasions. Why would he turn on her, and why would he kill her mother? Such unnecessary cruelty would be beneath any Guild member she had ever met while she had belonged. Denstal must have known she would kill him if she ever found out.

Her mind could not assemble the thoughts into any form that provided an answer, so she locked the shop door and took Vamma up to the parlour, where she let her confused thoughts tumble out, hopeful Vamma could organise them better than her.

Breathless with confusion and anger, Corelle finished her mangled tale. Vamma sat in her chair and stared into the fireplace. The cold, unreceptive charred wood from last night seemed as unpalatable as the idea Denstal had killed Corelle's mother after his attempts to persuade her to lead his pointless efforts to strike back at the Qagrue. When Vamma looked up, the fire in her eyes had grown hot enough to ignite the wood that remained in the fireplace, and she growled in anger. "He did it. I should have let you kill him. He has betrayed us and killed your mother."

"Why would he do such a thing?"

"Why he would do it, I cannot say. He tried to blame the Qagrue, doubtless in the hope you would go on a rampage against them and kill as many as you could before they cut you down, as they must at some point. That has been his wish from the first time I met him. I did not like him then. I despise him now."

Corelle did not want to believe Denstal would use her in such a cruel way. If he had killed her mother, there would be revenge. His ruin would be assured if he lay behind it. "Tomorrow, I will find us a house to move to. I fear this tale is not complete, and I want to ensure you are safe."

Corelle brought her work up to the parlour while Vamma lit the fire. Their moods had turned colder than the chill of the day, and Corelle focused on the dress to keep thoughts of vengeance and hatred from her mind. Deep into the night, she finished the dress and set it aside with care. Vamma had fallen asleep in her chair, so Corelle woke her and helped her wander to the bed.

The next day, Corelle set out early to find somewhere for them to move to. The husband of one of the shop's oldest customers owned several houses he rented to workers who travelled to Ryl to work for him, and she decided she would start with him since she already knew him.

She crossed the street, then re-crossed it and walked away from the customer's house. At the next corner, she crossed the street again and turned to walk in the direction of her destination. As she did so, she spotted a man who followed her. He glanced at her for a heartbeat before he entered the doorway of a shop that had not yet opened at this hour. Corelle stopped and studied his reflection in the window of a shop on her side of the street. The short, wiry man wore dull, unremarkable clothes. He had his back to her as he peered into the shop, but even though he had been good enough to track her this far, his eyes betrayed him; he used the shop door glass to watch her. Corelle hurried on and glanced into shop windows but did not see him reflected across the street. At each street corner she took random turns but took care to do nothing that might indicate she had noticed him. Even with Guild training, he would see nothing unusual in the pattern of her journey, as he did not know her destination.

Ahead of her stood one of the largest stores in the quarter, a store that sold expensive furniture to those with extreme wealth. It had a large glass front in which the owner liked to display his wares; well-made items that cost more coin than most Rylfolk would earn in a year, and she saw her pursuer reflected in the window. He had fallen some way back on the other side of the street. Corelle admired both his training and his skill. Few without the same training would have spotted him, even on the almost empty streets of the early morning.

To what end did he follow her? He might be bent on her ruin, although it seemed more likely he acted on Denstal's orders to check where she went and who she spoke to. If presented with a challenge, would the man abandon the pursuit or gamble she had not noticed him? To test his resolve, she headed for the Pyre ground from which her mother had been sent three days before, an open grassy space that a person would have little reason to visit unless they attended a Pyre.

When she reached the Pyre ground, Corelle walked across it without hesitation until she reached the plinth, where she stopped. A casual observer who knew her mother's Pyre had taken place on that plinth mere days before might reason she had gone there in some remembrance of her mother. She bowed her head as though out of respect and swivelled her eyes as far to one side as she could. He leaned on a wall across the road. He would be exposed if he crossed the Pyre ground, where he could find no cover other than the waist-high plinth. Would he follow, or abandon the pursuit?

Her ploy left him further away than he would have liked, and Corelle saw an advantage. He glanced away—standard behaviour; it did not pay to stand anywhere and stare at one's mark. As soon as he did so, she turned and ran. Corelle knew Ryl, and he might not. She ran across the far side of the ground. A street ran around it, so it resembled a square, with houses along each side and streets that led away.

She turned into one of the streets. The second house had a low hedge and she jumped over it, lay flat on her stomach in the garden, and hoped the owners were not at home. She strained to hear all the noises around her, and she caught the sound of footsteps as they hurried along the street, then slowed as they reached the corner. She imagined he peered around the corner, and now he no longer saw her, he might be confused. He must know now he had been seen, and his best move would be to abandon the pursuit and return to Denstal with the bad news.

Some Guild members disliked failure so much, they might take an unnecessary risk here and there. Arella, for example, while cautious and meticulous in all other regards, often told her marks her real name. With Corelle, all actions were weighted in favour of a positive outcome. She would have abandoned the pursuit in these circumstances and tried again another day. The man must know

Vamma remained at the shop, and Corelle would be sure to return. He could pick her up again there or wait until Vamma came out. Vamma would be a simpler mark to follow.

On the other hand, it hurt to admit failure. Corelle believed a successful assassin must be prepared to admit defeat and walk away. One's pride became embroiled in decisions it ought to play no part in otherwise. With a Guildmeister like Styrrach, it had never been easy to confess failure. It might mean death if Styrrach decided to shroud the member. It always led to humiliation. It seemed the old phrase had the right of it. Tricks easy to learn are difficult to unlearn. The footsteps crept down the street, slow and cautious.

His decision disappointed Corelle. He had been good until this moment, but now he continued the pursuit, even though he must know he had been seen. She could have run into any of the houses in the first half of the street to hide for a time. More conceivable, she lay in wait to ambush him. He had made a mistake, and she intended it to be one he would pay a high price for.

"Corelle, stop this game. I know you are nearby. Let us talk."

He had played another hand that disappointed Corelle. He gambled she lay hidden and would reveal herself to him, misled by his apparent friendship. A low hand, in her opinion. He would doubtless have his dagger drawn. Had he been authorised to kill her? Corelle must reveal herself to learn the answer to that question.

He continued along the street and passed within two paces of her, but she did not move. "All I ask is for you to tell me what you are about, and reassure me the two of you are safe. We know the Qagrue visited you yesterday. We wish to be sure you are both in no danger."

He had lied. They could have come to the shop to ask that question, but they had not. He had been a good tracker, but he must be simple if he believed these childlike lies would lure her from her refuge. She crawled forward until she could see him. He had his back toward her as he gazed around. If he looked back now, he might see her. She crouched low, then jumped the hedge, fan in hand.

He must have heard her jump or land, and he half-turned, but she had her blade at his throat before he could react to her presence. He did not have his own dagger in his hand. Another mistake. She hissed into his ear. "Tell me about the man Denstal killed three days ago."

He gulped as though afraid. "I cannot. I did not know he had killed anyone."

She could not judge whether he spoke the truth. "You served with Denstal in Torric?"

"That I did."

She imagined he would be loyal to Denstal. His face seemed familiar, and she reasoned she may have seen him at Raolos's house in Ort when she had killed Sisnop and Gillar. "He killed this man and said he had sold me to the Qagrue. He told me the Qagrue had destroyed my shop and killed my mother."

Something flashed across his eyes, something less than honesty. "Now I know the man you mean. He had indeed been bought by the Qagrue, and had been for some time, it turns."

"You wish to know where I am headed, you say?"

"That I do. We wish you to remain safe. We know the Qagrue visited you yesterday and we imagine they threatened you."

"That they did not. In fact, they claim they had nothing to do with the death of my mother."

He spat on the street. "Those vermin will tell any tale to retain their control over our land."

"Denstal would not lie to me, would he?"

"That he would not." He gave his head several vigorous shakes as if to reinforce his assertion. "We work for the good of Dur."

"So he says. He has asked me to lead you more than once."

"I know this. He would be delighted to have you join us. We all would."

She guessed she would learn no more from the man, and she wished to continue about her business this morning. She sweetened her voice and gave him a warm smile. "Will you give Denstal a message from me please?"

"I would be happy to. What is the message?"

She snarled. "Tell him I come for him." She slit his throat, stepped over his fallen body, and walked on her way.

CHAPTER 37
CORELLE

Corelle's customer became distraught when she learned her mother had been killed and furious Corelle had been threatened. Her husband had houses empty, and he made the largest available to her free of charge. Despite her argument she must pay, he would not be dissuaded—he would not accept a groat by way of rent. He gave her a key, and she hurried back to the shop, convinced none followed her, but she guessed as soon as Denstal discovered his dead colleague he would send men to the shop to kill her and Vamma.

They packed in a hurry, locked the shop, and set off. It proved more difficult to ensure they were not followed with Vamma to direct. She soon tired these days as the child grew within her, and before long, she ran out of patience as they criss-crossed streets and reversed direction. Corelle noted every face she saw and checked she did not see any of them a second time. She felt confident they had not been followed when they reached the house, where she unlocked the door and sent Vamma upstairs to rest on the bed while she stood near the window. She watched the street for close to an hour, she judged, but nothing suggested anybody had followed or watched the house.

As she watched, she weighed all Denstal's options in her mind. In his position, she would visit the shop late at night, or even in the early morning, while the women slept. She would unpick the lock and slip up the stairs to kill them both in their sleep, then burn the shop to the ground out of spite. Denstal might use a different plan, but he must err on the side of caution. He already respected her reputation, might even fear it. She had killed the Qagrue commander in his own home and escaped with her life, and now she had killed the man Denstal had sent to watch her. If he did not realise she would come for him, Denstal would also disappoint her.

Vamma came down the stairs and asked her what turned. Corelle said she admired the street and enjoyed the colourful fronts of some of the houses. To frighten Vamma any further would be a mistake, and she wanted Vamma to feel safe in the house. Too much stress might be harmful for the child, and they must avoid that outcome.

Corelle decided to watch the shop to see if the Guild came. She could not imagine Denstal would send only one or two members to kill Corelle and Vamma, but if he did, those men would not return alive. When she told Vamma of her plans, Vamma worried about Corelle's safety, as Corelle had expected. Despite promises Corelle would not act if it exposed her to any danger, it seemed Vamma accepted the idea with great reluctance. Vamma took the house key with strict instructions she must not open the door in any circumstances unless convinced Corelle and nobody else knocked on it. Corelle wished Vamma had the strength to push some heavy piece of furniture against the door as extra protection.

Senses heightened, Corelle used extreme caution as she made her way back toward the shop. At first, she walked in a different direction to the shop to ensure nobody followed her. If anybody saw her approach the shop, she wanted them to suspect she had come from another part of the city, and not the area where Vamma hid in the house. Satisfied she had not been followed from the house, she turned and took a circuitous route.

The surreptitious journey took far longer than if she had walked in a straight line, but she felt certain she had not been followed. Across the street from their shop, another shop sold provisions; food, essential household items, and some decorative trinkets to brighten a dull room. Corelle's family had shopped there for as long as she could remember, and may have done so before she had been born. Saboti, the old woman who ran it, had become a family friend after so many years of frequent visits to her shop, and they had often eaten at each other's homes. Her mother had always made dresses for the woman and pressed them on her with the tale they were cancelled orders. It would be hard to believe Saboti's shop brought her much coin, but no shopkeeper in the area wore finer clothes.

By the time Corelle arrived at Saboti's shop, twilight had descended at the end of a cold, cloudy day, and Saboti seemed about to close for the day. They greeted one other with the comfortable affection of long years of friendship. Saboti expressed her distress at the death of Corelle's mother and could make no sense of Corelle's story that jealous competitors had killed her. Corelle had borrowed Karaftaraluq Sumbrid Akh Aluq's tale to add some weight to her request she be allowed to watch over the shop from Saboti's parlour for a time. It delighted Saboti to help, and she offered Corelle some food. Since Corelle had eaten almost nothing since breakfast, she accepted and sat in a chair set back from the window. She and Saboti ate and talked, but Corelle always had one eye on the shop across the road, which she could see from the parlour.

Saboti cleared the dishes away, washed and stored them, then sat in her chair. She picked up two long wooden needles with thick wool wound around them. The needles clicked and clacked, and line after line of making flowed from them. Corelle had never learned the method, suitable for rough garments; shawls, over-shirts, covers for pots and such, but few people sought after clothes made this way. Her mother had told her people made most of their clothes with the needles many years before, but in recent years, thanks to a wooden device called a loom, higher quality cloth could be created, with patterns and colours woven into them from dyed thread. Corelle's family used only cloth made on a loom in their making.

The rhythmic clicks of Saboti's work soothed Corelle's anxiety, and she wondered whether she could take the practice up as a way to relax. The moon waned, and Corelle's fruitless watch continued on a dark night even as Saboti's needles gushed row after row of whatever she crafted. They spoke from time to time, but Corelle's eyes never left the shop doorway for more than a few heartbeats. Corelle begun to doubt Denstal would come to the shop after all else, and when Saboti yawned and put down her work, Corelle decided to head home to Vamma.

She stood but sat again at once as her keen eye spotted move-ment in the shadows below her. A cloaked figure could be seen pressed tight against the wall next to the shop, and it crept forward until it could peer in from one end of the display window. Saboti spoke, but Corelle did not catch her words. She held a finger to her lips in a gesture for Saboti to be silent and pointed to the shadowy figure.

The figure glanced behind it and made some gesture with an arm Corelle could not make out. Beside her, Saboti gasped as four more figures emerged from the deep shadow further along the street. They approached the door and one of them bent to the lock.

Saboti whispered, as though she wished to ensure the figures on the street would not overhear. "What are they about?"

"They work at the lock. They plan to enter the shop."

"This is shameful. I have never heard of any behaviour like this in my life. You should call the Portreeve's men."

"Saboti, there is no Portreeve any longer. The Qagrue will care little about these people, I am certain."

Below them, one of the men pushed the door open, and four of them entered the shop. Their caution and stealth marked them as Guild members without question. One remained outside the shop, and he slipped back into the shadows where Corelle could not see him. Doubtless he watched for any sign of trouble. The door closed behind the men; no passer-by would be any the wiser as Corelle and Vamma were murdered in their beds. Corelle's fury rose inside her, and her every instinct told her to go down to the street, kill the guard and take her chances against the other four.

"Saboti, it is late, and you should be in bed. I will leave now and head for an inn. I cannot stay in the shop tonight. I will go out of your rear door if you do not mind. I do not wish these ruffians to see me."

Only too happy to keep Corelle safe, Saboti unlocked her rear door, and once Corelle reached the alleyway behind Saboti's shop, she ran to the corner across the street from her own shop. With no easy way to approach the concealed man unseen, she pondered the dilemma. Voices carried to her ears, and the shop door opened. The guard appeared from the shadows to join the four who emerged. They whispered terse words to one another, and Corelle imagined their disappointment would be great when they had found the shop empty.

After a few moments' discussion, four of the men left. The other man crossed the street and approached a building on the opposite side of the street from Corelle. When Corelle had been a child, the building had been a storehouse for the furniture shop that had stood next to it. It now lay empty and had for many years. The man must intend to watch from the abandoned storehouse against the possibility the women returned. He closed the front door behind him.

An alleyway ran behind the storehouse, and another door opened onto it. Corelle faced a dilemma. She doubted she could enter the storehouse from the front unseen, since the man would watch from there. The rear door might be locked or blocked by debris inside, and the man inside might hear her enter. If he did not, she might be able to enter the storehouse, come up behind the man and kill him, all undetected.

A better idea entered her head, one that depended that the rear door had fallen into misuse. If she returned to the shop, he would see her and would doubtless slip away into the night to summon the others to return and kill her. She could follow him and learn the location of the others. Corelle reasoned their hideout might be the old Guild building, but they may have preferred a different location, since Corelle knew where the building stood. Better to know their location for certain and formulate some plan based on that knowledge.

If the rear door functioned, however, and he left through that door, she would not see him from the shop. She might have to roll the dice, even though she might roll ones and let him slip away.

Her rage told her to kill the man in the storehouse, but as pleasurable as that would prove, she yearned to kill Denstal to exact revenge for her mother. A deeper, stronger rage would be appeased by nothing less.

Flames of agony shot through her head, and she clutched at her temples. Her vision blurred, and it seemed a bright light shone behind her eyes for a time. When the pain passed, she leaned back against the wall as her breath came in short gasps. Doubtless the stress of the situation had triggered the moment, and she might now run the risk of death from the same brain issues that had taken Deineike. Corelle deserved death, but she must not die until she had killed Denstal. He had now become as much the target of her bitterness, fury and vengeance for the murder of her mother as Styrrach had been for the death of Deineike.

Corelle pondered the situation, no simple choice with a favourable outcome visible to her. All her efforts must be directed toward a result that saw Denstal under her blade. If her luck held, the watcher would leave the storehouse through the front door, which the Guild must have unlocked so the storehouse would be available for their surveillance. She imagined they had watched the shop since they learned she had returned to Ryl.

She rolled the dice.

CHAPTER 38

CORELLE

With a deep breath to calm herself, Corelle strolled across to the shop. She glanced around as she always did, discreet but observant. If the man in the storehouse had Guild training, he would expect her to be cautious, but she must not overact her caution. He knew of her skills, and if her behaviour strayed from their expectations, he could become suspicious.

She reached the door and fumbled in vain for the key in her trouser pockets. It must be in her pack—a setback she had not anticipated, but she rolled the dice again and tried the handle. The door opened. They had not re-locked it. A clumsy mistake, and difficult to explain. They may have been distracted when they had not found the women in their bed in the shop. Corelle dropped to a crouch and checked around the street. She imagined anybody would do so if they found an open door where they had anticipated a locked one. She pulled her fan from her boot and held it where she hoped the man in the storehouse would see it.

She hoped she had acted the part well enough. She slipped into the shop, pretended to lock the door, glanced around the darkened street once more, and strode toward the counter. Far back in the shop, she could no longer be seen from across the street. She stopped and pressed herself against a wall, eyes fixed on the storehouse, little more than a black shape in a blacker night. She could not make out the doorway. If she had not known where it stood, she could not have guessed.

For some time, nothing changed, and she worried he had left through the rear door. She did not know how far away Denstal and his men waited, and she could not wait for them to return. If they caught her, they would kill her through weight of numbers. As she prepared to leave, she spotted movement. The man emerged, turned right, and set off down the street. Corelle skipped to the door, pulled it open and crouched low as she peered around the corner. He had stopped in the time she had taken to leave the shop, and he stared into a shop window. She did not doubt he had no interest in the contents of the window. He waited to see if she followed him. She pulled her head back, counted to five then peered around the corner again. He had moved on in the same direction he had first taken. He walked at a brisk pace and had already walked so far from her, she felt she could follow him.

Corelle stayed as close to the wall as she could as she stepped around the corner and followed him. Ahead of her, he crossed to her side of the street and stopped. She sank back into the shadow of a shop front, motionless. He turned and stared back toward her for some time while she remained as still as the black of night. The slightest movement could draw his eye to her. She guessed he could not make out her shape in the dark shadow, but she could not risk any motion. He turned again and walked on. Corelle exhaled the breath she had held while he had stared back in her direction and set off behind him once more.

He made a sharp turn and crossed the street again. Corelle paused, sure that either he used excessive caution or he suspected she followed him. If he suspected, he must be one of the best she had ever seen when it came to awareness of one's surroundings. Despite her skill, either some sense had tingled in him, or her best efforts had not been good enough for such a skilled rival.

He headed further down the street and rounded a corner. Corelle moved forward again, but she did not cross the street. If he turned and looked round the corner, back the way he had come, he would first check his own side of the street, because anybody who followed him might first cross over so they could turn the same corner he had. He did not reappear, however, and she reached the corner. She stared along the street he had turned into but could no longer see him. Even when she stepped out of the shadows to open up the view of the entire street, he had vanished.

Still as death, Corelle scanned the street. He could not have reached the next corner in the time she had taken to follow him, no matter how fast he might be able to run. He had either realised she followed him, or suspected it. He had been a Guild member from when Styrrach ran things, she guessed, and a well trained one.

She stepped back into the shadows of the buildings, unsure of her next action. Her training screamed at her to abandon the pursuit. If she followed along a street where he might lie in wait, he could pounce on her and kill her. A small voice in her mind told her to press on. She feuded with the voice, anxious not to make the same mistake her pursuer had made earlier in the day.

Torn between the desire to kill Denstal and the need to protect Vamma, Corelle mouthed a silent curse. She prepared to abandon the pursuit and return to Vamma, but she heard a low cough from the first or second house in the street.

For the most part, the body could be controlled in dangerous situations. With sufficient expertise, a person could remain motionless for a long period. The breaths could be slowed and be all but soundless. Muscles might start to ache, but the pain could be ignored. The throat proved one of the hardest things to fight. If a small piece of spittle found the wrong pathway in the throat as one's entire body fought the nerves, muscles, and sinews that urged one to move, that spittle would aggravate the throat and insist it be coughed up and sent down the correct route in the body. It could be resisted for a time, but it would become so insistent that, of all the things Corelle could endure, that would be the one most likely to let her down. She managed her breaths in pressure situations for this precise reason.

The man's throat had let him down. A piece of spittle, a particle of dust, a slight irritation in the nose or throat; any small thing might have triggered it, and he could not fight it. He had coughed and betrayed his location. She gripped her fan and prepared to run forward to confront him, but light spilled out of the doorway of the house. The occupants of the house might have heard the cough. Who knew?

A man stepped out of the door, a lantern in his hand, and spoke to the Guild man. "Why are you in my garden?"

Corelle had no choice now. An innocent had placed himself in danger, and she could not allow him to be harmed. She yelled at the man to go back inside, and her prey stood, bathed in the lantern light. He glanced at her, and for a heartbeat seemed caught between doubt and uncertainty. As she drew closer, she yelled a warning to the man with the lantern. "He is dangerous."

The home's resident looked between them in shock. A dagger flashed in the lantern light, and the man staggered backward, his cry of pain a bitter blow to Corelle. The Guild man had stabbed him, and a vicious snarl tightened her lips. The Guild man stood sideways to her as the man fell back through his own door, and the lantern shattered as it clattered to the doorstep. Flames licked at the Guild man's feet, and he stepped back a pace.

Corelle leapt over the low wall outside the house, the one that had concealed her mark before his cough betrayed him. Furious, she thrust her blade into his side five times or more, and he cried out and slashed at her with his own dagger. Her free hand blocked his arm, and she drove her blade upward into his armpit time and again. His dagger clattered to the floor, and she grabbed the front of his tunic, kicked his feet out from beneath him, and dropped him to the ground. In a blind rage, she thrust her dagger into his stomach multiple times, and he moaned the low, hopeless lament of one who is about to die. Like his life, blood poured from his body and surrounded him.

Corelle jumped the wall again and walked off as fast as her lungs and the pain in her shoulder would allow. She did not look back, and she did not check on the resident of the house. She could not be caught here—she must return to Vamma. Her body shook as the violence and the speed at which she walked from the scene pumped her blood around it. Her heart pounded, and she heaved in deep breaths as she paused in a shop doorway, crouched low, alert for any sounds of pursuit. None came, and she glanced around to establish her location.

Satisfied, she rose and walked away at a comfortable pace, fan pressed tight against her thigh. With many turns and backtracks, she came at last to their house, convinced she had not been followed. Nobody had passed her, and she had changed direction on the few occasions she had thought she might encounter somebody in the street.

Her rage screamed in her head. The Guild member had attacked an innocent man who had come out of his home to investigate an unusual sound in his garden. If Denstal had sunk to the murder of civilians—Durfolk—in the pursuit of his ambitions, then those ambitions must be stopped. Corelle must kill him before he could hurt any more of her people in this disgraceful way.

When she tapped on the door of the house, a lantern flared in an upstairs window, then light crept out from beneath the door as though it longed to bring illumination to the dark streets. Such a peculiar thing, that light, Corelle thought. She could stamp on it, and it would climb to the top of her feet, then return to the ground when she moved her foot. It could not be killed by any weapon but could be stilled by the simple twist of a finger or a sharp breath on the lantern's wick.

She hissed at the door. "Vamma, it is me." The door opened, and the light leapt out into the street as if to celebrate its short-lived freedom. Corelle pushed the door closed behind her. The lantern illuminated the door as though angry its sojourn into the street had ended. Corelle stared at Vamma. A solitary tear trickled from the stallholder's eye.

"You are hurt." Vamma raised a hand to Corelle's tunic as she spoke.

The pain in Vamma's voice existed because of Corelle, and it hurt Corelle in turn, like a dagger thrust into her heart. "That I am not. This blood belongs to another." The man's blood covered Corelle, her tunic and trousers soaked by it. Vamma wiped at Corelle's face, and her hand came away red.

"Another? What has turned? Tell me now." Corelle poured out the story of the raid on the shop and the death of the Guild member at her hand. "They are determined to kill us." Vamma sighed, fear on her face.

"There is little to be afraid of for now. They do not know where we are, or they would not have tried to kill us at the shop. Their numbers dwindle. I have struck down two of them today alone."

Vamma gave no sign Corelle's words had reassured her. "Let us clean you up and get you into bed. Clothes into the basin please. Do not drip blood everywhere. This is not our house."

Corelle did not care for the flat tone of Vamma's voice, neither anger nor disappointment, concern or dismissal. Vamma almost sounded bored; bored of danger, bored of risk. Bored of a life that should be dull but had become complicated. No matter how Vamma felt, the blame lay at Corelle's feet. The moment Corelle had become involved with her in Yerrsun, she had embroiled Vamma in the complexities of her own life. After The Ictharelian sank, Corelle ought not to have returned for Vamma, who would have been better served if she had been left to her marriage to Raolos where they could raise their child together.

Corelle obeyed the instructions, and Vamma soaked a cloth in a bowl she filled with water before she wiped at Corelle. The cold water felt good on her face as it cooled her temperature and her temper both. Each time Vamma wiped, the cloth came away red, and soon the water resembled a bowl of the precious liquid Corelle had spilled so much of in her life.

She was twenty-eight years. The most recent summer marked the passage of another year for Corelle, who had no other way to record the precise moment of her birth. She had abandoned her life as a mariner in search of a quieter one, and now she had once more become embroiled in violence and death. The frequency of her headaches had increased, and she suffered from one even as Vamma wiped the blood of another of her victims from her. She often craved death, although she had lacked the will to end her own life despite many promises to herself to do so. For years, she had killed, fought, and fled. She might have damaged her brain down those dark years. If her fate led her to follow Deineike wher-ever she had travelled to afterward, she guessed it would be a relief to Ictharelian, and to Corelle.

They went up the stairs and climbed into the bed. Vamma blew out the lantern and lay close to Corelle, her arms wrapped around her lover in a grip that suggested she feared the night might sunder them. A desperate embrace followed by a desperate kiss. Corelle wept silent tears as grief and guilt threatened to over-whelm her.

Despite the tension that had coursed through Corelle's body earlier, Vamma's warm body formed a glow that carried her off to sleep. Her mother returned to her dreams, seated in a chair. Denstal stood behind her, his dagger at her throat, and Corelle cried out to him. "Do not hurt her."

Disembodied voices yelled from all around. "Kill Corelle. She loves her mother more than she loves us."

She recognised the voices but could not see the women they belonged to, so she shouted to them. "Show yourselves."

"Why should we? You will kill us if we do. You have always killed us."

Corelle screamed an angry denial. "That I have not." When she glanced down at herself, blood covered her. "Show yourselves."

"We are with you. We are the blood. We are in the blood. You kill us over and over."

Tears came from her eyes, and she wiped them away with the back of her hand. To her horror, the back of her hand turned red. She cried blood, and she screamed. Vamma appeared next to her mother, and Corelle pleaded with her. "Do not let him kill my mother."

Vamma smiled, turned to Corelle's mother, and picked a strand of the old woman's hair between her long, slender fingers. She allowed it to slide through her fingers until it all fell back onto her mother's head.

Corelle fell to her knees, her body wracked by convulsive sobs. "Do not let him kill her."

Vamma wagged a finger toward her. "Corelle, Corelle."

Corelle held up a hand to silence Vamma before she could speak the three words that would condemn her. Instead, Vamma's words condemned Corelle. "You will never see the child."

CHAPTER 39
CORELLE

Corelle's eyes opened, but when she turned her head, she lay alone in the bed, and panic squeezed her heart, an agony in her breast. She leapt from the bed and ran down the stairs. Vamma sat in a chair in the parlour, and she looked up as Corelle's feet pounded down the staircase.

Corelle stopped and slumped forward, her hands on her thighs as her heart ran rampant in her breast. She exhaled a loud, relieved breath as Vamma wished her a good morning.

Corelle shook her head from side to side. "I worried about you."

"I am sorry. You slept so deep, and I grew restless. I did not wish to wake you as I wriggled about in the bed, anxious to be up." She smiled. "I have washed your clothes from last night. I fear the tunic is ruined, but I will try to improve it later."

Corelle sat at Vamma's feet and draped her arms over her lover's knees. Vamma's stomach pressed against her dress, and Corelle suggested the seam could be let out a little if it would help Vamma to be more comfortable. "Do not fret. I know a garment maker."

"Oh." Vamma laughed. "Is she good?" Her voice teased Corelle.

"Not too bad, I hear." The jest made a welcome change from the sombre mood of the previous night. "She has made clothes for Portreeves, it turns."

"Portreeves?" Vamma raised her eyebrows in mock surprise. "She must be good then." A smiled formed on her lips, but a frown soon drove it away. "We need food. We have none."

"I will buy some later."

Vamma's frown deepened, her brows ponderous above narrowed eyes. "Why can we not both go?"

"We may be seen. I do not wish to place you in danger."

"You would not place me in danger."

"You know what I mean." Vamma could be so stubborn, and Corelle could not fathom it when her life could be at risk. "You are safer in the house."

"You cannot lock me up here for days on end. I wish to go out and buy food. What is so dangerous about that?"

"The house may be watched. These people are killers."

Anger crossed Vamma's face. "I know they are. I love one of them."

Corelle shook her head once in surprise at the retort. "What in the Five Cities does that mean?"

"Why are you so angry with me? I only wish to go out for some fresh air and to buy some food."

"I am angry because you insist on this stupid idea."

Vamma's eyes narrowed, and Corelle regretted the words almost before they had left her lips. "I am stupid now?"

Corelle tried to calm her temper. "Vamma, that is not what I meant. You do not seem to grasp the danger you are in."

"It must be because I am so stupid." Vamma folded her arms across her chest, defiant, put out.

Corelle slapped a hand to her forehead in despair, and Vamma rose from the chair. She crossed the room and opened her pack. Corelle heard the rattle of coins before Vamma turned to face her, her cheeks red and her eyes wild. "I will go to the nearest shop. If I do not return, I have been killed, stupid girl that I am."

Vamma unlocked the door and stomped through it. It closed with a bang as she pulled it behind her. Corelle sighed. Vamma's reaction irritated her, but she did not wish her to be in any danger. She pulled some clothes and her boots on and followed.

She caught Vamma with ease as she walked up the road. They wandered around three shops and Vamma piled Corelle's arms full of vegetables, bread and meat. When they returned to the house, Vamma placed all the food into the pantry before she flopped into a chair. "I am exhausted."

"I imagine you will become more tired as the child grows. By the end, you may no longer be able to move at all."

Vamma let out a loud laugh. Although it pleased Corelle to see Vamma happier, she could not understand what she had said to amuse her lover. "You know nothing about this, do you?" Vamma's laughter continued. "Unable to move at all. Oh my." Tears ran down her cheeks as she continued to laugh for some time. Corelle endured the mockery. Vamma had been placed in a difficult situation, and Corelle resolved to attempt to understand her frustration more.

The trip to the shops must have tired Vamma more than Corelle had realised, and she dozed off in the chair. Corelle's thoughts returned to the previous night, and she hoped the man the Guild member had attacked had lived. An idle thought crossed her mind, and she wondered what the Qagrue might do about the death of another person in the city. As the bodies piled up, it seemed certain some kind of investigation must take place.

She decided to walk over to the Guild building later in the day. Even if none of the Guild were there, she could, at the least, discount it as their hideout. If they did hide there, their numbers would be too great for her to attack alone, but she could watch the building from time to time. She might find some opportunities to thin their ranks even more. She might even kill Denstal, and that should end the conflict.

Vamma woke, and Corelle put some bread and cheese on a small platter. They shared the simple meal, and Vamma appeared much refreshed. Corelle outlined her plan. As expected, Vamma resisted. She argued the risks outweighed the benefits, that Corelle would be killed if the Guild saw her, but as they bickered back and forth about it, Corelle's temper worsened, and Vamma's face turned blank as she relented with a heavy sigh.

Corelle employed all her Guild craft to throw off any would-be pursuers as she made her way toward the poorer quarter. The building she sought lay in the middle of a street of identical houses built in one long terrace on each side of Smithy Row. The smithy the street had been named after had fallen into disuse long ago and had been knocked down while Corelle was a small girl. She had been down the street a few times as a child, but it seemed drabber now than she recalled. Some of the houses looked empty, with broken windows and doors battered down. Nothing had ever been built on the empty land where the smithy had stood. Corelle did not think the houses had been so damaged in the days before the Qagrue. The southerners seemed to have introduced an unwelcome element of lawlessness to Dur. The thought saddened her.

She entered an empty house almost opposite the Guild building and climbed the unstable stairs to the bedroom. The window gave her a view of the entire frontage of the Guild building and some houses either side of it. The Guild building had not been damaged, all its windows intact and its door closed. The shutters were closed in the ground floor window. The Guild's reputation may have preserved it, or somebody might now occupy it. The cold season had arrived, and Corelle shivered in the chill air, but no smoke rose from the chimney of the Guild building. The absence of smoke did not guarantee the absence of occupants, however.

Nobody came or went from the house as she watched for over four hours. The shadows lengthened as the sun sank in the west until it disappeared and handed its work over to the night sky. Darkness settled around the street and still no activity had been detected at the Guild building. Frustrated, Corelle returned to the house.

Vamma seemed irritated Corelle had been gone so long and said she had been worried. Corelle could not appease her and grew so angry herself, she declined any food and went to bed.

When they woke the next morning, Vamma wanted to talk about the previous day and about Corelle's temperament. Corelle sighed. "I have been awake mere heartbeats. Must we discuss this again?"

"Corelle, something is awry. Your behaviour is irrational and erratic."

"I realise I have been difficult. Denstal's men killed my mother not a sevenday since. I believe I am entitled to mourn."

"Then please mourn as a normal person would. You have turned your grief into the need for vengeance, and vengeance alone occupies your mind." Vamma paused, then, "What of me? What of our child?"

"I do all in my power to keep you safe. If I kill Denstal, you will be safer. What more do you wish from me?"

"I wish the woman I love to be as I remember her. You were never prone to such terrible outbursts of rage before you returned from that wretched voyage."

"Do you wish I had not returned? Is that it? Would you have been more content with Raolos and the child he gave you?" Corelle turned her back on Vamma, furious.

"Corelle, this behaviour is what I mean. I love you and wish you would be as you once were. Your return mended a life that had been incomplete without you. I know you cannot say the same, and I do not ask it of you." She paused, and her voice softened when she continued. "For three long years, I ached for you. I missed you more than I can say for every heartbeat of those years. When you returned, I thought I would die from happiness, but you have changed, and more since the death of your mother. Your moods are unpredictable, your temper never more than a look, a word away. I believe you were easier to miss than you are to live with."

Corelle stood and dressed. Vamma lay in the bed, tears in her eyes again. Since they had returned to Ryl, Corelle could no longer control her anger. Vamma had the right of it with her words about Corelle's temper, but once the fury bubbled up inside, it could not be stopped, so Corelle lashed out. Through ill fortune, it fell to Vamma to bear the brunt of Corelle's ire, but Corelle could not find the words to express her frustration at Vamma's constant complaints about it. Once she had slain Denstal, Corelle hoped she would calm down, but the death of her mother at his hands had driven her to this point, and she must have vengeance.

Vamma could not seem to grasp the level of danger the Guild posed to her. "Vamma, you are not the subject of my anger. You know it is Denstal. I must kill him. It is my hope things will return to normal when I have fed him to the flames, that we will be as we once were."

Vamma's red-rimmed eyes gazed at her, dejected. "You tell me your anger is directed at him alone, but every day I must tolerate the monster you become when you are in a rage. I know you do not love me. Do you, at the least, care for me?"

"By the fates. It rankles me you would ask this of me. All I do, I do to keep you safe, you and the child. How can you doubt that I care for you?"

"You care more for vengeance—"

"We talk in circles. This will not do. I cannot stand to begin this argument again." Corelle stamped down the stairs. At the bottom, she paused. "Lock the door behind me. Do not open it for anybody but me." As she crossed the room, she muttered in wrath, "If you can rise from the bed, that is." In her fury, she slammed the door behind her and set off for the poorer quarter. She could not stay in the house and bicker with Vamma all day. Far better to watch the Guild building for some sign Denstal and his men were within. Nobody could stay in a house for ever with never a trip to a shop or a breath of fresh air.

A pang of guilt flicked through her. Had Vamma not said those words, or similar, the previous day? She had no time to brood on her domestic situation while she hunted Denstal, so she dismissed the thought. He must come out at some point, she reasoned.

He did not. As darkness fell, she gave a grim laugh. Had she stayed in her own house and continued to argue with Vamma all day, nothing would have been missed here. The Guild must not be in the house, after all else. They may have deemed it too dangerous to remain in the building when they knew Corelle could come there at any moment. She reasoned Denstal, certain she bent all her endeavours to his discovery, feared to wait here where she would find him with ease. Corelle scoffed at her own thought. How many were they? It mattered little. Eight, ten, or twelve, they were many against one. Denstal would not fear her.

The riddle must be resolved, and she saw but one way to do so. She left her hideout and walked away from the Guild building at a brisk pace, then dashed across the road and checked the street behind her. Nobody had followed her. As she retraced her steps toward the Guild building, she checked every house she passed. No shutters twitched; no doors opened behind her. She jumped the low wall of the Guild building and faced the street as she pressed her back against the house, every sense on high alert. Silence rang in her ears as she strained to hear any sound from inside. She smelled no fire, no stale odour of men's long unwashed bodies as they cowered in wait within the house. Her hands pressed against the wall of the house, and the rough bricks scraped at her fingers and palms, each brick a small landscape in its own right, peaks and valleys carved into it by years and the elements. The time had come to act or to slink home to Vamma and more endless arguments.

CHAPTER 40

CORELLE

orelle crouched and shuffled beneath the house's ground floor window, then straightened at the door frame. As she strained to hear any telltale sound, she listened so hard she thought her ears might fall from her head.

She pulled her fan from her boot and laid a hand on the door handle. The door would not be locked; no Guild building ever had been as far as she knew. The door handle would be certain to squeak. Who knew how many times it had been turned, metal on metal as the small spindle in it drew back the latch? No oil would ever have been applied to the lock over the years. The more it squeaked, the more it warned occupants of the house somebody entered.

She turned the handle so slow, anybody who watched inside the house would have been hard pressed to see any movement. It made some small noises, but no sound came from within, and nobody pulled the door open from the inside. As the latch cleared the recess in the door frame, she opened the door a crack. No light spilled from inside the house.

Corelle released the handle and crouched, then pushed the door open and dived into the house away from the door. The moon cast a faint light into the room. Motionless and on one knee, fan in hand, Corelle waited with bated breath as her eyes adjusted to the darkness in the house. A parlour lay before her, chairs and a small table visible as shadow shapes. She closed the door, then moved forward until she spotted a lantern on the table and felt around beside it. Her fingers touched a flint and it fell from the table to the floor with a clatter that shattered the suspenseful silence, and Corelle jumped at the sound.

Corelle stiffened for moment upon tense moment as her eyes flicked around the room and her ears again strained for any sound. Nobody appeared, so she fumbled around on the floor for the flint and lit the lantern. A layer of dust covered every piece of furniture and the floor, but hers were the only footprints visible. Nobody had been in the parlour for some time.

A door set into one wall of the parlour led to Krage's office, she guessed. When she checked the room, nothing suggested it had been used for some time. The stairs wailed and sang of her every step as she climbed, and Corelle permitted herself a smile as she recalled the time Porl had abused her when she had attempted to repair the stairs in the Zhanghar Guild building. Memories of Arella ran through her head as she realised she now climbed stairs Arella's feet would have trodden while she had served in Ryl. Arella had sat in the chairs of the parlour, and her footsteps had crossed the floorboards. Corelle sighed. Arella could be found everywhere and nowhere, the worst legacy of their time in the Guild.

Upstairs, Corelle found nothing other than three empty, unmade beds and a chamber pot with a vile coloured liquid in it that almost turned her stomach. Flies buzzed around it, and she swatted at them as they hummed around her. A small scullery downstairs held nothing of interest, not even food scraps. She wondered whether Krage had a secret door in his office, as Styrrach had in Alcmouth.

A thorough search of the wall that adjoined the next house left her disappointed. She found no sign of any hidden portal, and she tutted. Another trunk of Styrrach's coin would have been welcome. As she prepared to leave the empty house, she heard the front door handle squeak. She cursed herself; her anger had led to a mistake. The likelihood eyes other than her own might watch the house had not occurred to her. Watch it they had, nonetheless, and they had summoned Denstal and his Guild. They had trapped her.

She had the door to the office ajar, and she crouched against the wall, careful to ensure the door would not strike her as it opened. The door would only hide her for a few heartbeats, but with nowhere else to conceal herself, she had little choice. She strained to pick up any sounds that might indicate how many assailants came into the house even though her heart pounded so loud in her ears, she feared twenty men could ride horses through the house, and she would not hear them. She struggled to control her breaths and lower her heart rate.

A soft footfall suggested somebody had stepped into the parlour. The front door closed. Corelle felt certain no more than one person had entered the house. Why would they close the door and risk a confrontation with her alone while they left their companions outside the closed door? The new arrival made neither sound nor movement, and their caution puzzled Corelle. They must know she had heard them, and they had the numbers to take her. She could hope for nothing more than to take some of them with her, Denstal among them with any luck.

Corelle thought of Vamma, safe in the house. Once she realised Corelle would not return, she ought to escape to safety. At the least, she could birth Raolos's child and raise it in relative peace.

"Corelle." The urgent whisper took her by surprise. The man knew someone had entered the house from the footprints in the dust, and he knew who those footprints belonged to, but he did not attack. She did not reply, and when he whispered her name again, she remained motionless and silent. "Corelle, curse you. Come out. You have little time." Corelle did not respond. His words could be a trap designed to lure her out. She did not understand the comment, in truth. Why did she have little time? Why would he say such a thing? He whispered again, a harsh sound in the otherwise silent house. "I must report you are here. You must be gone before we get back. That will not be long."

That meant their hideout lay close by, unless he bluffed. His feet edged forward, deeper into the parlour. "I know you are in the office. No footprints emerge from the doorway. I want to help you and do not wish to see you dead. They should not have killed your mother. We never killed innocents. I know you wish to kill us all in revenge, but I do not wish to die yet."

Corelle broke her silence with a whisper. "Then come into the office." Feet moved closer to her door, and the door swung open, but nobody entered the room. Corelle decided to act without delay and hope to gain the upper hand. She skipped out of the office and pressed herself against the man, her blade at his throat. He held no dagger and made no effort to resist or flee.

"Do not kill me. I am alone, but I must report you are here. You should leave now. We will all return in moments once I leave."

"Where is Denstal?" His name on her lips tasted as bitter as the outer layer of the oranges in Illfarlen.

"There is a house one street over, number seventeen. They are there, Denstal and nine others. Ten, when I return."

"How does he have so many men with him? There were no more than five or six of you in Ort, and I have killed two of your number already."

"Two others, from Zhanghar I believe, heard of us and joined. They had drifted after Styrrach's death but found nothing to fit their skills. He has recruited others from the population here, though they are not well trained. They are eager to oust the Qagrue, but most of them have never killed anything other than the occasional insect." Nothing in his eyes betrayed any falsehood in his words.

"They may not know I came. You need not report you saw me enter."

He let out a bitter laugh. "Your footprints tell a tale. The house has been left undisturbed for that sole reason. None of us visit unless to check whether you have been here. He fears you. He hopes to kill you with weight of numbers. You must leave."

"Why do you help me?"

"When they killed your mother, they betrayed us all, if they had but known it. She had done nothing to us, done nothing to warrant her death. She had nothing to do with your actions. I played no part in it, nor would I again in the same circumstances."

"My actions? I did nothing to antagonise Denstal."

"You would not join us. He sent men to destroy your shop and intended to blame the Qagrue in hopes you would join us to exact justice. Your mother resisted, and they killed her. He knew once the Qagrue told you you were cleared of the blame for the deaths of the commander and his wife, you would learn the southerners did not kill your mother. His fear of you is great, and he now wishes you dead."

Corelle saw the irony in the situation. She had refused to join Denstal, but she would never have betrayed him to the Qagrue if he had left her, Vamma, and her mother alone. He had made a different decision and killed her mother in the process. Now she marked him for death and would be his ruin. She looked at the floor. Both sets of footprints were clear throughout the parlour, with a large clear patch where they stood. Their feet had shuffled the dust around in such a way, Denstal could not fail to realise this man had spoken with her. Denstal would torture the man, who would admit he had tried to warn her. He would not enjoy the Guild justice that would follow.

He could not be trusted to say nothing as hideous things were done to him. With a small shrug, she slit his throat, and he collapsed to the floor with confusion on his face. Corelle gazed down on him as his life left him. His face seemed familiar, and she wondered whether she had met him in Ort when she first encountered Denstal. It mattered not. He had gone wherever he travelled to afterward, and Denstal's numbers had been further reduced.

She could learn nothing more from the house, so she closed the door behind her as she left. The man would soon be missed, and when he did not return, Denstal would send several of his men, likely to have guessed the fate of the one she had killed. The man had given her an address, but if he had spoken the truth, ten men waited there, armed and trained. She could not succeed against such odds, and it would not suffice for her to die and not take Denstal with her. Their numbers must be further reduced, or she must seek assistance. No allies could be found here anymore. Only Wilash still lived of those she had counted on for aid in the past, and he lived almost a pass away in Malkartas.

Defeated for now, she trudged back to the house. Nothing more dangerous than her own thoughts followed her home. It frustrated her that three of Denstal's men were dead, but he still lived, surrounded by too many men for any realistic chance she could kill him.

She knocked on the door and identified herself. Vamma stared at her in horror. "You are covered in blood again. What has turned?" She told Vamma the story. "He tried to help you, but you still killed him?"

Corelle shrugged and dismissed the suggestion she had done the wrong thing. "He served Denstal. If I let him live today, he would be another dagger to worry about when I do confront his leader." Vamma shook her head, and her reaction could not be gauged from her eyes. "They killed my mother. She must be avenged."

"Corelle, this is not like you. You have lost your compassion, your sense of reason. You cannot continue like this."

With a simple shrug, Corelle replied, "I am a killer. This is what I do."

"You have a heart." Vamma reached out and patted Corelle's breast as though to remind her that her heart still beat within her.

"I had a heart. Now I am nothing." Corelle accompanied her answer with a derisive snort. She had a heart once and had allowed Guild members to walk away from encounters with her. Little good that compassion had done her, or them. At least one had not heeded her words and had paid for it with his life. She would not make that mistake again. The time had arrived to accept what she had become and cease the futile attempts to deny her true nature. A killer, nothing more, vengeance for those who slew her mother. They would pay a fearsome price for that death.

"You did not react this way when Styrrach killed Deineike. Why has the death of your mother turned you into this... creature you have become?"

Corelle clenched her teeth and drew her lips back in a snarl. "You know nothing of how I felt when he took Deineike from me. It broke me. I longed for death. Now I long to bring death."

Vamma had taken a step backward at the outburst. "I do not understand." A tear fell from one eye.

"There is nothing to understand. I have always been this way."

"That you have not." Vamma took a step forward and pulled Corelle into her arms. "You cared for things, and for people. You gave that man in Yerrsun his life."

"He would have been better served had I given him a quick death." Bitterness gnawed at Corelle. "He betrayed my weakness, and they rewarded him with Guild justice."

Wide-eyed, Vamma appeared shocked. "Weakness? You call kindness 'weakness' now?"

"It is harder to take a man's life than to pat him on the head and tell him all will be well. Kindness is the easier path. The smoke from the Pyres of the kind would cloud the sky for a pass. I will not join them. Rather, I will feed Denstal to the flames. There is no more to be said on the matter."

Vamma remained silent for a time, and Corelle pulled herself loose of her embrace to sit in a chair. She brooded on how she could get to Denstal, but tiredness embraced her, and she could make no progress on her thoughts on the matter.

"You have lost your mind." Vamma's soft words interrupted Corelle's thoughts. "Mayhap the blow from that mast, or the countless times you have sustained similar injuries. It matters not, after all else. Come away with me. Let us return to Yerrsun, Corelle, please. I can take no more of this side of you. You come home every night covered in blood. You are angry all the time. It is terrible to behold."

"Then leave. Go back to Yerrsun. I will join you when my work here is done."

Vamma laid a hand on Corelle's head. "That you will not." Sadness dripped from her words like water from a punctured waterskin. "You will die if you stay here. You will not see our child." Corelle thought Vamma had the right of it, and she nodded in mute agreement. "I love you." Vamma would not relent as Corelle blinked back tears. "Is there nothing I can say to persuade you to come with me?"

"That there is not." The simple response might have shattered Vamma's heart, but Corelle could not abandon her hatred of Denstal.

"Then tell me how you will kill them all."

Corelle glanced up at her. "I will think of a way." She would; she must.

The next morning, she rose after Vamma and found her seated at the small table as she ate some bread and meats. Corelle sat and helped herself to some food.

They said nothing. Corelle guessed last night's conversation had hurt Vamma. It pained her, but her path could only end with Denstal dead, or her, or even both. She wondered whether Denstal had found the body of the man from last night yet, and her mind wandered through the conversation up to the point at which she had killed him. He had said Denstal had become more bent on her ruin once the Qagrue, Karaftaraluq Sumbrid Akh Aluq, had been to her shop, and he had suggested Denstal felt he could no longer trust her. Her blood boiled that he had thought so little of her, he had believed she would work with the Qagrue against him.

She stared at the bread on the table before her as she thought the unthinkable. Why not? Why could she not work with the Qagrue? Denstal outnumbered her, after all else, and she had no true allies. It seemed unfair Denstal should have the superior numbers, since he had initiated her vendetta against him when he had Corelle's mother killed. Denstal had sought her help in his plot to kill the Qagrue, or some of them at the least. If she told Karaftaraluq Sumbrid Akh Aluq that information, he might offer to lend her some of his men to bring down the plotters. That would even up the numbers and—

"What?" Vamma had concern in her voice.

Corelle looked across at her, puzzled. "What do you mean?"

"Something troubles you. You have not eaten for some moments, and your face is dark."

"It is nothing. I am fine." Corelle smiled at Vamma. "Lost in my thoughts, nothing more."

"And what were these thoughts that took you so deep into themselves?"

Corelle sighed. It would sound like madness to Vamma, she thought, yet she did not want to lie to her. She had brought enough pain and anxiety to her life already. She could not compound her bad behaviour with lies. Vamma deserved better than that. "I think I will seek help from the Qagrue."

Vamma stared at her as though she had lost her mind. "You jest. You would work with these southern invaders against your own people? That betrays everything you believe in."

"There is but one group of Durfolk I wish to see dead, and there are too many of them for me alone. Do you want them to kill me?"

Vamma shook her head. "I cannot believe what you have proposed. You have lost your mind, after all else. I had the right of it last night."

Corelle's anger grew again. "Do you have a better plan?"

"That I do." Vamma also sounded angry, and she slapped a hand down on the table. "Let us return to Yerrsun and forget all the madness you talk of here."

"I have already told you I cannot leave here until I have seen this through. Once Denstal is dead, there is nothing for me here in Ryl, and we can go wherever you wish."

"Please Corelle, do not do this. None of this is right. You must know it. You sound unbalanced."

"There is no time to lose. Once they find the body from last night, they may move to another location. They may guess he told me where they are."

Vamma shook her head. "Corelle, you are obsessed. It has twisted your thinking."

"This is the highest hand I can play. In truth, I have no other hand to play. I must do this. I cannot live with myself otherwise." She rose from the table. "I will speak to the one who came to the shop. They may help me. If not, I must find other allies."

Vamma bowed her head, defeated. "Come back to me."

"That I will." Corelle kissed the back of Vamma's neck.

"I love you." Vamma spoke as Corelle stepped out of the door, and she stopped. Something in Vamma's tone of voice touched some part of her. Had she lost her mind? Should she abandon the hatred and sail for Ort, then ride to Yerrsun with Vamma? The life she had wished for as she had struggled to reach Malkartas from Illfarlen and Argoya lay within her grasp. Could she walk out on that chance?

The memory of her mother on the floor of their shop, surrounded by a pool of her own blood, her stomach gashed open, swallowed any suggestion she could find peace if she did not avenge that foul deed. Corelle took another step outside the house but paused and turned before she closed the door. Vamma's eyes implored her to stop, to return to the house and not go through with the plan she had conceived less than an hour ago. Corelle hesitated, then pulled the door closed. As she walked down the street, she whispered, "That you do," but Vamma could not have heard her.

CHAPTER 41
CORELLE

No Portreeve served in Ryl these days. The Qagrue ruled Ryl now, and they did so from the former Portreeve's Offices. As Corelle stood in the square and gazed on the familiar building, she considered she might come to regret her next actions for the remainder of her life. Had anybody asked her before this morning how she felt about the Qagrue, she would have called them murderers, usurpers, invaders. Now she contemplated an approach to them to ask for their help to kill a citizen of Dur, a former Guild colleague. She had not known him in those days, but he had served and been manipulated by Styrrach, Sisnop, Krage, and the Guild as they all had been.

Her head throbbed in agony. It must be the pressure of a terrible situation, but she suspected the lengths to which she would go to avenge her mother played a large part in the headache. Her next move would betray Dur and ally her with southern trespassers, people who had no right to be in Dur. Some might say she worked to bring an end to the Guild, a ruthless band of killers with hearts of stone. Others would see Denstal and his men as heroes who resisted the invaders and fought to free Dur from their clutches.

She could see no other way to kill Denstal. He had too many guards. Without the Qagrue, she could not defeat him. Why, then, did she hesitate, here in the square? A few paces and she would be in the building and her request would be considered. Vamma, she realised. Vamma had suggested they leave and head for Yerrsun and the life they both desired in their hearts. Again, the memory of her mother's dead body came into Corelle's mind. She would ask for help, kill Denstal, avenge her mother, then leave Ryl. The Qagrue would have this one chance to be allied with her. Afterward, they would be enemies again.

A small voice inside her tried to reason an alliance of convenience could never be something to be proud of, so she strode into the building before it had time to change her mind. She asked for Karaftaraluq Sumbrid Akh Aluq, and a Durfolk clerk waved her to a chair to wait. Karaftaraluq did not appear for an interminable time, and more than once she considered she should abandon the scheme and follow Vamma's suggestion. The morning dragged on, and her doubts grew. Once she had the idea, she had acted on impulse, but the lengthy wait had given her too much time to consider the implications.

At the moment she stood to leave, Karaftaraluq Sumbrid Akh Aluq appeared. One of the women behind the long counter pointed her out to him, and he came across the lobby to greet her. Recognition appeared on his face as he reached her. "Corelle, am I correct? The garment shop?"

"That I am. You have a good memory for faces."

"Your face is not easy to forget. There are many stories in it, and I should like to hear them at some time. I fear some would not be pleasant for me or my people to hear." He laughed and extended a hand.

Corelle hesitated for a heartbeat, then shook his hand. With that handshake, she sold herself. Shame washed over her, as though the handshake were dirtier than the foulest deed she had ever done at

Styrrach's behest. She sighed, and he raised his eyebrows. "Can we talk somewhere more private? I seek your help with something that will also be of assistance to you. It is a delicate matter."

He led her through the large Ortwood doors behind the counter and along a passageway. They passed through an aides' office and into much grander one, the Portreeve's at some point in the past, she imagined. "This is my office. I have been appointed Commander of Ryl in place of Wimstredor Sumbrid Akh Stredor."

Corelle nodded, unsure how to begin the tale she must tell, and the doubts nagged at her even now. "I know of a group of men who plot against your people. They will kill your men if they can, and steal coin from you." She had thrown the mention of the coin in at the last moment to strengthen her story.

He pursed his lips. "Such a group operated in Ort, I hear. We had them cornered, or so we thought. It seems they fled. It is possible they came here."

Her anger returned, no longer dampened by her conscience. Denstal had lied. He had not come to Ryl to begin his operation. He had fled for his life. She saw no harm in that, but he had not told her the truth about why it took him three years to arrive in Ryl. Corelle should have known he had not been truthful. He might have felt ashamed, embarrassed even to admit he had almost been caught. "They are the same men. If you will make some of your men available, I will lead them to where these men are hidden, and we can take them into custody." She had no intention of taking Denstal anywhere other than to his ruin but thought it best to keep that to herself at this point.

He sat on one corner of the Ortwood desk that must have been left by the Portreeve. He rubbed his chin as he weighed her words. For a moment, Corelle feared he would refuse her request. "I cannot lend my men to you as you suggest. I would like to apprehend them, nonetheless. That would be an excellent way to start my appointment as Commander." He fell silent again and Corelle waited. At last, he reached a decision. "I will send my men, but you may not accompany them."

That would not suffice. If she could not go, she could not kill Denstal. He had given her the perfect excuse to end her uneasy alliance with his people. "Then I bid you farewell." Corelle turned and had reached the door before he could respond.

"Wait, where do you go?"

"I return to my home." She placed one hand on the door handle. "I know where these men are. You do not. If I cannot go, your men cannot go either."

He tutted. "Why do you wish to go with my men?"

"These men killed my mother. If you were me, would you not wish to see them captured?"

He held up a hand and beckoned her to return to the desk. She waited, her hand still on the door handle, while he seemed to wrestle with some inner conflict. "You had not told me these men killed your mother."

"That I had not, but now I have."

He fell silent again and seemed undecided, then snapped his head up, resolution in his eyes. "Very well. I can spare ten men. You may go with them, but you must observe, nothing more."

Only ten? They would be insufficient to best Denstal and his guards, Corelle felt. Did the Qagrue have so few men in the city they could only spare ten? For the first time, Corelle felt their numbers might not be as great as she had imagined. "There are ten of these men, and they are trained, skilful killers." His eyebrows shot upward. "Ten of your men may be insufficient. Some will die."

He shrugged. "So be it. Ten of my men it is, or you alone. If you kill them and somehow survive, I may hang you for their deaths."

Eleven against ten. She had no idea how good the Qagrue men's skills might be. They would need to be excellent to defeat ten Guild members. Some of Denstal's members might not be as well-trained as others, however. Corelle herself would be a factor also. It would have to be enough. She had this one chance to kill Denstal. "Ten will do, but please ask them to bring daggers. Those swords are next to useless in close quarters combat."

He led her out of his office and the building. They entered another building across the square where three Qagrue men in their distinctive tunics sat at a table. Karaftaraluq Sumbrid Akh Aluq spoke to one of them while Corelle waited near the door. The man disappeared through a door at the rear of the room, and Karaftaraluq Sumbrid Akh Aluq approached her. "The men will be here soon. I will leave you with them. I look forward to a successful outcome. Once we have apprehended these men, we will question them. Once we have all the information we require from them, we will deliberate." She nodded, non-committal. "Why do you betray your own kind to us?"

"I have told you. They killed my mother."

He studied her. "So you say. Do you have any proof of this?"

"I have my word. If that is not good enough, I do not know what else I can provide."

"They are trained killers, you say. How do you know this?"

"I am also a trained killer. I belonged to the same organisation as them." She saw no reason to deny the tale. She suspected he had guessed as much, after all else.

"I could have you hanged for this admission."

"That you could not. You were not in charge of Dur when I did these things. Your laws did not apply."

He smiled. "Indeed, you may be correct. It is a gamble for me to send my men to apprehend these Durfolk. I hope you have not misled me, and you do not lead my men into a trap. It will go ill for you if you have."

"It will not go ill for me. As you have guessed, it will go well for you. You will be praised, your name shouted from the rooftops."

He stared at her, his jaw set in determination. "It would best if we did not meet again."

"You may have the right of it." He left, and she waited some time. One by one, Qagrue men assembled at the door. One asked her name, and she gave it to him. They asked for the address, but she would not tell them. She would not risk detention at the building while they went without her. They did not seem anxious or worried for their lives and checked their equipment until all ten had gathered.

One of them spoke to her. "I lead this group. We are not regular soldiers. We undertake more difficult tasks for our tribe, tasks that ought not to be seen by our people." She guessed they were not dissimilar to the Guild in some ways. "Lead us to this house. You will wait outside while we take these men into custody."

They set off, and she led them by a circuitous route as she thought of a good reason to enter the house with them. "These men are trained killers. I have had the same training as them. It will not be easy to take them alive. I will follow you into the house. I may see things that will help you."

The man glowered at her. "What manner of things?"

"Poisons. If they have access to poisons, they may coat their weapons with them." Some Guild members had killed by the use of poisons, but she had never known any of them to coat their weapons with it. The Qagrue leader did not know that, however, and she needed him to allow her into the house. He nodded. She had won the first battle.

She stopped the men outside number fifteen in the street the man had told her about. She studied the houses. They all looked the same, but the shutters were drawn in number seventeen even though the midday had not long passed. She hoped the Qagrue would not notice that, or if they did, they would not recognise it as the target house. Corelle did not intend to be the last person into the building.

The leader whispered, impatient, she imagined. "What is the delay?"

"I am caught between doubt and uncertainty. I heard they are at number seventeen, but number fifteen looks more familiar."

He stared at both houses. "To my eye they are identical."

"Allow me to check a little closer, then you may lead your men in." Corelle crouched and shuffled forward. She did not need to crouch; they had been observed, or they had not. Ten men cannot approach a house unseen. The crouch allowed her to slide her fan out of her boot. They followed close behind her, and she reached the door to number seventeen. She turned to the leader. "It is this house."

"How do you—" Corelle reached out before he finished his question, turned the handle, and skipped inside. She heard some muttered words, curses in Qagrue she guessed, but she now focused on one task—the elimination of Denstal and his men.

Five men sat in a parlour, Denstal among them. Two lounged in chairs and three sat at a table in the middle of the room where they gamed with dice. Denstal sat furthest from the door and would be hard to reach until the others were down. He half-rose as soon as she entered, and the other four turned to see what turned. One of the men at the table sat with his back to the door and turned in his chair as she opened the door. He seemed slow to react, so she chose him as her first target.

The Qagrue ran in behind her and shouted in their own language as they charged toward the table. Most of them had their swords out instead of daggers. Corelle had no time for irritation. One step forward, and she had reached the man she had marked. She slid her fan around his neck and cut his throat with one swipe of her blade. His blood pumped from his throat and turned the table and everything on it vermilion.

In the corner of her eye, a man emerged from a door to one side of the room. He stepped toward her, and without hesitation he slashed at her with his dagger. His blade caught her high on her left arm, and she winced at the pain. It looked like a deep cut, and she guessed the arm would now wear an additional scar above the ones both Styrrach and Porl had carved in it.

Before the man could strike again, she thrust her blade into one of his eyes. He screamed in agony, and slapped the flat of a hand over the injured eye. His scream mingled with others in the room. The noise threatened to deafen Corelle. She had not heard such raucous cries since the fight with Styrrach and his men in Raolos's office in Ort. She pulled her fan out of the man's eye, took a step toward him, then thrust it into his stomach three times in quick succession. She pushed him, and he screeched with pain and fell to the floor.

Corelle glanced around the room. Three Qagrue men lay motionless on the floor, along with three of Denstal's. Two of the Qagrue fought with one of the men who had been in the chairs at the side of the room. They stabbed at him with their swords, and she guessed him to be dead or as good as dead. The other still sat in his chair, his head back as his lifeless eyes stared at the ceiling. One of the Qagrue fought with Denstal at the far end of the table. Three more Guild men had come down the stairs and had engaged in fierce combat with four of the Qagrue at the rear of the room. The Guild men fought with the ferocity of cornered animals. They might have been from the original Guild and seemed to have the upper hand.

Corelle tried to close on the melee to aid the four Qagrue, but the floor swam with blood, and she slipped and fell forward. She landed on her hands and knees and lost her grip on her fan, which skittered away from her toward the rear of the room. She reached up and used the table to pull herself to her feet. Denstal had slumped down in his chair, and blood poured from a head wound. The remaining Qagrue had taken on the three Guild members at the rear of the room. Weight of numbers atoned for the inequality of skill, and swords cut the Guild men down, although they took one more Qagrue with them.

The chaos of the combat faded, the feral screams gone, replaced by the groans of the injured survivors. She turned to the table. Denstal still sat in his chair and glared at her. She stepped behind him and grabbed a handful of his hair, then heaved his head around so he could see her.

He smiled his bitterness up at her and croaked words in a weak voice. "I did not think you would join these vermin." Blood spurted from his head wound, and he had already turned pale from its loss.

"Then you did not think the matter through with enough care." Hatred and anger gripped at her insides. "Do you know where Krage is, or did you tell yet another lie?"

He coughed blood from his mouth. He had other injuries she had not noticed before. Cuts covered his body, but one Qagrue lay at the foot of his chair. "He is in Argoya. His aide, Ricrid, sent word they sailed for there after they heard of your great discovery." He laughed, but the laughter gave way to another series of coughs that showered the table with even more blood.

"You know this Ricrid?"

"That I do, a little. We stayed in touch over the years since he left. He lives, you know. The boy."

"What boy?" His words perplexed her.

"The one you mentioned in Ort. The bailiff's son. Krage asked Ricrid to kill him, but he could not do it. Neither could I, it turns. I must be softer than I believed."

Corelle gasped at his words. He might have lied, but there seemed little reason for him to have done so. Raopul had not been killed? It all but took her breath away, and she forced herself to remember why she had come to the house. She reached for two dice from the table, both covered in blood. "I will roll for you. You must hope I do not roll ones." He gave a small laugh but did not reply. She looked at the vermilion dice in her hand, then closed her fist around them. She threw them onto the table. They came up five;

a two and a three. She glanced around. The dead Qagrue nearby still held his sword. She bent and picked it up.

Denstal objected, but no fear of death shone in his eyes. "I rolled five."

She stared at him in contempt. "You rolled ones the day you killed my mother." She raised the sword and thrust it down through his back. Its point passed through him, emerged from his chest, and stuck into the table. He coughed again, more blood spurted from his mouth, and his head slumped forward.

She had killed him with a sword, and the irony did not escape her. Her contempt for swords remained, but she had finished Denstal off with one. The Qagrue stood around her. Two clung to colleagues, too injured to stand unaided. They all bled from cuts, and Corelle felt weak as her hatred and nervous excitement subsided. None of the Qagrue spoke, but their eyes told her the fight had taken a toll on more than their bodies. Their leader lay dead, along with four others. Nine Guild men lay or sat around the room, all dead. If the man she had spoken to last night had told her the truth, one remained unaccounted for. He may not have been at the house, to his good fortune. Corelle guessed he would not now remain in Ryl, and since she did not know him, she reasoned she must be satisfied with the vengeance she had taken from his companions—Denstal dead, and her mother avenged.

One of the Qagrue said they would send for a cart. They needed to take their dead for their Pyres. "We will need another cart for these nine. We will burn them without honour."

She did not understand what it meant to burn them without honour but felt too tired and weak to ask about it. "I will walk part of the way with him. I must return to my home. You must explain to Karaftaraluq Sumbrid Akh Aluq how this turned awry. They attacked us."

"They did not attack us." Corelle wheeled on the one who had spoken, and whatever he saw in her eyes stilled his tongue.

She found her fan, wiped it on Denstal's back, and slid it into her boot. Blood covered her, and much of it must be her own. Corelle clutched at her arm as she walked alongside the Qagrue. Neither of them spoke, and when she turned toward the house and left him to walk on to the square alone, they did not bid each other farewell. She had used them to her advantage and would not work with them again. They were her enemies once more.

VAMMA

Vamma sat in a chair in the parlour. She held little hope Corelle would return and had decided that if she did not, she would take their coin and return to Yerrsun where she could birth the baby and hope to give it a peaceful life. She cried often, as much for Corelle as herself. It horrified her that Corelle would work with the Qagrue under any circumstance. Only Corelle's desperate desire for vengeance drove her to such a course of action. To cooperate with the invaders who had taken over their land seemed unthinkable to Vamma, and she feared, even if Corelle killed Denstal, in years to come she would find it difficult to forgive herself for her alliance with the Qagrue. She already carried so much guilt and self-hatred for all that had turned in her life, and there must come a point at which she could no longer bear the weight of that guilt. It must kill her, if the injuries to her head or the blade of some opponent did not do the job first.

When she heard the knock at the door, her breath caught in her throat. She rose from the chair and hurried across the room. Corelle's voice called her name, and Vamma unlocked the door and wrenched it open. She had intended to throw herself in joy into

Corelle's arms, but the woman before her was drenched from head to foot in blood, and this time it seemed some of it must be hers. She pressed her right hand to her left arm, and blood ran out between her fingers.

Vamma dragged Corelle into the house, through the parlour, and into the scullery. A small yard lay at the rear of the house, and she pulled the door open and took Corelle outside, where she sat her on the ground. "What must people have thought as you passed them?" Corelle did not answer, and Vamma scampered inside to fill a pail with water so she could clean her lover and investigate the injury. Corelle sat in silence as Vamma washed the blood from her face, then tore the sleeve from Corelle's tunic and washed her arm. A deep cut ran across it, high up near her shoulder. The old familiar scars would have a new companion. Blood oozed from the gash as soon as she cleaned it, and she tied the sleeve around Corelle's arm above the cut to try to stem the flow of blood as she cleaned it. From inside, Vamma brought a clean tunic and tore it into strips. She folded the rest of the material and bound it tight across the wound. The makeshift bandage would have to suffice until they could get a healer to close the wound.

Her work finished, Vamma sat on the ground next to Corelle. "Every day you return soaked in blood. This cannot continue."

"It need not. It is done."

"You have killed him?"

"I have killed them all."

Vamma heaved a sigh of relief. Mayhap now they could leave Ryl, a city that had brought them no joy. They could build their life together and put these horrors behind them. "We can leave once you are strong enough to travel. I will bring a healer soon."

She moved to stand, but Corelle's face gave her pause. "Krage is in Argoya, and Raopul lives."

Her flat, emotionless voice distracted Vamma from the news in her words for a moment. "What? Raopul lives?"

"Denstal claimed it."

Vamma's chest tightened with concern. "Do you believe him?"

"I know not. The story about Krage seemed unlikely to me. Raopul may not have been killed. Nobody knew for certain when I met Raolos outside Delcan."

"Where is the boy?" Vamma worried these two pieces of news might lead Corelle to seek the boy, which she believed would be a mistake, or head to Argoya in search of even more vengeance.

"I know not. Denstal did not say."

"Corelle, you cannot seek Raopul."

"Why is that?" Corelle turned to look at her, pain etched on her face.

"He might be angry or resentful."

"Why would he be?"

Vamma looked up to the sky, frustrated by Corelle's apparent blindness to the folly of her words. "Because you killed his father." She almost feared to give the words voice.

"Not on purpose."

Vamma gave a short, sharp laugh of derision. "I imagine that will be a great help to him." Corelle stared at her but made no reply. "Corelle, do not seek him. What if he became angry and attacked you?"

Corelle blinked twice before she replied. "I would have to kill him."

"What?" Vamma could not keep her disbelief and anger out of her voice. "He is… what, fifteen years?"

"Then it would be sensible if he did not attack me."

Vamma stared at her. Corelle stared back, her eyes almost glazed, and Vamma imagined she had lost a lot of blood. She seemed not to realise how horrendous her words had been. "Who are you? This is not the Corelle I knew. What has become of you?"

"Nothing has become of me. The boy deserves to know his father is dead."

Vamma blew a long breath from her lips. Corelle appeared oblivious to the significance of the things she said. "That he does, but not from the woman who killed him." Vamma's exasperation threatened to crush her. She could not believe the direction the conversation had taken.

"Who better, after all else?"

"And after you have found or killed this young boy, you will sail to Argoya against the slim chance you have not been lied to and you may seek further vengeance on Krage?"

"That I will."

Vamma could tolerate no more. She had tried to help Corelle, to stand at her side as her comfort and support. The madness had gone too far. "Corelle, I cannot stand this any longer. You have lost all sense of reason. You are out of your mind and dangerous. I am afraid for you. I am afraid of you."

"Vamma, have I not told you I would not hurt you?" Corelle's voice and eyes held no emotion. The words she spoke seemed instinctive rather than reasoned.

"You say that, but you say so much these days, and so little of it makes sense. I will return to Yerrsun. I will visit my grandfather if he still lives. You must seek a healer who can guide you back and help you to become the person you once were. To become again the woman I love, not this monster you have turned into."

"Nothing is wrong with me. I had to kill Denstal."

"Corelle, do you remember any part of this conversation?" Corelle remained silent. Vamma felt as though she talked to herself. Corelle gave no indication she heard or understood the import of Vamma's words, her concerns. "It may be you did have to kill him. You did not have to enjoy it so much. You did not have to kill that man yesterday. You have lost your way. I am sorry, but I cannot stay."

Corelle shrugged. "You must do whatever you desire. It matters not. I must stay and search for Raopul."

Vamma wiped at her tears as she replied, her voice as broken as her heart. "Please do not seek him. I beg you, Corelle. If you have any sense or compassion left in you, do not look for him."

Corelle stared into Vamma's eyes. "Then what will I do, alone here?"

"Seek help." Vamma sobbed. "Please."

Corelle nodded, but Vamma guessed it had not been a nod of agreement. She may not even have realised she had made the gesture. "When will you leave?"

"As soon as I can gather my things together. I cannot stay. I fear you. I will send a healer to you. Please let them in so your arm can be attended to, then seek help for these problems you have, I beg you. If you come to your senses and wish to join me, you know where you can find me." She wiped her tears away again and kissed Corelle's lips. "I love you. You brought so much joy to my life. I would live and die beside you if you would become again the Corelle I knew when we first met."

"Take the coin." Corelle seemed detached from reality, as though she were a spectator who watched a carnival performance. Vamma sighed and went up the stairs to pack her belongings. She took some of the coin but left enough for Corelle to pay a healer and for a ship to Ort. When she came down the stairs with her pack, Corelle stood in the parlour.

Vamma embraced her, the coppery smell of the blood that covered her clothes thick in her nostrils. "Please seek someone to help you. It breaks my heart to see you this way. I hope you find somebody who will put you back together again. Come and find me if you do." Corelle kissed her. "Goodbye Corelle. I love you."

She pulled the door open, took a backward glance, stepped out into the street, and pulled the door shut behind her.

CHAPTER 43
CORELLE

As Vamma left the house and closed the door, Corelle collapsed into a chair and closed her eyes. How had she managed to drive away the woman who loved her? Four women had said those three terrible words to her; five if she included her mother. Only five women, yet four had died, and the fifth had walked out on her. The horror of her dream as a young girl had come true over and over. It would be best for her to live alone from now on. At least no other women need die or have their hearts shattered by her.

Where had things gone so wrong with Vamma? Corelle had been focused on revenge for the death of her mother, without doubt, and had wanted to keep Vamma safe. Those motivations had counted for nothing with Vamma, in truth. She had wanted more from Corelle than Corelle could give.

Corelle stood and pumped some water into a pitcher. Her thirst had turned her throat as dry as sand, and she needed to drink. She poured a cup of the water and threw it down her throat in one gulp. A clear head would be needed before any decisions could be made, and that would be achieved best after a night's sleep. In truth, too many options lay before her. One clear-cut path would have been preferable, not this thorn bush of options that threatened to shred her to pieces if she turned in the wrong direction.

Her heart screamed for her to chase after Vamma and persuade her to return with promises of change, or at the least to travel with her to Yerrsun. If Corelle stayed in Dur, then Krage would live, and that would tear at her mind until it drove her into the flames. The news that Raopul lived brought further complication, and she felt she owed it to him to tell him his father had died. So many choices.

Corelle tipped the pitcher, poured another cup of water, and guzzled it down her throat. Had her deadly work always made her this thirsty? She could not recall. When she glanced down at her tunic, it ran red with the blood from her arm and those she had fought.

She drained the pitcher, then slumped back into the chair where she brooded on her choices as an hour passed, then another, and the decision seemed to become more difficult with every beat of her heart. A knock at the door interrupted her contemplation, and dizziness washed over her as she stood. She swayed and steadied herself on the arm of the chair before she could move to open the door. The light-headedness and imbalance felt worse than when she stood on firm ground after time aboard a ship. When she composed herself and pulled the door open, a man stood there in dark clothes. He carried a black satchel, and Corelle did not recognise him.

"Are you Corelle?" She nodded in confirmation. "I have been asked to help you with an injured arm, and I see my help is needed. You have lost much blood, and we must address that at once, or you may bleed to death."

"The blood is not all mine. Some belongs to others. Only my arm is hurt."

He looked startled, as though her words horrified him, but she had only told the truth. He shook his head. "Please, let us go inside, and I will examine you." He gestured toward the parlour.

He sat her in one of the chairs, then unbuttoned her tunic. He pulled the saturated tunic from her body and took in a sharp breath when he saw the cut on her arm. "How did you get this?" He touched the wound with his fingertips and sounded distracted.

Blood poured from the wound, down her arm and onto the arm of the chair. "A dagger."

"A dagger?" He stared into her eyes, and she smiled at him. "I must close this wound."

"Just a small dagger." Why did he find daggers unusual? Corelle could not imagine why that part of her story seemed odd to him. It did not matter; she had other things to consider, and his frail sensibilities could not interfere with the decisions she must make.

He reached into his satchel and produced a needle and thread. "Do you have a candle?"

Corelle gazed around, bewildered. The hour had moved on toward the sunset, but plenty of light remained in the day, and she could see no need for a candle. "It is not yet dark."

"I do not need it for light. I must heat the needle before I close the wound."

More mysteries. This healer must be the most peculiar in all Dur. "Why must you heat it?"

"To ensure it is not covered with dirt or things that might cause an infection in the wound."

"Inflammation." She nodded her head, proud of herself.

"You have the right of it." Corelle sat and gazed at him, and he gave a small, exasperated sigh. "The candle?"

"I will bring one, although it is not yet dark." In the scullery, she found several in a drawer near the pump and brought them over to the man. He took one, then told her he needed a flint. Corelle huffed her displeasure. Why had he not mentioned that while she had been on her feet? She fetched a flint, and he lit the candle.

He nodded his head at the chair, so she sat again. He waved the needle in the candle flame for some time, then threaded it. "Now." Corelle waited, but he did not elaborate. He pushed the needle through the flesh of her arm without further discussion.

She gasped aloud. The needle had hurt, but it had been nothing compared to the pain when the Guild man had slashed her arm open. As he pushed the needle through her arm, first in this direction, then that, Corelle watched him work with interest. Blood oozed down her arm and pooled on the arm of the chair like a lake of red wine. "Your making leaves much to be desired." She laughed at his crude stitches in her arm.

"Be that as it may, it will save your life." He glanced up at her. "There. It is done."

"My thanks. I will see if Vamma left any coin so I can pay you." Corelle went up the stairs and found her pouch, which still held some coin. Vamma had not taken it all, after all else, so she took the pouch downstairs and handed it to him. "Take as much as you want. I have no need of it."

He stared at her, then picked up the candle and blew it out. "Are you all right? You seem disorientated, forgetful even. Have you taken a blow to the head along with this cut?"

Corelle laughed. He would be here long into the night if she recounted all the injuries she had received. "A mast fell on me." She hoped the explanation would satisfy him.

"A mast?" He squinted at her and held a finger up before her face. "Follow my finger." He moved the finger to one side, and she turned and took half a step in that direction. "What are you about?"

"You told me to follow your finger." Even though Corelle had followed his instruction, he seemed irritated.

"I meant follow it with your eyes, not walk after it."

He sounded annoyed, but Corelle could not understand why. "Sorry." She could not resist a small, foolish laugh.

He repeated the movement of his finger and moved it from side to side several times as she tried to focus on it. "You need further investigation, I think." He sighed as he spoke. "I fear something is broken inside your head. It may have been when the mast fell on you." He shook his head, and Corelle tilted hers to one side as she tried to fathom why he seemed so exasperated.

"Very well. Will you do it now? Is there enough coin in the pouch?"

"Not by me. I am no expert on the head. Few are, in truth. Nonetheless, you are not in possession of your faculties, that much I can determine." He bent to his satchel and muttered. "No surprise, when masts fall on a person cut by a dagger." He straightened, then took some coins from the pouch before he handed it back to Corelle. "My thanks for the coin. Please, seek somebody with expertise in head injuries. I fear something is wrong in your head."

Vamma had said something similar. When Corelle showed him to the door, twilight had come on the city, and as he walked off, she called out to him. "This would be a better time to light a candle." He stopped, turned, then shook his head and walked on.

Alone in the house, Vamma's face swam in Corelle's mind. Vamma had been a kind, considerate woman, but Corelle did not love her, and now she had left, unable to tolerate the death that came with Corelle, it seemed. The death that accompanied Corelle would not abandon her soon, and she believed Vamma had made the right decision. It might have been pleasant to see the child, and Corelle resolved to travel to Yerrsun at some future time and meet him or her.

Tiredness washed over her, the emotion of the day too much to hold back, so she carried the lantern upstairs, blew it out, and fell into the bed. Denstal hounded her dreams, a giant sword embedded in his face as he tore off his own manhood and tried to thrust it between Corelle's legs. He persisted even as she tried to fend him off and cried out, "I do not wish the foul thing."

He laughed, then shouted. "You shall have it whether you wish it or not. You shall have it because I love you."

"We all love you." Female voices joined Denstal's, and Corelle whirled around to see Arella, Deineike, Pettra, and Vamma in a line before her, her mother behind them. Denstal rammed his manhood into Corelle's sex from behind her, and Raolos appeared, a baby in his arms. He caressed its tiny pink manhood as everybody yelled in unison, "I love you."

CHAPTER 44
CORELLE

The next day, Corelle woke to the sound of rain as it pattered against the window, driven by a wind that sighed through the gaps between the window frame and the wall of the house. She reached for Vamma, then remembered she had left for Yerrsun. With no reason to rise, she lay in the bed and listened to the song of the rain and wind. They seemed to sing to her of all her imperfections, but if they intended to bring her guilt, they failed. She already despised herself so much, nothing the elements could say would worsen her self-loathing.

Hunger drove her from the bed, and the pain in her arm smothered even the agony of another dreadful headache. She grimaced as she picked her way down the stairs, slow and deliberate. No more than the end of a stale loaf remained. All the food Vamma had bought when she stormed out of the house a few days ago had gone. Either they had eaten it, or Vamma had taken it. Corelle shrugged. "She needs to feed the child, after all else." Her voice echoed around the empty parlour, and she sniffed. She missed Vamma already. Should she forget about Raopul and Krage journey after Vamma? If Corelle could keep her temper under control, they might yet find happiness.

She tried to gather her thoughts, and her stomach growled in protest at the lack of sustenance the piece of bread had provided. A trip to a shop would remedy the lack of food in the house, so she struggled back up the stairs to find some clean clothes. She grabbed the pouch from the table in the parlour on her way out of the house and set off up the street.

Exhaustion took hold of her within a few moments. The injury appeared to have drained her strength, but she pressed on until she could go no further. She leaned against the wall of a tavern and tried to heave breath into her lungs, but the air seemed reluctant to enter her body, as though it knew the monster she had become and wished no taint from her to ruin it.

The door of the tavern opened, and a man emerged. He nodded at her as he walked up the street, and the smell of roasted meats followed him out. Unlike the air around her, the odour of the food slithered into her nose and whispered of relief from her hunger. Corelle's mouth watered at the smell, and since she lacked the energy to go far, she gave in to the seduction of the aroma and staggered into the tavern, found a table that faced the door, and slid onto the settle with a wry smile. *"Old habits die hard,"* she thought, not for the first time in her life.

The innkeep brought her a goblet of wine and a plate of food, greasy and overcooked, but plentiful. One goblet led to a second, and a dim memory of a previous time, when her consumption of wine had been out of control, pestered her. She tried to push the memory into a corner out of the way, but it needled her to leave, to go home before she became intoxicated. Corelle persuaded herself she lacked the energy to return to the house yet, and she would leave as soon as her strength returned.

Two hours and many goblets later, the room blurred, and there were more people than she remembered in the tavernroom. She had known how to resolve the problem at one time, and a vague recollection chattered in the back of her mind, suggested she should close one eye. "It is an old trick, but it just might work."

She giggled as she said the words, and a man nearby turned toward her. "What did you say, girl?"

"I am no girl." The words sounded thick in her mouth, and her tongue felt clumsy, awkward to wield.

"You are to me." The man laughed, and his companions joined in.

Corelle frowned and closed an eye so she could focus on his face. He had pale, blemished skin and lank, greasy hair. "You are ugly, and you should be careful how you address me. I am a killer, after all else." She giggled again, delighted by her jest.

The man lowered his tankard to the table in front of her and leaned forward. "You are inebriated, nothing more. I never strike a woman, but you could try my patience, I think."

Corelle half-rose, but the innkeep appeared before her table. He stared at her. "He has the right of it, at that. You have had more than enough young woman. I suggest you take yourself off home."

Who were these people who thought themselves important enough to speak to her with such contempt? "I am a friend of the Duke."

The men gathered around her laughed, and their amusement at her friendship with the most important man in Dur angered her. Somebody said there had been no Duke for years, and the disdain in his voice stoked the fires of her rage. She sat again, pulled the fan from her boot, then rose and leapt at the innkeep with an animal growl.

CHAPTER 45
WILASH

Wilash and Derkhata walked down the ramp onto the dock. They waited for a mariner to deliver the small trunk they had brought with them on the voyage. For almost an entire pass they had sailed, from Malkartas to Alcmouth, then to Zhanghar, and at last on to Ryl.

Wilash pulled the letter out of his pocket and read it again. It had arrived some time ago at his smithy in Tanasttra. It was from Vamma, back in her old house in Yerrsun, a torrid tale of agony and vengeance. It claimed Corelle's mother had been killed, and Corelle had lost her mind in the grief. It said she had worked with the Qagrue to extract her revenge on the Guild for the death of her mother. It told him Vamma had been unable to stay with Corelle, so dangerous had her moods become.

He had agonised over the letter for days. His business had become well-established, and while Vamma pleaded with him to travel to Ryl and check on Corelle's safety, he had been loath to close his smithy for an extended time. In the end, Derkhata persuaded him to make the long voyage north. She had never seen Dur but wished to do so, and she reminded her husband friendship mattered far more than a few coins. His skilled work had become so in demand, he need not worry about the smithy for a pass or two. He had taken little time away from his work for over a year, and it would do them both good to have a break.

Now they found themselves on the dock in Ryl on a cool day toward the end of the cold season. Wilash sniffed the air. "Spring will be here soon." Derkhata smiled as she gazed around at the unfamiliar sights.

She took his hand. "It is small, Ryl."

"That it is. It is the smallest city in the Duchy. There are towns that are bigger. I suspect it has more to do with Styrrach and the Guild than any other factor, although it is a wealthy city for its size, by all accounts."

"How long will we stay here?"

"That will depend on how long it takes us to track Corelle down. We will find an inn, and I will begin the search. I will start with her shop. She may have returned to garment making."

"Why do you not start with The Council, or whatever it is called here? In Malkartas, they keep records of many things. They must be able to aid you."

He looked around at the land of his birth in misery. The Qagrue walked the dock, interspersed with the Durfolk, but the two did not much mingle together. "I do not know what system the southerners use to govern. I could visit the old Portreeve's Offices, I imagine. We will find the better inns near the square, after all else." He hoisted the trunk onto his shoulder. "Come. Enjoy the sights of Ryl."

He had never been to Ryl and had to ask for directions before they found the square. They found a good inn and left the trunk in their room while they returned to the square. Derkhata wanted to peer into every shop they passed, and it took them almost an hour to arrive at the Ortwood door, guarded by four Qagrue. They were a strange people, Wilash thought. He had seen them at the docks in

Tanasttra, and around the taverns of the poorer quarters, and while they resembled the Durfolk, they had darker skin and were shorter, for the most part. They all had black hair, as black as the darkest night.

A large counter with one man and one woman, both Qagrue, behind it stood in the lobby of the Portreeve's Offices. The man looked up from his work as they entered and gave them a smile of welcome. "What can we do for you?" His accent lengthened the vowels. To Wilash, it sounded as though he had asked "Whert cern wey der fer yer?"

Wilash smiled in amusement and hoped the man would mistake it for a friendly grin. "I seek an old friend. I have not seen her in many passes, and we are here for a visit. I long to see her."

"What is your friend's name?"

"Corelle. She owned a high-quality garment shop on Varayn Street."

The smile went from his face. "Yes, this person is known to us." Wilash thought the statement sounded ominous, as though they sought her as a criminal or some such. "Wait here please." The man turned and whispered something to the woman behind the counter before he disappeared through a door behind them.

The woman gestured at the chairs against a wall. "You may seat."

They sat, and Derkhata whispered in Wilash's ear. "Take a sit, my love." They laughed, and the woman glanced over. Wilash's laughter died from embarrassment, and he looked at the floor and shuffled his feet. If he had not taught Derkhata to speak Dur, she would not have made the jest, and he would not have been caught as he laughed at the woman.

The man returned through the door and smiled at them. "You will be seen soon." Wilash nodded his thanks. They waited for some time and Wilash grew restless. He wandered the lobby, unable to remained seated. Some parts of the wall were a different shade from the wall around them, and he reasoned some pictures or signs had been removed by the Qagrue, although they must have hung there for a great many years. It annoyed him the invaders seemed intent on the removal of Dur history and culture in this way, more so since they had not replaced the removed items with any pictures of their own.

He heard a cough, and when he turned, a man hovered between Derkhata and himself. He had some braid on the shoulder of his tunic, and some symbol Wilash could not recognise on the left breast. "I am Karaftaraluq Sumbrid Akh Aluq. I am the Commander of Ryl." He held out a hand toward Wilash, who shook it for a heartbeat before he released it. "Please follow me."

He turned, and Wilash spoke to his back. "There is no need for a formal conversation." His experience in the Portreeve's Offices in Zhanghar remained emblazoned in his mind. He knew etiquette and did not desire a lengthy walk to the man's office only to have their business concluded in a heartbeat. He might have no information on Corelle's whereabouts, after all else. She had never been the type of person who permitted the bright lantern light of authority to shine into her life. "We seek information about a friend, nothing more."

The man stopped and turned his head. "I know this. Please, let us go to my office."

Wilash frowned and glanced at his wife, unsure what to make of the Commander's words, whose name he had already forgotten. Had Corelle got into some sort of trouble? They might seek her in connection with some crime, and Wilash and Derkhata might be questioned about their potential involvement. He had rolled the dice, and he had little choice. They followed the man through the door and down a long corridor, through one office into another, much bigger.

The Qagrue gestured to a long couch, and Wilash and Derkhata sat. The other man sat in a chair opposite them and smiled again. "You are…?"

"I am Wilash, and this is my wife, Derkhata Perozel. We have travelled from Malkartas in search of an old friend."

The man nodded. "This friend's name?"

"Corelle. She came from Ryl but has travelled a great deal. She sailed on the voyage that proved Ictharelian is a globe."

The Qagrue smiled. "I have heard of this journey. Until I can make the voyage myself, I must remain sceptical." He laughed. "How could we be on a globe but sail to the other side of it and not fall off?"

Wilash resented his doubt about Corelle's achievements. "I am no scholar who can answer your question. Corelle is a friend. A good friend. I would trust her with my life. If she tells me she made the voyage, then I believe her."

The Commander appeared taken aback, but he gathered himself. "Quite right. I have such friends, but none of them sailed aboard this ship. It sank, I hear."

"That it did." Wilash's anger at the man's disbelief over Corelle's voyage grew within him. "Corelle continued the journey by other means. I have not, however, come to Ryl to discuss whether we might fall off the other side of the globe. I have come in search of Corelle."

"Yes, I realise this." Wilash had not known the Qagrue used 'yes' and 'no' in the same way the Malkartasians did. "How long have you known her?"

"I am not a scholar, as I have already explained. I do not reckon the passage of the years, but if I must guess, I would say not less than nine years."

"You know she is a killer?"

Wilash forced a blank expression to his face. "A killer?"

"Well, this is what she told me. I would have expected such a close friend to know this."

Wilash wrapped his words in a bedsheet of caution. "I am certain anybody Corelle has killed would have deserved death."

The man stared at him as though he sought a lie in Wilash's eyes, his expression. "I see. You seek her because…?" He waved a hand as if to invite a response.

Derkhata interjected. "Forgive me, this is my first time in Dur. Is it a crime here to seek the company of an old friend whom one has not seen for many passes?"

He smiled at her. "No, it is not. Forgive me for my questions. Some who might arrive here, unknown to me, and ask of Corelle's whereabouts might have less than noble intentions toward her, I hear."

"My intentions are nothing more complicated than that I am a friend, I long to see her, and I hope to find her well." Wilash remained annoyed at the tone of the entire conversation.

He nodded; Wilash had noticed he seemed prone to do so. "I have some bad news, I am afraid."

A cold dagger pierced Wilash's heart, and he took Derkhata's hand. "Bad news?"

"Yes. I am sorry to tell you Corelle is dead."

"Dead?" Derkhata squeezed Wilash's hand as his stomach tied itself in knots. "Dead? How can this be?"

"Killed in a tavern, four or five passes ago. She became involved in an argument with a customer and the innkeep. She killed the customer with a blade she had concealed about her person, but it turned he had been a mariner, and his crew-mates were in the tavern with him. A brawl erupted. The ship departed with four fewer crew members, but Corelle fell." He hesitated before he continued. "I am sorry."

A tear dripped from Wilash's eye onto the leg of his trousers. He sniffed. All the misery of the globe could not match his own at that moment. Many years he had known Arella, and had watched the vivacious, cheerful girl with whom she had returned from Ryl turn into a creature she would not have recognised, were she to have met her again later in her life. Corelle had been corrupted by death, as had so many who joined the Guild. It had not been her fault, in truth. The fates written for her were unkind, and she bore them with a strength most could not have summoned. To hear she had died at all devastated him, but that she had died in such mundane circumstances might prove too much to bear. He had lost them both —Arella and Corelle. Klordia too, taken by this tale that would not cease to gnaw at his heart. "Are you certain?"

The man nodded. "That I am. I knew her. She helped us with a small matter. Short, with skin a similar colour to ours. Short hair, brownish. A terrible scar on the top of her head, where no hair would grow. The guards called me to the tavern that night. I saw her body. I am sorry."

Wilash leaned back and placed both hands behind his head. He had arrived too late. Could he have saved her if he had left as soon as he had received Vamma's letter? He doubted it. It sounded as though she had died not long after Vamma had scribed the letter, before he even had it in his hands.

She had gone. Corelle had gone.

CHAPTER 46
VAMMA

Vamma stood at the basin in her scullery and washed some dishes. Her grandfather still lived and had been delighted to see her return to Yerrsun. She had waited for Corelle to appear for two passes before she scribed to Wilash. She felt he deserved to know some of the things that had taken place with his friend and her lover. Even after she sent the letter, she still sat in her parlour for hours and stared at the door, desperate for a knock to come so she could tear open the door and see Corelle outside her home, returned to her, whole again.

A pass. Two passes. Corelle did not come, and Vamma abandoned her ceaseless vigil. She pondered how to earn some coin to keep herself and the child when it came. She could think of nothing other than the stall and decided she would return to it once the child had been birthed.

Vamma twisted a dress in her hands, and water poured from it back into the basin. She held it up to the light to inspect it. Satisfied with its cleanliness, she slung it over a shoulder and headed toward her rear yard to hang it on a cord to dry, but a knock came at the front door.

She froze, but her heart did not. It leapt up in her breast and pounded, faster and faster, harder and harder. She turned, and the knock came again. The second knock broke her paralysis, and she ran to the door and pulled it open, ready to leap into Corelle's arms at last. The smile died on her face. Wilash and his wife stood at her door. "Wilash." Vamma forced the smile back to her lips. "How lovely to see you. Come in, both of you. You must be exhausted from such a long journey." She held the door open wide, and they stepped into the parlour. On the floor nearby stood a wooden crib. "Meet Raolinda, my daughter."

Wilash smiled, and his wife bent to the crib and purred. "She is beautiful. How old?"

"Almost two passes."

"Such a delightful name." Vamma saw something in Wilash's eyes as he spoke, something she feared.

She moved toward the scullery. "Can I offer you some food or drink?" She was unprepared to hear whatever they had come to say.

"Our thanks, but we are not hungry."

She did not turn to face him. "Did you go to Ryl?"

"That we did." His voice sounded heavy and mournful.

Vamma turned to face him. "Did you find her? Is she all right?" She fought to bring lightness into her voice.

Wilash raised his hands to his face, and his shoulders sagged. Vamma glanced down at his wife and realised she could not remember the woman's name. Tears ran from the woman's eyes and dripped onto the side rail of the crib. Vamma staggered back a step and reached for a chair to steady herself. "How?" She shattered into myriad pieces inside, shredded beyond repair. She would never recover, could never be whole again.

"A fight in a tavern, it seems. Somebody killed her, we hear. She killed four before they overwhelmed her." If there had been any attempt to force pride into his voice, Wilash had failed. His words oozed misery, and his tone had become as desolate as the wretched emptiness in Vamma's heart.

Raolinda cried, as though she was not prepared to be the only person in the room who did not weep uncontrollable tears of grief. Vamma bent and picked her up, kissed her head, and clutched her daughter tight.

Vamma looked at Wilash through the haze of her tears. She gave him a feeble smile. "She is at peace with herself at last."

Through his sobs, he managed a tortured reply. "That she is. That she is."

ACKNOWLEDGMENTS

Cover by Adrian DSGNS

Torr Sea map by Lara Mitchell

Dur map by André Barbeto

SPECIAL THANKS

Ailsa. Another book I could never have published without you.
Jo & Rob, Wendy & Danny, Joseph. How can I ever thank you enough for your support?
Christopher Cross. I tried so hard to get Sailing into this book.
Rosie. How lucky we are to have such a fabulous cat.
Everybody who reads my books. It's one thing to write a book, but when people buy and read it, it is a humbling thing. Thank you all.

ABOUT THE AUTHOR

HAYLEY PRICE has always been a storyteller. Throughout her life, she has told her story through songs as the principal songwriter in several bands, most recently Adventures With Alice, whose songs feature in many of her books.

A New Zealander, Hayley currently lives in Canberra, Australia with her long-time partner and a grumpy, bossy cat called Rosie. She loves baseball and suffers eternal torture as a fan of the San Francisco Giants. Music has been a major part of her life, and outside her own compositions, she is an enormous fan of Christopher Cross as well as Daryl Hall & John Oates and underrated 80s UK prog-rock band Voyager, who once named her their #1 fan.

Hayley's first book, The Vermilion Ribbon, received an Honorary Mention in the 2024 The BookFest Award for LGBTQ Fantasy, a 2024 Indie BRAG Medallion, and was a finalist in the ABLE Golden Book Awards 2024. Her second book, The Vermilion Cross, won third place in the BookFest Awards for LGBTQ Fantasy.

LINKS

Here are some links I hope you will find useful.

My website: https://hayleyprice.net

Please leave a review for this book at: https://books2read.com/u/
m2DwRj

9 781763 799851